ALL ON A SUMMER'S DAY

ALL ON A SUMMER'S DAY

John Wainwright

St. Martin's Press
New York

For information, write: St. Martin's Press,
175 Fifth Avenue, New York, N.Y. 10010
Manufactured in the United States of America

Library of Congress Cataloging in Publication Data

Wainwright, John William, 1921-
    All on a summer's day.

    I. Title.
PR6073.A354A79   1982   823'.914   81-14517
ISBN 0-312-01983-1   AACR2

The raw recruit to the police at the start of professional policing in this country was assumed to be stupid but trainable.

The Idea of Policing in Britain: Success or Failure?

The Police We Deserve
T.A. Critchley

POLICE PERSONNEL

Bordfield Regional Headquarters
Assistant Chief Constable (Crime) Harris
Head of C.I.D. Detective Chief Superintendent Blayde

Beechwood Brook D.H.Q.
Chief Superintendent Blakey
Detective Chief Inspector Tallboy

Sopworth Section
Inspector Rowe
Detective Constable Evans
W.P.C. 1324 Pearson

Night Shift
Sergeant 2828 Noble
P.C. 1116 Wooley
P.C. 1662 Barker
Office Reserve P.C. 1871 Higginbottom

Early Shift
Sergeant 1728 Ramsden
P.C. 2324 Pollard
P.C. 1555 Witherham

Late Shift
Sergeant 1871 Cockburn
P.C. 2564 Sowe
P.C. 1956 Hinton

Upper Neck Beat
P.C. 2004 Cooper
P.C. 2121 Kyle

Rimstone Beat
P.C. 1404 Pinter
P.C. 1235 Karn

FRIDAY, JUNE THE TWENTY-SIXTH

Midnight   The sweep hand of the office wall-clock moved past the vertical, and it was the start of a new day. So easy. So little pother. Time, like the geometrician's dot, didn't exist other than in the imagination; 'now' became 'then' merely by reason of noting it. What didn't exist couldn't form a fuss, couldn't make its presence felt, couldn't trigger off fireworks, or bring in a brass band, or deliver itself of some monumental utterance. It couldn't even be there. It could only *pretend* to be there and, with each spin of the earth, it gave birth to a new day. Nice going . . . a pretence which brought about a reality. Something of a miracle which was performed every twenty-four hours.

Not that the three men in the Charge Office went in for miracle-watching. Not that they even believed in miracles. Working coppers don't allow their fancies to wander along such philosophical back alleys. Believe what you see, son. What you see with your own two good eyes. Believe what you smell. Believe what you hear . . . as long as *you* hear it. Believe only that, son, and keep the door ajar in case you're being conned.

Harry Noble stirred a pint pot of instant coffee with one hand and eased the lid from a plastic sandwich box with the other. Both pot and box were on the top of a four-drawer-high filing cabinet; a steel filing-cabinet whose green paint was chipped and scratched and whose surfaces were bulged and marked from rough usage. The bottom drawer wouldn't close properly and the chrome locking-button near the top right-hand corner of the cabinet was jammed open because, since time immemorial nobody had ever known where the damn key was.

Noble said, 'Johnny, get Coop, eh? He's off at one. Tell him I'll meet him going off duty.'

'Will do.'

Police Constable John Henry Higginbottom pushed himself upright from the chair in front of the battered and ill-used Remington and walked to the tiny anteroom which housed the switchboard, the teleprinter and the microphone. The Sopworth mike was okay for the local beat-bashers; assuming the patrolling constable wasn't in one of the dozen or so 'blind spots', where buildings goofed up the

7

transmission from Sopworth nick, a flick of the button brought oral contact to a range of up to two miles and, in places, a little more. But P.C. Cooper was an 'outside beat' man — a village constable — whose patch stretched almost fifteen miles into open countryside. And, what was more, Coop rode around in a Minivan, complete with radio. His was no walkie-talkie link with Sopworth Section. His wireless waves were pushed out from the top floor of Beechwood Brook Divisional Headquarters.

Higginbottom rammed a plug into a switchboard socket marked 'DHQ' and spoke to his opposite number in the Fuzz Palace itself.

Noble sipped the instant coffee, pulled a face, opened one of the sandwiches built of ready-sliced bread and pulled another face.

'Cheese!' he muttered.

The third occupant of the Charge Office said, 'Mine, too, five gets you ten.'

'How's the Arrest Report going?' Noble carried the pint pot towards the table desk, and spoke through a mouthful of cheese sandwich.

'About ten minutes. Then his property to itemise.'

'How is Nibbo?' Noble jerked a head in the general direction of the Cell Area.

'Stoned, but surfacing.'

'Will he . . .' Noble sent his tongue on a quick safari round his teeth, searching out doughy bread and mousetrap cheese hiding from the journey down his gullet. He gulped a mouthful of instant coffee, then said, 'Will he be fit to travel by the time I get back from Upper Neck?'

'At a guess.'

'Okay. Make out a Bail Form. Monday's court. Fifty quid. Then — while you're in here — you might as well hang around and have your supper.'

The instructions brought a grunt of understanding, touched with disapproval.

Noble grinned to himself. Wooley wasn't a bad copper. But a bit of a wide lad; thought he knew all the answers; kidded himself he'd invented some new twists to old gags. But . . . no way, youngster. No *way*! He (Noble) knew all the gags in the joke book; knew 'em, had pulled 'em, while Wooley was still carrying a school satchel. And now he was a section sergeant he could see 'em coming before they'd left the launch-pad. One Drunk-and-Dizzy coming up; at just the right time; tool around long enough with the paper work and, with luck, half the night has slipped by. That one had been a passenger on the ark.

But not while he, Sergeant Noble, was around. Get writing, lad, have your snap, then try the streets for temperature; test a few more doorknobs; give Barker a spell inside.

Not that Police Constable Barker minded too much. Barker was working Sopworth Town 'B' Beat; the beat with the Market Square, the banks, most of the shops and the cinema-turned-Bingo Hall. Not the residential area — assuming a one-horse dump like Sopworth could claim to have a residential area — therefore not lumbered with a few score honest householders, away on holiday and expecting their vacant homesteads to be 'tried' at least once every night to ensure that villains hadn't nipped in and nicked the T.V. set. 'B' Beat was, in the main, torch work. A quick flash of the beam across the windows; the would-be-masterminds favoured windows when it came to what they counted as 'a big job', and hick crooks couldn't perform a window caper without leaving a gap big enough for a double-decker to drive through.

P.C. Barker was, perhaps, one of the oddball crowd. He really *loved* bobbying. He also hated crooks, but not in the way some members of the C.I.D. crowd hated them. To him it wasn't a personal thing, it wasn't a war. It wasn't, for example, like Coop's burning fury. No . . . Barker hated crooks much as a good doctor hated disease. The object was to stop them. Not 'cure' them. (Most of them were well beyond hope as far as 'curing' was concerned.) Just to discharge them. And certainly not to *punish* them.

Like earlier on this evening. Half-eleven, thereabouts, he'd seen Alf Rayon; deliberately crossed the road to speak to him.

'Night Alf.'

'Eh?' Rayon had stopped and scowled.

'Just wishing you good night.'

'Oh, aye?'

'On your way home, are you?'

'Why? Wot's it to you?'

'Politeness.' Barker had smiled gently. 'Just being polite.'

Rayon had had some drink; it had made him nasty.

He'd snarled, 'Get off my back, copper.'

'The last place I want to be.' Barker had retained the smile.

'Eh?'

'On your back.'

'Shag off, Barker.'

'Me, too,' Barker had murmured.

'Wot?'

'*You're* not *my* pin-up boy, either. So, straight home. And good night.'

Rayon had deliberately spat on the pavement, then turned and walked away.

Barker smiled as he recalled the incident. Nothing to it. Simple crime prevention; one aspect of crime prevention never mentioned.

12.30 a.m. Alf Rayon was a wrong 'un. Always had been, always would be. But the only muscles he had came in liquid form from a pint glass. A runt, in other words. And runts rarely took risks. Alf would now know — even his booze-befuddled mind could work it out — he'd been seen and noted, so stay on the straight and narrow tonight, Alfie boy. Or else . . .

Bobbying the 'Barker' way. It worked and, whilever it worked, he was a happy man. A knob-tryer, okay, a knob-tryer. *Somebody* had to try the bloody doorknobs. Somebody had to walk the streets. Somebody, in short, had to graft away at the grass roots. And that was his job, and he was a contented man.

Something even his missus couldn't quite understand. She accepted it, but she couldn't understand it. He didn't *want* promotion. The hell with promotion. He refused even to *sit* the promotion exams. Nor was it because of a lack of ambition. Sure, he was ambitious. But in his own way, and a very personal way. Come Pension Day he wanted somebody — somebody whose opinion counted for something — to sigh and say, 'That Barker. Christ, he was a cracker of a copper. We'll miss him. We'll *really* miss him.' Damn-all to do with stripes or pips or crowns. Just being a copper, but not common-or-garden. A copper good enough to be missed.

He stepped into the doorway of Truform, eyed the display of ladies shoes, checked the door, then lighted a cigarette and listened to the sounds of the night.

Nice just standing there. Very private. Very solitary. Up there, the old Milky Way as plain as any man could wish. No clouds. A moon only days past its birth. And more stars than the eye could count. A funny old science, astronomy. Not too much unlike pulling the wings from a butterfly. I mean, who the hell wanted to *know*? And, once you did know, what *good* did it do you? They were *there* — be satisfied. They were beautiful — leave it at that. Who cared what they were made of? Why they were there? How far away they were? A light year: what the hell was a light year? The distance light

10

travels in one year. *In one year!* A stupid, dream language. Flash language beyond any real understanding. No, the mind wasn't made which was capable of genuinely comprehending those sort of distances. One light year — ten light years — a hundred light years — a thousand light years: crap piled high upon crap. Stars. That's all. 'Twinkle twinkle little star'. The only snippet of astronomical knowhow he'd ever been able to understand. The nursery rhyme was correct; stars twinkle, planets don't. So you watched and, if it winked at you, it was a star. If it didn't, it *might* be a planet, but on the other hand it might still be a star whose winking wasn't too obvious. Who cared? Call 'em all stars. Because that's what they were. *Stars.* Old Ma Nature's fairy lights. Enjoy 'em. You won't see 'em forever.

He stood there, smoking his cigarette and soaking in the balm of night silence.

Well, no it was never *quite* silent. Thanks to the invention of the internal combustion engine there were few moments when you didn't hear some car in the distance, either passing or driving away. And, up on Dolly Hill, the brickworks baked twenty-four hours a day and in the dark 'silence' the sound of stoking carried, and could be heard. Other sounds, too. Especially in summer when bedroom windows were left open. Snores, a creaking bed, a door being opened and closed, mumbled voices. And of course (and always) the slap of the flagpole line atop the council offices. All over Sopworth you could hear that slap-slap-slap in the small hours. First time he'd heard it . . . Christ, it had puzzled him for more than an hour. But, by now, it was part of the night shift. Expected. Listened for. You could damn near tell the velocity of the wind by the slapping of that flagpole line.

Not quite silence, then. But, instead, a down-soft cushion of sound upon which the silence might rest. The sound of a tiny market town as near to sleep as it ever could be.

Barker savoured it and was content. Content with his job, content with the way he did his job. Content with the responsibility of 'B' Beat.

Until the crash came.

Its suddenness and its relative violence made him start. But wise man that he was, he remained still for a moment. Plate glass? Certainly. Plate glass for sure. Some shop window. But where? The streets and corners played hell with pinpointing the exact location of a sound. The Market Square, probably. It *seemed* to come from that direction.

11

Then, clear in the night's near-silence, he heard the sound of running footsteps. The Market Square . . . definitely!

Barker tossed the stub of his cigarette into the gutter and was already running as he unclipped his walkie-talkie.

Higginbottom cursed the infernal 'o' on the Remington for the umpteenth time. The bloody arm was bent, must be. Every time he typed an 'o' the damn thing stuck and the following letter made a splodge on the sheet. Not that he was a typist, or even a policeman clerk come to that. Just Night Office Reserve . . . until further notice. Police politics on a minor scale. On a very petty scale. Okay, a constable was free to go his own way when off duty. As long as he kept within the law, he was as free as any other citizen of the U.K. He could play cricket with the Sopworth team, if he liked. Sure, why not? And if some thunder-and-lightning speed merchant on the opposing side bowled a yorker and chipped a bone in the batsman's ankle, too bad. It was part of the game and, if nothing else, it gave the lie to hairy-chested types who figured cricket as a game for sissies.

A few weeks off duty on full pay. It happened. It was bloody boring, but these things *do* happen.

Then the medic: 'It's knitted nicely. Back to work, but take things easy for a while. Have a quiet word with your boss. It'll be a weak point for some time yet.'

But unfortunately 'your boss' is a chief superintendent. And, more than that, a chief superintendent like Blakey.

'What's 'taking things easy' mean exactly?'

'Well — er — till it's properly healed, sir.'

'Weeks?'

'Yes, sir. I think so.'

'Months?'

'I — er — I don't know, sir. I shouldn't think many . . .'

'During which time you'll be little more than a passenger.'

'I'll try not to be a passenger, sir.'

'Can you guarantee that?'

'Well . . .'

'No. Of course you can't. I'll have a word with Inspector Rowe. Suggest you be Night Office Reserve till further notice.'

Nice going, Blakey. Police politics at its lowest level. A night shift, stuck in the bloody Charge Office, till you say 'when' . . . because *you* aren't civilised enough to like cricket.

12

From behind his back Wooley said, 'I'm going into the back to brew-up. Ready for yours?'

'Aye.' Higginbottom stood up from the chair, walked to where a stained, World War II respirator carrier was parked alongside the steel filing-cabinet, then handed Wooley a plastic pill-container filled with a mixture of tea and sugar and a small medicine bottle filled with milk.

He said, 'As hot as it comes . . . and let it brew.'

Wooley nodded and left the Charge Office.

The teleprinter began to chatter and Higginbottom walked into the alcove. He read the message as it came through. One more stolen vehicle. The fourth that night. Friday nights were great nights for nicking cars. Friday nights and Saturday nights. Four in Beechwood Brook Division alone. Throughout the U.K. one every five minutes average, night and day. Some arithmetical clown had worked it out. Why? Because it *looked* good, no better reason. There was no other reason. Like this teleprinter message, it *looked* good. Short of the bloody motor car being driven into the Charge Office it wasn't going to *do* any good. The Motor Patrol lads would have had it more than thirty minutes ago and, if it was going to be found the chances were it would be found by the Motor Patrol lads. But, no matter, shove it out on every teleprinter line available. It *looked* good. It was being 'circulated' . . . which was the big thing.

The teleprinter ceased its clatter, Higginbottom tapped the 'Received' letters on the keyboard, then tore the message from the machine. He returned to the Charge Office, tossed the original of the message into the 'In' tray for Noble to glance at when he returned, then reached for the gooed up bottle of Gloy and pasted the carbon copy in the Telephone and Teleprinter Message Book.

All clever stuff. The British Police Service; the best in the world; the finest equipment money could buy . . . like a gummed up bottle of Gloy and a bloody typewriter that wouldn't work!

Mind you this was Sopworth . . .

Specifically it was Sopworth Police Section which, in turn, was part of Beechwood Brook Police Division. Population around the eighteen thousand mark. Industries: textiles, brick-making and a few tupenny-ha'penny small firms tooling around with plastics, paper bag manufacture and the like. Thus, Sopworth. Unapproachable, other than downhill . . . which seemed appropriate. Like a badly shaped soup bowl; as if somebody had slammed his fist hard into the lower reaches of the Pennines and said, 'There! That's where I want Sopworth. The uglier the better.'

13

The original muck-and-brass dump. Mill chimneys, brickwork chimneys, household chimneys, chimneys which seemed to have no other purpose in life than to churn out volumes of thick, black smoke. More chimneys than *that*. And forget all the 'clean air' crap. Sopworth hadn't seen clean air since they cut the first sod for the first wattle-and-mud hut. Nor did Acts of Parliament cut much ice. The law 'ran' — so the pundits preached — but it hit a brick wall when it came up against money like Sopworth money. More million-aires per acre than anywhere else in the U.K. That was the local boast, and it wasn't an empty boast. They didn't *live* here. Hell, nobody lived at Sopworth from choice! But this was where they made their loot; this was the home of their 'registered offices'; this was one of the last bastions of what the mind conjured up when it was fed the phrase 'Industrial Revolution'.

But y'know ... Sopworth money also meant Sopworth bobbying.

Originally it had been part of the County Constabulary area and, with amalgamation, it had been gobbled up within the newly formed Lessford Metropolitan Police District, but that hadn't changed things one little bit. Sopworth: the only police section in the whole damn force up to 'authorised strength'. A uniformed inspector, three uniformed sergeants, a detective constable, seven 'town' beat men, one 'town' policewoman and four 'outside' beat men covering the two detached beats of Upper Neck and Rimstone. Seventeen bloody coppers, of varying sorts and sizes, where as things stood in the force — and had the place not been Sopworth — you'd have been damn lucky to have four men and a sergeant.

'Tea up.' Wooley strolled into the Charge Office, carrying a steaming pot in each hand.

At the same time the loudspeaker near the opening leading to the alcove crackled and a very tinny reproduction of Barker's voice said, 'Sopworth. Barker, here. I'm on my way to the Market Square. There's a window gone. Sounds like a shop window.'

Sergeant Noble eased his car into the lay-by within sight of P.C. Cooper's house, switched off the lights, lighted a cigarette and settled back to wait. It was peaceful up here, on the Upper Neck patch; peaceful and as near to open countryside as anybody working out of Sopworth Section could hope for. A nice place, a nice patch ... so why in hell did Coop insist on calling it a 'punishment posting'? Cross swords with an assistant chief constable, mate, and if Upper Neck Beat is all you get you've fallen on your feet. Some-thing Coop wouldn't have. Instead, a shoulder-chip on a par with a railway sleeper and the refusal to accept that he'd never be a detective constable again.

Noble wound down the window and stared out at the yellow sodium street lighting of Sopworth. From above they looked very picturesque. At ground level they seemed to give more shadow than illumination: Noble's personal opinion was that they were too far spaced and too high, but from up here they were very picturesque.

He'd almost finished his cigarette when he saw the lights of the Minivan pulling into the lay-by behind his car. He leaned across the front passenger seat and unlocked the nearside *1 a.m.* front door. Then he tossed what remained of his cigarette from the window, dusted non-existent ash from the front of his tunic and waited.

As he opened the door and climbed into the car, Cooper said, 'A call from D.H.Q. Some clown's pushed a shop window in on the Market Square. Wooley and Barker are attending.'

'Accident? Some drunk?'

'I wouldn't know. I didn't ask.'

A typical 'Cooperism'. A deliberate refusal to take an interest in anything beyond his immediate concern and, by this refusal, to goad a little.

'All quiet?' Noble refused to be drawn and, instead, asked the standard 'meeting-point' question.

'Up here, what else?' countered Cooper bitterly.

'Y'know . . .' Noble opened the packet of cigarettes, held the packet out towards Cooper and, when they were both smoking, said, 'It's not a bad beat.'

'I'm no village bobby,' growled Cooper.

'Kyle's happy enough. So is Pinter and Karn. And Rimstead's a damn sight worse beat than Upper Neck.'

'It's all they've ever known.'

'Whereas you . . .' Noble drew on his cigarette.

'I'm a better jack than Evans.'

It wasn't a boast. It was a simple statement of belief and, from what he'd heard, Noble wasn't willing to argue. But, good bad or indifferent, Taffy Evans was the Sopworth detective constable, and Cooper was an outside beat man covering Upper Neck.

Cooper glanced towards his home and said, 'It's in there.'

'What?'

'My ticket. All it needs is dating.'

'What the hell good's resigning going to do?' demanded Noble.

'I can get a job.'

15

'Where for Christ's sake? Doing what? Outside the force, we're unskilled labour and, if you've an ounce of gumption, you know it.'

'Security firms.'

'Coop.' Noble shook his head sadly. 'Ex-inspectors, and above, queuing for the plum jobs. You'll end up wearing a crash helmet and riding in the back of a van.'

'Detective agencies.'

'Oh, for God's sake! Keyholing on some miserable bastard having it off with some slag somewhere.'

'I'm getting out,' said Cooper doggedly.

Noble smoked in silence for a moment, then he said, 'Okay, park your van.'

'Eh?'

'You're on overtime. That shop window . . . maybe summat, maybe nowt. If it's theft you can show us all how.'

Wooley arrived in the street leading from the Market Square in time to see Barker dive for the fleeing Rayon, grab him by the wrist then turn and, using centrifugal force as an ally, slam him, face first, into the boarded-up window of a shop under alterations. For a moment Rayon's knees buckled and, before he could recover sufficiently to fight back, Wooley had his other arm and all hope of escape vanished.

'Thanks,' gasped Barker.

'Any time.'

'Hartley's Radio Store.' Barker continued to gulp in air.

'This nerk?'

'I reckon.' Barker nodded. 'He was running away.'

'Whad y'wadda . . .' began Rayon.

'Shove it!' snapped Wooley.

Rayon obediently 'shoved it', but looked hurt. The truth is he *felt* hurt. Having your face hurled, nose first and at a tidy rate of knots, into a sheet of eight-ply does not make for instant and lasting friendship. Added to which, it plays merry hell with the nose. A steady stream of gore flowed from Rayon's nostrils, screwed up what little conversation of which he was capable and was rapidly ruining his Marks and Sparks shirt and his Burton's suit. He winced as Barker jerked him round, pulled his hands behind his back and snapped on the handcuffs.

Wooley tightened his grip on Rayon's arm as Barker unclipped his walkie-talkie and contacted Higginbottom at Sopworth Section Station.

'Sopworth. Barker here.'

16

'Okay, Ron. What's happening?' Higginbottom's voice sounded thin and metallic.

'There's a window gone in the Market Square. Hartley's Radio Store. Charlie's with me. We've arrested Rayon.'

'Which Rayon?'

'Eh? Oh, Alfie.'

'Nicked something has he?'

'We're going back to check. Meanwhile, can you contact the key-holder and get him out here.'

'Will do.'

'Thanks.'

'Okay. Keep me up to date.'

Higginbottom moved from the microphone, went into the Charge Office, opened a book entitled *Keyholder's Register* and, within five minutes, had telephoned a certain Mr Albert Hartley and told him that his radio shop window had been smashed, that the chances were that (despite the hour) a smash-and-grap caper had been pulled, and would he please get to his premises as soon as possible in order to give necessary information. He recorded the message in the Telephone and Teleprinter Message Book; this time in red ink, because it was an *outgoing* message.

As Higginbottom might have put it . . . all clever stuff!

But, to be fair, John Henry Higginbottom, Police Constable 1871 had a lot on his mind. Nothing to do with police work. The sheer inconvenience apart, he could do Night Office Reserve on his head. Nevertheless, he had a *lot* on his mind.

Mabel, his wife . . . of all the stupid times to tell him. At half-nine last night. Just as he was pulling his shoes on ready to come on duty. And Betty . . . well, God alone knew where Betty was.

'Johnny, I think you should know.'

'What?' He hadn't even looked up.

'These.'

He had looked up and seen a strip of tinfoil-backed cellophane containing a row of capsules.

Mabel had said, 'I found these in Betty's handbag.'

The tone of her voice had had that brittle, look-out-for-squalls quality he'd grown to recognise.

He'd stared at the capsules and said, 'What the hell are they?'

'Pills.'

'I can see they're pills. What sort of pills? What's wrong with her?'

'There's nothing wrong with her. They're — y'know — *pills*.'

'If there's nowt wrong with her, why is she . . .'

'Pills, you fool. *Pills!*'

'Oh!' The light had gradually dawned. He'd taken a deep breath, then repeated, 'Oh?' but this time it had held a questioning ingredient.

'Well?' Mabel had snapped the counter-question straight back at him.

'When did you find 'em?' he'd asked.

'This afternoon. I was cleaning out her room. I happened to glance into her handbag.'

'Happened to?'

'I like to know what my child's up to.'

'Aye', he'd sighed. 'I'm not criticising.'

'She got them from somewhere.'

'Aye.' He'd bent to fasten his laces.

'Some doctor. Wilkinson.'

'I dunno. Can you – y'know – buy 'em at a chemist's?'

'How do *I* know?'

'Dammit!' For a moment he'd almost lost his temper. 'Women use 'em. Not men.'

'You know perfectly well we've never . . .'

'All right,' he'd soothed. 'All right.' He'd dusted the bottoms of his trousers, then straightened. 'Don't let's fly off at half-cock, Mabel. Not something we might regret.'

'She's a fifteen-year-old child. She's no *right* . . .'

'Not something we might both regret,' he'd repeated.

'All right.' She'd taken a deep breath. 'Tomorrow morning. Call in at Wilkinson's surgery. Ask him. If it's him, tell him not to any more. That we forbid it.'

'I'll call,' he'd promised. 'We'll start with that.' He'd stood up from the chair and reached for the tunic draped over the back of the sofa. 'Meanwhile, what about Betty?'

'I'll leave it till you've seen Wilkinson.'

'Aye.'

A complete non-solution. That's what it boiled down to. A fifteen-year-old schoolgirl – a well-brought-up lass – carting contraceptive pills around in her handbag. It wasn't a nice thought. And if she missed them – and she *would* miss them – what then? Contraceptive pills meant but one thing. She was going out with a man – a lad – hopefully only *one* lad. And not just 'going out' with him. A lot more than that. A hell of a lot more than that. Fifteen! Fifteen, for

1.30 a.m.

18

Christ's sake! Dammit, it wasn't even *legal*. This bloody 'permissive society' — 'putrid society' more like. What the hell had happened to morals? What the hell had happened to pride and decency? What the hell had happened to *everything*?

All right . . .

Mabel and him. When they'd been 'courting' . . . funny nobody 'courted' these days. It was a big laugh. 'Are you courting?' The stock funny-man-cum-quiz-master question. But in those days it wasn't funny at all. Very serious. Very enjoyable, but very serious. A little frightening, too. That engagement ring . . . Jesus wept, he'd almost trembled when he'd slipped it on her finger and realised exactly what it *meant*.

And yet . . .

Okay, okay, they'd 'done it', too. And before marriage. Before they'd even become engaged. But it hadn't been a quick, throw-away thing. Not a 'one night stand'. And Mabel . . . hell's bells, that first time it had almost amounted to rape. And she'd wept after it. And he'd felt an absolute sod. That was the 'done thing' in those days; the recognised reaction as far as ordinary decent folk were concerned. The man acted out the role of bastard. The woman acted out the equally important role of ravished innocent. And — okay — it had been a complete put-on, but that was the 'done thing' and it was part of respectability, and only tarts carried contraceptives around with them and admitted to any degree of enjoyment.

And now, Betty. At fifteen. And in this crazy day and age she wouldn't even think she was doing anything wrong.

He heard the outer door open, then a second or two later the Charge Office door opened and Barker pushed Rayon into the room.

Higginbottom stared and said, 'What the bloody hell!'

'It's all right.' Barker pushed Rayon farther into the Charge Office, closed the door and said, 'It's only a busted nose. He was trying to run for it.'

'The keyholder's on his way down.'

'Champion.' Higginbottom pushed Rayon onto a chair. 'The sergeant got back yet?'

'Not yet. I asked 'em to contact Coop . . . to tell him.'

'Shouldn't be long, then.' Barker pulled Rayon forward in his chair and unlocked the handcuffs. 'We'd better get something for this nose.'

'Cold water.' Higginbottom made for the Charge Office door. 'I'll fix it.'

19

'Ta.' Barker cocked an eye at Rayon and said, 'You've made a right cow's arse of it this time, Alf, haven't you?'

'I'm sayid dowt,' mumbled Rayon.

'Your prerogative, mate.' Barker removed his helmet and placed it on a side table. He unbuttoned the flap on the breast pocket of his tunic, took out notebook and ballpoint, flipped the pages, then said, 'You've heard it all before, Alf. Here it comes again. You're not obliged to say anything unless you wish to do so. Whatever you say will be taken down in writing and may be used in evidence.'

Rayon scowled and repeated, 'I'm sayid dowt.'

Barker chose a line in the notebook and wrote, *The accused was arrested. When cautioned he said, 'I'm saying nowt'.*

By this time Rayon was stone cold sober. Shock, followed by fright, followed by a bloodied nose, followed by arrest had more than offset the evening's consumption of booze. He was up the creek and, as far as he could see, there was only one way in which he might reverse the canoe. And he didn't want to *take* that way. Maybe . . . if things became too hairy. He could be 'fixed' — *really* 'fitted up' — he realised that. He wouldn't be the first one. He wouldn't be the last. But, for a copper, Barker was at least half-decent. Let things ride a while. Don't get mouth-happy. Don't rock the boat. Just see how things went.

Higginbottom returned carrying a cloth dripping cold water. He placed the cloth across the lower half of Rayon's face and said, 'There. Hold it in place. And hold your head back.'

Rayon tilted back his head and pressed the soaked cloth hard against his nose.

Barker replaced his notebook in the breast pocket of his tunic and said, 'Empty your pockets, Alf.'

'Eh?'

'The usual routine. You know it by this time. Your pockets . . . everything onto the table.'

'How d'bloody 'ell . . .' Rayon kept his head tilted back and the soaked cloth to his nose.

'One handed,' said Barker flatly. 'There won't be much. There never is.'

The loudspeaker crackled and Wooley's voice said, 'Sopworth. Wooley here.'

Higginbottom walked to the alcove and picked up the microphone. 'Okay, Charlie. What is it?'

'Mr Hartley's here. The missing property. A Pioneer CT-F1250 cassette deck.'

'Just that?'

'A pricey piece of equipment, so I'm told. Big enough to grab and lug off, but pretty heavy. One of the better pieces of the window display.'

'I'll pass it on,' said Higginbottom. 'Meanwhile, what about you?'

'Hartley knows a man. A joiner. He's going to ring and get him up here before he leaves. Get the window boarded up. I take it Ron's busy?'

'He's busy.'

'I'll cover the town till I hear from you, okay?'

'Okay, Charlie. Keep in touch.'

They came back from Upper Neck via the town; via the Market Square. They braked at Hartley's shop and intercepted Wooley as he was about to resume patrol. From Wooley they obtained the basic details of the smash-and-grab and what was missing.

Cooper glanced across the square to where a light shone behind a curtain above a chemist's shop.

'Old man Willis. He keeps all hours,' explained Wooley. 'A real insomniac. When you're on 'B' Beat you can reckon the back's been broken when you see a light in his bedroom.'

Cooper nodded and grunted.

'Had a meal?' asked Noble.

'Not yet. I was going to . . .'

'Give the property a quick whip-round. Then come in for a snack. We'll bail your drunk while you're in.'

'Thanks.'

They drove to the police station, parked the car up the side street, then walked into the station and the Charge Office. Higginbottom was pasting one more teleprinter message in the Telephone and Teleprinter Message Book. Barker was carefully itemising a small collection of junk in his notebook. Rayon was leaning back in the chair, holding a wet and, by now blood-soaked, cloth to his nose.

Noble glanced at Rayon and said, 'What's up with *him*?'

'Resisting arrest.' Barker didn't even bother looking up.

'Oh, aye.' Noble hesitated for a moment, then said, 'Ron . . . let's have a quiet word.'

'Sure.'

Barker put down his pen and followed Noble into the corridor, beyond the Charge Office door.

'I've brought Coop down,' said Noble quietly.

'Uhuh.'

21

'Your case. Don't get the wrong idea. But – y'know –.'

'He wants to get back to the Flash Brigade,' smiled Barker.

'It might help.' Noble knew what he was asking. He also knew the man he was talking to.

'I'm happy here,' said Barker.

'That's what I thought.'

'*His* case?' Barker was prepared to go the whole hog.

'No. You're the arresting officer. Just – y'know – let him "assist".'

'With the appropriate wording.'

'It's your case, Ron. Top to bottom. I'm not even asking.'

'It's okay, sarge. Word it properly, and it makes me look a dim bulb.' The grin broadened. 'Then it becomes *his* case, with *me* "assisting".'

'I leave it to you.'

'I'll fix it.' Barker hesitated, then added, 'Y'know, sarge, I wouldn't mind Upper Neck Beat . . . if it ever comes empty, that is.'

'I'll have a word.' Their eyes exchanged secret, but friendly, messages. 'If it ever comes empty.'

The measure of this man, Police Sergeant 2828 Harry Noble. He wouldn't stay sergeant; he was far too adept at 'man management' ever to remain a mere sergeant. By far the best of the three uniformed sergeants responsible for the running of Sopworth Section. Miles ahead of Inspector Rowe who carried the final sectional can. And yet, he hadn't learned it. It came from the covers of no book. It was just *there*: a God-given gift of which he seemed unaware.

To Noble it was quite natural to be trustworthy; to back the men under him all the way . . . just as long as they didn't chance an arm and try to let *him* in the soup. Bobbying was a job. The hell it was a job! It was a bloody work of art. To take tarted up language from a law book and make it work; to kick the germs up the arse and, at the same time, make 'em believe you were patting them on the head; to know that, way up there in the rarified atmosphere of Headquarters, some goon who'd never worked the streets (or who, if he had, had forgotten the basic nuts and bolts of the job) was waiting to pounce. One slip . . . that's all. That was the goon's reason for living. To grab as many balls as possible and swing on 'em. Never mind that he wouldn't know how the hell to start should *he* meet a given situation. He wasn't going to meet that situation, ergo he knew all the answers.

Noble's job, as he saw it, was to chop his bloody fingers off before he had time to grab. To wrap things up in a neat parcel, complete with pink ribbon, and deliver it, registered mail . . . and minus all the clangers it might have collected down in the working sewer. The good old NCO. Like the NCOs ran the army, the NCOs also ran the Police Service. They took the bright ideas, modified them, passed them down the line and made them work.

Noble and Barker returned to the Charge Office.

Higginbottom was just closing the Telephone and Teleprinter Message Book. He re-opened it, in case Noble wanted to see the latest griff.

'Anything interesting?' asked Noble.

'Stolen cars, mainly. Not much else.'

'I'll sign it before I go off.' Noble turned to Rayon and said, 'Well? What have *you* to say for yourself?'

Rayon lowered the bloody rag, and spoke the immortal words, 'I wanna solicitor.'

'Any particular solicitor?' asked Noble sarcastically.

'No. But I'm entitled to . . .'

'At the moment, sonny-boy, you're entitled to breathe. And not much else. In case it's slipped your memory, you've just lobbed a brick through a shop window. You've just nicked a very expensive piece of electronic equipment. You've just thrown the bloody thing in some dark corner somewhere, which won't have done it a power of good. And you've just resisted lawful arrest. At a pinch I'd say you've enough to worry about without risking an overheating of the brain thinking up "entitlements".'

'I haven't pinched owt,' muttered Rayon.

'Of course not. You were out jogging.'

'Eh?'

Noble turned to Cooper and said, 'Take him into the Interview Room, constable. Whisper words of wisdom into his shell-like ear.' And to Rayon, 'Be advised, son. Come clean. I'm not promising you anything if you do . . . don't get any wrong ideas. But, knowing this officer, I'm pretty safe in promising you something if you *don't*.'

A frown of worry touched Barker's face, then cleared, and he said, 'I'll get the paperwork under way.'

'Thanks.' Cooper stepped towards the cringing Rayon, grasped him by the elbow, hoiked him up from the chair and growled, 'C'mon, squirt. You and me have an agreement to reach.'

Interview Rooms. A whole book, indeed a whole library of books, could be written about Interview Rooms. The name itself carries strange and worrying suggestions. An interview can, when all is said and done, be carried out in *any* room. In a bedroom. In an office. Across a table in a restaurant. Anywhere. But that there should be

23

specific rooms, purpose-built for *interviews*. And, be it understood, not merely in police stations. In every department of the Establishment. Rooms there for that single purpose . . . a place in which to conduct an interview.

Privacy, perhaps? Perhaps, but if so privacy among *other* things. Because an Interview Room — all Interview Rooms and every Interview Room — is womb-like in its complete isolation.

2 a.m. The door is closed and, thereafter, no other person is invited to enter. Just the interviewer and the interviewee. And every aspect of the room is geared to favour the former while, at the same time, it intimidates the latter. Not, perhaps, deliberately so, but by the very nature of the room's purpose. There is warmth, but not too much warmth; not enough warmth to bring on drowsiness; not enough warmth to give more than token comfort. There is light. Too much light; the strip lighting is of unnecessary strength, as if to pierce the exterior of the person being questioned and thus see the truth before a word is uttered. There is a window, but the pane is of pebbled glass; a mere makebelieve window, there to remind the person interviewed that there is another world . . . to which he might return if he performs the correct tricks. But he can't *see* this world any more than, in most cases, he can hear it, most Interview Rooms being situated in a position whereby the noises of the place of which they are a part *can* be heard, but not the noises of that other outside world. There is also standard 'Interview Room' furniture. A table: a simple, ordinary table, sometimes with a drawer, sometimes without a drawer; sometimes the surface of the table is polished, sometimes it is unpolished, but always on the surface of that table (polished or unpolished) there is a cheap, tin ashtray. One table, two chairs. If a third chair is needed it is *brought* to the Interview Room. If a third chair is not necessary . . . two hard-bottomed, uncomfortable chairs.

Thus a police Interview Room. Where men are questioned. Where terrible secrets are teased from men's minds. Where murder (and worse) is confessed. Where a deadly rapport is woven between questioner and questionee. Where, eventually, men unburden themselves far more than in any confessional. Where, in time, the evil and horror spoken seems to soak into the walls and furniture until the room becomes . . . an Interview Room. It has the correct 'feel'. It has the necessary 'atmosphere'. It becomes what it was meant to be. A place to be feared.

Cooper ushered Rayon into the Interview Room, waved him to a chair, then closed the door. And had that simple movement of closing the Interview Room door been recorded on film, Cooper would have swept the board of Oscars. The impression was — indeed the *certainty* was conveyed, as if in neon letters a yard high — that the door *might* be re-opened this side of Christmas . . . if everybody trod carefully and said the right things at the right time.

'Put that filthy cloth down.'

Cooper spoke softly and without real expression. He moved a disdainful hand from the wrist and that, too, was a deliberate gesture. Cooper knew. This was his last chance. Thanks to Noble, thanks to Barker, he had been given an opportunity to regain what he mistakenly believed to be his 'manhood'. His 'dignity'. This tiny piece of human scum floating on the sea of criminality was his personal sacrificial lamb. If he goofed it . . .

Rayon placed the stained and soaked cloth on the surface of the table. And he, too, knew. This was going to be no buddy-buddy session. This copper whom he knew but slightly — whom he'd seen only occasionally in the town — was unlike the rest. This one was a real mad bastard.

The nose-bleed had stopped, but the front of his face throbbed slightly and *that* didn't help.

Cooper unbuckled the belt of his tunic and asked, 'D'you wear spectacles?'

'Eh?'

'Glasses? D'you wear 'em? In a case, in your pocket somewhere?'

'Er — no — why?'

Cooper didn't answer the question. He didn't even seem to hear it. He removed his peaked cap, placed it on the seat of the vacant chair then, slowly and deliberately, began to unbutton his tunic.

Cooper complemented the Interview Room. He 'belonged'. It was his natural habitat. The combination of the Interview Room *and* Cooper brought Rayon out in a muck sweat.

Brotherly love — okay, brotherly love — but he, Alfred Henry Courtland Rayon, had always sucked the hammer. Always! As kids he'd always been the one to have his earhole clouted. As youths going out on blind dates he'd always been the one who finished up with the cross-eyed, gormless bint. On the booze-ups he'd always been the one tanked-up stupid and blamed for everything. It wasn't fair . . . was it hell as fair! Bert always ended up as the smart bastard while he, Alfred Henry, ended up with his arse in a sling. But this time . . .

'Dentures?'

'Eh?'

'False teeth,' amplified Cooper.

'W-why?'

'D'you wear 'em?'

'Er — no.'

Cooper slipped his arms from the sleeves of his tunic, folded the tunic and placed it carefully over the back of the vacant chair.

'Er . . . why?' ventured Rayon.

Cooper allowed his lips to curve into a momentary smile.

'You're — you're not gonna thump me?'

'Don't you think so?' countered Cooper flatly.

'You've — you've no right to . . .'

'No.' The mock-sadness was a deliberate insult. 'People do these things. Things they've no right to do.' He unbuttoned his cuffs and began to roll up his sleeves. 'Like nicking cassette decks. Like belting blue shit out of you. Human nature, I suppose.'

'I — I wanna lawyer.'

'Get knotted.'

'I — I didn't do it.' Rayon pushed himself and the chair a few inches away from the advancing Cooper. He gabbled, 'Not me . . . I swear. Our kid. Bert. He did it. I saw him. I just blew.'

Wilf Pinter shuffled in his armchair, felt the pins-and-needles in his right shoulder move towards a painful cramp and awakened from his cat-nap. His first thought was, 'In God's name, how much longer?' and, having given birth to the thought he felt shame. It was almost like wishing her dead. As evil, as selfish, as that.

He stood up from the armchair, worked his shoulder, then rubbed it, then glanced at the near-dead embers of the tiny fire in the grate. Even in late June it was cold Rimstone way; cold and shivery in the small hours. Some sort of fire was needed; a fire or a warm bed. He took a poker from alongside the hearth, teased the embers into a brighter red with a shallow near-invisible blue flame atop, then chose a couple of split logs from a wicker basket and placed them carefully in position. He waited, poker in hand, until the logs began to spit and splutter — until the blue flame spread into the yellow of burning wood — then he replaced the poker, picked up some tongs and, from a scuttle, took pieces of coal and stacked them in an irregular pyramid around and on top of the logs. The only light in the living-kitchen was from a tiny, glowing bulb fitted into a table lamp perched on top of the kitchen cabinet. He leaned the tongs against the scuttle, rubbed his shoulder again, then walked to the inner door of the kitchen and switched on the light.

26

As he turned the tap to fill the kettle he tried to think, to *really* think. It wasn't possible. The hurt, the worry and the accumulated loss of sleep was like a foam mattress through which clear thought was unable to penetrate.

The door opened and his mother-in-law entered the kitchen.

His mother-in-law . . . and forget all those stupid jokes about mothers-in-law. This one was a gem. The finest, kindest woman he'd ever known . . . bar one.

She said, 'I heard you.'

'You should get some sleep, ma,' he said and, even as he said it, he knew how silly it sounded. Nevertheless, he meant it. He added, 'Did you look in?'

'She's the same.'

He nodded and spooned tea from the caddy into the teapot.

She said, 'She can't feel anything, Wilf.'

He whispered, 'How the hell do *they* know?' and the words held a savagery born of heartbreak and helplessness.

She didn't answer. She pulled her blanket dressing-gown a little tighter around her tiny, thin body and turned to stare at the growing fire.

The truth was, there was no answer to his question. How *did* they know? 'They'. 'Them'. The doctors, the specialists. Until *they* were in a state of coma, until *they* were within touching distance of death, until *they* had suffered the tortures of the damned and had had drugs pumped into them every few hours – how *did* they know? Nobody knew.

She knew – *had* known – and now Wilf knew. A good husband. And now a good daughter. The old 'iron crab' . . . that's what some-body had once called it. Gripping, tearing, crawling. Deep inside. And, as fast as the surgeons sliced away one of its claws, another grew. Not always, of course. Thank the good Lord not always. Some people had it and lost it; enjoyed a re-birth. The lucky ones. Her husband hadn't been lucky. And now her daughter . . . another unlucky member of the family. And the same routine. Home to die. Everything possible had been done. Nobody could ever fault the dedication of those who fought the foulness. But, when the fight was finished, when further fight was hopeless . . . home to die.

She knew how Wilf was feeling. *Exactly* how Wilf was feeling. Hannah was dying. A few days . . . no more. Dying. Technically still alive, but in effect already dead. A massive drug dosage would keep her in a sleep deep enough to counter the agony, but she would never awaken from that sleep. She'd spoken her last words. She'd seen

27

her last sight. She was still breathing, her heart was still beating, her blood was still circulating, but beyond that . . . nothing. Nothing ever again.

She stared into the burning coals and remembered the last time.

'Tea, ma?'

She turned and took the proffered beaker of scalding, sweet tea. Together they sipped the drink and neither knew the right words to say.

She said, 'What time are you on duty?'

'Six o'clock. Off at ten, then on again at two till six tonight.'

'You should tell them,' she said gently. 'Ask for . . . what is it?'

'Compassionate Leave.'

'I think you should, Wilf.'

'No.' His jaw tightened. 'I'll not make her public property.'

'Wilf!' she said softly.

But that, of course, wasn't the real reason. They knew she was ill — of course they knew she was ill — but what they didn't know was *how* ill. And whilever he worked — whilever he went on duty — she *might* get better. Compassionate Leave. That would be like a form of surrender. A capitulation. A tacit acceptance that she *wouldn't* get better. An acceptance of her death.

'You can get me,' he muttered. 'The number's there by the phone. Ring D.H.Q. They'll radio me. I'll be here as quickly as possible.'

She nodded. She thought she understood, but she didn't.

The truth was, he didn't want to *see* her die. Didn't want to watch. Was prepared to be told, but didn't want to witness. Something he'd accepted with great shame, but the truth. To actually stand there and *watch* her die. Dear God! That would really drive him mad.

They sipped tea in silence for a few minutes.

Then she said, 'You could get a couple of hours' sleep in before you go on duty.'

'No.'

'How long is it now?'

'What?'

'Since you went to bed? Since you slept?'

'About a week . . . something like that.'

'Nearer a fortnight. Wilf.' She looked at him with a perfect mix of admiration and affection. 'You're a fine man, Wilf. She knows that . . . she's always known. She wouldn't want you to — y'know — like this.'

'I'm all right, ma. I'll catch up on sleep when it's over.'

Noble said, 'Feel like a spell on the street, Johnny?'

Higginbottom stared, then said, 'Blakey ordered me to . . .'

'Always obey the last order, Johnny.' Noble grinned. 'Chief superintendents sleep the sleep of the just at this hour. I'll make it an order, if you like.'

'No.' Higginbottom looked delighted. 'Suits me fine.'

Noble said, 'Tell young Wooley to come in for his meal. An hour, eh? The good people of Sopworth can rest easy in their beds. Police Constable Higginbottom's on the job.'

'Thanks.' Higginbottom went to the alcove to radio Wooley.

Barker was still busy 'making up his notebook', prior to filling in the forms required to justify the arrest of Rayon. 'Making up your notebook'. It was a complete contradiction, in that it was a necessary impossibility. The Civil Liberties lunatics went a bomb on this barmy instruction from on high. On paper you'd better do it — or else — but anybody not short on marbles knew damn well it *couldn't* be done.

Like tonight. Rayon haring for his life. You racing after him. The tussle when you caught him. Everybody out of breath, everybody heaving and pushing, and then — at that *very* moment — you were supposed to blather out the Short Caution, grab your notebook and write down his immediate reply. Then, not later. Do it later and you're up a gum tree. Christ Almighty, how many arms, how many hands were you supposed to possess? Which meant . . .

All right, don't let's fanny around choking on cherry stones, it meant you committed perjury, time and time and time again. 'I arrested him, told him why I was arresting him, administered the Short Caution, and he replied . . .' It meant you went out on a limb — a very dangerous limb — every time you did your job. Because you *didn't*.

Did you hell as tell him what he was being arrested for. Ninety-nine times out of a hundred he knew bloody well what he was being arrested for, he didn't have to be told! And as for the Short Caution. Struggling, towing — Rayon having a go and trying to knee you in the balls — you're going to say, 'You're not obliged to say anything unless you wish to do so.' The hell you are. You've arrested him. Your first job — your *only* job — is to make damn sure he *stays* arrested.

He wrote: *12.45 a.m. Gave chase and arrested Alfred Henry Courtland Rayon. Administered the Short Caution to Rayon and informed him I was arresting him on suspicion of having committed a felony. Rayon did not reply. Escorted Rayon back to Sopworth Police Station.*

And pick the bones out of *that*, Mr Defending Solicitor. He 'did not reply'. Whereas, the old boys sitting up there on the Bench know that an innocent man *would* have replied. My oath, wouldn't he just! He'd have screamed the place down. He'd at least *2.30 a.m.* have asked questions. Only some nutter as guilty as sin 'doesn't reply'. But nobody can pull a 'fitting-up' accusation. He kept his trap shut and if, by keeping his trap shut he did the right thing, but also screwed himself solid as far as the beaks are concerned . . . whose fault?

And yet, had he been asked, Barker would have insisted that he was a fair-minded police officer. Would have taken an oath that he was. And, indeed, he *was* . . . by some yardsticks. The Law was wrong. The bewigged pundits who periodically revised The Judges Rules were wrong. The whole crazy set-up was wrong. Because the starting point was that the copper was going to twist. All coppers. Every copper. The whole shooting match started with that proposition . . . that no copper will tell the unvarnished truth unless he's hemmed in by judiciary do's and don'ts. And the result? He *has* to twist. There's no other way.

Barker ran his fingers through his hair and pondered upon what next 'near truth' he could record in his notebook.

Cooper guided Rayon into the Charge Office, then closed the door. Wooley watched from where he was eating sandwiches and drinking tea. Noble glanced up from where he was making out the Overtime Cards. Barker stopped writing and waited.

Cooper was carrying his tunic over one shoulder, his sleeves were still rolled high and he was carrying his peaked cap in his free hand.

As he nudged Rayon to a vacant chair, Cooper said, 'He'd like to make a statement.'

Noble looked a question at Cooper and Cooper's eyes smiled and his head moved in a barely perceptible shake. Slight relief showed itself on Noble's face.

Barker began, 'In that case we'd better . . .'

'Later.' Cooper began to roll down his sleeves. He said, 'You arrested the wrong brother, Ron.'

'Eh?'

'Alf, here, was in the Market Square. So was his brother, Bert. Nothing pre-arranged. One of those coincidences.' He buttoned the cuffs of his shirt sleeves. 'Brother Bert slammed the brick through Hartley's window and pinched the cassette deck. Alf, here, saw him . . . he'll *say* he saw him in the statement.'

30

Cooper pulled on his tunic and fastened it as he continued, 'The chemist . . . what's his name?'

'Willis.'

'Willis was going to bed at the time. Standing at the window, drawing the curtains. Bert scarpered. Alf scarpered. Alf was scared . . . sure Willis must have seen him. Certain we'd nail him for the theft. Chances are Brother Bert had the same idea.' He chuckled. 'My bet is that Willis didn't see a damn thing. A well-lighted room . . . who the hell can see what's going on outside after dark?'

'So Albert has the cassette deck?' said Barker.

'*Had* it.' Cooper put on his peaked hat. 'We'd better get round there.'

'With pleasure.' Barker stood up and took his helmet from the table.

'Need a car?' Noble held the keys of his car towards Cooper.

Cooper said, 'No. We'll stretch our legs.' Then to Wooley, 'Shove sonny-boy into a cell until we get back, okay?'

Cooper and Barker left the Charge Office. Wooley guided the wretched Rayon to the cells and locked him up and, when he returned, said, 'The guts . . . d'you think?'

The tone was that of an inquisitive schoolboy seeking authoritative information concerning the facts of life.

Noble scooped the Overtime Cards together, straightened them, then slipped them into a manilla envelope.

'Coop,' amplified Wooley. 'He's obviously given Rayon a real roughing up.'

'Has he?' Noble slipped the envelope into a desk drawer.

'He's coughed. He's ready to . . .'

'Son, they *all* cough.' Noble swung round in the swivel chair. His voice was paternal, tinged with a little impatience. 'How long have you carried that number?'

'Two years . . . going on three.'

'And how many times have you seen a prisoner thumped? I mean *seen* him thumped? Known for a fact that he *has* been thumped? Not just heard some second-hand yarn about some prisoner having hell belted out of him?'

'None, until tonight.'

'No. Not tonight, either.' Noble leaned forward and helped himself to one of Wooley's sandwiches. He bit into it, then continued, 'A thing to remember, son. The shyster lawyers. When all else fails — when they haven't the ghost of a leg to stand on — swear blind the client's been manhandled while in police custody. It sometimes works. It works a bloody sight more often than it *should.*'

'There's a lot of police-bashers, these days. Pillocks who make a lot of noise . . . usually about sod-all. Police violence. It's talked about. On the box. At damn near every political meeting. All our coppers are bomb-happy. Thugs. Refugees from the Gestapo. And it's all balls!'

Noble swallowed, then took another bite at the sandwich.

He continued, 'Lemme tell you lad. I've seen it *once.* Just the once. And the bastard needed it because *he* started it. But I've also stood in a witness box and been accused of damn near crippling men I haven't laid a glove on. Not me, not anybody. But that hasn't stopped me from sweating. And it hasn't stopped some people from believing I *did* punch him around. It's a very nasty accusation, but . . .' Noble chuckled gently. 'It comes in handy sometimes. All this hot gospel crap about what goes on behind closed doors in a nick. Lunatics like Rayon believe it. Believe every word of it. They believe it, because they *want* to believe it. Because they've listened, open-mouthed, to all the moonshire their pals have invented. And it terrifies 'em.' Again Noble swallowed then popped what was left of the sandwich in his mouth. 'That's what brought on the bout of coughing, son. Not what Coop did — Coop didn't do a damn thing — but what Rayon *expected* Coop to do. He thought he had a straight choice. To talk or to bleed. At a guess Coop played on that, and Rayon talked.'

It was very nice being on the street again. That's what bobbying was all about. Not sitting in an office all night answering telephone and teleprinter messages. That wasn't bobbying. *This* was bobbying.

Higginbottom strolled along the parade of shops, checking each door as he passed. A sweet and steady number; official walking speed two-and-a-half miles per hour . . . that's what the book of words said and the book of words was always right. In the distance he could hear hammering as some joiner boarded up the window of Hartley's Radio Stores. A neat piece of collar-feeling on the part of Ron, that. It might even earn him a commendation from the chief. Maybe. Nobody ever knew how those things were dished out. A bloke pulled a beaut — like Ron had done tonight — and 'Good work lad', and not another sausage. Some other bloke did damn-all and had a commendation pinned to his backside. There was no telling. Except, of course, for runaway horses. Bloody funny that, stop a runaway horse and you were a stone cold cert for a chief constable's recommendation. Always! Look through the files. Every runaway horse, one C.C.R. Rumour had it — when horses were a lot more plentiful on the streets — that the old coppers used to work deliberate flankers. One scared the nag into galloping, his pal waited for it and grabbed. A couple of months later they changed places . . . tit-for-tat. There was a fiddle to everything. Enough commendations and three stripes were there for the taking. Even the promotion exam was fixed. You couldn't fail. He was a bloody hero — he stopped runaway horses — he *had* to be a sergeant.

He tried one more knob and the door gave against his pressure.

All thoughts of runaway horses left Higginbottom's mind. He held the door steady for a moment, then gradually, silently, released the pressure on the knob. He listened, but could hear nothing. He'd borrowed Wooley's torch, truncheon and walkie-talkie. He transferred the torch to his left hand and slipped his right thumb through the thong of the truncheon. Gingerly, slowly and with infinite care he eased the door open. It was a pork butcher's shop and, as he opened the door, the faint smell of the place touched his nostrils.

When the door was part-way open, he went in with a rush and at the same time switched on the torch. There was nobody there. The till had its drawer open but, on examination, he found it not to have been forced; wise shopkeepers empty the till at night, then leave it open in order to show thieves that it *is* empty . . . and thus save a wrecked till. He shone the torch under the counter, then under the display shelf of the window. Nothing.

Obviously, some bloody fool had forgotten to lock the place up. He shone the torch beam on the door. It had a latch-lock — a Yale — therefore he could drop it as he left and save the inconvenience of dragging the owner from his bed.

He was about to leave when he heard the sound beyond an inner door. It sounded like voices. Muttering. Murmuring. That and the sound of movement. He went to the inner door, turned the handle and pushed, and immediately the door was slammed back in his face.

So easy, eh? So near to a clanger. The bastards were in there; in the living quarters, perhaps. Whatever, helping themselves to whatever wasn't too hot or too heavy. Right. So this was where he (Higginbottom) showed Blakey just how wrong he was; how he (Higginbottom) was well above fannying around in a sectional office all night.

It was meant to be a flyer and, indeed, it *was* a flyer. Torch in one hand, truncheon in the other, Higginbottom shoulder-charged the door and, as he arrived, he slammed down the handle of the door with the hand holding the truncheon. It really was quite spectacular. The door flew open, Higginbottom entered the room like a world-beater then, on the second stride, hit the 'trip-wire'. The torch flew and went out. His injured ankle felt as though some bastard had driven a knife into it. His feet tried to untangle themselves while the upper part of his body continued momentum and, as he fell forward, the arm of a sofa came up and smashed all the breath from his body. Then they started trying to smother him; with an old, wet and smelly rug; at least six of the mad sods. He couldn't fight back. The truncheon dangled on its thong from his wrist, but they refused him freedom enough to grab it. He yelled and fought as well as he was able, but it was no good, he was out-numbered and this was *it*.

A light was switched on and a voice bawled, 'What the bloody 'ell!' followed by, 'Down Sheba. Down.'

It wasn't a rug, of course. It was the biggest bloody St Bernard's dog Higginbottom had ever seen. And the 'trip-wire' was its lead; a long lead, fastened to a socking great hook screwed into the skirting board.

Nor was the man with the voice in the sweetest of tempers. He stood at the foot of the stairs and held a particularly nasty-looking butcher's cleaver in his right hand.

'What the 'ell's going on?' he demanded.

Higginbottom heaved what felt to be a ton of friendly dog from his body and gasped, 'For Christ's sake, why don't you lock your front door?'

The man turned his head and shouted, 'Elsie! Did you lock the shop door?'

From upstairs, a woman's voice called, 'Eee . . . now you mention it, I didn't. I forgot all about it.'

The dog was returning its attention to Higginbottom.

The man said, 'It's all right. She's friendly. She'll no'an bite.'

'She's too bloody big to be friendly,' snarled Higginbottom.

'Happen so,' agreed the man.

Higginbottom pushed himself up from the sofa and almost buckled as he tried his weight on the injured ankle.

'It's our kid's dog,' volunteered the man. 'He's on holiday, in Switzerland.'

'Why didn't he take the damn dog with him?'

Higginbottom hobbled around and collected the torch and his helmet.

Somewhat grudgingly, the man said, 'Thanks for finding the door unlocked. I'll lock it after you.'

Barker twitched his nose, sniffed, then looked up at the chimney of the house they were approaching. It was one of a row of terrace-type houses and from its chimney thick smoke drifted upwards against the cloudless sky. Smoke that stank to the high heavens.

'They're burning the thing,' said Cooper.

'In that case . . .'

'In that case, they haven't a cat in hell's chance. Guilt. That's what you can see. That's what you can smell.'

Barker was prepared to accept Cooper's word without argument. Dave Cooper had proved himself. In that Interview Room. Hell knows what he'd said, hell knows what he'd done, but he'd *done* it, and in a fraction of the time he (Barker) could have done it.

'Down there.' Cooper moved his head to indicate an alley. 'Take the back door. I'll go in at the front.'

'If they let you in.'

'They will.' Cooper grinned.

Barker didn't argue. He stepped into the road, counted the houses, then hurried into the mouth of the alley.

Cooper strolled towards the house. He paused at the curtained window and listened to the muted voices from within the lighted room then, very gently, he tapped on the glass.

He moved to the side of the window — between the window and the door — and pressed himself against the wall. The curtains were parted and a shaft of light shone into the street before the curtains were closed again. Cooper waited, then he moved to the window and again tapped on the glass. A little harder this time. Again the curtains were opened for a few moments then closed. Cooper listened and heard footsteps from inside the house. He heard a door-chain being slid along its fastening. He heard a bolt withdrawn. He heard a key being turned. As the door opened he whipped round the jamb, bundled the woman back into the house and sneered, 'Curiosity killed the cat, missus.'

The woman yelled, 'Albert!' and an inner door began to close.

Cooper met the closing door with the heel of a well-placed boot and the door, and the man closing it, were thrown backwards and into the room.

It was there — what was left of it — a very expensive cassette deck. A tangled mass of wire, melting plastic and a twisting steel chassis. The fire was doing its best, but the Pioneer CT-F1250 was not a very combustible piece of equipment.

The woman rushed into the room, screaming abuse and with her hands held ready, fingers bent and eager to claw. Cooper bent, lifted an upholstered pouffe and threw it hard at her knees. It brought her

35

down and she remained on the floor, beating the carpet with her fists.

The man was standing and waiting. He was enough of a criminal to recognise the end of the line when it arrived. He was nursing a hand which had taken the brunt of the edge of the door when Cooper had kicked it open.

Cooper said, 'I've a friend at the back door. Let's have him inside.' As Rayon turned Cooper added, 'And a bucket of water.'

When Barker and Rayon returned to the room the woman was still on the carpet. She'd quietened; she merely sobbed her frustration and, now and again, hammered at the carpet with the side of a fist.

Cooper took the pail of water, stepped as far back as the furniture would allow and threw the contents onto the fire. A great cloud of soot-heavy steam billowed into the room. What had once been moderately clean was now filthy.

'One more should do the trick.' Cooper handed the bucket to Barker, who returned to the tap in the back kitchen.

'Like to tell me?' suggested Cooper, without too much interest.

Albert Rayon nodded. It was the usual story of brainless, spur-of-the-moment theft. A pint too much to drink. A brick. A shop window. A nice looking cassette deck. Then, as he'd held the loot, the turning on of a bedroom light above the chemist's shop and the surprise of seeing Alf, his brother, less than fifty yards away. He thought he'd been seen. He was damn sure Alf would break under questioning. His only hope — a very long-shot hope — was to destroy the stolen property.

'You win some, you lose some,' he sighed.

Cooper took the second bucket of water and threw it at the almost-extinguished fire. The cloud of steam wasn't as big this time.

'Something to put it in,' said Cooper.

Rayon yanked a stretch-cover from one of the chairs. Barker held it, while Rayon picked what was left of the cassette deck from the soaked ashes and dropped it carefully into the makeshift carrier.

'That the lot?' asked Cooper.

'I think so,' said Rayon.

'Okay, Ron.' Cooper turned to Barker. 'He's all yours. Take over.'

'The — er . . .' Barker motioned towards the woman who was still on the carpet. 'His wife?'

'She married a bent bastard.' Cooper shrugged. 'If he promised her a rose garden . . . now she knows.'

If you would see human nature at its weakest, at its most susceptible, at its most pathetic, visit a police station in the small hours of a morning and witness the end product of that transfiguration from roaring drunkenness to wretched self-pity. All that fighting booze has evaporated. All that cock o' the walk arrogance has shrivelled into nothingness. A lot of money has been spent, and the end-product is discomfort, a mouth like a dried-out sewer and, very often, a feeling of shame.

Harry Bodkin was one of those gaunt, prematurely bald men, in his mid-fifties. He would change very little however long he lived. Such men seem to reach a plateau as their hair falls out and, from that moment, they are 'elderly', but will never grow 'old'. He was quietly dressed in a clerical grey suit, a white shirt, a wine-coloured tie (which was still rolled neatly on the desk, ready for him to place around his neck) and black shoes. He sat on a chair and fastened the laces of his shoes with trembling fingers.

'Was I . . . *very* drunk?' he asked in a low voice.

Wooley said, 'You were tanked.'

'Oh, my God!' It was a whispered exclamation of despair.

'You were really enjoying yourself,' chuckled Wooley.

'No.' The voice was heavy with defeat. He straightened and reached for the tie. 'The silly thing is, I don't drink much. Hardly at all. This is the first time I've been drunk in my life.'

'There's a first time for everything.'

'I'll lose my job.' It wasn't a plea. He wasn't seeking sympathy. It was a simple statement of fact.

'Be damned,' scoffed Wooley. 'You get a skinful on your own time. Who's likely to . . .'

'Check the Previous Conviction Book, Charlie.'

Noble interrupted Wooley, left his own desk in a corner of the Charge Office and walked over.

Wooley stared for a moment, then went to a wall-cupboard and pulled out an indexed ledger.

'From where?' Noble stood in front of Bodkin and stared into the miserable face.

'I beg your pardon?'

'Where are you from?'

'Oh, Bordfield.'

'And if we ask *them* to check for previous convictions?'

'I once . . .' A sad smile touched the lips for a moment. 'I once parked on a double yellow line. About two years ago. If that's recorded.'

'It might be.' Noble waited, then said, 'Anything else?'

'No.' Bodin shook his head. He straightened his collar and began to knot the tie. 'I'm not a criminal, sergeant. A fool, yes, but not a criminal.'

'What happened last night?'

Wooley closed the ledger and said, 'No previous cons here, sarge.'

'Last night?' repeated Noble.

'An old school friend.' Bodkin tightened the knot. 'It was my day off. I hadn't seen him for years. Something of a celebration, but it got out of hand. Very much out of hand.' He sighed, then added, 'I'm sorry, sergeant. Sorry for the trouble I've caused.'

'It's what we're paid for,' said Noble flatly. 'You say you'll lose your job?'

'I don't think there's much doubt.'

'Why?'

'Respectability.' Bodkin moved his hands. 'It's understandable. I mean, who wants drunks . . .'

'You're not a drunk.'

'It's a poor argument, sergeant. It won't get me far.'

'What is your job?' asked Noble.

'Bordfield Crematorium. I'm a gas-chamber attendant.'

Wooley gave a short laugh.

Noble turned his head, and Wooley explained, 'It explains things, sarge. Marching up and down Queen's Street, bawling, 'I burn the buggers! I burn the buggers!' at the top of his voice.'

Bodkin breathed, 'Oh, my God, was I?'

Wooley said, 'Sure. That's why I nicked you.'

'So, you'll lose your job?'

'There's nothing more certain. When *that* comes out in court.'

'It will,' said Noble tonelessly.

'I know.' Bodkin nodded. 'Look, I'm not blaming you. I'm not blaming *anybody*. I should have . . .'

'The hell it will,' said Noble softly.

'What?'

'Eh?' Wooley's eyes opened.

Noble said, 'Get dressed, Bodkin. Take it as a lesson. I think you will. Go home, and don't get drunk again.'

'You — you mean that?' Bodkin frowned his puzzlement.

'You've been lucky,' growled Noble. 'Go home.'

Bodkin collected his belongings then, stammering his thanks, left the Charge Office, left the police station.

Wooley's outrage was tempered by his respect for Noble. Nevertheless, the outrage had to be voiced.

He said, 'You can't *do* that, sergeant.'

'No?' Noble raised a sardonic eyebrow.

'That was my case. If I'm asked . . .'

'Is it in the Charge Book yet?'

'No. But it's in my notebook. I can be right in the shit if somebody happens to . . .'

'Tear those forms up.' Noble glanced at the official documents which had already been made out by Wooley. 'And give me your notebook.'

Wooley handed Noble his notebook.

As Wooley tore up the forms and dropped them into the waste-paper basket Noble flipped the pages of the notebook and found the entry covering the arrest of Bodkin. He took a ruler, drew two slanting lines across the entry then wrote, *Cancelled. No action by order of Police Sergeant 2828 Noble.* Then he signed, dated and timed the cancellation and handed the notebook back to Wooley.

Wooley read the cancellation, then muttered, 'That — that isn't official, sarge.'

'Right. You've got me by the short hairs. All it does is get *you* off the hook. That's all it's meant to do. Flash it in front of Rowe and I'm in trouble. Don't think you're telling me
3 a.m.   something I don't know, son. I'm chancing my arm. With Bodkin. With you. But I'm damned if I'm going to stand by and see a man lose his job just because, once in his life, he got pissed.'

'I'm — I'm sorry, sergeant.' Wooley looked shamefaced.

'Don't be.' Noble's voice softened. 'You had the guts to object. Finish your meal, then go out and spell Johnny.'

And at that moment Police Constable 1871 John Henry Higgin-bottom limped through the door of the Charge Office.

Noble gazed at him for a moment, then said, 'And what have we here? The remnants of Ney's Last Stand?'

There was a break. There is always a break somewhere within the night shift of every police station. It is never planned; nobody ordains that between such-and-such a time and such-and-such a time the pace of action shall ease to a speed which is almost stationary. It just happens. Like half-time at a football match. Like the eye of a hurricane. It has no specific duration, nor has it a determined o'clock. Somewhere in the small and impossible hours the brakes are applied for a time, and everybody sighs with relief, accepts the breather and asks no questions.

In the Charge Office Noble brought the Sectional Diary up to date; the entry of events, the graph showing the men on duty and the beats covered; a neat system which showed, at a glance, the weak points and the times when policing was thin enough to be near-transparent. The police 'day' began and ended at 6 a.m., therefore he, in turn, could see what activity and what police cover the previous day had brought. A fatal road accident had been recorded by the Late Shift sergeant, Cockburn. The Early Shift sergeant, Ramsden, had recorded two petty thefts; ladies' underwear from a clothes line and a bicycle left unattended outside the town's main supermarket. The Sopworth detective constable, 'Taffy' Evans, had handled both thefts, and, knowing Taffy, he'd made a five-course meal of both incidents. There was a Missing From Home, which had been duly recorded and circulated, but not to worry, *that* little trollop had been 'missing' four times previously and, given time, the London boys would pick her up in some West End pin-table arcade. The seamy, 'yucky' side of life. The temporary lunacies. The minor disasters. Not a word about the thousands of ordinary, decent citizens who went about their own ordinary, decent business. The Sectional Diary . . . it recorded only what went on in Sopworth's crotch.

Higginbottom was bent forward in a chair, within the telephone and teleprinter alcove; ready to answer any call should that be necessary. He'd removed his shoe and sock and was gently kneading the ankle-joint of his foot. The hell he was going to go off duty 'sick' again. The hell he was going to give Blakey the chance to gloat. He'd come on duty in a wheelchair first. But the wrestling match with that bloody great dog had done his ankle a power of no-good. And when he got home he'd let Mabel get cracking with cold compresses. Maybe some comfrey — the old 'knitbone' beloved of herbalists — perhaps some of these old wives' remedies really worked. When he got home! Those blasted contraceptive pills . . . that was *another* problem. When he got home.

Bloody women! Bloody wives! Why couldn't they bring their daughters up properly? Why couldn't they tell 'em? Dammit, that was the *job* of being a mother. Not just potty-training 'em. Other things. Things a father couldn't do; couldn't explain; couldn't talk about to his daughter. Why the hell hadn't Mabel . . .

Ah, but a lad. If it hadn't been Betty. If it had been a son. Oh, my word. That would have been *something*. Cricket, for a start off. He'd have taught him all the craft of the finest game in the world. A batsman, perhaps. An opening batsman. Steady as a rock; tearing all the

40

thunder and lightning out of the opening speed merchants; driving 'em into the ground. Then, when the ball was a big as a balloon, opening his shoulders and letting fly. Square cutting. Driving into the covers. Flicking it between slips. A great batsman. A county player, perhaps . . . perhaps even opening for England.

And *not* being hit on the bloody ankle.

He kneaded the hurting ankle and dreamed great dreams.

Cooper and Barker sat, huddled together, and completed the required entries in their respective notebooks.

'Show you arresting him,' murmured Cooper.

'Nay, be damned. You were the one . . .'

'You the arresting officer,' insisted Cooper. 'I was present. I'll be witness.'

'If you're sure.'

'I'm sure.'

They wrote in their notebooks. They exchanged broad details of the arrest, the taking possession of the stolen property and the escorting of Albert Rayon to the police station.

'Cautioned and charged, he said what?' asked Barker.

'What the hell *didn't* he say?' observed Cooper.

'Well, he said he must have been bloody mad. He said that a few times.'

'That'll do. It's as good as an admission. Cautioned, charged, he replied, "I must have been mad".'

'Great.'

Again, they bent their heads and wrote in their notebooks.

Barker said, 'A statement, you think?'

'We don't need one. Get the cassette deck identified. There'll be a chassis number, somewhere. Get Hartley to identify it. We have him by the goolies.'

'Aye. I suppose.'

'Ron.' Cooper lowered his pen and spoke as an expert to an enthusiastic amateur. 'Statements — voluntary statements — don't let some of the smart types fool you. Sometimes they're needed. If you've damn-all else a voluntary statement can swing a case. But not for the *sake* of 'em, see? If you don't need a voluntary, forget it. The magistrates. The judges. They're not mugs. A bent bugger doesn't give a voluntary unless it's kidded out of him. That makes it suspect. But come up a few times with an open-and-shut job — and *without* a voluntary — and when you *need* a voluntary they'll give you the benefit of the doubt. Get it? And when you're giving evidence, say all the good things you can about him — within reason. That makes you a nice, unbiased policeman. Then, when you go on to tell 'em what a ringtailed bastard he is, they'll believe *that*, too.'

'You must have been a damn good jack,' said Barker quietly.

'I was.' Cooper smiled. 'Y'know . . . I enjoyed tonight.'

'And Upper Neck?'

'I hate the bloody place.'

'As bad as that?'

'I'm not just a bobby, Ron.' There was a sad, sighing quality about the words. 'I'm not knocking the job — being a bobby, I mean — but I wasn't cut out for it. I'm a thief-taker. And if I can't be that, I don't want to know.'

Outside, too, this time of rest and inactivity had taken over. Police Constable 1116 Charles Wooley sat in the shadows of the tiny wooden shelter, in the pocket-handkerchief-sized Garden of Rest, legs stretched out in front of him, feet crossed and relaxed. He was struggling with the intricacies of pipe-smoking.

He fancied himself as a pipe-smoker. Very masculine. Very 'steady' looking. Somebody had once said — one of the older hands he'd met on his last Refresher Course.

'A pipe, young 'un. When you're on nights. It's more than just a smoke. It's a *pal*. You get the old pipe cracking, and you aren't alone any more. Fags? Ah! Gimme a pipe, every time.'

Unfortunately this pipe-smoking wiseacre had also been something of a nutter. He'd had all the lore of pipe-smoking at his fingertips. And he'd been anxious — almost eager — to pass on the know-how.

'A cherry wood, see? Only flake in a cherry wood. No mixture. Mixture smokes hot in a cherry wood . . .'

'At least half a dozen. Not like fags. Never — *never* — refill a warm pipe. Give it time to cool. Time to breathe . . .'

'Flake . . . you rub it. Like this. Rub it well. Tease it. And don't take the pipe to the tobacco. Get the flake rubbed up well, hold it on your open palm, like this, then turn the pipe upside down and ease the baccy up to the bowl of the pipe and roll the baccy — like this — until it eases itself into the bowl . . .'

Yards of it. The do's and don'ts of expertise in the use of a briar. And he, Wooley, had listened and had resolved to become a real, honest-to-God pipe-smoker.

But, until now, he'd made a right cock-up of it. He spilled more tobacco down the front of his trousers filling the damn thing than ever ended up in the bowl of the pipe. And having filled and packed the thing — having poked around with a match organising the correct 'draw' — how in hell's name did you keep the tobacco smouldering? A match a minute. That was the average. That, or sucking like the clappers until you were gasping for breath. He must have got it all wrong, *somewhere*. The bloke — the bloke who'd told him all the ins and outs — had stroked the surface of the tobacco with the flame from a single match and, from then on, gentle, peaceful puffing until every shred of tobacco was grey ash.

Wooley towed and tussled with his newly chosen vice, and one part of his brain remembered Bodkin, the crematorium worker. Christ, old Noble had chanced his arm on that one! Supposing he, Wooley, had been one of those crawling buggers; one of those hounds out to make a name for himself, even if it meant treading on other men's necks? They were around; in the force, out of the force; the trawl for coppers was pretty wide these days, and some genuine beauties wore the uniform.

Nevertheless . . .

Okay, he was a comparatively 'new boy' and Noble had felt more collars than *he'd* had hot dinners. Okay, accept that. He'd still chanced his arm. And another thing. Why in hell wasn't that sort of thing mentioned — even if only hinted at — at the Police Training College. Yards of crap about 'definitions'. Hour after hour of yap about 'police/public relationships'. First Aid. Swimming. Marching . . . marching, for Christ's sake! Standing at make-believe crossroads, directing make-believe traffic. Piddling about, wasting time, thinking of cock-eyed situations nobody was ever going to encounter. But not so much as a hint of *that*.

The important thing. The most important thing that had happened to him since he'd joined.

It made him feel . . . no, not *trusted*. Not just trusted. More like *accepted*. A fully paid-up-member of a very select club; a club some coppers would never be allowed to join, however long they wore uniform. Bloody strange. The difference it made. Now he *was* a copper . . . he didn't just wear police uniform.

The pipe died for about the tenth time. He sucked, then blew, then sucked again. Nothing.

He muttered, 'Sod it!' shoved the pipe into his tunic pocket and took out a packet of cigarettes.

Noble yawned, stretched, rose from his chair, strolled across to where Cooper and Barker were still checking notebook entries, and said, 'How's it going?'

'Just about tied up.' Cooper caught Noble's yawn and he, too, yawned. 'Ron takes the kudos. I perform the I-was-there-sir routine. Sunny Jim gets it where the bottle gets the cork, and everybody's happy.'

Barker said, 'I'll nip home at six. A quick wash and shave. Then I'll come back and get Hartley to identify what's left of his property. Then . . . a special court?' The last three words were a question.

'I'll leave word,' said Noble. 'Ten o'clock. One magistrate. Police custody till Monday. Then we'll think about bail.'

'What about Alf?' asked Barker.

Cooper's grin was wolfish as he said, 'Easy, mate. Bail to appear here in — say — fourteen days. Withdraw the bail. Meanwhile a nice juicy statement all about what he saw his big brother do. Lean a little, he'll say whatever you want him to say. Then — after the case — leave him to Albert. With luck, we'll get 'em both for Breach of the Peace.'

'You,' smiled Noble, 'are a devious bastard.'

'I know. It makes life very interesting.'

'Ready for home?' asked Noble.

'I reckon.' Cooper turned to Barker. 'Anything we've missed?'

'No, and thanks a lot.'

'Okay.'

Cooper stood up and touched Barker on the shoulder in a quick gesture of comradeship.

In the car, on the way back to Upper Neck, Noble said, 'Good of you, Coop.'

'Eh?'

3.30 a.m.   'To help Ron, like that.'

'Barker's a good copper.' Cooper sounded strangely uncomfortable. 'I didn't do a thing he couldn't have done.'

'That pantomine in the Interview Room,' murmured Noble.

'I enjoyed myself.'

And that, thought Noble, is no more and no less than the truth, Coop old son. You *did* enjoy yourself. Maybe that's why . . .

'I've never asked,' said Noble slowly.

'What?'

'This beat.'

'Upper Neck?'

'You don't like it.'

Cooper grunted.

'You don't even like uniform work.'

'I'm not a wooden-top,' said Cooper bluntly.

'I — er — I never knew why.'

44

'Why I'm not a wooden-top?'

'Now, don't be thick, Coop.' Noble smiled. 'You know what I'm asking.'

'Yeah.' Cooper moved his head in order to squint up at the sky. He said, 'It's a nice night, sergeant.'

'And, that's me in my place.' Noble's smile broadened.

'It *is* a nice night,' said Cooper pleasantly.

And for the rest of the journey they talked inconsequentialities.

Coppers — without being deliberately secretive — can make clams look like loudmouths if, and when, they consider a given subject *verboten*. Noble knew he'd transgressed the unwritten code of the force, but it had been well worth a try. Equally, Cooper was aware of the general curiosity concerning the incident which had dumped him on Upper Neck Beat as a form of 'punishment'. No hard feelings. A try and a failure. Because Coop (and Cooper himself knew it) was a walking question mark. Damnation, he was a born jack. To waste him on a hick beat like Upper Neck amounted to an outrage. A complete misplacement of talent. In the past, he'd tangled with some really tough birds; tangled with them, and planted them where they'd belonged . . . behind granite. All things being equal, he should have made steady progress up to (and perhaps beyond) detective chief inspector. But — obviously — all things were *not* equal. Hence Upper Neck.

Nevertheless . . .

Noble braked the car to a halt by the gate.

Cooper said, 'There's coffee. Thermos, I'm afraid, not fresh. Marian leaves it. And some sandwiches. You're welcome.'

'Okay. Thanks.'

The fact was that, had Noble not allowed his inquisitiveness to get the better of his tact, he might not have accepted the invitation. But he *had* been nosey . . . and the acceptance of the proffered hospitality amounted to an indirect apology. He therefore switched off the ignition, climbed out of the car, locked the car doors and followed Cooper through the gate.

Cooper was standing on the concrete path which led from the gate to the door of the house. He was shining his torch at something on the path.

'What the hell's *that* doing here?' he remarked.

'That' was a cheap, buy-one-at-any-hardware-store, twin-battery torch which was lying on the path.

'Not yours?' asked Noble.

'Not that I know of.' Cooper stooped and picked up the torch.

His thumb slid to the switch of the strange torch as he said, 'Some silly young . . .'

Those were the last words he spoke for almost fifteen hours.

Later Noble was to say, quite truthfully, that he heard nothing. (Or, to be strictly accurate, that he couldn't *remember* hearing anything.) He saw the flash. He felt the push of the blast; a push which lifted him from his feet and sent him sprawling into the vegetable plot alongside the path. In the light from the flash he saw (or thought he saw) the glass of the ground floor windows shatter. The whole thing happened in a split second, and yet it seemed to last for minutes. A strange, slow-motion, not-of-this-world feeling.

And yet, blast being one of the most unpredictable things in the world, Cooper remained upright. Minus a right hand; with the jagged bones of the wrist showing pink and shiny; with a curtain of blood lowering, then dripping from his mangled face . . . but still standing, with his elbow bent as it had been when he'd switched on the doctored torch.

Noble scrambled upright and literally hurled himself at the maimed Cooper. He caught him as his knees buckled, lowered him onto the path, then whipped off his tie, pulled his truncheon from its pocket, fastened tie and truncheon to the lower arm above the shattered hand and, almost savagely, twisted the truncheon until the makeshift tourniquet had reduced the pump of blood to a gentle ooze.

After which came kaleidoscopic jumble of sound, movement, feeling and experience. Not now 'slow-motion'. The reverse, in fact. Like one of the old films, shown at an incorrect speed; silly, laughable, hysterical and monstrously unnatural.

Within himself, Noble fought to regain control of warning emotions and thoughts. He was a copper. He was a sergeant. Nothing — *nothing!* — must make him panic. Coppers — good coppers — retain control of a situation. Any situation. If *they* panic . . .

There was a dull and growing pain in his left eye. Things were out of focus. Only two-dimensional. He held the tourniquet tight with one hand and raised the other to his left eye. The probing fingers touched a warm, gooey mush and, without being able to control himself, he bent his head and spewed all over Cooper's blood-soaked tunic.

Thank God for telephones. Thank God for radio waves. Thank God for motor cars. Without a combination of all three one man (perhaps two) might have died. Like the doctored torch, the messages exploded, faster than the speed of sound in all directions . . .

'Operator. Which service, please?'

'Ambulance. And police. And hurry, please.'

'Where are you speaking from?'

'Upper Neck callbox. It's urgent. Can you . . .'

'Where's the site of the emergency, please?'

'Here. I can see it from here. Will you please . . .'

'Stay where you are, caller . . .'

'Beechwood Brook Ambulance.'

'A nine-nine-nine emergency call from Upper Neck. Within sight of the telephone kiosk.'

'Any details, please?'

'No. Sorry. The caller insisted it was urgent.'

'Thank you, operator. We're on our way . . .'

'Beechwood Brook Police.'

'A nine-nine-nine from Upper Neck. Within sight of the kiosk.'

'A road accident?'

'No idea. The caller said it was urgent. The ambulance is on its way.'

'Okay, operator. We'll have a car there as soon as possible . . .'

'Control Alfa calling Fox Fifty-Nine. Come in Fox Fifty-Nine.'

'Fox Fifty-Nine here.'

'Your present location Fox Fifty-Nine, please.'

'Fox Fifty-Nine. We're travelling south along Sopworth Road. Approaching Dolly Hill.'

'Incident at Upper Neck. Details not yet known. Ambulance on its way. Please attend and report details.'

'Fox Fifty-Nine. Will do. Fox Fifty-Nine, out . . .'

Higginbottom yanked the plug from the switchboard and continued to massage his ankle. Barker was putting the finishing touches to the file relating to Albert Rayon, prior to taking to the streets for a final check of property.

Higginbottom said, 'Summat at Upper Neck. D.H.Q. just had a triple-niner.'

'The sergeant and Cooper should just about drop for it,' observed Barker.

'Aye.'

'Might be as well to give Coop's house a ring. See if they want reinforcements.'

'They'll ring us, if they do.' Higginbottom flexed the ankle, then reached for his sock.

* * *

The hamlet of Upper Neck — the hamlet itself, not the beat which carried the same name as the hamlet —numbered less than five hundred.

A typical North Country hamlet, where people tended to mind their own business. Other, that is, than in an emergency. In an emergency the inhabitants worked to shake aside their natural reticence and people who hardly spoke to each other from year end to year end accepted the necessity to combine into a single unit.

And this *was* an emergency.

Simpson-Jones, the retired army officer whose bullet-shattered knee required that he use a walking stick to move around, limped back from the telephone kiosk and, to nobody in general, said, 'They're on their way. Police and ambulance. Just keep 'em quiet, eh? Give 'em plenty of air.'

He wore a heavy dressing-gown over striped flannelette pyjamas, with a silk scarf tied, cravat-style, at his neck. His bare feet were encased in expensive leather slippers and his normal, parade ground bark was modified to suit the seriousness of the situation.

Again, to nobody in particular, he said, 'I — er — I shouldn't touch anything, what? Do what you can to make 'em comfortable, of course. But don't touch anything. The police might want to search for things.' He glanced at his wrist watch, as if to double-check that it was still working, then added, 'I make it zero-three-fifty hours — thereabouts — when the explosion occurred. I wasn't sleeping too well. It awoke me, and I glanced at my watch. Zero-three-fifty, I make it. The police'll want to know.'

'I reckon,' agreed John Palmer.

John Palmer was the only person fully dressed . . . and everybody knew why. As the local poacher 'zero-three-fifty hours' was the o'clock when he was ready to set out on his rounds.

And yet Palmer was a tower of strength at that moment. Blood, vomit, broken and splintered bones left him unmoved. He could handle. He could touch. He could examine. He could take the basin of warm water and, with a relay of newly laundered handkerchiefs, clean the faces of Noble and Cooper until some estimation of the injuries could be made.

The water in the basin was a deep pink by this time.

Mrs Johnson, the 'retired gentlewoman' who guarded the privacy of her cottage and its grounds with all the fury of an angry wild cat, brought a fresh basin of warm water to replace that already used.

'I put a handful of salt in it,' she said. 'I hope I didn't do the wrong thing.'

48

'Do no harm, missus,' growled Palmer.

Palmer continued his ministrations, assisted by Cooper's wife, Marian.

Marian Cooper. Not too popular in Upper Neck. Too overtly independent, perhaps; all this Women's Lib rubbish was frowned upon by rural (or even semi-rural) Northerners. Home-making . . . that was a woman's job. And, to do it right, it was a full-time job. Marian Cooper worked, part-time, at Beechwood Brook Cottage Hospital. Which was all right, as far as it went — and no doubt she did a good job, her being a State Registered Nurse and all that — but what about her man? Working all hours, day and night . . . what about his meals? What about a little home comfort to which he was entitled?

Well, nobody could accuse her of not looking after her man at that moment.

She and Palmer handled the bulk of the emergency treatment.

Palmer wiped the blood and mush from Noble's eye with a gentleness usually reserved for tickling trout. For a moment, before the blood gushed in to cover it again, he and Marian Cooper saw the glitter of chrome-plated metal.

'Whatever it is, it's bedded deep,' said Palmer quietly.

Marian Cooper said, 'Leave it.'

'Aye.'

'If we try to dislodge it we might do more harm than good.'

'I'm with you there, missus.'

Marian Cooper looked up at the staring faces of the crowd and said, 'A pad, somebody. Something thick to place over the eye. Then some bandage.'

A woman said, 'I've some sanitary pads handy.'

'Really!' Mrs Johnson allowed her outrage to surface for a moment.

'That'll do,' said Marian Cooper. 'Two if possible.'

'I'll get them.' The woman hurried away.

Marian Cooper said, 'And bandages. Thick, wide bandages, to hold the pads in position.'

Mrs Simpson-Jones said, 'I've an old sheet. Clean, but old. Flannelette. We could tear it into strips.'

The landlord of the village pub pushed his way through the tiny crowd. He, too, was in pyjamas, dressing-gown and slippers. He carried glasses in one hand and a bottle in the other. He was a short, fussy man and, to him, all answers came in liquid form.

'Brandy,' he said. 'They need a sip of brandy. Give 'em some brandy.'

49

'No brandy,' said Marian Cooper firmly.

'It won't do them any harm. They . . .'

'No brandy.' Marian Cooper turned to her husband; she left the padding and bandaging of Noble's eye and face to Palmer. She raised her head a fraction and said, 'Blankets. Something to keep them warm until the ambulance arrives.'

Two women detached themselves from the crowd and hurried — almost running — to their homes in order to bring blankets.

Marian Cooper examined the tourniquet, frowned her worry, then pulled the bowl of blood-stained warm water nearer. With infinite care — a care, combined with a sureness, which comes only with years of nursing experience — she eased the cuff of Cooper's tunic a few inches higher than the splintered bones. She unbuttoned the bloodied cuff of the shirt and turned it back. Then she eased the unconscious Cooper onto his side. A man from the crowd — a farm-worker who'd pulled on his trousers over his pyjamas, but who was still bare-footed — stepped forward, knelt and helped her.

She said, 'Easy. Hold him there.'

She guided the torn stump of his hand to the warm water, immersed it, then slowly moved it around. The water became a deeper shade of pink and the gentle movement soaked away tiny shreds of flesh and pieces of dirt which had embedded themselves into the tissue.

There was a minor commotion as a woman at the front of the crowd fainted and, just in time, a man caught her and prevented her from falling across the unconscious Noble.

Palmer snarled, 'Jesus wept! Keep back. Keep well back.'

'More water,' said Marian Cooper calmly, and Mrs Johnson hurried away to do her bidding.

And, in the distance, the sound of the ambulance could be heard speeding to the scene and, behind the ambulance, a squad car, its roof blue light revolving and sending an eerie beam sweeping the countryside.

Tim Burns of the Motor Patrol Division was the man who triggered off all the high activity. Like so many world-weary coppers he figured himself immune from shock; he'd watched post mortem examinations, he'd shoved his hands, armpit deep, into the blood and carnage of multiple pile-ups on motorways, he'd seen *everything*.

And yet . . .

Maybe because they were fellow policemen. Maybe because there was no known *reason*. Maybe because he'd expected some form of minor shunt-up with little more than cuts and bruises. Whatever the reason, his voice was a little unsteady as he spoke into the car's microphone.

'Fox Fifty-Nine here.'

'Go ahead Fox Fifty-Nine.'

'This — this incident at Upper Neck. It's bad. An explosion of some kind. We need assistance.'

'A gas explosion?'

'No . . . no, I don't think so. Explosives. Y'know dynamite . . . something like that. Sergeant Noble and Police Constable Cooper are on their way to Bordfield General. They're both in a bad way.'

'You say *not* a gas explosion?'

'Not a gas explosion,' repeated Burns. 'We need some rank out here. C.I.D. We need assistance . . . fast.'

'Understood. Stay there, Fox Fifty-Nine. I'll get assistance there as soon as possible.'

Edmund Blakey, chief superintendent, uniformed Big Daddy of Beechwood Brook Division. How in the name that all was holy in hell he'd clawed a way to that particular rank was one of those unsolved mysteries which punctuate every police force in the United Kingdom . . . at a guess in the world. The expression 'pissing in the same pot' sprang readily to mind whenever that mystery was discussed. He 'knew' people. More important, perhaps, he knew when to smile a sycophantic smile and agree . . . or *not* agree, as the case may be. His eye never strayed from the main chance. He was a Gilbertian character; figuratively speaking, his arm muscles were hard and strong from years of 'polishing the knocker on the big brass door'. A Gilbertian figure, but without the saving grace of being even remotely humorous. Humorous, indeed? There never was a man more full of his own importance. More contemptuous of his underlings. More convinced that he ruled by reason of some peculiar divine right.

'Why?' He sat up in bed, held the telephone receiver to his ear and sneered the question into the mouthpiece.

The Beechwood Brook D.H.Q. telephonist said, 'P.C. Burns — he's Motor Patrol, sir — he's at the scene.'

'And what does that prove?'

'It's serious, sir.'

'Because P.C. Burns *says* it's serious?'

'Well, yes, sir. Sergeant Noble and P.C. Cooper had been taken to Bordfield General.'

51

'What does that prove?'

'Sir?'

'An ambulance was requested . . . am I right?'

'Yes, sir.'

'They have to justify their existence, constable.'

'Sir?'

'Good grief, man, use your imagination. It wouldn't look good for the ambulance to return empty. There's nothing to suggest that either Noble or Cooper are *seriously* injured. We have the word of Burns that there was an explosion. Some Gas Board . . .'

'Sir, he was quite sure the . . .'

'I want proof, constable. I want far more than the word of a Motor Patrol Division driver. I'd look something of a fool if I attended some fiddling little incident, at this hour, on the strength of what *you've* told me.'

The telephonist sighed, 'Yes, sir. I'm sorry, sir,' and jerked the plug from its socket in the switchboard.

It was a mistake, of course. The great and almighty Blakey had dropped a great and almighty clanger. The D.H.Q. telephonist felt duly peeved. He also felt in dire danger of catching a draught should the Upper Neck flap turn out to be something a deal larger than Blakey seemed to think it was. He therefore logged the outgoing message (in red ink) and the incoming reaction (in black ink) . . . and cherry *that* stone, Mr Chief Superintendent Blakey if you find yourself up a ladder without any rungs!

The ambulance raced fast and smoothly toward Bordfield General Infirmary. Already a radio message had been sent, from ambulance to infirmary, warning of a possible amputation, plus a second possible emergency operation . . . and please have a theatre and a team standing by.

In the rear of the ambulance Noble and Cooper were on stretchers, tucked warmly within the folds of scarlet blankets. An attendant, Marian Cooper and Motor Patrol Constable Burns busied themselves, holding the injured men steady against the roll of the vehicle and wiping the ooze of blood which still disfigured their faces.

Burns had left his partner, Tyler, at the scene. Maybe he'd done the wrong thing, he wasn't sure. But other squad cars were converging onto Upper Neck, and the man, Simpson-Jones, seemed to have standing in the community and was forming a formidable back-up authority to whatever suggestion was made.

A tiny community. A rural community. Everybody stunned;

everybody wanting to do the right thing, but at the same time nobody wanting to do the *wrong* thing, because they didn't know better. And a decision had had to be made.

4.30 a.m.

Nobody knew what the hell had happened. An explosion . . . beyond that, nothing. Just that Noble and Cooper had been at the receiving end and, any time now, somebody would be asking questions.

He'd said, 'I reckon one of us should go.'

'You go, mate.' Tyler hadn't hesitated. 'These people won't take much handling, and there'll be somebody else along in no time.'

'To — y'know — find out exactly what *happened.*'

'We need to know. They're the only two who can tell us. Go in with 'em, Tim. Go in with 'em. If anybody asks, I'll tell 'em where you are . . . and why.'

Tyler. A nice guy. A nice guy with whom to share a squad car; a guy prepared to go along with any suggestion. But at the same time a guy to be trusted.

Burns held his arm across the chest of Noble and did what he could to counter the sway of the vehicle. The ambulance attendant gently dabbed a mixture of sweat and blood from Noble's face. Noble made a move as if to try and push himself upright.

'Easy, sarge,' crooned Burns. 'You're okay. We'll soon have you between cool sheets.'

'Coop . . .' It was a mumbled word which trailed off into muttering silence.

'Coop's fine,' lied Burns.

'His — his hand . . . Coop's . . .'

'Everything's fine, sergeant. Everything's under control. Just relax.'

'A — a — a . . .'

'Please,' pleaded Burn. 'Relax. There's a good chap.'

Noble's unbandaged eye suddenly opened wide. Glaring. Angry.

He croaked, 'A bloody torch. Who'd *do* a thing like that? A bloody torch. And when Coop switched it on . . .'

The eye closed. The head fell back onto the pillow. Burns tightened his grip fractionally, across the stretchered body. The attendant dabbed moisture from Noble's face.

Police Constable 1871 Higginbottom, John Henry, passed the buck. And why not? Night Office Reserves were not expected to *think*. They were expected to stick silly bloody messages in silly bloody books. After that . . . nothing. Ask Blakey. Blakey knew all the

53

answers. Blakey carried one crown and one pip on his shoulder epaulets. And Blakey was getting away with nowt . . . however gormless the Beechwood Brook man was.

That stupid, non-productive telephone conversation.

'Beechwood Brook D.H.Q. here.'

'Sopworth.'

'Blakey wants some more information about the Upper Neck thing.'

'Bully for Blakey. What the hell can *I* do?'

'I thought you might have heard something.'

'From whom?' Higginbottom had asked carefully. Sarcastically.

'Dammit, it's in your section.'

'I've yet to develop second sight, mate. Noble's out there. Put a call through to Cooper's house. They should . . .'

'Cooper and Noble are both on their way to Bordfield General.'

'Oh!'

'And from what Motor Patrol say, they've both been badly injured.'

'Christ!'

'An explosion of some sort.'

'Gas?'

'Everybody asks that same question, how the hell do I know?'

'But Blakey wants to know?'

'Blakey wants to know.'

Higginbottom had said, 'Tell the stupid bastard to open his. bedroom window and sniff.'

'Don't think I wouldn't like to.'

'Okay,' Higginbottom had taken a deep breath. 'Leave it to me. I'll have Rowe out.'

'Do that, eh?'

Ergo, Police Constable 1871 Higginbottom, John Henry, passed the buck. He yanked the plug from the socket marked 'DHQ' and rammed it into the socket marked 'INSP'. He pushed forward a toggle on the switchboard and knew that one more gold-plated copper was about to have his slumbers disturbed. The thought heartened him a little.

A voice said, 'Inspector Rowe.'

It was a strange 'pastel-blue' voice; high-pitched and squeaky. It was a voice (thought Higginbottom) which went with the man; gutless and ever eager to agree with anybody holding higher rank than its owner.

'Higginbottom here, sir.'

54

'Yes, Higginbottom?'

'There's been an explosion at Upper Neck, sir. We don't know what caused it. About the only thing we know is that Sergeant Noble and Constable Cooper were injured, and are on their way to Bordfield General Infirmary. Chief Superintendent Blakey has been notified and he wants somebody to visit the scene and let him know more details.'

'Ah . . . Oh . . . yes. I'll – er – I'll get there right away.' Rowe paused, then added, 'You'd better notify Chief Inspector Tallboy, Higginbottom. Tell him I'll meet him there.'

'I'll do that, sir.'

'And – er – you won't have a sergeant?'

'Not until Sergeant Ramsden comes on at six, sir.'

'Er – get him out, get him out, as soon as possible, Higginbottom. And Kyle. What time should Kyle come on duty?'

'Six o'clock, sir.'

'Good. Good. Get him out, too. Tell him to meet Mr Tallboy and me at the scene.'

'Yes, sir.'

Higginbottom pulled the plug from its socket. He chuckled to himself. Good old Rowe. Good old panic-pants. He doesn't know what the hell's happened, but he wants a line of bobbies between himself and whatever *has* happened.

Before he began telephoning, Higginbottom called in Barker and Wooley on the walkie-talkie waves.

'Stand by your beds, lads. Rowe's up and about. Summat's happened at Upper Neck. Ramsden's coming on. Who knows, even Big Boy Blakey himself. So, fags out and keep your thumbs in line with the seams of your trousers.'

Pinter ran hot water into the bath. He was already stripped. He'd already shaved and cleaned his teeth. The bath served a dual purpose. He liked bodily cleanliness therefore, whenever he had a night without sleep, he always had an extra bath; a morning bath in addition to the daily evening bath. But, in addition, hot water tended to relax him; helped to take the ache out of his bones; helped to prepare him for one more day, after one more night without sleep.

He stared at his face in the bathroom mirror. He squeezed in his cheeks with a thumb and forefinger. Christ, if he didn't get some real sleep soon . . . If she didn't . . .

He breathed, 'You bastard!' at his reflected face.

And, in return, the reflection mocked him. His skin was the colour of putty. His eyes were set deep beneath cavern-like brows and above half-moons of dark purple. He'd seen healthier-looking faces on morgue slabs.

He broadcast a handful of salts into the hot water, then stepped into the bath and allowed his weary body to soak.

The trick was to give his mind other things to think about; to guide it, like driven sheep, away from the chasms of despair. This bath, for example. A hot bath; one of life's less expensive luxuries; a relaxation of the body and a relaxation of the mind. Then a brisk towelling; warm towels, straight from the radiator; an exertion which, along with the warmth from the bath, made the blood circulate and the skin tingle. Then a slow donning of clothes; slow; deliberate; a mild and harmless form of eroticism. Then breakfast; a simple breakfast of scrambled egg on toast, done to a turn; eaten with hot, sweet tea. All the time in the world, mate. More than an hour. The sun well above the horizon. An early morning heat haze rising from the fields; the fields of Rimstone Beat. Rimstone Beat . . . maybe not quite as 'rural' as Upper Neck, but a beat which gave variety. The hell, you couldn't call the flash houses a 'dormitory district' of Sopworth. Of Bordfield, perhaps, but, even then, you'd be pushing things. Just houses. Fancy houses. Expensive houses, standing in their own grounds. And then — less than half a mile away — the brickworks, Dolly Hill, then the boundary with Upper Neck Beat. A few farms. The golf course, the common, the . . .

And in the next room his wife was dying.

In God's name, Hannah — dear, sweet Hannah — get well if you can, but die if you must. Die quickly. Not like this. Get rest . . . and *give* rest. If I could make you well I'd never sleep again as long as I lived. And count it a small enough price to pay. But 'they' say you'll never come out of the coma, and 'they' are the experts. But Hannah — dear, sweet Hannah — I'll not pray. I'm not a praying man . . . and to pray now would be hypocrisy. To pray *now* and never to have prayed before. It wasn't on. Definitely not on. And if there was Something — Somebody — *if* there was Somebody. Credit him with knowing. Credit him with being able to tell the truth. To pray *now* . . . that Somebody wouldn't be too pleased.

Hannah — dear, sweet Hannah — can't you see I'm trying. Everything! I'm trying so bloody hard it's almost driving me mad . . .

Tallboy was still fast asleep.

Christopher Dennis Alaric Tallboy; the 'Dennis' and the 'Alaric' bits were a closely guarded secret; they were included on his birth certificate, his marriage certificate and very little else. To his friends he was 'Chris'. To his underlings (and, when they weren't using naughtier names, to his enemies) he was Detective Chief Inspector Tallboy.

A copper. More than that . . . a fairly high-ranking copper.

But at the moment he looked anything *but* a copper. At some time in the night he'd thrown the bedclothes aside to reveal the eye-searing splendour of a very snazzy pair of pyjamas, bought for him by his wife in one of her less sedate moments. He was on his back, with his grey-speckled hair all-and-every-way on the crumpled pillow and from his partly-open mouth came a soft, rhythmic, gurgling snore.

His wife, Susan, hoisted herself up on one elbow and cocked a cynical eyebrow at the man in her life.

She smiled to herself, then murmured, 'Some detective!'

For Susan Tallboy it had been a restless night. Some nights are like that. For no good reason you *can't* sleep. The most you can do is lie there, staring into the gloom, silently singing snatches of favourite tunes, silently reciting half-forgotten stanzas of girlhood verse . . . anything but sleep. Not sleepy. Not really *wanting* to sleep. Remembering. Remembering long-dead parents; parents who loved each other like nothing on earth but parents who, for a while, were driven apart by this infernal police force. Such a lot to answer for this police force. The daughter of a copper, the wife of a copper. Nobody could kid *her* about the force.

Much as the skin of a coalface worker becomes pitted with the telltale marks of his trade, so with policemen. But with them it is not an external sign. The greying hair apart, the difference between them and non-police types is an 'inside' thing. They handle filth, they handle corruption, they handle twisted and bestial minds. To survive their own minds must become hard . . . almost harsh.

To them 'grey' as a colour is a lighter shade of 'black', it is never 'off-white'. There is a difference and, to know that difference, it is necessary to be a policeman's wife.

Susan Tallboy knew the difference. Over the years she'd watched it change her man. Much of what he laughed at these days were strictly 'in' jokes; jokes whose point was lost other than on fellow policemen; jokes with cruelty attached. And yet he was not a cruel man. He was a good man — a fine husband — but at the same time, a policeman.

She raised a hand and gently straightened a strand of his hair.

Then the bedside telephone rang.

* * *

57

Another police wife — Marian Cooper — held her unconscious husband steady in the swaying ambulance. A nurse, she'd seen mangled limbs galore. She knew her husband had lost a hand . . . at least a hand and possibly a forearm. The thought made her sick with worry. Coop (even she called him 'Coop') was a thick-headed, ramrod-backed, bloody-minded Yorkshireman, and an 'incomplete' Coop was something she doubted whether she could cope with. The code of this husband of hers. He was right — *always* right — and, in fairness, he very often *was* right. But the reverse side of the coin . . . he was 'right' even when he was monumentally *wrong*.

An abrasive man and, over the years, that abrasion had worn away much of their original love for each other.

Opposition — especially opposition he could not overcome — brought bitterness. Always. The run-in with Harris, the A.C.C. In God's name, how could a detective constable face up to an assistant chief constable (crime) and even *expect* to come out on top? But Coop had . . . *and* been surprised when he'd been slapped down.

'Dammit, I'm right,' he'd snarled.

And she'd listened and known that he was only partly right.

'He was on the fence,' he'd stormed.

'You think so.'

'Damnation, woman, what the hell do *you* know about these things? He was there, sitting on the fence. Maybe he did it, maybe he didn't. That's not important.'

'To *him* it's important.'

'Him!' He'd spat the word contemptuously. 'He's a nothing. Scum. One of a family. Every last member bent. And he was on the fence. All I did was give him a push. And don't give me all that innocent-till-proved bullshit. That's for Persil-minded old ladies. Policing — *real* policing — doesn't work that way. He was guilty. Guilty as sin. And because I couldn't bloody-well prove it, he sat there. On the fence. Grinning at me. *Daring* me. All I did was topple him onto the side he belonged to. It's what I'm paid for. It's what I'm *there* for.'

'You verballed him,' she'd murmured sadly.

She knew the language. The expressions. 'Fitting up'. 'Sorting out'. 'Nailing'. 'Verballing'.

'What else?' He'd rounded on her. Eyes blazing. 'Him or me . . . and it wasn't going to be *me*! You're like Harris. Soft-centred. Of course I verballed the lying young hound. Why not? The only way. He broke in. He belted an old lady until she was black and blue. And for what? Less than ten lousy quid.'

'Harris doesn't think so.'

'Harris can get stuffed. He's thick. Thick! Harris can't even see when he's being conned.'

End of argument. Indeed there'd *been* no argument. Coop had been right. Coop was always right. Coop always *would* be right.

She held him and wiped the welling blood from his torn face. Like a giant. Like a god. But who can love a god? Who can ever do more than respect a god?

It was daylight at the scene. That cold, brittle daylight which, even in summer, lacks warmth until the sun has hauled itself farther from the horizon. Three squad cars were at the scene by this time. Uniforms enough to keep the front garden well clear of rubber-neckers. By this time the villagers had thinned out to return to their homes; they had jobs to go to, homes to organise, kids to get ready for the school bus; their inbred phlegmatism refused them the ghoulish luxury of remaining at the scene for the sake of mere curiosity. The double-stain on the concrete path, and Noble's torn and blood-darkened helmet, could be seen from the closed gate. The shattered windows of the police house testified to the force of the blast. Look carefully and, even from the gate, you could see the bruised tops of lettuce and young cabbage plants, where Noble had been thrown. Things the forensic people and the scene-of-crime boys might be interested in. But not Motor Patrol Division. The men on wheels *stayed* on wheels; the force, like every other force, was pigeon-holed and, if he'd any sense, a man stayed on his own nest.

5 a.m.

An elderly, sardonically inclined driver said, 'The Sherlocks won't like seeing the streets before they're warm.'

'D'you know 'em?' asked his companion.

'Noble? Cooper?'

'I think I met Noble, once.'

'Good copper.'

'Can't remember Cooper, though.'

'Used to be a jack. A real tree-tearer.'

Mrs Johnson, having returned to her cottage in order to wash, dress and tidy up her hair, returned carrying two Thermos jugs.

She said, 'Soup. Tinned, I'm afraid, but it should be warming.'

'Thanks, ma'am.' The elderly driver took the jugs. 'These things — y'know — they tend to overlook meal breaks.'

'Any news?' asked Mrs Johnson.

'Not yet, ma'am.' The driver allowed his lips to curl into a quick, crusty smile. 'We're just here to keep the dogs away.'

'The — er — dogs?'

'Figuratively speaking. They don't tell *us* much.'

'Oh!' Mrs Johnson nodded, pretended understanding and left for her cottage.

As he poured soup from one of the jugs into the plastic top-cum-cup, the elderly driver mused, 'Nice beat, this. It'll be going. I wouldn't mind . . . see me through nicely to pension time.'

Odd, thought Higginbottom sourly, the place *still* smells like a wrestler's jock-strap. Open all the doors, open all the windows, get the draughts moving left, right and sideways . . . it *still* stinks. Something to do with the time. Summer, winter, autumn, spring . . . a nick, in the last few hours before a night shift ends, pongs like the very clappers. Always. The smell of tiredness, perhaps. The smell of boredom . . . although this night hadn't been too boring. No matter. Peruvian brothels weren't in it!

Higginbottom limped to the open window of the Charge Office. His limp was more pronounced than it had been when he'd come on duty. Thanks to some stupid cow who'd forgotten to lock the door of a shop. That and a bloody great man-eating St Bernard.

Now, why? Why, in God's name, do people keep dogs as big as young elephants? I mean, *why*? Summat to do with inferiority complexes, that at a guess. Little men, big dogs. Like cars. Little men, big cars. They have to have *summat* that's big. But that flaming dog. Christ, it must cost as much to keep as a houseful of kids. And a useless bloody article, to boot. Those damn things needed mountains and a few feet of snow. Brandy flasks round their necks . . . that sorta thing.

Sergeant Ramsden bustled into the Charge Office through the open door. Bustled. The only word to use. He was one of those chubby men who never walk; their normal mode of progression verges upon the canter. Twinkling legs. Busy arms and hands. The impression is that somewhere inside they have a dynamo, spinning away for dear life . . . and getting nowhere. Men around whom jokes and anecdotes are told; not disliked, but never wholly trusted.

He said, 'What is it, then? What's happened?'

'Upper Neck,' said Higginbottom briefly.

'Yes, but *what*?'

'Some sort of explosion.' Higginbottom almost yawned. 'Sergeant Noble and Coop. Badly injured, so they say. Who the hell tells a Night Office Reserve anything?'

Detective Constable William 'Taffy' Evans joined them in the Charge Office.

'What's to do, then?' he asked of nobody in particular.

Ramsden said, 'An accident at Upper Neck. Sergeant Noble and Constable . . .'

'An accident?' Evans widened his eyes.

'Sounds like it. Sounds as if . . .'

'I'm not here to deal with *accidents*,' protested Evans. 'Crime . . . that's my job. Nobody said anything about . . .'

'Argue the toss with Rowe,' growled Higginbottom. 'He said get you out. All I do is pass messages.'

'What's happened, then?' demanded Evans.

'If and when,' said Higginbottom, 'some moderately sensible bastard sees fit to tell *me*, I'll tell *you*. Meanwhile, I do what Rowe tells me to do. I'm off duty in less than an hour . . . and thank God for that.'

'Rowe can't bring me out for an . . .'

'Rowe can do anything.' Higginbottom's patience was running out. His ankle was giving him hell, and he'd those contraceptive pills to sort out within the next few hours. He almost snarled, 'Rowe can put little nobodies like us in the family way if he feels so inclined, or didn't you know? He can give us babies. The only thing he can't do is make us love 'em.' Then, before Evans could jump in and prolong the exchange, he added, 'Tallboy's up there. If *he* can go to an accident, I'm bloody sure *you* can.'

'It might not be an accident,' said Ramsden.

'He's just said . . .'

'I don't know.' Ramsden always treated Evans with a degree of respect. C.I.D. and all that. The one thing Ramsden *didn't* want was rockets from Rowe *and* Tallboy. He said, 'I think you should go. Then let me know the details.'

A scowling, unconvinced Evans left the Charge Office. Ramsden walked to the Sectional Diary, examined the open page, then said, 'Two arrests?'

'The Rayon brothers. Alfred and Albert. Albert lifted a cassette deck from Hartley's. Alfred saw him. It's Barker's case . . . Coop witness.'

'Bail?'

'Barker knows the details.'

'Fine.' Ramsden ran his finger along the graph showing the men on duty. 'Contact Barker. Tell him to make for Lloyd's Bank. I'll meet him there.'

Higginbottom hobbled to the microphone. Good old Ramsden. Meet Ron outside the bank, sign Ron's notebook – time and place – a neat way of 'checking on duty'. Not too far removed from a punch-clock. Play for safe, boy. Prove you came on duty before six o'clock. Show what a conscientious little sergeant you are . . . and screw whatever's happened at Upper Neck.

Tallboy reached Upper Neck only minutes before Rowe, but those minutes were important. Tyler from Motor Patrol, peaked hat pushed back from his forehead, half-consumed cup of hot soup in one hand, felt an invisible weight leave his shoulders as the Capri braked at the scene. 'Weight'. The name of the game. This little parcel weighed far too much for a mere working wheelman; two of his buddies maimed and, because he and Burns had been first at the scene, they – specifically *he*, Tyler – held the responsibility pending the arrival of real rank. In other words pending the arrival of 'weight'. 'Weight' required 'weight', and Tallboy had earned himself a good reputation.

As Tallboy climbed from the Capri Tyler walked across to him. It was significant that Tyler neither straightened his cap, nor made any attempt to hide the cup of soup; Tallboy wasn't interested in trivia.

'You first at the scene?' asked Tallboy.

'Yes, sir. Me and Burns . . . Burns has gone in with the ambulance.'

'Right. What do we know?'

The two fell into strolling step as they walked towards the police house gate.

Tyler said, 'An explosion. Just before four. Most of the villagers heard it. We caught the nine-nine-nine. When we arrived Sergeant Noble and Constable Cooper were both unconscious. On the path leading to the house.' They stopped at the gate and Tyler said, 'Cooper's hand's gone.'

'Gone?'

'Blown off at a guess. Both their faces were in one hell of a mess.'

'Bad.' Tallboy stared past the closed gate.

'Burns has gone in with the ambulance,' repeated Tyler. 'As soon as he knows anything definite he'll be in touch.'

'The garden?' Tallboy nodded to beyond the gate.

'The villagers were doing what they could, naturally. Once they were in the ambulance we closed the gate. Nobody's been into the garden since. That . . .' Tyler pointed. 'Gold-coloured. From here it looks like torn metal. There could be others. We haven't searched.'

'Mrs Cooper?'

'She hasn't been questioned. She went with her husband. None of the villagers have been questioned yet. Just the time of the explosion. They all seem shocked . . . for what that's worth.'

'Mrs Noble been informed?'

'I — er — I don't think so.' Tyler sounded unsure.

'I think she should be . . . don't you?'

'Yes, sir.' Tyler accepted the mild and implied criticism without rancour. Mrs Noble *should* have been informed. One of those things — one of those *important* things — which had slipped through, and which *shouldn't* have slipped through.

'Right.' Tallboy seemed to reach a decision. 'We need a telephone. We need an Incident Centre. The Police Office . . . is there a way in without walking through the front garden?'

The Upper Neck Police Office was a squat, square building alongside the house. It was separate from the house and its red brick and flat roof gave it the appearance of a cheapjack addition to the Yorkshire stone and high-pitched roof of the house. In the village it was a never-ending bone of contention; for years, the boom had been dropped on planning permission, even for expensive bungalows, but here was a square-cornered eyesore, okayed by the local Police Authority, and about as much 'in place', as far as the surrounding houses and countryside was concerned, as a performing giraffe in an Old Vic production of *Hamlet*. A lot of harsh words had been bandied around concerning Upper Neck Police Office; hints of backhanders; gossip concerning wheeling and dealing by mysterious powers-that-be. But the plain fact was that the modern copper was no longer prepared to set aside the front room of his own home as a place wherein he might interview complainants, drunks, petty thieves and the like. His home was his home . . . period. And if the big-wigs required him to perform 'office work', it was only right and proper that they provide him with an 'office'.

Tyler said, 'There's a back door, sir. Coop'll have the key. But Inspector Rowe has a master key for the two outside beat offices.'

And, as if on cue, Rowe arrived at that moment.

Yo-yo. Like a damn yo-yo. Which was stupid, because the yo-yo went out with . . . Damn it, what *did* the yo-yo go out with? Something equally crazy. Like dance marathons, maybe. Dance marathons? What the hell did *he* know about dance marathons? He'd never seen a dance marathon in his life. The film — okay, the film — *They Shoot Horses Don't They?* He'd seen the film. He'd read the book. Damn good film. Damn good book. But what in hell's name did dead horses have to do with a yo-yo. Dead horses didn't go up and down. Up and down. Hearing things, not hearing things. Seeing things, not seeing things. Dammit, what crazy bastard had wrapped a string around the world? What crazy bastard was playing yo-yo with the world?

At the top of the string a strange voice said, 'Not too many questions, officer. I realise you need to . . .'

Then the world spun around the wrapped string, and the voice faded into the distance. Up and down . . . up and down . . . up and down . . . The trick? Sure, there was a trick. There was *always* a trick. Find the trick and everything becomes easy. And this trick wasn't too hard to find. On the upward journey . . . see? As the string shortens start talking. Start trying to make sense. As the string lengthens — forget it — the world spins faster, the words get jumbled and you move farther and farther from meaning anything.

'. . . remember what happened, sergeant? It's important. We need to know.'

'The torch. Just a torch. On the path. On the path to the house. And Coop . . . Coop . . . Coop . . .'

'. . . which torch? Whose torch? Try, sarge. We *have* to know.'

'Nobody's torch. Just there. Coop picked it up. Switched it on. But it didn't. It was . . . it was . . .'

'. . . enough, Officer. They're preparing the theatre. At the moment, *our* priorities matter. And I can't allow you to . . .'

Sopworth was easing itself from sleep. The newspaper delivery vans were zipping along pre-determined routes, braking long enough for the drivers to hurl twine-bound bundles of morning editions at newsagents' doorways with practised accuracy. The clatter of milk bottles added itself to the gradual increase of sound. The 'early men' — bus drivers, railway workers and the like — walked or rode bicycles to work. Barker had returned to the police station with Ramsden, in order to complete the bailing and statement-taking relating to the Rayon brothers.

Wooley strolled the pavements and felt content. The whole of Sopworth — a few thousand souls and umpteen million pounds worth of property — and, in effect, he was the sole guardian.

A nice feeling. A sweet mix of humility and importance. A feeling in which dreams took upon themselves the status of possibilities. Even probabilities.

He liked being a copper. No doubt about it . . . he really *liked* being a copper. Nor could he understand the gripers. Okay, so you worked Bank Holidays, you worked weekends, you spent a third of your life bashing paving stones when, by all rules of nature, you should be asleep. So what? You joined the force — any force — on that understanding. Nobody told you. Okay, nobody told you. But plain honest-to-God marbles should make you figure that out for yourself.

Meanwhile . . . this morning.

A beautiful June morning; a sunrise you've actually been *paid* to see; wispy smoke curling up from the kilns Dolly Hill way; less than an hour, then a nice warm bed after one of Mrs Jones's breakfasts . . . and, boy, when that motherly landlady of his made a breakfast it was *some* breakfast.

'Now, Charles, eat it all up. My Bill, when he was alive, used to say, "No man can live a full life on an empty stomach". One of his favourite sayings it was. He lived by it.'

Like saying grace before every meal. She always quoted that saying of her dead husband. People do. Funny that, the way people look back on the dead and build up false images. From what he'd heard — from snippets of gossip collected from neighbours who'd known the old man when he was alive — he'd been like a sow at a trough. Forever stuffing himself. *And* not treating the old lady too well.

'Mean — y'know — real mean. Boozing every night. Never taking her on holiday. I dunno. I dunno how she stuck him for that long.'

Police Constable 1116 Charles Wooley. A happy and contented man. A man who, if he gave much thought to whatever was happening at Upper Neck, wasn't unduly worried. Sergeant Noble was there. Sergeant Noble and Coop . . . between 'em they could tame tigers.

Tallboy hogged the telephone at Upper Neck Police Office. Rowe didn't mind. Whilever Tallboy used the phone he had a legitimate excuse for not being able to contact Blakey, and the truth was Rowe was scared sour apples of Blakey. Blakey had a knack — all his career he'd had this knack — of sounding reasonable but, in effect, asking the impossible. It didn't matter what the hell Rowe reported, Blakey was going to ask some fool question he couldn't answer. Therefore Rowe, along with Tyler and the newly arrived D.C. Evans, stood around while Tallboy handled the telephone.

5.30 a.m.

He spoke to Sopworth Police Station.

'How many men can you rustle up, sergeant?'

'We've — er — ' There was the sound of pages being turned. 'Pollard and Witherham. They're on earlies. Hinton and Sowe are on late shift. And, of course, the outside beat men.'

'The outside beat men,' said Tallboy.

'Pinter's on at six at Rimstone. Then there's Kyle, the other Upper Neck man. And Karn — Rimstone — it should be his Weekly Rest Day.'

'Cancel it,' said Tallboy. 'Contact Pinter. Tell him to cover both beats. I want Kyle here as soon as possible.'

'Yes, sir.'

'And Policewoman Pearson, there's a job for her.'

'Sir?'

'Both of you. Get her down to the station, then take her along to Sergeant Noble's place. Tell his wife what's happened.'

'What — er — what *has* happened, sir?'

'Some sort of explosion. Sergeant Noble's taken a battering on the face, that's as far as I know at the moment. He's at Bordfield General. If Mrs Noble wants to visit contact Motor Patrol, use my authority.'

'I'll do that sir. And the town men?'

'Leave 'em for the moment. Keep the town covered, if we can.'

'Yes, sir.'

Without returning the receiver to its rest Tallboy pressed the prongs of the telephone, then dialled Beechwood Brook Regional D.H.Q.

'Chief Inspector Tallboy, here. I'm at Upper Neck, Sopworth Section. Major incident. Pass the word. I want the complete Ringling Brothers. Photographs, plan drawing, scene-of-crime . . . the works. And ring round the other divisions. I want some C.I.D. men. *And* uniform. Say twenty — half of each — if we need more, I'll let you know. And fast. I'll telephone Detective Chief Superintendent Blayde myself.'

Robert Blayde was already up and about.

Stripped as he was, and towelling himself after a shower, the expression 'lean and hungry' would easily have sprung to mind. He was a few years older than Tallboy; a few years older and a few degrees fitter.

Only once in his life had he ever loved a woman and that was more than twenty years ago. Since then? Well, bachelorhood suited him fine. No ties. No family. Few friends. The tiny cottage on the outskirts of Beechwood Brook was far more than his home. It was his retreat; the womb substitute to which he returned in order to steady his world and prepare himself for another foray. That's what it all boiled down to. Forays. Battles. A form of polite – and sometimes not too polite – guerrilla warfare.

And why?

Because the men who were his friends – his colleagues – should have been his enemies. Fate. Kismet. Call it any name you chose. They were his friends and that they *were* his friends gave proof of their stature, it also gave proof of *his* stature, but Blayde was not a man given to self-analysis.

Harris – Robert Harris, assistant chief constable (crime) for the Bordfield Region of the Lessford Metropolitan Police Area – the same Bob Harris who, when they were younger men and less exalted coppers, had taken his woman and made her his wife.

Tallboy – Divisional Detective Chief Inspector Tallboy – the son-in-law of an unlaid ghost called Charles Ripley . . . and before moving on to be Bordfield Regional Head of C.I.D. Blayde had sat in Ripley's chair, and a lot of people (probably including Tallboy himself) *still* figured his backside was a few sizes too small for that particular seat.

As he dressed Blayde pondered upon the now-deceased Ripley.

Odd how some men – some coppers – can be a basis for legends. Mark of Scotland Yard. Sillitoe of Sheffield and Glasgow. St Johnston of Lancashire County. Seedman of New York City. A handful – no more than a dozen – men who had become myths. And of course Ripley of Beechwood Brook. Hell's teeth, *nobody* could follow such men. The stories were stretched a little more with each telling. Even youngsters new to the force – straight from the college and not yet knowing how to *walk* like a bobby – within weeks the greybeards had fed them the Ripley pap and, from then on, Blayde would always be second horse in that particular race.

Good men. (Don't belittle 'em, Blayde.) Mark, Sillitoe, St Johnston, Seedman, Ripley . . . all the others. Good men. Unique men. Even great men, great coppers. But not gods! They could be equalled. They could be bettered.

But . . .

Having dressed as far as trousers, shirt and tie, Blayde left the bedroom, descended into the tiny kitchen, filled and plugged in the electric kettle then, while it boiled, strolled into the garden. His 'green moat' as he called it. Little more than half an acre and most of it close-cropped lawn; the pensioner he paid to come in, two afternoons a week, chased the weeds, encouraged the flowers in the border-beds and kept the grass well mown. His 'green moat' which encircled the cottage and, in turn, was hedged by head-high beech.

By strict horticultural standards not much of a garden, but *very* private . . . which was all he asked.

A black and white tom — pure 'moggy' from some neighbouring farm — squirmed its way through a tiny gap in the hedge and, tail held high, wandered towards him across the grass. They were buddies. They knew each other well. They each respected the other's right to 'walk alone'.

The cat followed him round to the front of the cottage. It purred as he collected the newly-delivered milk. It returned with him to the kitchen door, then waited on the flagged path.

As he placed the saucer alongside the step, he said, 'Cat, you're no fool. You always get the top of the milk.'

The cat purred and lapped at the same time.

From inside the cottage the telephone bell rang.

Woman Police Constable 1324 Muriel Pearson pushed a thickness of hair aside in order that she could hear more clearly.

She said, 'I see . . . How badly? . . . Okay, I'll be down, sergeant. Just give me time to get dressed.'

She returned the receiver to its rest on the wallphone.

Her boyfriend sat bolt upright in the large divan bed and said, 'Shit!' in a low, but very disgusted voice.

'You know the rules of the game.' She smiled at him. 'Duty calls, and my job is just as important as yours.'

W.P.C. Pearson was a very modern miss; so modern, in fact, that had her parents known of certain facets of their daughter's life they might have seriously considered disowning her. They would, of course, have been wrong, but wrong for all the right reasons. The tag-end of the twentieth century equated with honesty rather than hypocrisy, and honesty included sexual honesty. Miss Pearson was a dedicated career woman; which, by her reckoning, meant she could forget disabling ties of marriage and (for sure!) the even more disabling ties of a family.

Okay, but marriage was only an official document, and no girl in this day and age need have kids if she didn't want them. Which, in turn, meant she could have a boyfriend if she so desired. And *if* she so desired — and because she rented a neat little self-contained flat — what she did, and who she slept with, was strictly *her* business.

Mind you, she was no whore. She was no one-night-stander.

She and Tony were married in everything but name. He, too, had a flat — in Bordfield where he was a male nurse at Bordfield General — and, just as her flat was his whenever he felt like it, so his flat was hers. She was in her late twenties. He was in his early thirties. No wife, no husband was involved in the arrangement. Nobody was being either hurt or deceived, what the hell? A red-blooded male, a red-blooded female, both in their prime and each more than just 'liking' the other. Love? Okay if (as the sob-sisters claimed) sex *wasn't* love maybe that extra something would gradually develop. Meanwhile they jelled, and sometimes they *really* jelled.

She walked across the bed-sitter, towards the shower cupboard. She was quite naked and, equally, quite natural and unaware of the fact.

Tony flung the clothes aside and said, 'I'll make the coffee.'

'Thanks.' She pulled the glass door of the cupboard closed and turned on the shower.

Tony padded across the carpet to the miniaturised kitchen. He, too, was quite naked; pyjamas and nightdresses being strictly for the birds, and anyway he was going to follow her under the jets of the shower while she was towelling herself.

As he began the ritual of quick-brew coffee-making he shouted, 'What is it?'

'Wassat?' She eased the door of the shower-cupboard open a little.

'The flap. You're not supposed to be on duty till nine.'

'Sergeant Ramsden,' she called.

'Yeah, I know Sergeant Ramsden. What about him?'

'He wants me on. Sergeant Noble's been hurt.'

'So?'

'Mrs Noble doesn't know. He wants me along when he tells her.'

'Badly?'

'Eh?'

'Noble. Is he badly hurt?'

'Sounds like it. He's at your place.'

'He's in good hands.'

'What's that?'

'He's in good hands. They don't come better.'

'Oh, my word.' She turned off the jets, stepped from the shower-cupboard, reached for a towel and began to dry the droplets of water from her body. 'Such modesty. How come you're not heading some P.R. team?'

But it was no less than the truth. Bordfield General Infirmary *was* one of those oiled-bearing organisations which got on with the job and filled in the forms later. Two men had been brought in. That they were coppers made not a scrap of difference.

6 a.m. They were people, they were badly injured and they needed immediate attention. That's what they were given. Operating Theatres Numbers Three and Four were used and, as they lay on the tables, skilled teams performed near-miracles upon Noble and Cooper.

In Number Three Theatre the surgeon concentrated his attention upon Noble's left eye. A nurse wiped perspiration from the forehead of the masked and gowned surgeon. A second nurse handed him forceps in exchange for a stainless steel probe. Behind the mask he talked; partly to himself, partly to the team without which he could not have worked.

'Easy does it. Gently. Gently . . .

'Nurse, keep that eyelid well clear . . .

'Come, my little beauty. That's not where you belong . . .'

Then with feeling, 'You're a nasty little sod, aren't you?'

For a moment he held the screwed base of a cheap tin torch in the forceps. The spring was still attached. The base and the spring were dripping blood and eye tissue.

He dropped his find into a steel kidney bowl, then said, 'Right. Swabs. Let's get the muck out and see what damage we have to deal with.'

In Number Four Theatre it was more of a joinery job. Cooper's face had taken some of the blast and would, eventually, need stitching together, but it was the right hand which presented the problems. Or, to be strictly accurate, the *absence* of most of the right hand.

The surgeon and his assistant discussed matters.

The surgeon said, 'The lower joint of the thumb, it *could* be saved.'

'For what?' The assistant was a middle-aged woman; blunt to the point of rudeness. 'A useless stump. No size at all. He won't even be able to use it to scratch himself.'

'It's tricky at the wrist.'

'A clean job,' said the woman dogmatically. 'Leave him a six-inch stump below the elbow. A good artificial hand. With practice, in six months' time, he won't know the difference.'

The surgeon pondered the problem in silence for a few moments. Then he nodded and said, 'Get the arm ready, please. About six inches below the elbow.'

Police Constable Pollard and Witherham wandered into the Charge Office. Something was 'up'. That much was obvious. In the first place, Ramsden didn't give the impression that he'd just come on duty; he was simmering a little and, in the normal course of events, it took a good hour to reach his normal, on-the-boil state of near-panic.

It was an open secret that Police Constable 2324 Edward Pollard 'carried' Ramsden. Even Ramsden admitted it. Ted Pollard didn't mind; he was the oldest officer in Sopworth Section — within three short months of retiring age — and he had an answer for everything. A gentle answer. The sort of answer which only comes after a lifetime of common-or-garden beat work; of handling hysteria at accidents; of quietening down screaming wives and raving husbands at 'domestic disturbances'. You name it, Pollard had had experience of it. He was the fount of knowledge; the paterfamilias of the section; a walking encylopaedia of police lore.

He and Witherham walked into the Charge Office and were immediately aware of an 'atmosphere'.

'Something?' asked Pollard.

It was his way of talking to colleagues. A verbal shorthand which in many cases could be reduced to a single word.

Ramsden said, 'Noble and Cooper caught a packet. They're both in Bordfield General at the moment.'

'What?'

'Some sort of explosion. Some of the heavy boys have been called out.'

'Who?'

'I haven't heard owt. No names have been mentioned yet. They'll let us know things . . . when they're ready.'

The teleprinter began its rattling urgency.

Pollard said, 'I'll take it,' and walked towards the alcove.

Higginbottom looked relieved, checked that he'd collected all his pens and pencils, then made for the door and the end of his night shift. Witherham flipped the pages of the Telephone and Teleprinter Message Book, glanced at the entries made since he'd last been on duty and scrawled his initials in the margin.

Ramsden said, 'Ted, stick in the office for a while. Miss Pearson's on her way. We have to tell Noble's wife.' Then to Witherham, 'Cover the town, Joe.' He compressed his lips in disgust. 'How in hell's name we're expected to bobby the bloody place beats me. One man on the street, one man in the office. All it needs is . . .'

'We'll cope, sergeant.' From the alcove Pollard interrupted Ramsden's outpourings. The voice of unruffled sanity.

Ramsden nodded, walked to the main desk, made the last few

entries in the Sectional Diary, signed his name then turned the page and (as far as 'police records' were concerned) scrawled the date and began a new day.

Pinter drove his Minivan slowly; deliberate third gear progression. Had he been asked he might not have been able to give any reasonable explanation. Just that he wanted to 'see things'. It was the beginning of a summer and, for him, that summer would be a turning point in his life. Never again would he view the waist-high cow parsley in the verges with quite the same emotion; now and for the rest of his life, the cow parsley, the green of the hedges, the wild flowers generally, would be part of a memory.

Indeed, it already *was* a memory. Something he'd come to terms with. Something he'd forced himself to accept. No more springs — no more summers — with Hannah. The way he felt at the moment . . . no more springs, no more summers, no more *anything*. The girl next door . . . *literally* the girl next door. Kids playing out in the street. A gradual acceptance that the other was there and always *would* be there. School and waiting for each other in the playground, then walking home together. Kids talking. Forever talking. Funny, kids always have a million things to tell each other. Even holidays together; their parents had been good friends, they'd always holidayed together . . . so even on holidays he'd always had Hannah. Sand, sea and rock pools. Never ever bored. What was boredom? Kids — happy kids — they don't know the meaning of the word.

Then jobs. Working for a living. She'd ended up at Marks and Spencers, not a firm to employ odds and ends. A good firm and she'd been respected. As for himself . . . he hadn't really known. A list of real dead-enders. And she'd known. She'd always been the one with brains. With the capacity to see ahead.

'You'll need a better job, Wilf.'

'Uhuh. I'll — er — I'll look around.'

'Something with a future. That's what I mean.'

'I'm doing my best, Hannah. Honest I am.'

'I know.' Then she'd paused and, almost timidly, continued, 'What about the police force?'

'Me? A bobby?'

'Why not?'

'I'm . . .' He'd moved his hands helplessly. 'There's an examination of some sort. Y'know what I'm like.'

'It's not *so* difficult.'

Well, he'd passed the examination. As she'd said, it hadn't been too difficult. The medical had been a walk-over. The three months initial training at the college had pushed him a little, but he'd made it.

And then . . .

Getting married had been no surprise at all. The surprise would have been if they *hadn't* married. The suggestion that he become a copper had been part of the acceptance of what was going to happen. And yet, dammit, he'd never asked her. He'd never said, 'Will you?' and she'd never said, 'Yes.' Think about it. He'd been a louse. No proposal. No engagement . . . no engagement ring. That had been a dirty trick. Not deliberate. God help him, he wouldn't deliberately hurt Hannah. Not deliberate, just thoughtless. And he wished . . . He wished . . .

Funny. He'd enjoyed being a copper. From that first day. He'd *enjoyed* the job. Not throwing his weight around. Nothing like that. Just — y'know — easing things along a little. Sorting out problems. He was no court fanatic. Never had been. A quiet word. A warning to the right person. Mind you . . . Just occasionally. Some right bastard had tried it on and asked for it. Crown Court three, maybe four, times since he'd joined. Nothing personal, just that some hard-faced bugger had tried it on once too often.

And then Rimstone Beat.

'I think you have the right attitude of mind, Pinter.'

His old super (a gem and not at all like this brainless twit Blakey) had smiled up at him, and said, 'Take Mrs Pinter along. See if she likes the house.'

'Yes, sir.'

'If she does, the beat's yours. I think you'll like it.'

Like it! It had fitted him like a second skin. And Hannah had fallen in love with the house on sight; two cottages knocked into one then 'modernised', but without destroying its crazy but happy proportions. Seven years now. Seven of the happiest years of their married life. Like the T.V. advert said, 'Happiness is a thing called . . . Rimstone Beat'.

Until . . .

Just one reason, eh? Just one logical — even half-acceptable — reason. Not a load of mealy-mouthed religious crap. Something. Anything! Not comfort — he didn't want comfort — he wanted Hannah . . . and if he couldn't have Hannah he wanted to know *why*.

Witherham — Police Constable 1555 Joseph William Witherham — strolled the town pavements and felt good. He liked the Friday early shift. Friday was Sopworth Market Day, and already some of the traders were busy hauling the framework and the planks from the yard behind the Council Offices and erecting the stalls. The vans and the lorries were easing their way into their allotted places. The men and women — members of that particularly hardy race which make up the open-air traders — made it look so easy. In an hour — little more than an hour — the whole shooting-match would be there, ready for the first customers.

Witherham; a run-of-the-mill cop; reliable but not outstanding. He usually doubled up with old Pollard, and to that extent he was forever overshadowed. Pollard was pretty unique. Some of the lads — some of those eager to grab limelight — wouldn't have liked working in double-harness with Ted Pollard. But that was okay with Witherham. To have Ted there as long-stop . . . that was okay with Witherham.

He strolled into The Market Cafe. It was already doing good business. The stall-holders were damn near as addicted to tea-drinking as coppers. Some of them raised a hand in greeting as he eased his way to the counter. He took his pint mug of hot, sweet tea and joined an Asian gentleman at one of the stained tables. 'Ranji' . . . whether his name was Ranji or not Witherham didn't know. Or, come to that, care. It was the name every stallholder called him. It was the name by which Witherham addressed him. To anyone listening their talk would have sounded innocent, but between Witherham and Ranji the words had subtle and understood meanings.

'Holidays. I'm away on my holidays, soon, Ranji. Next month.'

'I hope the weather holds, Mister Witherham.'

'Aye, so do I.' Witherham tasted the tea. 'I'm looking for shirts. A couple of shirts.'

'I sell shirts, Mister Witherham. I sell very good shirts.'

'I'm not talking about "seconds".'

'My shirts. I get them from Bradford. From Manchester. I buy in bulk therefore I can . . .'

' "Seconds",' repeated Witherham. Again he tasted the tea. 'Your wife's a clever woman.'

'My wife. My daughter,' agreed Ranji solemnly.

'Those fancy boxes you tart 'em up in.'

'The presentation . . . most important, Mister Witherham.'

'I want a good shirt. A *good* shirt. *Two* good shirts.'

'But of course.' Ranji nodded solemnly.

'What I'm not prepared to pay for is a bloody box.'

'I — er — I understand.'

'And I'm not interested in "seconds".'

74

'What — er — what price range have you in mind, Mister Wither-ham?'

'A fiver.'

'I can get you a very fine shirt for . . .'

'Not each . . . for the pair.'

'Ah!'

'Next week,' said Witherham gently. 'I'm on nights. I'll call round in the afternoon, okay?'

'I'll do all I can, Mister Witherham.'

'Not "seconds", Ranji. Not even *good* "seconds".'

'I understand.'

'And not boxes. I'm not paying for fancy boxes.'

'Of course.'

'Two nice shirts for my holiday, that's all.'

'Next week, Mister Witherham. Call at my stall next week. I'll have them waiting for you.'

Witherham nodded and took a first long drink from the mug of tea. Ranji smiled, nodded, then left the cafe.

Witherham lighted a cigarette and set about enjoying his early morning pint of tea. He tipped his helmet slightly towards the back of his head and congratulated himself on getting the message across to old Ranji. 'Perks' . . . that was the name of the game. And why not? Those shirts. They'd be waiting. Nothing surer. Two damn good shirts, each well worth more than he was going to pay for the pair. So what? They'd already been nicked; some sticky-fingered employee — some slippery van driver somewhere — they'd already *been* nicked. Nothing surer. Them and a few dozen others. To use the expression . . . "off the back of a lorry". Somewhere they were waiting to be bought and sold, and Ranji knew where.

Ranji was on the hook. Jesus wept, they were *all* on the hook. Those shirts on his stall. Very flash . . . until you'd bought 'em, taken 'em home and opened 'em up. Very cheap. And so they should be. "Seconds". Every last one flawed somewhere; not one of 'em with the maker's name sewn inside the collar. Some other bloody name. Some name some clown had come up with. The real maker wouldn't even *own* 'em. So, buy a few score labels, buy a few score fancy boxes, then get your wife and daughter cracking. Set 'em up, all neat and jazzy, then wait for the suckers.

The world was a con, friend. Everybody was on the hook. So, tell me, why not Joe Witherham?

Never had Upper Neck Police Office held so many coppers at the same time. Detective Chief Inspector Tallboy; Inspector Rowe, Tyler and two of his pals from Motor Patrol Division; Kyle, the colleague of Cooper from Upper Neck beat; Karn from Rimstone Beat. It was only a tiny office — literally a 'one-man' office — and the waiting officers watched Tallboy as he replaced the telephone receiver onto its rest.

Tallboy said, 'Right, that was P.C. Burns. From what he learned in the ambulance — from what little he's been told by the medics — this is the picture. A torch, presumably an electric torch. On the path of Cooper's house, here. Cooper picked it up. Maybe because he picked it up. Maybe because he switched it on. We can't be sure. But it exploded. Cooper's lost a hand — his right hand. Sergeant Noble's lost an eye — at least one eye. Those are the main injuries. They've both taken some stick about the face and upper body. But — the good news — they'll live.'

Somebody mouthed, 'Thank God!' and a sigh of relief whispered through the gathered police officers.

Tallboy continued, 'Okay, we know when Cooper began duty. Nine o'clock, last night. The thing exploded just before four. That means it was *put* there between those times. This is one case where house-to-house might mean something. Upper Neck. A village community. Somebody *has* to have seen something, heard something. I want to know what and when. There's enough of you. You should be able to strip this village clean of all possible information within the next two hours. There'll be foolscap around somewhere in this office. I want every person — not every house, every *person* — interviewed. And by that I mean questioned, *really* questioned.' He paused, then added, 'Two of your mates are in operating theatres and, what the hell the surgeons do, they'll be maimed for life . . . at least that. That isn't allowed. Somebody did it. I want that somebody behind a cell door before I go off duty.' Once more he paused, then asked, 'Any questions?'

Rowe said, 'Er — terrorists — possibly?'

'No, Inspector Rowe.' Tallboy's contempt for the question wasn't quite concealed behind his polite reply. 'Unless, of course, you know of any reason why a place like Upper Neck might attract terrorists?'

'No — er — no, of course not.' Rowe's face coloured.

'That's it, then.' Tallboy jerked his head. 'Move to it. Start asking questions . . . and keep clear of that front garden.'

Evans, the Sopworth D.C. entered the office.

'Where the hell have *you* been?' demanded Tallboy.

'I — er — '

'The rest of you,' interrupted Tallboy. 'Get out and get cracking.'

When only Rowe, Evans and Tallboy were left, Tallboy said, 'Well?'

'My — my car,' muttered Evans. 'It was parked awkwardly, you see, sir. I didn't want to . . .'

'Great God!'

Rowe said, 'You're supposed to set an example, Evans. You're a detective constable. I expect you to . . .'

'Get out of here,' snarled Tallboy. 'Start asking questions. House-to house. And — for your own sake — pray to God you come up with something.'

They rode in Pearson's second-hand Volvo. For the life of him Ramsden couldn't see how in hell a mere woman police constable could afford to run a socking great Volvo; one of the larger models. Okay it was second-hand, but it was *good* second-hand. They hadn't given it away with tops from soap flake packets. And, what is more, it was a very greedy beast. It drank petrol at an alarming rate and, these days, petrol was like liquid gold. He, himself, ran one of the medium-range Fiats, and *that* took some doing. But a Volvo!

6.30 a.m.

However . . .

He leaned back in the front passenger seat, decided it was none of his business (which, in fact, it *wasn't*), stretched his legs and gave thought to the task in hand.

W.P.C. Pearson had breezed into the Charge Office and said, 'When you're ready, sergeant.'

Just like that. No pause for a plan of campaign. No discussion about how the job should be done. Very cold-blooded, or, if you wanted to bend over backwards and be charitable, very efficient. A damn sight too efficient for a man like Ramsden. Efficient females tended to scare the hell out of him.

He chewed at his lower lip for a moment, then said, 'How d'you think?'

'What?' She flicked the gear-stick with the smooth indifference of a grand prix driver.

'Tell her.'

The Volvo nipped between a bread van and a parked Merc with (or so it seemed to Ramsden) not much more than three coats of paint to spare.

'Tell her,' said Pearson bluntly.

'Just like that?' Ramsden put mild sarcasm into the question.

'Do you know an easy way?' she countered.

'Well – no – but . . .'

'It's like messing about with a bad tooth. You either have it out or suffer for a long time . . . *then* have it out.'

Ramsden sighed. She was right. Of course she was right. But this from a woman! Dammit, the so-called 'weaker sex'. This one wasn't weak. She was as hard as tempered steel.

He said, 'One good thing. He isn't dead. He isn't . . .'

'Only blind,' she interrupted bluntly.

'I know. But . . .'

'Me, I'd sooner be dead.'

'He's only lost one eye,' argued Ramsden weakly.

'Hopefully.'

'From what we're told.'

'Sergeant.' She seemed suddenly to lose patience. 'He's lost one eye. There's a chance – there's always a chance – he'll also have lost the sight of the other eye. Now, I don't know any easy way to break that sort of news to a man's wife. I don't think there *is* an easy way. But what I *do* know is this. If you arse and fart about, instead of telling her straight out, she'll think the worst. She'll think he's dead. I don't want that to happen. I know Mrs Noble, slightly. She's a very nice person. So, if it's all the same to you, *I'll* tell her.'

'If – if you think that's best.'

'I'm sure.'

'Right.' Ramsden seemed relieved. 'We'll do it that way.'

Ted Pollard could stonewall. Nobody better. He had the knack of presenting a completely expressionless face, blinking a little owlishly and blocking every question by a counter-question. Till the cows came home, if necessary. It was his forte. And, moreover, he'd developed the knack into a near-art form.

Added to which, he disliked newspaper reporters. Once long ago – when he'd been a moss-green recruit – some smooth-tongued reporter had wheedled information from him. Not a lot of information, and not very important information, but enough and important enough to earn him a stern warning from his then divisional officer. And P.C. Pollard *never* made the same mistake twice.

The reporter didn't know this past history, of course. The reporter was only doing his job. Somebody – there's always 'somebody' – had lifted a telephone receiver, dialled a number and asked for the news editor of the local daily. Then the news editor had telephoned the reporter and (because it seemed the sensible thing to do) the reporter had hot-footed it to Sopworth Police Station and thumbed the bell-push on the public counter.

Pollard strolled from the Charge Office.

'Upper Neck,' said the reporter in a deliberately important, you-don't-have-to-tell-me-I-already-know tone of voice.

'Upper Neck?' Pollard turned the words into a surprised question. 'What, exactly, has happened?'

'Where?'

'At Upper Neck. At Constable Cooper's house.'

'Constable Cooper?'

'The Upper Neck constable.'

'Oh, *that* Constable Cooper.'

'He's been injured.'

'Has he?'

'So I'm told.'

'Who by?'

'Well, *hasn't* he?' The reporter's cool was beginning to melt.

'I only came on at six.' Pollard spoke the words as if they were the final answer to every question under the sun.

'Look, I'm Press.' The reporter fished an identification card from an inside pocket and placed it on the counter. Pollard picked the card up, read it slowly and carefully, then handed it back to the reporter.

'Very interesting,' he observed.

'All I'm after,' said the reporter, 'is a few facts.'

'Facts?'

'About Constable Cooper.'

'I haven't seen Cooper for — lemme see — at least three days.'

'About Upper Neck,' said the reporter desperately.

'Upper Neck?'

'Surely to God you know . . .'

'Nowt,' said Pollard flatly.

'I find your attitude obnoxious in the extreme,' blustered the reporter.

'Oh, aye?'

'Almost insulting.'

'Lad.' Pollard leaned fractionally over the counter. 'Nobody asked you to come. Nobody's asking you to stay.'

Blayde and the 'circus' arrived at the same time.

The 'circus' . . . the colloquial, collective noun used by ordinary coppers for what was known as The Specialist Services. It was meant as a term of contempt and it was grossly unfair. These officers (in this case six men and one woman) had been responsible for the detection of more than their fair share of crime.

Their history?

Way back, Sir Bernard Spilsbury had taken the then contemptuously viewed profession of forensic medicine and turned it into an acknowledged science. Later Professor Keith Simpson had honed that science into something not too far short of an art. To visit the scene of a crime — to examine a murder victim — and, by scrutinising the minutiae, perform near-magic. The When, the Where, the How . . . and, very often, the Who. These two giants had proved it possible. Regional Forensic Science Laboratories had been created as a direct result of their skill; laboratories, available to Prosecution and Defence alike, whose staff worked to add to the mountain of knowledge accumulated by Spilsbury and Simpson. Police liaison officers had been attached to each laboratory and, as major crime proliferated, teams of Scene of Crime Officers, fine-trained to the task of searching for and collecting possible minute clues to be taken to the laboratories, there to be examined by various specialists. Almost as a matter of course — and certainly as a matter of expediency — experts from Photographic Section, Fingerprint Section and Plan Drawing Section had been added to the expanding team.

Thus the 'circus'. And, having arrived at Upper Neck, they subjected the front garden of Cooper's house to an inspection which (literally) left no square inch unsearched or unphotographed. They were at work until past noon. Peering. Measuring. Tabulating. Sealing scores of tiny pieces of possible evidence in cellophane envelopes. In effect, forging tiny links of a chain which, hopefully, would enmesh whoever was responsible for the crime and create a situation wherein a plea of 'Not Guilty' would amount to a forensic frivolity.

Blayde watched them go to work for a moment, then walked to the rear of the Police Office and joined Tallboy and Rowe.

'So far . . . what?' he asked, bluntly.

Tallboy said, 'House-to-house. Somebody *must* have seen or heard something.'

'Need more men?'

'Not at the moment. If we have to expand the enquiries . . . maybe then.'

'How are they?'

'In the operating theatre.' Tallboy frowned. 'From what I gather Noble's lost an eye, Cooper's lost a hand. Other injuries, naturally, but those are the basics.'

'Who's at the infirmary?'

'Burns, Motor Patrol, he went in with the ambulance.'

'Inspector.' Blayde turned to Rowe. 'I think you should be there. In uniform. If necessary, sling your weight around a little. We need to know as much as possible and as soon as possible.'

'Yes, sir.'

Rowe felt relieved. Since his arrival he had suffered a form of mental flatulence; his inside had been churning over and, more than once, it had needed a physical effort not to break wind. Rowe was no headline-chaser. A quiet life at all costs, that was his creed. And to sit in a comfortable armchair in some lounge of Bordfield General Infirmary was all *he* wished to contribute to this unexpected act of sickening violence which had occurred within the area of his authority.

'Oh, and inspector.' Rowe stopped as he reached the door. Blayde said, 'Send Burns back here. We can use all the good men available.'

When they were alone, Blayde took cigarettes from his pocket and, when he and Tallboy were smoking, he said, 'Now, Chris, what do we know, what do we guess?'

Tallboy filled in the details as well as he was able. They didn't amount to much but, when professionals talk together as friends, a little goes a long way.

'A torch on the path, waiting to be picked up,' mused Blayde. 'Something very deliberate, wouldn't you say?'

'Aimed at somebody who was going to use that path,' agreed Tallboy.

'Cooper. Possibly his wife, but we'll take the obvious and stick with Cooper.'

Tallboy contributed, 'Somebody – other than Cooper or his wife – somebody known to have been going to visit the house? No!' He waved the hand holding the cigarette. 'As you say, let's stay with the obvious whilever we can. Cooper. More than that . . . somebody who knew when Cooper was coming on duty and when he was going off duty.'

'Cooper,' agreed Blayde. Then added, 'Not Noble?'

'Who'd know? A section sergeant. He's given free rein. The chances were *against* him being with Cooper.'

'Okay. Cooper. Next question, *why* Cooper?'

'A good copper? Perhaps *too* good a copper.'

'Chris, you know better than that.' Blayde smiled. 'They all swear vengeance. It never means much.'

'He was a jack,' murmured Tallboy.

'Ah!' Blayde seemed to suddenly remember.

'Harris dumped him back in uniform.'

'For pulling something of a fix, as I recall.'

'Something like that.'

'It couldn't be *so* easy.' Blayde's expression was of exaggerated wonder as he added, 'Could it?'

In the cobbled square of the market the stall-holders were setting up their wares. It was Friday, it was market day and, for a pleasant change, rain didn't even seem a possibility. The two brothers who sold cheap lino arranged a tarpaulin sheet very carefully; none of the tack they sold had any quality; some of it was little more than tar-paper; get that stuff under a blazing sun for a few hours and you'd end up with rolls of goo. The woman on the china stall humped wicker baskets filled with crockery from the rear of a van; baskets full of assorted beakers; baskets full of plate and saucer oddments; baskets in which were stacked mock-willow-pattern tea and dinner sets — each piece with some tiny flaw in either design or glaze — to be sold at a price well below competition from any established shop in the town. At the fruit and veg stalls muscular, brown-skinned men and beefy women slashed open sacks of potatoes, onions and cab-bages — ripped the thin wooden tops from boxes of apples, pears, oranges and grapefruit — and carefully selected the best of their produce for pride of place in the pyramids built up along the front of their planked counters.

Police Constable Witherham wandered among the stalls. He approached a fruit and veg stand and spoke to a man busy polishing the shine on apples.

'Nice day, Harry.'

'Looks promising, Mister Witherham.'

'Anything out of the ordinary?' Witherham cocked an eye at the produce on and around the stall.

'Nice Jerseys. *Very* nice Jerseys. Best potatoes we've had this season.'

'Four pounds?' suggested Witherham.

'I'll hand-pick every one,' promised the stall-holder.

'Fine.'

'Just before two?'

Witherham nodded and said, 'I'll collect 'em as I go off duty.'

Hilda Noble sat hunched in the armchair and trembled. She seemed incapable of speech, incapable of movement, incapable of coherent thought; as if she was in some massive deep-freeze — had been locked in the deep-freeze for hours — and had lost the ability to do anything other than shake from head to foot.

'I'm — I'm sorry, Mrs Noble,' muttered Ramsden. 'We're all sorry. Very sorry indeed.'

W.P.C. Pearson said, 'He's going to need you, Mrs Noble. He's not dead . . . be grateful for that. But he's going to need you.'

Hilda Noble seemed neither to hear nor understand. She continued to stare at the carpet and tremble. For the moment her mind was incapable of grasping anything other than the monumental injustice of it all. The inequity. The unfairness. The utter and absolute wrong-fulness. Three weeks ago — less than a month ago — her father had had a stroke. Last week the letter from the College of Technology . . . *with real regret that I must inform you that your son lacks the necessary application. I need hardly say that he could take full advantage of his tuition, if only his priorities allowed him so to do, but in view of the fact that his present activities are tending to disrupt the smooth running of . . .* The three men she loved. The three men she lived for. One half-dead. One a trouble-maker. And now Harry.

'Mrs Noble,' said W.P.C. Pearson gently.

That old saw: 'Troubles never come singly, always in threes'. How true. How very true. But where the courage? Where the moral strength? How to cope, what to do, which way to turn? There was evil abroad in the world. There *must* be. There *had*

7 a.m.   to be. Killing and torture and senseless destruction.

It was no place for ordinary, decent people. To be left alone. To be allowed to live in peace. But that wasn't allowed any more. That was forbidden. Just war and threats of war. Just — just . . . *Harry*!

'Mrs Noble.' W.P.C. Pearson squatted alongside the wretched woman, took one of the trembling hands and squeezed it gently. She said, 'You're not alone. We're here. *I'm* here.'

Ramsden cleared his throat. He wanted to say something; he felt he *ought* to say something. Something sympathetic. Something comforting. Something helpful. But what? In God's name, what *did* a man say in such circumstances?

Pearson looked up and murmured, 'Tea, sergeant. Hot and sweet with something strong in it, if you can find something.'

Ramsden took a deep breath, nodded and almost tiptoed into the kitchen.

Police Constable Pollard heard the buzz from the bell-push at the public counter and squashed a half-smoked Woodbine into a heavy glass ashtray somebody had 'won' from one of Sopworth's pubs. He walked from the Charge Office and smiled a greeting at Preston.

Charles Preston was one of the firers, employed up at the brick-works. Like coppers, he worked 'shifts'. Unlike coppers, his shift-change took place monthly. Pollard and Preston were of an age and, despite the difference in their jobs, of a similar disposition. When their night shifts coincided Pollard regularly called in at the brickyard and enjoyed a smoke and a chinwag with Charlie Preston. Depending upon the season, their talk usually centred around either cricket or football.

'Charlie,' greeted Pollard.

'I'm glad it's you, Ted,' said Preston somberly.

'Me?'

'Not one o' the young 'uns.'

'Oh, aye?'

Preston was dressed in what he might have called his 'Sunday Best'. A moderately well-fitting, off-the-peg suit of navy blue, a white shirt, a dark, quietly patterned tie, brightly polished black shoes. The skin of his face shone from the recent use of a razor. His greying hair was carefully parted and combed and slicked into unusual tidiness.

Pollard noticed all these things.

Preston glanced at the door leading to the Charge Office and said, 'Anybody else in?'

'No.'

'The sergeant, maybe?'

'Just me.'

Preston nodded as if satisfied. As if relieved. He said, 'Can I — y'know — have a word?'

'Aye.'

'In private?'

Pollard lifted the flap of the public counter, waited until Preston had passed, then lowered the flap and followed Preston into the Charge Office.

'So, this is where it's all done?' Preston raised a weak smile and swung his gaze around the room.

'Sit down, Charlie.'

Pollard motioned to a chair, then offered the open packet of Woodbines. When they were both smoking, Pollard said, 'Well?'

'I — er — I hardly know where to begin.'

Preston looked embarrassed. As if he was an intruder. As if he had no real right to be in the police station, and was trespassing upon the kindness of a friend.

Pollard waited.

Preston said, 'I should have been up at the kilns last night. I wasn't. I took the night off.'

'Oh, aye?'

'Unbeknown, of course.' Preston paused for a reaction and, when none came, he continued, 'I didn't tell anybody I wasn't going in. I just stayed away. Walked about most of the night.'

The two men smoked in silence for a moment or two. One waiting. The other not knowing how to begin.

Preston moistened his lips and said, 'I — er — I don't have to tell you about May.'

'Your missus?'

'There's — er — y'know, there's been a lot o' talk.'

'I don't listen to it,' said Pollard gently. 'People talk that stuff. Half the time they don't know what they're talking about . . . the rest is none of their business.'

'It's right, though,' sighed Preston. 'Her and Sammy Sutcliffe.'

'I'm sorry,' growled Pollard.

'I . . .' Preston wiped his mouth with the back of a hand. 'I don't blame her. Not really. She's a deal younger than me. I knew that when I married her. I knew I was taking a chance. I — y'know — I thought it was worth it. *She* was worth it. An' she was. Till Sammy Sutcliffe clapped eyes on her.'

'Talk it over with her,' suggested Pollard.

'Nay, that I can't.' Preston dropped his head for a moment, then inhaled cigarette smoke, exhaled and said, 'Last night I went home. Y'know . . . early this morning. About four. Happen just before four. I — I hadn't my boots on. Stocking feet, see? I'd taken my boots off. Deliberately. An' — an' I heard 'em. Upstairs. In *my* bed. I heard 'em. *Our* bed. *Our* bedroom. Dammit, Ted, *my own house*. I wouldn't have cared — happen I wouldn't have cared — ' Preston raised a hand and nipped the root of his nose, as if denying the sorrow a right of exit. He continued, 'I — I went upstairs, see. And — and there they were. Dirty. Dirty. Dirty! And — and I couldn't help myself. I just — y'know — did it.'

'What?' asked Pollard softly.

'That — that old twelve-bore of mine. You've seen it. I take it to work sometimes. An odd rabbit for the pot.'

'What did you do, Charlie?' insisted Pollard gently.

'Both barrels,' breathed Preston. 'I used both barrels. I blew both

85

their bloody heads off, then I had a bath and a clean up and came down here.'

The teleprinter began to clatter.

Pollard said, 'Be with you in a minute, Charlie,' and walked to the alcove.

Pollard allowed the teleprinter to chatter out its message, glanced at the text, then picked up the mike which linked him with Witherham's walkie-talkie.

'Joe. You receiving me, Joe? Pollard here.'

'Okay. I'm with you, Ted.'

'Come back to the nick for a while. Take over for half an hour or so. Something's cropped up.'

'Okay, Ted. I'm on my way.'

Back in the Charge Office, Pollard said, 'Just us two for the moment, Charlie. We'll have a walk to your place. Then we'll play things nice and easy.'

'It's not an odd rabbit or two this time, Johnny.'

Police Constable 2121 Angus Kyle — 'Andy' to his army of friends — wore an unaccustomed expression of sad solemnity. As partner to Cooper on Upper Neck Beat he, more than anybody else, knew where possible information might be available. To him house-to-house enquiries meant more than moving from one door to the next. Hence his call upon John Palmer, the one man in the district to whom poaching was a near-profession.

He said, 'I know you didna like Coop over much. And maybe he was a mite hard on you, at times. But this is no time to keep your tongue between your teeth if you know summat.'

Palmer compressed his lips for a moment, then growled, 'I had a Churchill, once. A damn good gun. I'd a licence for it, too. Cooper took it away from me for the sake of a measly pheasant.'

'The court, not Coop.'

'Would you have done the same?' demanded Palmer.

'Maybe.'

'Not in a thousand years you wouldn't. A Churchill for a pheasant!'

'Dinna bet your life on it, Johnny.' Kyle's voice hardened. 'After last night . . . dinna bet your life on *anything*.'

The tiny cottage had an earthy, gamey smell; not overpowering; not even unpleasant, but *there*. The smell of creatures of the wild. The smell of nature, uncultivated and timid; of hares, of rabbits, of ferrets, of partridge and pheasant. Gamekeepers' cottages and poachers' cottages share this masculine, 'brown-earth' scent.

Kyle said, 'Johnny, I coulda nailed you a hundred times these last few years. I didna. But by God I *will* if I ever find you know things and won't say.'

'You'll need to catch me first.' Palmer smiled.

'Half-Crown Meadow,' said Kyle. 'I know where the gin trap is. The row of snares along the bottom of Marshall's big field. The hide you've made for yourself on the north side of Belltop Wood.' Kyle paused, then added, 'On duty. Off duty. I've watched you, Johnny. I know the runs — the roosting places — as well as you do, maybe better. I've bided my time. I'm no unpaid gamekeeper. But dinna think I can't put you out of business in a month. Every snare. Every gun. Every ferret. Aye . . . and maybe a short stretch in prison.'

'And you *would*?' Palmer sounded shocked.

'Try me.'

'*If* you could.' Palmer wasn't giving up without a fight.

'Laddie,' warned Kyle, 'I'm no Gorbels steet boy. Dinna ever have that idea. I'm from the Highlands. I've dodged more gillies than you'll *ever* dodge. Aye, and taken more from the land in a day than you'll *ever* take. I've changed sides, that's all. That doesn't mean I've lost the knack. I'll tell you.' Kyle stared at Palmer, and it was patently obvious that this was no game of bluff and counter-bluff. 'To keep my hand in, see? I've followed you for miles, Johnny. More than once.' Kyle wagged a warning finger. 'More than once — *more* than once — I could have taken the bird right out of your hand: and dinna call me a liar, Johnny, or I'll do just that next time you're out.'

'That good?' said Palmer heavily.

Kyle nodded.

'All right.' With some reluctance, Palmer capitulated. 'There was a car . . . a pick-up. Until I saw it, I thought it was a car. It stopped and started again.'

'You saw it?'

'I heard it stop. I went outside and saw it. A pick-up.'

'Where did it stop?'

'Just along the road there. Between here and Cooper's place.'

'Time?'

'Midnight. Just before midnight.'

'Who was in it? Who was driving?'

'I dunno. A man. There's no lighting in the village. Just a man . . . I couldn't see more.'

'And you call yourself a poacher,' sneered Kyle. 'Which way was it facing?'

'Away from here. Towards Cooper's place.'

'There'd be a rear light. A rear number plate.'

Palmer nodded.

'The number?'

Palmer shook his head sadly.

'Man, you saw the number plate. You're supposed to notice . . .'

'I can't read,' said Palmer in a low growl.

'You can't . . .' Kyle turned and faced the shelf above the hearth. There was a clock on the shelf, and the clock had Arabic numerals. Kyle said, 'Just before midnight?'

'Yes.'

'You checked with that clock?'

Palmer nodded.

'Right, so you can tell the time?'

'Everybody can tell the time.'

'Figures.' Kyle reached the clock down from the shelf. 'Numbers. That pick-up had numbers on its rear plate. Which numbers?'

'I tell you I can't . . .'

'These.' Kyle pointed to the dial of the clock. 'Which of these numbers were they *like*?'

'The — the same number, I think.'

'Which number?'

'That.' Palmer pointed to the number three.

'All of them that number?'

'I reckon.'

'Thanks.' Kyle returned the clock to its place on the shelf. He said, 'You're not a bad man, Johnny. I'll tell 'em — I have to tell 'em, but not where the information came from.'

Palmer grunted embarrassed thanks.

As he turned to leave, Kyle said, 'Last night — before I went off — I checked the snares in Marshall's big field. Two rabbits . . . should be four by this time. But take some gloves. One of the snares has a cat in it. One of Marshall's farm cats. It'll tear your hands to ribbons if you dinna have heavy gloves.'

Not at all like the man-in-the-street's idea of things. No tyre-screaming car chase. No cornered killer yelling, 'Come and get me, copper!' No police cordon. Nothing like that. Just two middle-aged men strolling, side by side, along the street. One of them in uniform. One of them neatly dressed and smoking a Woodbine. They didn't talk, but they were obviously friends. The one in uniform looked a little sad. The one not in uniform looked quietly resigned.

They turned a corner, then stopped at a neat terraced house. The man smoking the Woodbine felt in a pocket, brought out a key-ring, chose a Yale key and unlocked the door. The door led directly into the front room of the house.

Pollard said, 'Front bedroom, Charlie?'

'Aye.' Preston nodded.

'The gun?'

'Where I dropped it. Near the bed.'

'Right. Stay here, mate. Shove your hands in your pockets. Don't touch anything.'

Preston screwed the Woodbine into a brass ashtray, shaped like a curled leaf, then pushed his hands into his trouser pockets.

Pollard, too, thrust his hands into the pockets of his trousers, then climbed the narrow stairs. On the tiny landing he eased the partly open door on his left with his elbow. He'd seen blood before. He'd seen bodies before. He'd seen most things, but nothing quite like this.

The trick was to detach yourself. Completely. To be a pair of eyes and a brain. Just that and nothing more. As impartial as a camera. As objective as a computer. Forget Charlie Preston. Don't let personalities intrude. Don't bugger things up by letting so much as a hint of emotion past that closed door in your mind.

Item: one double bed; the bedclothes giving the impression that they'd been hosed down in blood, then liberally scattered with shattered bone, teeth, brain-tissue and torn pieces of flesh.

Item: one corpse, female, naked, headless, folded forward at the waist, multiple pellet wounds around the shoulders and upper breast.

Item: one corpse, male, naked, headless, half out of the bedclothes, as if attempting to reach some person standing at the door, positioned at a slight angle on top of the bed on its front, multiple pellet wounds around the shoulders and down the back.

Item: one head-board, originally ivory-coloured P.V.C., torn and pellet-blasted, splatter-dashed with great blotches of blood and brain tissue.

Item: wallpaper, bloody almost beyond belief.

Item: carpet squelching blood.

Item: twin-barrel, twelve-bore shotgun on carpet near the foot of the bed, bloody from drips from bed.

Item: blood, blood, blood and more blood.

Pollard closed his eyes for a moment and whispered, 'Charlie! When they show photographs of *this*!'

He stood on the tiny landing for a few seconds then slowly descended the stairs. Preston was waiting where Pollard had left him.

The two men left the house, Pollard dropping the Yale latch-lock as they left. They walked in silence back to Sopworth Police Station.

Back in the Charge Office Pollard said, 'Okay, Joe. I'll take over.'

Witherham stared, then said, 'You — you all right, Ted?'

'Aye.'

'You look — y'know — ill.'

'I'm fine. Off you go. Make sure the market's still there.'

'If you say so.'

When Witherham had left, Pollard motioned Preston to the chair he'd used before their visit to the house. Then he walked to the alcove, plugged in for Beechwood Brook D.H.Q. and said, 'Pollard, here. I want Detective Chief Inspector Tallboy. Know where he is?'

One day some enterprising, would-be-Ph.D will do a treatise on tea. Its recuperative powers. The mystical manner in which it steadies nerves and chases away near-hysteria. Indeed, the work might well include the serious proposition that the difference *7.30 a.m.* between the extroversion of the average U.S.A. citizen and the introversion of the average U.K. citizen is, in effect, the difference between coffee-drinkers and tea-drinkers. U.S. cops slosh coffee around at the drop of a Kojak, U.K. cops brew-up whenever they find their hands unoccupied. Each man to his own poison but, certain it is, that hot, strong, sweet and brandy-laced tea worked marvels on Hilda Noble.

She stood up from the chair and said, 'I'll get dressed, then I'll go see him.'

'Take your time.' W.P.C. Pearson levelled her voice to a more businesslike tone. 'Something special. Look smart. Give his good eye something worth looking at.'

Hilda Noble smiled quickly, then left the room for upstairs.

Sergeant Ramsden frowned and said, 'That was a little — y'know — uncalled for.'

'What?' Pearson looked puzzled.

'The remark about his *good* eye.'

'Sergeant.' Pearson tilted her head slightly. 'What you know about law may earn you the title of Copper of the Year. But what you know about women . . . you're not yet past kindergarten.'

'I don't see what . . .'

'It'll make *her* feel better. She looks a frump, she'll behave like a frump.' She paused then, in a sombre voice, added, 'Anyway, he might not *have* a good eye. The chances are against it.'

'It was only his left eye. As far as I know his . . .'

90

'I have a boyfriend. He works at Bordfield General. He knows about these things. One eye gets a real socking . . . if it's bad enough the whole system goes.'

'Oh!'

'Sometimes it's only temporary. Sometimes it's permanent.'

'In that case . . .'

'He's not going to be able to see her, sergeant. He'll be bandaged, that at the very least. But if she *feels* good she'll *sound* good.'

'I wonder how . . .' Ramsden stopped, scowled and rubbed the nape of his neck.

'What?'

'The section. I should be at the station.'

'Pollard's there.' Perhaps without meaning to she made it sound as if Sergeant Ramsden was a supernumerary whilever P.C. Pollard was around.

Ramsden said, 'Drop me off. On the way to Bordfield, drop me off at the police station.' He paused, then added, 'I hope nothing's happened while we've been away.'

Kyle had reported his findings to Blayde and Tallboy. Everything Palmer had said, but without giving Palmer's name.

'He'll have to be seen,' said Blayde bluntly.

'Sir, I gave him my word.'

'Kyle, old son.' Tallboy tried to put it more reasonably. 'He's the only lead we have. I know — 'The identity of informants shouldn't be revealed' — that's what the book says. But is he an informant? A *regular* informant?'

'No, sir,' admitted Kyle.

Blayde grunted, 'I don't give a damn if he's Judas himself.'

'He *has* to be interviewed,' insisted Tallboy.

Kyle said, 'He's *been* interviewed. *I* interviewed him.'

Blayde sniffed, very pointedly.

Kyle argued, 'Sir, he can't read. He can't write. If . . .'

'A proper little Einstein.'

'. . . If anybody takes a statement from him, it'll be useless. A moderately good defending lawyer . . .'

'I'm not arguing, Kyle. We're not taking a vote on the subject. I want that man's name . . . *now*.'

The telephone bell rang and Tallboy lifted the receiver.

After the initial resigned sigh of, 'Good God!' there was little to be learned from Tallboy's end of the telephone conversation. An occasional Yes — I see and Good made no sense, but the expressions which chased each other across Tallboy's face brought an almost impatient curiosity as far as Blayde was concerned.

Tallboy replaced the receiver slowly. Gently. As if the sudden dropping onto the prongs might damage the instrument.

'Well?' asked Blayde.

'A double murder,' said Tallboy heavily.

'Y'mean Noble and . . .'

'No, at Sopworth. A man called Sutcliffe. A woman called Preston. Preston's husband found them in bed together, shot them with a twelve-bore, then gave himself up.'

'When for God's sake?'

'That was Pollard.' Tallboy glanced at the phone. 'Constable Pollard. Preston's in custody. Pollard's visited the scene. Nasty. I know Pollard — a very steady type — if he says it's nasty it's *nasty*.'

'Where's Ramsden?' asked Blayde.

'Out with Policewoman Pearson, notifying Noble's wife. He should be back at the station within the next half-hour or so.'

'Damn!' Then Blayde repeated his first question. 'When did this happen?'

'About the same time as *this*.' A quick, wry smile touched Tallboy's lips. 'Preston took his time. Washed and brushed himself up, then walked into the nick and told Pollard.'

'Right.' Blayde seemed to change gear. The cold-blooded efficiency — one of the reasons why he held the rank — slipped into place and he rapped the orders out without hesitation. 'You stay here, Chris. Handle this lot. I'll get down to Sopworth and sort out the shotgun artist. When the boffins have finished here, send 'em down to me. You . . .' This to the waiting Kyle. 'Find Evans. Tell him to meet me at my car. And that's *all* you tell him.' When Kyle had left, Blayde added, 'Keep me in the picture, Chris.'

'Will do.'

'And . . .' Blayde hesitated, then reached a hand towards the telephone and said, 'Yes, damnit, why not? Let's have Harris out. A double murder, a double maiming . . . what the hell does he get paid for?'

'What'll happen to me, Ted?' Preston asked the question in a quiet enough voice but, buried deep inside the tone, there was a fear of the unknown.

'Prison.' Pollard saw no reason for anything other than honesty.

'How long . . . d'you reckon?'

'Depends.'

92

'On – on what?'

The two men were still in the Charge Office. By the rules of the game – by every rule of the game – Preston should have been locked away in a cell by this time. But what the hell? That would come soon enough. Enough cells – enough prisons – why lock him away before it was strictly necessary? He'd killed. On paper he was a murderer. The hell he was a murderer! He was a guy caught up in as neat a web of circumstances as anybody could imagine.

Pollard knew things. Things even Charlie Preston didn't know. May Preston was a bag – had *been* a bag – anybody's meat for the asking. Sammy Sutcliffe? Okay, if she'd *had* a special ram it had been Sammy Sutcliffe. But there were others. Pollard could have named at least three others. Poor old Charlie. Poor old inoffensive Charlie Preston. Look at him. The realisation taking over. His guts tying themselves into knots.

'You'll need a solicitor,' said Pollard.

'Who?' Preston seemed startled at the idea of a solicitor.

'Try Ranson,' suggested Pollard.

'Is he – y'know – good?'

'He's straight. And he fights.'

'I – I don't see how . . .' Preston's voice tailed into silence.

'Ranson'll get it reduced,' soothed Pollard.

'Y'mean . . .'

'Manslaughter. Diminished Responsibility.'

'Y'mean I'm daft? I'm off my head?'

'No, meaning you've done what most men would have done.'

'Ted, you're not . . .'

'I'm telling you the truth, Charlie.' Pollard sighed. 'Get Ranson, but don't say I *told* you to get Ranson. Do what he says. You'll be charged with murder. But that's only the first step. After that, leave things to Ranson.'

'Christ!' Preston suddenly folded. He dropped his head into his cupped hands, rested his elbows on his knees, and groaned, 'What the hell made me do it, Ted? What the hell made me *do* it?'

It was a question which did not admit of an answer. Pollard didn't try to answer it.

Think of a cart horse; a particularly awkward cart horse, with legs over which it has only partial control, with great yellow teeth too long for the upper lip and a head proportionally too large for its body and, moreover, a head which seems forever to be either shaking or nodding with unnecessary vigour. A pantomime cart horse, in fact. Clothe that cart horse in ill-fitting clerical grey plus (of all things) a wine-coloured bow-tie . . . and there you have the Market Superintendent.

Nobody took the poor guy seriously. Whoever chose him as Market Superintendent must have been blind, barmy or possessed of a very off-beat humour. He just *wasn't*. He just never *could* be.

And yet he did his best, and was *doing* his best.

The argument was with the cut flowers man; the man whose site was on the very corner of the market square and who (according to the Market Superintendent) had trespassed well beyond his allotted area.

'Up there.' The Market Superintendent waved his arm wildly. '*That's* your pitch. You're *yards* too far this way.'

'And what about the lorries?' demanded the cut flowers man. 'They come round the flipping corner. They have to take a wide sweep. If I set up *there,* they either knock my containers over or shift all my customers. It's happened too many times. I *know.*'

'That's your pitch, Perkins. You know that an' all.'

Witherham rounded the corner causing the controversy and the cut flowers man called, 'Constable! Constable Witherham!'

'It's nothing to do with him,' said the Market Superintendent. 'It's no good appealing to him. He hasn't a say in the matter.'

Nevertheless P.C. Witherham strolled across to the arguing men.

'That corner.' The cut flowers man pointed. 'Flipping great lorries — bowsers and things — turn right there. They knock my containers over sometimes. And I've not enough room to serve my customers.'

'Seems room enough for me.' Witherham measured the corner and road width with his eye.

'But he shouldn't be here,' explained the Market Superintendent. 'He should be up there. *Yards* up there.'

'He's not taking over anybody else's pitch, is he?'

'That's not the point. Perkins knows where his own pitch is. He's just trying to be awkward.'

'No, I'm hanged if I am. All I'm saying . . .'

'*If,*' mused Witherham, 'If some vehicle did come round that corner. Too fast, maybe. Too big, maybe. And *if* it knocked somebody down. Somebody buying flowers say.' Witherham looked hard at the Market Superintendent. 'I wouldn't be in your shoes, mate. Some kid gets killed while its mother's buying flowers.' Witherham pursed his lips into a silent whistle. 'Mate, what's the coroner going to say to you? Especially now *I* know you've deliberately put him back there.'

94

'It's my job,' wailed the Market Superintendent. 'I don't decide the pitch placing.'

'I doubt if he'll wear that,' said Witherham solemnly.

'Who?'

'The coroner.'

'All right! All right!' The Market Superintendent sucked at his great yellow teeth with open annoyance. 'But you'll also note, I hope, that I pointed out to him that he wasn't on his correct pitch.'

'I'll make a note,' promised Witherham.

The defeated Market Superintendent stomped away. If anything, he looked even more like a clumsy cart horse dressed in clerical grey.

The cut flowers man said, 'Thank you, constable.'

'Nice flowers.' Witherham eyed the display approvingly. 'That pot of miniature chrysants . . . *very* nice.'

'Shall I put it aside for you?' suggested the cut flowers man.

'Would you?' Witherham raised his eyebrows in mock-surprise.

'With — er — with my compliments, of course.'

'That's bloody civilised of you, old son. I'm obliged.'

Blayde threaded his car through the growing crowd milling around Sopworth Market Square. He spotted the uniformed figure of

8 a.m.
Witherham talking to some oddball type in a grey suit near a flower stall. He didn't know the officer; to the best of his knowledge he'd never clapped eyes on him before. But he knew the type. Odd how you could tell 'em after a few years in the force. Not exactly useless, but never much bloody *good*. The way he held himself. The matey-matey attitude. Ten-to-one he was on the make. Nawpings, that's what they used to be called. What they probably still *were* called. Not exactly bribery. Just — y'know — for services rendered. One day with luck — *bad* luck — he'd make sergeant, and on that day the local shopkeepers, the local publicans, the local bookies, the local *everything* would be taken for a steady but never-ending ride.

Blayde muttered, 'Stupid bastard,' and turned the car from the square, along a couple of streets, and braked at the police station.

He strode into the Charge Office with Evans trotting at his heels.

Pollard looked up from the Telephone and Teleprinter Message Book, and said, 'Sir.'

'A double murder . . . so I'm told.'

'Yes, sir.' Pollard motioned with his head. 'Preston. Charles Preston. He shot his wife and her boyfriend. Found 'em in bed together. Then came along and gave himself up.'

'Why isn't he in a cell?'

'He hasn't yet been arrested.'

'What the . . .' Blayde took it with little more than a blink of the eyes, then turned to Evans, and said, 'Right. Take him to a cell. Tuck him in. Read him his rights . . . then let me know.'

When he was alone with Pollard, Blayde said, 'You've more than a little wool on your back, constable. Mind telling me why?'

'I know him,' said Pollard simply. 'She was a slag. He's no tearaway. Just ask . . . he'll tell you everything.'

'But *you* haven't asked?'

'I haven't pushed things, sir.'

'Why not?'

'I don't want the case,' said Pollard bluntly. 'A few weeks time, I'm out of this job. If possible, I don't want to be called as witness. A double murder . . . it might do somebody some good. Evans, maybe. Not me.'

'To you it's just a blasted nuisance?'

'That's about the size of it, sir.'

'Let me tell you something . . . what's your name?' snapped Blayde.

'Pollard.'

'Let me tell you something, Pollard. You're a copper. Till the last minute of your last shift. You're a copper.'

'If I take the case . . .' Pollard stared straight into Blayde's eyes. 'As you say, sir, I'm a copper. An ordinary flatfoot. If I take the case, the chances are I'd make such an almighty cock-up of the file. You wouldn't believe.'

'You would?' Blayde met Pollard's gaze, and silently called him a liar.

'A real old woodentop. That's me, sir.'

'Now,' said Blayde gently, 'between these four walls — as "woodentop" to "Sherlock" — the *real* reason?'

Equally gently, Pollard said, 'I've got thirty in.'

'And you don't want to go out on a murder?'

'I don't want to go out on *this* murder.'

'Because he's your pal?'

'Because I know him. Because I knew *her . . . and* her fancy man.'

'They deserved it?'

'I'm not saying that.' Pollard shook his head slowly, then added, 'When you see that room.'

'Y'know what?' Blayde almost smiled. 'I think you're a stubborn old bugger. I think you might just do it.'

96

'What's that, sir?'

'Make a real cow's arse of the file . . . deliberately.'

'Off the record, sir?' said Pollard calmly.

'Depends.'

'Evans needs it. I don't. He's a detective constable, but nobody takes him seriously. A double murder — even this one — and he'll have a name. It might even do *him* good.'

Blayde pulled at his nose for a moment. Then he sniffed. Then he scowled.

Finally he growled, 'Evans's case, then. He won't thank you — not at first — but, later, if he's any gumption.'

'He'll have to come to Hove,' grinned Pollard.

'Eh?'

'That's where I'm retiring to.'

'God help Hove!'

Blayde left the Charge Office for the cells.

Marian Cooper carried the plastic beaker with exaggerated care. It was vitally important that none of the tea spill onto the polished surface of the corridor's floor. *Vitally* important. As, when she was a girl and returning home from school, it was equally *vitally* important that she shouldn't tread on any of the cracks between the paving stones. Not a game. No glorified hopscotch. If she trod on a crack — just one crack — there'd be something in her homework she wouldn't be able to do. She'd make a hash of it and, next morning, Miss Watford would have her out before the class and make her feel a fool. Miss Watford's way. An old cow — all the girls knew she was a wicked old cow — but that didn't stop them from giggling whenever some girl was subjected to the Watford sarcasm. But if she *didn't* walk on a crack — if she walked slowly and carefully — it would be all right and she'd be able to answer all the questions, and some other girl would be the recipient of the sarcasm and she (Marian Cooper) would only be expected to giggle dutifully.

Only this time it wasn't homework. This time it was Coop. And if she spilled so much as a drop of tea from the beaker . . .

Coop had everything nailed down. Rigid. No wavering. Black, white. Up, down. Left, right. No in-betweens. No excuses. No 'never minds'. A hard man to live with. An impossible man to please. Maybe because he'd been brought up in an orphanage. A 'charity child', that was one of his own expressions. A curl of the lips, then the sneer, 'I'm a charity child. Didn't you know?' That orphanage! God knows what they'd done to him, how they'd treated him, but they'd created a form of monster. Not evil. He wasn't evil. Indeed, at times his kindness had almost choked her. But to *himself*!

How can a man be a monster to himself? Self-hatred, self-contempt, honed razor-sharp and forever cutting and slashing. A monster, buried deep inside, and satisfied only when it was inflicting torment on its own creator.

In God's name, what was he going to be like with a hand missing?

The plastic of the beaker was paper-thin. The tea was painfully hot, and reached the very brim of the beaker. But not a drop of it must fall — not a crack must be stepped upon — otherwise, all hope vanished.

She steered herself into the lounge, bent and placed the beaker carefully onto one of the low tables. Then she gave a sigh of relief and settled back into one of the worn armchairs.

She saw the man in police inspector's uniform. His peaked cap was on the table alongside his chair, and he was reading an old *Readers' Digest*. She recognised him, pulled her dressing-gown tighter around her nightdress, then said, 'Inspector Rowe.'

'Eh? What . . . oh!' Rowe lowered the *Readers' Digest,* then said, 'It's — er — it's Mrs Cooper, isn't it?'

She nodded.

'How is he?' he asked.

'He's in the theatre.' She hesitated, then added, 'They're taking his hand off.'

'Aah.'

The noise (it couldn't be called a word) was pure 'Rowe'. It meant nothing, but it could have meant *anything*. Sympathy, perhaps. Or — equally — congratulatory relief. A hand? What's a hand? It might have been his head. Rowe had developed non-committment into a fine art. Without effort he was able to mouth words and noises in various tones which completely screwed up their meanings.

Marian Cooper sipped the scalding hot tea, replaced the beaker on the table, then said, 'What's going to happen to him?'

'Oh, he'll — er — ' Rowe waved a hand in a vague gesture. 'They have wonderful artificial limbs these days.'

'I'm a qualified nurse.'

'Oh?'

'I wasn't asking about his hand. I was asking about *him.*'

'Er . . .' Rowe lifted one shoulder. 'Something, I suppose. There's bound to be *something.*'

'Do you give a damn?' Her voice was steady. The question was quietly asked.

'I . . .' Rowe dropped the *Readers' Digest* onto a table, then muttered, 'You're – er – distraught, Mrs Cooper. You really mustn't upset yourself so . . .'

'I'm not upset.' Her voice was as steady as ever.

'Well . . . of *course* we care.'

'How much?'

'We'll . . . We'll do something. Of course we'll do *something.*'

She paused long enough to sip her tea once more, then she said, 'He was a detective. You know that, of course?'

'Yes. Before he . . .'

'Before Harris dumped him on Upper Neck Beat.'

'It's a good beat, Mrs Cooper. Few officers would complain about a beat like Upper Neck.'

'A demotion,' she said bluntly.

'Hardly that.' He tried a smile for size, decided it didn't fit the occasion and discarded it. 'He was only . . .'

'A detective. Reduced to village bobby.'

'The village policeman . . .'

'Coop was never a "village policeman" type,' she interrupted. 'Harris knew that . . . that was the "punishment". Like putting him in a straitjacket. Like caging an eagle. Well . . .' Her eyes hardened. 'You caged the eagle. And now you've smashed one of its wings. Is that enough, do you think? Has Harris – the rest of you – have you all had your full pound of flesh?'

'Isn't it time you went to bed, Charles?' Mrs Jones cast a motherly eye upon Police Constable Wooley. As if he was unaware of the fact, she added, 'You're on night duty again tonight.'

Dear Mrs Jones. She was plump . . . not yet fat, but decidedly plump. Childless, nevertheless she had a natural maternal quality. Since the death of her husband ('her Bill' as she always called him) she had 'taken-in' unmarried police officers. The force (every force) is grateful whenever it finds such a lady. For a pittance called 'lodging allowance' they provide a home for some lonely copper. In the main they are middle-aged widows; they open their house and they open their heart to a strange young man. By definition because he's a copper (and because care is exercised in the choice) he is a young man not likely to cause trouble or make a nuisance of himself. He is neither moody nor garrulous. He is grateful. He has a good billet, and he knows it.

In their own way – in a very different way – these ladies are as legendary as theatrical landladies. A strange (sometimes rather timid)

99

young man enters their front door and, in no time flat, they have adopted him. No hanky-panky; the relationship is strictly a mother-and-son affair. Complete, be it understood, with mutual affection which can grow to *equal* that of a mother and her son.

And all for a few quid a week. Nobody ever grew rich on 'lodging allowance'. More often than not the good lady is out of pocket on the deal. Ah, but you see they once more have 'a man in the house' . . . and that is the crux of the matter. A man shares their roof and without bringing with him that feeling of guilt which might accompany a second marriage. Their pledge to their dead husband remains intact . . . and yet they have 'a man in the house'. A policeman. It adds to their feeling of security. It brings out the best in them. It makes them feel *wanted*.

One day somebody will write a book about police landladies, and in its own way it will be a love story.

And Wooley, having downed a giant's breakfast, knew that Mrs Jones was right. After an all-night stint on the street, bed *was* the place for him.

And yet . . .

'I — er — I think I'll take a walk first,' he said.

'Sergeant Noble?' The question was asked gently and with understanding. She added, 'He's a good man.'

'Just to the station. See how things are,' muttered Wooley.

'And the other one?'

'Coop?'

'I've never met him.'

'The Upper Neck man. A nice chap.' But the sorrow with which he'd mentioned Noble's name was missing.

Mrs Jones squeezed his shoulder, then began to clear the table. Wooley stood up from the table, went upstairs, exchanged his tunic for a sports jacket and left the house. There was complete rapport between the two. Words had been unnecessary.

Sopworth was coming to life. Kids were about, people were walking the pavement, goods vehicles and the occasional bus joined the steady growth of traffic. A market town. Not a metropolis, but busy and becoming busier. The traffic wardens had begun their slow, self-important saunter along the rows of parked cars.

He entered the police station via the rear door. Passing the row of cells he heard the mumble of voices from behind one of the closed doors. In the Charge Office Pollard greeted him with a single nod of welcome.

'No real news,' said Pollard, without waiting to be asked. 'They're still in the operating theatres.'

'Who the hell *did* it?' Wooley's tone was low and furious.

'Five minutes with him,' agreed Pollard. 'Just him and me . . . old as I am.'

'Ted.' Wooley seemed to have difficulty in saying what he wanted to say. 'Coop . . . it was meant for Coop. Noble just happened to be there.'

'Aye.' Pollard nodded.

'Why?'

Pollard shrugged.

'I mean . . .' Wooley struggled on. 'Coop. We all have — y'know — not exactly enemies. People who don't like us. But *that*!'

'Coop has enemies,' said Pollard simply. 'He's that sort of bloke. He *makes* enemies.'

Wooley whispered, 'Jesus!'

'Some are like that.' Pollard spoke sadly. Softly. From a lifetime of experience. 'Every man has his own way of bobbying. There's no fixed way. That's *their* way.'

'But for Christ's sake . . .'

'Sometimes the *only* way.'

Pollard fingered a Woodbine from its packet. He offered the packet to Wooley, but Wooley shook his head. Pollard lighted the cigarette and watched the emotions make shadow-play across the younger man's face.

Outside a car stopped, a door slammed, then the car started up again and drove into the distance. Ramsden bustled into the Charge Office.

He said, 'Wooley. I thought you were off duty at . . .'

'I came back for news.'

'Oh?' Ramsden turned to Pollard and said, 'Anything?'

'A double murder.' Pollard made it sound like a throw-away remark.

Ramsden's jaw dropped.

'Charlie Preston,' amplified Pollard calmly. 'He used a shotgun on his wife and her fancy man. He's in the cell. Blayde and Evans are with him.'

'How . . .' Ramsden boiled up to his normal point of everlasting near-panic. 'I mean . . .'

'He gave himself up.'

'Oh?'

'Charlie *Preston*?' Wooley stared disbelievingly.

'The kiln firer,' said Pollard.

'But Christ . . . I only saw him the other night.'

'You didn't see him last night.' Pollard drew on the Woodbine. 'Last night he had other things on his mind.'

'In the cell?' said Ramsden.

'Aye.' Pollard nodded.

'With Chief Superintendent Blayde?'

'And Evans.'

'I'd — I'd better . . .'

Ramsden hurried from the Charge Office. He almost ran along the corridors to the cell area. He paused, touched his tie, cleared his throat then, hearing voices from inside one of the cells, he tapped on the cell door.

From inside the cell Blayde called, 'Yes? Who is it?'

Ramsden turned the handle, pushed open the cell door, then said, 'It's me, sir. Do you — er — want me at all?'

Blayde glared from across the length of the cell, then snarled, 'Why the hell should I want *you*, sergeant?'

Technically (as per entry in Sopworth Sectional Diary) it was known as Double Beat/Twenty-four-hour Discretional Cover. Which, in layman's language, meant he was responsible for Rimstone Beat and Upper Neck Beat, from 6 a.m. until 6 a.m. and that, between those times, he could come on duty and go off duty as he pleased with the proviso that the 'on duty' bits added up to no more than eight hours. Chinese mathematics wasn't in it. Up and down, in and out, like a fiddler's elbow. And (other than on paper) it couldn't be done.

Pinter wasn't complaining. Driving the Minivan kept his mind occupied. Deliberately double de-clutching. Carefully keeping his hands at 'ten minutes to two' on the steering wheel. Killing time . . . until time 'killed' Hannah.

He didn't want to go home. Home was the last place to which he wanted to return. His home. Hannah's home. *Their* home. The guilt welled up and threatened to choke him. The guilt and the cowardice. To love a woman, as much as he loved Hannah, and to almost pray *not* to be with her at the end. *Not* to be holding her hand. *Not* to ease her into the darkness.

All the books he'd read, all the films he'd seen, all the T.V. plays he'd watched. It wasn't like that at all. Those endings . . . all wrong. *Wrong!* You can't love a person, then sit there and watch them die.

The medics said she wouldn't know. She'd slip away. From coma to nothingness. Well, maybe. That would be nice — no not 'nice' — but *something*. If it happened. But what if it *didn't* happen? What if

— y'know — just for a moment? Before the end? *At* the end? And she knew. She knew she was . . .

He pulled the Minivan into a lay-by and braked to a halt. He gripped the steering wheel in a wild effort to stop his hands from trembling. To stop his thoughts from racing. To stop the world — to stop time — to *reverse* time . . . to bring back those days before she . . .

He choked, 'Oh, God! Oh, God . . . what am I going to *do*?'

Tallboy replaced the receiver and said, 'WQW 323D. Morris pick-up. Registered owner Ronald Peacock. Ronald Peacock, general contractor, occasional demolition work. Address — and works address — Winchester Avenue, North End, Lessford.'

'Thanks.' P.C. Kyle nodded his gratitude.

'Don't thank me. Thank Criminal Intelligence, fortunately they have it filed and cross-referenced.'

Kyle nodded, this time a little reluctantly.

Criminal Intelligence. It was a new thing. A new ball game. In the old days it was known as 'local knowledge'; to have control of a beat to an extent that nothing — but *nothing* — happened without your knowledge. To know that Joe Bloggs had bought a very fancy greenhouse; to know that, on the wage he took home equated with the input of booze he habitually consumed at the local pub equated with the manner in which his wife and kids were dressed, Joe Bloggs couldn't *afford* that fancy greenhouse . . . not if they quartered the price. That sort of thing. Multiply it a thousandfold and it became 'local knowledge'. A crime was half-way towards being detected before it was even committed. Kyle was a great believer in 'local knowledge'. His Beat Book — that very private volume which remained at every outside beat police house, regardless of who worked the beat — was kept up to date with near fanatical zeal. The local snouts. The local troublemakers. The make and number of the cars of those who just *might* try something on. The drunks, the wife-beaters, the wide-boys. The vantage points, and which parts of the beat to be viewed without being seen. The late-go-to-bedders and the early-get-uppers. Who was pally with who and (perhaps more important) who was *not* pally with who. Sneaky stuff, 'local knowledge'. Sneaky, but of great importance . . . the reason why Kyle had gone straight to John Palmer.

But this comparatively new thing. Force Criminal Intelligence. For a handful of guys to sit on their backsides, surrounded on all sides by card index files. For these same guys to be in a position to make 'local knowledge' look like a sick cat . . . and, be it understood, some forces had scrapped the card index system and taken on computers. Andy Kyle was a simple soul. He mistrusted computers, and he wasn't over-keen on card index systems. A Beat Book was one thing, but the new-style collation of knowledge — this systematic gathering together of tiny scraps of information — smacked of 'Big Brother' bureaucracy. The one-to-one element was missing. It wasn't *bobbying*, and, if that was a crazy way of looking at things, Kyle knew he wasn't alone in his thinking.

Nevertheless . . .

'If your informant's innumerate — as you say he is — he could well have mistaken three-two-three for triple three.'

'Yes, sir.' Kyle nodded agreement.

'And Peacock . . .'Tallboy glanced at the scribbled notes he'd jotted as Criminal Intelligence had fed him the facts. 'Peacock is the father-in-law of Tony Shanks. And Tony Shanks was the last villain Cooper put away before he took over Upper Neck Beat.'

'There was some trouble,' said Kyle gently. 'At the trial, I mean. Cooper was criticised . . . so I'm told.'

'He was threatened.' Tallboy's voice gave nothing away.

'Yes, sir. But . . .'

'It happens, Kyle. Often. The threats are rarely carried out. This time . . . who knows?'

Meanwhile, out in the street, the population of Upper Neck had just about doubled itself in a time span measurable in minutes. The 'mass media' was going about its business. National and local radio were there, complete with microphones and recording gear. Two T.V. groups had sent men and women, armed with portable cameras and video tape. The newspaper reporters and cameramen jostled and pushed in their endless search for new angles and differing accounts.

And, of course, the rubbernecks.

A puzzle which tantalises so many police officers. What is there about blood, muck and general mayhem which attracts hordes of otherwise decent, clean-living people? Some sub-conscious, primaeval 'pull' which stretches back to the carnage of the sabre-tooths? A morbid fascination with death itself? A whistling-in-the-dark attitude which forces an examination of horror, coupled with the unspoken thought that when the final enemy does arrive the chances are it won't be as terrible as *that*? For whatever reason, they came to gawp. Men,

8.30 a.m.

104

women and, often, even kids; a trip with the family to view the gore; an outing to gaze at a real-life chamber of horrors.

By this time extra officers had been drafted in from neighbouring sections and divisions. Jacks, to help in the house-to-house enquiries. Uniformed men, to stand in groups at a point beyond which the public were not allowed to trespass. What was officially known as 'A Major Crime Situation' had been created.

Nevertheless, by one-o'clock news time the radio listeners would be fed basic details. The evening editions of both locals and nationals would have enough meat to pad things out into a full story. The early evening T.V. news slots would carry pictures of people being interviewed.

Gradually, the inhabitants of Upper Neck had lowered their defences. They talked. They voiced opinions. They answered mildly loaded questions about Police Constable Cooper . . . and Mrs Cooper.

A happy couple were they? Well, if not quite still in the honeymoon stage, moderately happy, would you say? They kept themselves very much to themselves, did they? I understand he was in C.I.D. before he took over this beat . . . d'you know *why*? Why he was transferred from plain clothes to uniform branch, I mean? He never spoke about it? He never discussed it with you? Not even when he was off duty? Did he have many friends in the village? Just acquaintances? Why was that d'you think?

Oh, those questions. Politely asked, but demanding an answer. And each answer was one more nudge in a predetermined direction. The media had made a decision . . . that Police Constable 2004 David Cooper was not the all-English, red-blooded, couldn't-tell-a-lie copper beloved of police recruiting adverts. He wasn't too popular. He had a background. He was, despite his injuries, a potential Aunt Sally.

Whereas Charlie Preston . . .

Evans had made him remove his boots, his tie, his braces, his belt and even his suspenders.

'You might want to do yourself in,' Evans had explained, with all the subtleness of a charging rhino. 'You might want to hang yourself. We can't have that, can we?'

'Hang myself?' Preston had gaped.

'You never know.'

'With my *bootlaces*? With my *suspenders*?'

'Just take 'em off, man. I don't make the rules.'

'A bit daft . . . innit?'

'I don't make the rules,' Evans had repeated.

Then, bootless, tieless, without braces, belt or suspenders, Preston had lowered himself to a sitting position on the cell bed . . . and Blayde had arrived.

Blayde had closed the door and said, 'Your case, Evans.'

'*My* . . .' Evans had paled visibly.

'Pollard . . .'Blayde had cleared his throat. 'Pollard's getting a bit too old for it. Ever handled murder before, lad?'

'No, sir — er — never.'

'You'll enjoy it,' Blayde had promised. 'Right. Get your notebook out.' He'd turned to the slightly flabbergasted Preston and snapped, 'Been cautioned yet, Preston?'

'I — er — '

'You're-not-obliged-to-say-anything-unless-you-wish-to-do-so-but-whatever-you-say-may-be-taken-down-and-given-in-evidence. Right . . . you've been cautioned. Now, say your piece and Detective Constable Evans will write it all down.'

And now, Evans had cramp in his fingers, but Blayde was still shooting the questions at the bemused Preston.

'You had the gun handy?'

'It's an old twelve-bore, sir. Constable Pollard'll . . .'

'Forget Pollard. You had the gun handy?'

'Yes, sir. At home.'

'Loaded and ready?'

'No, sir. Not loaded. The cartridges were . . .'

'The cartridges were handy?'

'In a drawer, where I keep them.'

'So, you loaded the gun?'

'Yes, sir.' Preston moved his head in a miserable nod.

'Deliberately?'

'Well — aye — I loaded it . . .'

'Downstairs?'

'Eh?'

'You loaded the gun downstairs. Before you went up to the bedroom?'

'Yes, sir.'

'You meant to use it?'

'I — I reckon.'

'Downstairs. You deliberately loaded the gun, and meant to use it?'

'I could . . . hear 'em.'

'The question was: you loaded the gun downstairs?'

'Yes, sir.'

'Meaning to use it, when you reached the bedroom?'

'I – I reckon so.'

'Would you have loaded it otherwise?'

'I – I dunno. That was my May upstairs. I – I could hear 'em. I didn't really know . . .'

'You knew enough to load the twelve-bore.'

Preston swallowed, then croaked, 'A – a solicitor.'

Blayde raised an eyebrow.

'Ranson,' breathed Preston. 'I'd – I'd like Ranson here, before I answer any more questions.'

'Ranson?'

Preston nodded.

'You know how to pick 'em,' observed Blayde.

'Am I – am I allowed . . .'

'You're "allowed",' growled Blayde. He motioned to Evans. Evans closed his notebook with a sigh of relief. Blayde led the way from the cell. Evans slammed the door on Preston.

Blayde said, 'Okay. You visit the scene. I'll contact Ranson's office and tell him he's a new client.'

W.P.C. Pearson guided Hilda Noble along the corridors, up the gentle slopes and around the various corners within the labyrinth of Bordfield General Infirmary. The early morning bustle of a large hospital surrounded them; hurrying hospital staff; white-coated ancillary workers pushing huge, wheeled baskets of soiled linen; uniformed porters steering stretcher-trolleys with almost uncanny accuracy.

A factory. A huge, fine-tuned factory geared to the alleviation of suffering. Big enough to tackle just about anything. Maybe too big. Too impersonal. Maybe (the thought frightened Hilda Noble) . . . maybe big enough to make mistakes and not even *notice* them.

They ended up in a huge room upon whose door was printed *Staff Lounge*. Wall-to-wall carpeting, brightly painted walls, dozens of armchairs, sofas and low tables. And in one corner a great, gaudily coloured monster which delivered tea, coffee, soup or milk at the insertion of a coin and the press of a button.

Pearson deposited Hilda Noble in one of the armchairs, and said, 'Something to drink?'

'No, thank you.'

'I won't be a minute.' Pearson walked across the room and returned with a tall, angular woman in nurse's uniform. She said, 'This is Nurse Bowtree. She'll look after you. I'll see what news I can get.'

107

'I don't need . . . .'

But already Pearson was hurrying towards the door.

'I'm sorry.' Hilda Noble managed a weak smile. 'She's quite over-powering, isn't she?'

'She'd have made a great nurse.' Bowtree returned the smile. 'We all know her. One of our male nurses is her young man.'

They sat in awkward silence for a few moments.

Then Hilda Noble said, 'It's — it's my husband. Sergeant Noble. He's a police sergeant. And last night — in the early hours of this morning, apparently — he . . .'

'He's in my ward.' Bowtree made it sound as if all worries need now be forgotten. 'The night staff made the beds ready. Sergeant Noble and Constable Cooper. They're still in theatre.'

'Oh!'

'He'll look rough.' Bowtree's smile was not far short of a grin. 'They all do after surgery. Especially the men. Very often we discourage people from seeing them for the first few hours. Men's Surgical.' The near-grin came and went. '*I* like it. The real "Florence Nightingale" feeling. They're so infernally helpless when they're hurt.'

'It's — it's his eyes,' muttered Hilda Noble.

'I know, luv.' Bowtree was suddenly very serious. 'I'm being flippant. I'm sorry. I know how you must feel. But — truly — we've a great team on Men's Surgical. Especially on Appleton Ward.'

'When — when can I see him?'

'Soon,' promised Bowtree. 'When he's out of theatre. Give us an hour — thereabouts — to make him presentable.'

'Presentable?'

'To bring him round, luv. That's all. He'll still be dopey, but he should be able to recognise your voice.'

At Sopworth Police Station Harris arrived.

That simple word 'arrive'. A cricket ball hurled by Mr F.S. Trueman in his prime and at his most aggressive, could have been said to 'arrive'. Equally, the goodnight punch of Mr Rocky Marciano, the touch of a match to a powder-keg, the splitting of a tree by forked lightning.

Thus, Harris 'arrived'. Robert Harris. One-time Detective Chief Superintendent Harris of the now defunct county force. Present office, assistant chief constable (crime), Bordfield Region of the Lessford Metropolitan District.

As he strode into the Charge Office, he rapped, 'Something about a double murder?'

'Detected. All it needs is the pink ribbon.' Blayde was in no way intimidated by A.C.C. (Crime) Harris. Harris resented this a little, but that was okay by Blayde because Harris knew that within the resentment was a core of reluctant respect. Blayde added, 'At Upper Neck . . . two uniformed officers badly injured by an explosion. That's *not* detected.'

'Who's handling the Upper Neck incident?'

'Tallboy.'

'And this double murder?'

'I'm here,' said Blayde calmly. 'The Sopworth D.C. and one of the local lads — a Constable Wooley — have gone to the scene.'

'And you?'

'Preston — the killer — he's in the cell. His solicitor, Ranson, is on his way. I want to be around.'

Harris compressed his lips for a moment, then seemed satisfied, and said, 'Blakey?'

'Chief Superintendent Blakey?' Blayde passed the question on to Pollard.

Pollard chose his words carefully, and said, 'I haven't seen him since I came on duty at six, sir.'

'He *was* notified?' Harris draped storm warnings around the question.

'Yes, sir.' Pollard flipped the pages of the Telephone and Tele-printer Message Book. 'Four-thirty-five. Message from D.H.Q. From Chief Superintendent Blakey. To contact Inspector Rowe and notify him of the Upper Neck incident, and ask him to attend.'

'And Rowe?' Harris's voice dropped a semi-tone.

Blayde said, 'Rowe's at Bordfield General, waiting for something specific about Noble and Cooper. I sent him there.'

'And Blakey?'

Blayde shrugged.

Harris turned to Pollard and said, 'Get me Beechwood Brook Divisional Headquarters, Constable.'

'Yes, sir.'

Blayde added, 'Then make yourself scarce for a few minutes. Brew some tea . . . or something.'

'Yes, sir.'

Harris took the receiver from Pollard's hand, and Pollard left the Charge Office.

Harris growled, 'Bob, if that nebulous bastard *isn't* on duty, I don't give a damn *who* hears me . . .' Then, into the telephone, 'Assistant Chief Constable Harris, here. Put me through to Chief Superintendent Blakey's office.'

The D.H.Q. operator voiced the immortal words, 'I'm sorry, sir. The chief superintendent doesn't usually get to his office before nine.'

'Does he not?' said Harris, slowly. 'In that case, put me through to his house.'

'Yes, sir.'

After the necessary pops and crackles, Blakey's voice said, 'Yes?'

'Chief Superintendent Blakey?'

'Yes.'

'The Beechwood Brook divisional officer?'

'Yes. Who wants to . . .'

'Assistant Chief Constable Harris wants to know.'

'Oh!'

'Recognise the voice now, Blakey?'

'Yes, sir. Of course, sir.'

'Chief Superintendent Blakey. I am curious.' Harris's growl was almost ponderously slow. Each word was enunciated carefully and at near-dictation speed. 'I am curious,' continued Harris, 'to know what — short of the end of the world — is likely to get you on duty before nine o'clock in a morning. Would you be so kind?'

'Sir?'

'To tell me what the hell it needs!' exploded Harris.

'Sir, I . . .'

'A double murder. Two officers at the receiving end of an explosive device . . . both in Bordfield General needing major surgical work. What the hell *does* it take?'

'I — I didn't know,' pleaded Blakey.

'No?'

'I wasn't informed.'

'The hell you weren't informed,' snarled Harris. 'It's here, in the Message Book. Four-thirty . . . that's when you were informed.'

'I — er — I notified Inspector Rowe. I instructed him to . . .'

'You notified Inspector Rowe.' Harris's voice dropped to its slow, deadly rumble. 'And that's *all* you did, eh? You notified Inspector Rowe. Then you turned over and went back to sleep. Does that sum up the situation, Chief Superintendent Blakey? Is *that* what you think the ratepayers pay you a damn great salary for?'

'Sir, I . . .'

'Get yourself down here, Blakey. Fast! I'm at Sopworth nick. I want to see you coming through that door within the next fifteen minutes.'

Harris slammed the receiver back onto its hook. He took a few moments to cool down, then he said something which almost surprised the shockproof Blayde.

'Tallboy.'

'He's at Upper Neck. I left him there to . . .'

'No. I don't mean that. I mean as a man — as a copper — what's he like?'

'Above average,' said Blayde.

'Aye.' Harris nodded. 'Verification, that's all.' Harris paused, then said, 'In charge of Beechwood Brook.'

'Tallboy?' Blayde raised an eyebrow.

'Your old patch. Ripley's old patch . . . and Ripley was Tallboy's father-in-law. Let's play nepotism.'

'And — er — Blakey?'

'Blakey can measure his future as a chief superintendent in days,' said Harris grimly.

Blayde grunted.

Harris said, 'You don't approve?'

'Tallboy,' said Blayde, 'is only a chief inspector.'

'By next week he'll be superintendent. When he takes over the division he'll be *chief* superintendent.'

'He's a jack. He's always *been* a jack.' Blayde was arguing for the sake of argument.

'You were always a woodentop. Now you're C.I.D.' Harris gave a quick, mirthless smile. 'As I recall, the uniform never prevented *you* from sandpapering elephants down to greyhounds.'

'And you can do it?' asked Blayde with interest.

'A quiet word to the chief.' Harris sounded confident. 'He listens to what I say . . . *he'll* do it.'

'The king-maker,' murmured Blayde gently.

Harris's eyes narrowed slightly, as he growled, 'We'll soon see.'

'You can smell it. If you touch it with a damp fingertip, you can taste it. Gelignite. Nitrogylcerine, nitrocotton, potassium nitrate and wood-pulp.'

'Oh, aye?' The detective sergeant refused to be impressed. This forensic science liaison bloke was being 'flash'. Blinding a poor old question-asker with science.

The liaison officer held up the cellophane bag and displayed the

111

torn and buckled metal. Thin tin; cheap tin which had been painted with gold metallic paint when new.

The liaison man said, 'Easy. A two-battery torch. Use one battery, stuff the rest of the inside with gelignite, a simple wiring job, a good detonator . . . bingo!'

'Pity you can't make it talk,' said the D.S. sardonically.

'Eh?'

'Tell us the name of the clever bastard responsible.'

The D.S. was one of the old school; the bobbying-by-the-seat-of-the-pants crowd. All this high technology gave him a pain. The name of the game was collar-feeling. 'How' didn't matter. Only 'Who' mattered. Ask around, find out 'Who', lean a little . . . the 'How' arrived with all the other information.

'Where's Tallboy?' The liaison man changed subjects.

'Sorting out the turd responsible.'

It was a slight exaggeration, but the D.S. thought it time to take the initiative. All this scientific garbage. It meant sod-all, without a name attached.

'Y'mean . . .'

'Oh, aye.' The D.S. nodded solemnly. 'We find 'em, you fix 'em. That's the way it goes . . . innit?'

Meanwhile Detective Constable Evans was bringing up his breakfast. His breakfast, last night's supper, last week's fish and chips . . . the lot. He leaned, with his hands flat against the wallpaper above the cistern, and emptied his stomach down the toilet in Charlie Preston's bathroom. He seriously thought he was going to die. All that blood, all that ripped flesh, all that splintered bone . . . all that horror.

Wooley touched his shoulder and said, 'Easy, Taffy. You've seen it. The worst's over. You'll be able to go back into the bedroom without it affecting you.'

Evans retched and shook his head at the same time. His nose dribbled, his eyes spouted tears, and bile — the only thing left in his guts — turned his mouth sour and hung in saliva from his lips.

'If this is being a detective,' he groaned.

Wooley almost smiled . . . almost. Then he remembered the scene. There really was nothing to smile about in two headless corpses and enough blood to float the QE2. But (the reason for his near-smile) that was what detective work included. That, too, was included on the agenda. Not (as Taffy seemed to think) nicking milk bottles, lifting bits and pieces from supermarkets, grabbing ladies' underwear from clothes lines. Poor old Taffy. To him (and until this morning)

C.I.D. had been a very soft touch. Recording crime, rather than detecting it. Mooching around the boozers, chatting up the town drunks and making believe they were 'informers'. Well — as Andy Kyle might have said — he knew the noo.

A car braked to a halt outside the house. Wooley nipped into the spare bedroom, glanced down at the street, then returned to the bathroom.

He said, 'The Kodak lads are here, Taffy. Buck yourself up a bit. It's *your* case, remember.'

'I — I can't . . .' Evans remained stooped over the toilet, with his hands against the wall.

'You bloody-well *can*,' snapped Wooley. He reached across, flushed the toilet, then said, 'Right. Splash some water over your face. Take a grip. The team. Sopworth. Don't let the team down. It's no worse than some fatal road accidents.' Wooley knew he was telling a deliberate lie; it was a damn sight worse than *any* road accident. He turned on the cold tap at the washbasin, and said, 'Come on, Taffy. You've had your spew. Clean yourself up.'

Wooley left the bathroom and walked down the narrow stairs to meet the police photographers.

'Smoke, sir?'

P.C. Kyle tentatively offered the opened cigarette packet to Tallboy.

'Thanks.' Tallboy accepted the cigarette, then asked, 'There — on the dashboard — shove the lighter button in, will you?'

Kyle pushed the button until it clicked into place.

He said, 'You think Peacock, sir?'

'Possible,' said Tallboy quietly.

'I mean — y'know — he's only Shanks's father-in-law.'

'He's the father of Shanks's wife,' said Tallboy. 'Criminal Intelligence have him tabbed as a violent man. He's a demolition man. That suggests explosives. If I was a gambling man . . .'

Tallboy lifted a hand from the wheel-rim long enough to turn it palm upwards in a gesture of personal opinion.

Odd, thought Kyle, some blokes . . . blokes like Tallboy, here. So easy to get on with. Despite the rank, so easy to get on with. Blayde, for instance. If that telephone hadn't interrupted their talk, Blayde would have demanded the name of the informant. He'd have made it an order. And for why? What difference did it make? Palmer had said all he could say. A poacher — not even a very good poacher —

but he had his pride. He couldn't read, he couldn't write, he couldn't add up, but that was *his* secret. And he, Kyle, had promised to keep that secret. Not in as many words, maybe. But an understood thing. Not to rob Palmer of his pride. Not to name him. But, for Blayde, that wasn't good enough.

For Tallboy, okay. Tallboy hadn't pressed. Hadn't even mentioned it. Just telephoned Criminal Intelligence, gathered a few facts, and here they were on their way to see this bloke Peacock. Because, if it *wasn't* Peacock, it didn't matter. Palmer had said all he *could* say and, if it wasn't Peacock, hard lines. Naming Palmer wouldn't *make* it Peacock. And this bloke − this Tallboy − seemed to understand that. But Blayde? No way.

The lighter button snapped out. Kyle held the glowing wire, first to Tallboy's, then to his own cigarette. He replaced the lighter to its tiny hole in the dashboard. They smoked in silence for a few minutes as the car gobbled the miles towards Lessford.

Then Tallboy said, 'Cooper. Work well together?'

'He's never ducked his share, sir.' Kyle grinned. 'He's a townie. Other than that, I like him fine.'

'If,' mused Tallboy, 'somebody left a rigged torch on *your* path?'

'I canna think of anybody who'd . . .'

'*If* somebody did?' pressed Tallboy.

Kyle drew on his cigarette, then said, 'I'd worry, sir. I'd resign . . . maybe.'

'Why?'

'It's not a pleasant thought. That somebody wants to kill you. I think I'd resign . . . for sure.'

'Run?' It wasn't a criticism. It was a simple man-to-man question.

'Aye.' Kyle nodded solemnly. 'Run. Back north . . . back to Scotland. And . . .' He paused, then continued, 'I'd have a rare good look at myself. Try to find *why* somebody wanted to kill me.'

In the Interview Room at Sopworth Police Station Harris and Ranson faced each other. If you want a comparison, think of a mace and a rapier; each deadly, each able to kill or maim. Harris (because he *was* Harris) disliked solicitors . . . *all* solicitors; he saw them as agents of the civil libertarians, sent to prevent him from clearing the streets of scum. Some were out-and-out shysters. Others, like Ranson, were mere 'opponents'; people whose profession it was to make policing just that bit more difficult. The shysters he bludgeoned into the ground by weight of sheer personality plus the bull-roar of a voice

114

which could out-bawl any amount of smarm. The rest? He grunted and growled but, grudgingly, allowed that they were there to protect the interests of their clients.

Timothy Ranson knew Harris. Knew him to be basically a fair-minded man . . . *second* to being a copper. Knew that flash legal quotations of 'rights' merely made things more difficult. Not too friendly, but not too stroppy. That was the way to handle Harris. Don't give the impression that you're sucking up. Equally, don't give the impression that the rank of A.C.C. (Crime) doesn't matter a damn. And, for good measure, respect the difference in age. Harris could have been Ranson's father.

'You'll want to see your client,' grunted Harris.

'Eventually.' Ranson lowered himself onto one of the two chairs which made up the seating arrangement of the Interview Room. He placed his brief-case on the table. 'First, I'd like the details.'

'Know what you're up against?'

'That, too.' Ranson smiled. 'I'd like the truth. Then I'll hear *his* side of the truth.'

'There's only one side to truth.'

'A bottle, Mr Harris.' Ranson continued to smile. 'It's half empty. Equally, it's half full. Two truths . . . that's what I mean.'

Harris sniffed, then folded himself onto the second chair.

He said, 'Charles Preston. He works at the brick kilns. His wife, May Preston . . . according to some of the officers, a bit of a scrubber. Anybody's meat. Preston heard things. Specifically, about one of the town's rams, Samuel Sutcliffe. Preston stayed away from work last night. Found 'em at it — Sutcliffe and his wife — at around four this morning. There was a shotgun. A twelve-bore. He loaded it, went up to the bedroom and blasted 'em both to hell. Then he washed, shaved, put on his Sunday best, walked down to the station here, and told us what he'd done.' Harris heaved his shoulders. 'That . . . in a nutshell.'

Ranson jotted notes on a foolscap pad.

He looked up and asked, 'He's been interviewed?'

'Bare details.' Harris nodded. 'Detective Chief Superintendent Blayde and Detective Constable Evans.'

'Cautioned, of course?'

'Of course,' said Harris sardonically.

The smile returned, and Ranson said, 'Don't get me wrong. I don't expect him to have been cautioned before he *said* anything. Before he told whoever it was what he'd done. But at the earliest opportunity.'

'At the earliest opportunity,' agreed Harris.

'Has he been charged?'

'Not yet.'

'I'm obliged . . . I'd like to be present.'

'That's why you're here.'

'Murder?' Ranson raised questioning eyebrows. 'Or . . . manslaughter?'

'Murder,' said Harris flatly.

'Diminished Responsibility?'

'That's your job, Ranson.' Harris mellowed slightly, and added, 'You shouldn't find it difficult.'

'Bail?' Again the raised eyebrows.

'He's nothing previous,' said Harris. 'A good man driven daft by a cock-happy wife. You give assurances . . . we won't raise any objections.'

'I'm obliged.'

'Make it easier,' mused Harris, 'if he made a statement. I'm not pressing,' he added hastily. 'Just . . . it might save time. Get things over with.'

'Less work for the police,' smiled Ranson.

'Less waiting for your client,' countered Harris. 'It's up to you. You advise him.'

'It might be best,' conceded Ranson. 'I'll talk to him, then decide.'

'In the cell? Or here?'

'Here, I think. A little less intimidating.'

'I'll send for him.' Harris stood up. As he reached the door, he added, 'Nobody'll be listening outside.'

'The thought never entered my head.'

'I'll bet!'

Higginbottom sat in the Waiting Room and scowled. His ankle ached like the very clappers. Thanks to a flaming bowler who sent 'yorkers' down with the intention of crippling inoffensive batsmen — thanks to a bloody great dog whose sole aim in life was to smother the whole of the human race with unwanted affection . .. . thanks to such things, his ankle ached like the very clappers. Or maybe rain was in the offing. He knew men and women, rheumatic sufferers, better and more accurate than any weather-glass when it came to forecasting rain. But, Christ, they were *old*. Doddering old codgers crawling around with a stick in each hand. It couldn't be *that*. He wasn't quite on his last legs . . . not yet. Just — y'know — his ankle ached like the clappers. That was all.

116

And this blasted Waiting Room didn't help.

The surgery started at nine. Bags of time. A quick nip home. A bite of toast and a mug of hot tea, into a jacket and down to the surgery. Bags of time. He *had* to be first in the queue.

The hell he had!

Four in front of him. Coughing, sneezing, spreading germs all over the place. In hell's name why couldn't they stay in bed and get Wilkinson to visit. Wilkinson . . . or one of his partners. Five of 'em. Five medics, all able to run socking great cars — *and* a runabout for the wife — and socking great houses and fancy holidays anywhere in the world . . . and between 'em they couldn't cure a bloody cold! But magazines for the Waiting Room? *Readers' Digests*, months old. And, even money, they slipped *those* in on their tax returns. 'Reading matter for Waiting Room' . . . a very flash way of making the poor old taxpayer cough up for expensive magazines. Ancient copies of *Punch*. Some Sunday supplements. Thumbed, torn, tatters and (one of 'em) sticky where some kid had daubed it with mucky paws.

And the four in front of him.

Jesus, they must have spent the night there. At the very least, been there since dawn. Sod-all else to do with their miserable little lives; put the alarm on, get out of bed before the sparrows and let's have a nice long morning at the doctor's. Strewth! The way some people lived. The first three — all right — straight in, straight out. A renewal of a certificate, at a guess. But the fourth. The big bloke, built like a brick wall. He was making a real meal of things. A quarter of an hour he'd been in there. A fag and a natter, maybe. Some long drawn-out bloody yarn, conning the medic stupid. As fit as a Derby winner, that, for sure. Obvious. You could *see* it. Out to be thrown on sick. Out to have a few weeks' holiday on the state. Out to fix things so he could laze around in the sun for a bit, instead of going to work. No wonder the damn system was falling apart. A combination of flash doctors and idle buggers . . . no wonder the wheels had snapped off.

And this crowd here in the Waiting Room. Humanity with a boil on its bum . . . that's all it amounted to. That woman over there. What the hell sorta life did *she* live? Thin as a rail. Like something from an Oxfam poster . . . and, if she was thirty, she wasn't a day older. Clothes from some jumble sale by the looks of things. And two kids she could no more control than she could fly to the moon. She was dead . . . all bar the coffin and the funeral service. Chances were she'd never even *lived*. Poor little bitch. She'd no idea what . . .

A buzzer sounded and, from behind her desk in a corner of the

Waiting Room, the white-coated receptionist said, 'Mr Higginbottom. Will you go into Dr Wilkinson now.'

Higginbottom rose from his seat and limped into the surgery.

Wilkinson waved him to a seat alongside the roll-topped desk.

Wilkinson; a very modern medic. Very 'with it'; sideburns, long hair, drooping moustache . . . the lot. And clothes to match. Not *quite* as eye-searing as the stage rig of the late Max Miller, but climbing in that direction.

'The old foot. The old ankle,' said Wilkinson cheerfully. He scanned the buff-coloured envelope containing Higginbottom's medical history as he spoke. 'Playing you up a bit, is it?'

'Eh?' Higginbottom stared. He didn't know what this medical clown-dog was on about.

'The ankle.' Wilkinson glanced at Higginbottom's feet.

'Oh . . . that? No.' Higginbottom shook his head. He took a deep breath and said, 'It's about Betty.'

'Betty?'

'Betty, my daughter.'

'Ah!' Wilkinson leaned back in the swivel-chair and clasped his hands at the back of his neck.

'The — er — the pills,' said Higginbottom.

'The pills,' repeated Wilkinson.

'Bit young, at fifteen, isn't she?' muttered Higginbottom, awkwardly.

'I'm sorry. I don't get your meaning.'

'Birth-control pills,' said Higginbottom.

'Oh, *those.*' Wilkinson grinned.

'She — er — she got 'em from you, I take it. The prescription, I mean.'

'Uhuh' Wilkinson nodded, *'Minovlar* . . . as I recall. I can check, if you like.'

'No. It doesn't . . .' Higginbottom moved a hand in a vague and meaningless gesture.

'Y'know . . .' Wilkinson unlinked his fingers and, as a variant, linked them on top of his head. He swung gently, left and right, in the swivel-chair. 'They grow up quicker, these days. They mature much earlier.'

'Aye. Happen so. But fifteen . . .'

'Her libido's fully developed.'

'Is it?' Higginbottom looked dutifully surprised. He mentally decided to check with the dictionary when he got home. Probably wouldn't be in there. One of those peculiar bits and pieces women have, but don't talk about. For safety's sake, he added, 'I didn't know that.'

'Oh, yes.' Wilkinson nodded. 'That's why I agreed to prescribe oral contraceptives.'

'Oh!'

'She's my patient,' said Wilkinson gravely. 'I know she's your daughter, but she's also my patient. I have to take that into account.'

'Oh, aye. Of course.'

'It was a decision . . . *my* decision. I took it.'

'Aye.' Higginbottom nodded.

'Rather that than she become impregnated, surely?'

'Oh — er — of course. I wouldn't — y'know — I wouldn't deny that.'

'Happy, then?' Wilkinson smiled.

'I — er — well . . . not exactly *happy.*'

'Satisfied?' suggested Wilkinson.

'I — er — I reckon.' Higginbottom nodded his head.

'Good.' Wilkinson lowered his hands and smiled. He stood up from the chair. 'I'm glad you called in. On the whole better that you know, don't you think?'

'Better,' agreed a dazed Higginbottom. 'Much better.'

Higginbottom limped from the surgery. He was a much bemused man; a simple, decent man lost in a maze of problems and double-talk. Bloody doctors! Like their handwriting — like their prescriptions — God alone knew what they meant. They could poison you . . . *you* wouldn't be any the wiser. Libido? What the hell was a woman's libido? *Where* the hell was a woman's libido? One thing, for sure, he couldn't ask Mabel, his wife. He *daren't* ask her. He'd be in the dog-house for a month . . . even assuming *she* knew.

Wilf Pinter replaced the hand-mike after radioing off duty, then climbed from the Minivan and walked slowly through the rear door of the bakery. It was the village bakery — *Rimstone Village Bakery* — and Dave Rhodes, the proprietor, was about as close a friend as Pinter had. Had ever had. The two men were much alike in temperament; solemn, slow to anger but with a depth of feeling kept hidden from public gaze. Pinter knew the working habits of Rhodes; knew that, at about this time, the baker would have kneaded his second batch of dough of the day, and would be taking a spell for the 'rising' time.

The inside of the bakery was white with the dust of flour. The tang of good yeast touched the nostrils. It was warm — hot almost — from the ovens, despite the open windows with their insect-proof gauze. But cosy. Like a womb. A refuge, in which nothing was hurried, nothing was slipshod, nothing was taken for granted. Like Rhodes himself. Tranquil and reliable. Like the bread he baked. Nothing false, nothing fancy; good, solid . . . the genuine staff of life.

Rhodes smiled a nodding greeting and, without being asked, stood up from the ancient kitchen chair upon which he periodically rested, unhooked a beaker from its hook on the wall and poured tea from an old-fashioned brown teapot. He added sugar and milk, then dropped a spoon in the liquid and handed the beaker to Pinter to stir.

'Buttered teacake?' asked Rhodes.

'Please.'

The butter was farm-made and a deep yellow. The teacake was still warm. Rhodes handed it to Pinter and, in return, Pinter handed over a 10p piece. It was an understood thing. Pinter never cadged. The price of a buttered teacake, in the shop beyond the bakery, was 10p . . . and good value at that. Pinter paid for what he wanted. Standard price. To have offered it free would have been an insult. Not to have paid would have lowered Pinter in Rhodes's estimation. The beaker of tea was different. Making tea wasn't part of Rhodes's livelihood . . . the tea was an act of friendship. The line was as thin as that. The limits as clearly defined.

Pinter didn't sit down. He could have done — and welcome — but the flour dust would have marked his uniform. Instead, he stood and chewed the teacake, sipped the tea . . . and talked.

Rhodes said, 'Hannah?'

'No better.'

The three-word question and answer sufficed. The question was far more than a politeness; it was as quietly heartbroken as was the soft-spoken answer. Pinter knew, and Rhodes *knew* Pinter knew. Between these two men outward emotion was unnecessary. Thereafter they talked of other things. The Upper Neck incident; villagers using the shop had already passed on the news. They talked gardening; do-it-yourself decorating, music . . . they were both choral music enthusiasts. Like skaters, skilfully avoiding thin ice, they weaved a pattern of conversation around the one subject uppermost in both their minds. To dwell on that subject wouldn't have helped. To leave the obvious unspoken granted Pinter a few minutes of make-believe peace.

In the privacy of Rowe's office Blakey sought comfort from Blayde, but received none. Two chief superintendents. One C.I.D., one uniform. But the difference went much deeper than that. Blakey was terrified of Harris, Blayde was terrified of no man. Blakey was the typical midget in giant's britches, Blayde was (figuratively speaking) the giant.

'You never *have* liked me,' said Blakey petulantly.

'I wouldn't say that.' Blayde puffed at a well-burned pipe as he allowed Blakey's tantrums to break themselves upon his calm.

'I know for a fact . . .'

'You've never been important enough for me to like . . or dislike.'

'That's a foul thing to say to a fellow officer.'

'Two fellow officers have been maimed,' said Blayde calmly. *'They* weren't important enough to get you out of bed.'

'I sent Rowe. I gave him firm instructions to . . .'

'Bobbying by proxy never was much bottle, Blakey.'

'You're . . . ' Blakey waved his hand. 'You're going to back Harris. That's obvious. You're going to . . .'

'Harris,' said Blayde softly, 'doesn't need me — doesn't need anybody — to skin *you* alive.'

'Oh!'

'I'll be out of this office before he's finished with Ranson.'

Blakey ran worried fingers through his hair.

'Need advice?' asked Blayde gruffly.

'I — I . . .'

'What service have you in? Thirty? Thirty-one?'

'Thirty-two, actually.'

'Resign,' said Blayde.

'What?'

Blayde removed the pipe from his mouth and said, 'That way you'll end up with a chief superintendent's pension.' Blayde gazed into Blakey's eyes for a moment, then added, 'That's good advice, Blakey. Take it or leave it . . . it's a damn sight more than you deserve.'

Blayde strolled from the office and closed the door gently behind him.

And, of course, there was Nick Karn — Police Constable 1235 Nicholas Karn — the officer who, in normal circumstances, shared Rimstone Beat with P.C. Pinter.

At the best of times Karn was only there for the ride. A man of whom other officers, when asked, said, 'Karn? *9.30 a.m.* Karn? Oh, aye . . . Karn. He's on Pinter's Beat.' And that was the measure of the man; that was the

121

size of his unimportance. Karn was something of a mathematical genius when it came to working out how many buckshee days off duty he could swing. Three days 'unofficial' Sick Leave, without the necessity of a doctor's certificate. It wasn't a perk. It was a small humanity – an accepted necessity – in order to allow a man or a woman to clear a cold in the head (say) without going through the rigmarole of form-filling. But . . . not with Nick Karn it wasn't. Karn knew to the day – to the minute – when he could claim another three days U.S.L. And he claimed them. Never missed. Indeed, within the section his name was synonymous with U.S.L. Somebody came on duty with a streaming nose, a cough, a blinding headache. After sticking it for so long he (she) might remark, 'Oh, God! I'm sorry, I'll have to take a "Karn".' And no further explanation was necessary.

And this was Karn's Weekly Rest Day.

After the initial briefing by Tallboy, at just after six, Karn had strolled from the Upper Neck Police Office, turned a couple of corners, vaulted a post-and-rail fence and, within ten minutes, had vanished from the face of the earth. As far as Karn was concerned, it was *still* his Weekly Rest Day. The hell with working in pairs. The hell with house-to-house enquiries. House-to-house enquiries? One big horse laugh. Whoever saw or heard anything? And, if they did, whoever admitted seeing or hearing anything?

The trick was to take things easy. *Very* easy. Bobbying was a cushy number if you played your cards right. A job. That's all . . . just another job. Upper Neck Beat? Rimstone Beat? If you pounded both those beats, inch at a time, what difference was it going to make? What *difference*? It wouldn't stop the next Great Train Robbery. Two hole-in-the-corner dumps . . . best thing, just sit back and enjoy things.

Which was exactly what Karn was doing. Sitting back . . . specifically, sitting back in the hay, up near the roof of a Dutch barn. Enjoying things . . . specifically, enjoying a thick paperback, written by one of the top American pulp writers, wherein if there wasn't a blow-by-blow description of off-beat fornication every ten pages or so, the impression was that the author was losing his touch.

Hilda Noble had been joined in the Staff Lounge of Bordfield General Hospital by Marian Cooper. W.P.C. Pearson was with them, as indeed was Motor Patrol Constable Burns. Burns had gravitated to the lounge, having met Pearson in one of the corridors, and Burns was stranded at the hospital, pending transport back to Upper Neck;

ambulances not being vehicles available to shuttle coppers between scenes of incidents and hospitals. They formed a tight group in one corner of the lounge; a quartet well-versed in the less-advertised aspects of bobbying. Like stranded climbers, huddling together to keep themselves warm, they huddled together in an attempt to ward off the equally cold touch of worry. Somewhere, in another part of this strange world of sickness and pain, two of their number – two loved ones, two colleagues – were being cut and sliced and stitched. Don't think about it! The very thought brings on goose-pimples. Probes, scalpels, saws and needles. For God's sake . . . don't even *think* about it.

How long? That was the unasked question. The question to which none of the four had an answer. How long? And, when the waiting was over, what would be the result?

They spoke little. Even W.P.C. Pearson had run out of comforting clichés. The other two women seemed to have evened each other out; Hilda Noble's near-panic had quietened, while Marian Cooper's efficient calm had heightened into pale-faced concern. As for Burns . . . he wanted to know the worst and was prepared to stay on duty all day if necessary.

Plastic beakers of cold and scummed coffee were on the low table. Around them uniformed men and women hurried and joked, flopped into chairs and lighted cigarettes. Eased up for a moment. Relaxed while they were able. Lived . . . while the quartet in the corner seemed to have temporarily suspended life.

Nurse Bowtree thrust her way past the swing doors and approached. Solemn-faced, but working hard not to look *too* serious.

She bent over the group, and four faces turned up to look at her.

She said, 'Sergeant Noble's out of theatre. Constable Cooper should be on his way to the ward.'

They waited expectantly.

Bowtree continued, 'We've given them a two-bed sideward. Just the two of them. Private. We thought they'd like it that way.'

Marian Cooper nodded. Still nobody spoke.

Bowtree lowered her voice a little and said, 'I'm sorry. Constable Cooper's lost his hand – part of his arm, almost to the elbow – he'll be fitted with an artificial limb.'

Hilda Noble's right hand felt around until it touched the fingers of Marian Cooper's left hand. Then the right hand squeezed the left hand in silent comfort.

Bowtree said, 'Sergeant Noble – I'm sorry – both his eyes have gone. It – it sometimes happens that way.'

123

W.P.C. Pearson swallowed, then muttered, 'Thanks, luv. Thanks a lot.'

Bowtree ended, 'Give them another hour or so, eh? Y'know . . . to come round. Then I'll take you along.'

The two hands squeezed tighter and tighter. The two women nodded, silently. Unable to trust themselves to speak.

Police Constable 1555 Witherham was having trouble. And, be it plainly understood, Police Constable 1555 Witherham could handle trouble. He never looked for it. He never sought it out. But when it was handed to him on a plate he could handle it . . . in his own way.

The swarthy stallholder — the man who hawked hand-made and hand-tooled leather goods — had caught the youth red-handed. Nicking (in fact *trying* to nick) a particularly fancy belt. He'd grabbed and held. The youth — a latter-day apostle of the near-defunct 'punk' fraternity — wore a striped 'Burglar Bill' sweat shirt, weathered jeans and ancient climbing boots. His hair was cut to brush-bristle length. Various dingle-dangles of cheap brass and other metal draped various parts of his anatomy.

Witherham did not fall in love with him on sight.

Between them, and without difficulty, they marched the would-be-thief around a few corners, up a back-alley and into an enclosed space which stank to the high heavens. Then, at a sign from Witherham, the stallholder returned to his leatherwork.

'Well?' asked Witherham politely.

'Well wot?' The punkie was obviously not prepared to play ball.

'You have a name?'

'So?'

'Don't keep it a secret, lad. Let's be knowing.'

'Get knotted.'

'I'd like your name, lad,' said Witherham gently.

'That's *your* bleedin' job, pig.'

'You want arresting . . . that it?'

'If yer think yer can.'

'So you can go home, and tell all your pals. What a tough baby you are. How you've been nicked. How it took ten bobbies to hold you. How you deserve a tripe medal for the way you fought back.'

'Think you can do it?' sneered the punkie.

'I could try . . .'

'That'll be the bleedin' . . .'

'. . . but I won't. Because that might mean fumigating the cells.

And the rates are high enough already. Last time of asking, lad. What's you name?'

'Go screw yourself, copper.'

At which point Witherham slipped into overdrive. A sudden, and very muscular, shove on the chest sent the punkie staggering backwards until his short-haired head hit a particularly filthy brick wall. On the rebound, Witherham grabbed the very handy chain which was draped around the punkie's neck, twisted, then stepped forward and held the punkie hard against the filth of the wall with the pressure of his own body.

The punkie gasped, 'This ain't a police state, copper. You can't . . .'

'Listen, arse-face.' Witherham's voice was little more than a whisper. 'Know where you are? No? I'll tell you. You're behind the cattle-market wall. Where all the farmers come when they want a quick piss.' Witherham twisted the chain a little more, then jerked it higher. The punkie's face began to change colour. Witherham continued, 'That's why nobody comes round here. Nobody. Ever! Just a quiet little world inhabited by two people. You and me. A world in which fifty per cent of the population are coppers. Now, I'd call *that* a police state . . . wouldn't you? And if half the population — the coppers — thought the other half weren't fit to live . . . the other half would have problems. *Your* half. Right?' Again a fractional twist and lift of the chain. 'You're not from Sopworth. We'd have smelled you years ago. Where are you from?'

'B-B-Bradford,' choked the punkie.

'Good. Now I'd like you to go *back* to Bradford.' Soft and reasonable was Witherham's voice. 'But, first of all, take those boots off.'

The punkie made as if to offer objections — or, perhaps, to ask a question — but a further slight tightening of the chain changed his mind and, instead, he contorted himself and, eventually, stood bootless.

'Now the trousers,' said Witherham.

Again, there was hint of argument which died before it was born. The punkie took off his jeans.

Still gripping the chain in one hand, Witherham stooped, picked up the boots and jeans and tossed them over the wall. The punkie was, by this time, gasping for breath; mouth gaping and face turning a deep shade of puce.

'Right.' Witherham smiled. 'The police state at full throttle. Now, I'm going to allow you to breathe. Isn't that kind of me? Any heroics on your part and I'll break your arm, then bounce you through the market shoppers — Y-fronts and all — and slap an indecent exposure round your filthy little neck. In short, you're fixed, sonny. Fixed, fitted up and paddling through your own private fertiliser farm.' He paused then, in a most reasonable tone, added, 'On the other hand, you could climb the wall, put your pants and boots back on .. then disappear back to Bradford in a cloud of following dust. On the whole, that might be best. Less pain for you. Less paperwork for me. But . . .' he moved his face an inch or so nearer to that of the punkie and whispered, 'Come out of your cage once more — let me see you in Sopworth once more — and I won't throw the book at you . . . *I'll throw the whole bloody bookcase.*'

Witherham loosened his grip on the chain and stepped back. The punkie's knees buckled slightly, he fought for breath then, after a few seconds, turned and jumped to catch the top of the wall. With some difficulty he hauled himself up the face of its slimy surface, then dropped out of sight.

Five minutes later Witherham was in The Market Cafe once more.

He strolled up to the counter and said, 'Tea, old pet. Hot and strong. Plenty of sugar . . . I'm a growing lad.'

He took the mug of tea. It never entered his head to pay for it.

Pollard replaced the receiver and walked slowly from the alcove and into the Charge Office. He sighed heavily.

Blayde looked at the elderly constable questioningly.

In a sad voice, Pollard said, 'Burns . . . from the hospital. Cooper's lost a hand. Sergeant Noble's blind. Both eyes.'

Blayde breathed, 'Oh, Jesus!'

In the face of such news all differences in rank were forgotten. They were two men, of an age, suddenly feeling the hopelessness of a job which would never be completed. To combat evil. That was their trade. To make the streets clean and safe to walk along. And for a few moments the burden seemed too heavy. The price too high.

Pollard shook cigarettes loose in a Woodbine packet. He offered the open packet to Blayde. Blayde shook his head and, instead, fished his pipe from a jacket pocket. He struck a match and held it first to Pollard's cigarette, then to the half-filled bowl of the pipe.

'Right,' sighed Blayde, 'I'll tell Chief Superintendent Blakey. If Mr Harris finishes with Ranson before I'm back . . .'

'He's on his way to Upper Neck,' interrupted Pollard.

'Harris?'

'While you were in with Mr Blakey.'

'Okay.' Blayde nodded. 'Give 'em a ring. Tell 'em. Then contact Public Relations . . . let *them* know. And – from me – we don't want the hospital swarming with reporters.'

Lessford was a city with a population of close to a million people. It was the twin city of Bordfield, but almost twice the size of Bordfield. At best, a sprawling, industrial giant; smoke-ridden, soot-encrusted, intimidating. At worst . . . North End.

Tallboy murmured, ' "Sullivan Territory".'

'It's still called that.'

They'd picked the detective sergeant up at Lessford Regional Headquarters. A lanky, laconic man; if his normal expression was a guide, 'a man of sorrows and acquainted with grief' . . . but Tallboy had known some damn good coppers who *never* smiled. It was an adopted mannerism. A deliberate, poker-faced front.

'Know Peacock?' asked Tallboy.

'Aye.' It could have meant anything. It could have meant that the D.S. had once seen a photograph of him . . . or, equally, that he'd married Peacock's sister.

'Could he have done it?' asked Kyle.

'He's a North Ender.'

And that (as far as the D.S. was concerned) explained everything. A complete answer, with diagrams attached.

Tallboy knew what the D.S. meant. Tallboy had know North End when Sullivan had been its chief superintendent. Before amalgamation. When the city had had its own force and when, within that force, North End had been a division and, at the same time, almost a separate entity. When Sullivan (and coppers who'd refused promotion rather than work under another gaffer) had daily 'gone to war' against the North End gangs, and the individual hooligans who'd lived in this, the slum quarter of Lessford.

He eyed the high-rise flats and said, 'It's changed.'

'Perpendicular instead of horizontal,' droned the D.S.

'Still as bad?'

'It never could get worse . . . but it keeps trying.'

The tower blocks hemmed them in as they drove towards the very heart of North End. Scattered between the towering monstrosities were odd streets and alleys of the once-upon-a-time North End; hovels, where the vermin of the city had bared their teeth and fought off every attempt of the city fathers to dislodge them. The result was the worst *of* the worst; an ugliness beyond hope; anti-establishment gnomes squatting between anti-establishment giants.

'Will he be at home?' asked Tallboy.

The D.S. said, 'He won't even be up.' And there was certainty in the answer.

The D.S. gave directions, and the car eventually stopped at the entrance to one of the tower blocks. Winchester Court — part of Winchester Avenue — an upturned, vandalised concrete box, set in a sea of dried mud and general garbage. The D.S. motioned Tallboy and Kyle to remain in the car. He opened the car door, closed it, then stood staring at a group of coloured youths who, in turn, stared back.

One of the youths — a big lad, with the body of a heavyweight — sauntered across and for some moments the youth and the D.S. stood facing each other. Silent. Each sending out invisible waves of contempt and loathing.

Softly the D.S. said, 'The Goofs won't like it, Eddie.'

For a shaved second terror touched the coloured youth's expression.

'This car.' The D.S. moved his head. 'We need it when we get back. Including the wheels.'

The coloured youth grunted, turned his head and waved a hand. The rest of the group — all coloureds, Asian, African, West Indian — hurried across and, at a signal from their leader, took up positions around the parked car.

'Okay.' The D.S. opened the car door, and Tallboy and Kyle joined him.

As they walked towards the entrance to the tower block Tallboy said, 'What the hell was all that about?'

'Pics and Goofs,' drawled the D.S. 'Coloureds and whites — the two main groupings — the Piccaninnies and the Goofballs. Gang warfare. It breaks the monotony.'

'And?'

The entrance hall of the flats stank of urine. Slogans were paint-sprayed on every wall surface.

The D.S. drawled, 'This week the Goofs are on top. Eddie — the lad I had words with — he's the Pic's king.' The D.S. sighed. 'He has brains. Outside this jungle he could make something.'

'And?' repeated Tallboy.

'Not the lift.' The D.S. spoke to Kyle. 'There *isn't* a lift. If they could have pinched the shaft that wouldn't be here.' As they began to mount the stairs, he said, 'Would you believe "love" . . . in a dump like this?'

'Let's say I believe,' grunted Tallboy.

'Eddie and one of the Goof-queens. If the Goofs get so much as a whiff, they'll slice his balls off.'

'That's rough,' observed Kyle.

'That,' said the D.S. 'is one of the rules in this particular cockpit. Knowledge. I've used it . . . that's all. The Pics guard the car. Or else!'

The stench of urine (and worse) assaulted their nostrils as they climbed the stairs. Filth and filth upon filth. And (presumably) people paid rent — or were *expected* to pay rent — to live in this hell-hole. Had the walls, floor and ceiling of a public toilet been defaced and vandalised in the manner of the walls, steps and ceiling of this block of flats there'd have been a public outcry. Here it was accepted. Here it was 'normality'. The male, the female, the off-springs — here they were not human beings — here they were less than animals.

When they reached the third landing, the D.S. said, 'Okay if *I* talk?'

'Sure.' Tallboy nodded. 'You know the details?'

'Enough.'

The D.S. tapped on a cracked and paint-peeling door and, almost immediately, a woman answered his knock.

She was a huge woman. Massive. Obese. Something from a seaside postcard come alive. Her upper-arms, in the cheap cotton frock, were like hams and the frock showed sweat-stains at the armpits. The rest of her was in proportion. She was gross — any side-show would have welcomed her as 'the fat lady' — and yet her eyes were beautiful. Genuine corn-flower blue, with lashes like those film stars buy at expensive beauty parlours. Her voice, too. Gentle, crooning and with each word clearly enunciated.

10 a.m.

'Mr Kelly,' she greeted the D.C. and smiled a welcome.

'Is he around?' Kelly led Tallboy and Kyle into the flat as the fat woman stood aside.

'In bed.'

There was no disgust in her reply. No censure. It was a simple statement of fact. The impression was that this woman had quietly come to terms with life. With the grossness of her body, with the dirt of her environment, with the helplessness of day-to-day living. Within the context of the building the room was clean. Not eat-off-the-floor clean, but at least the signs were there that the cheap furniture was not allowed to gather filth *ad nauseam.*

'Detective Chief Inspector Tallboy. Constable Kyle.' Kelly performed the quick introductions as the woman closed the door.

The woman nodded a greeting. In some strange, magical way the

129

nod looked remarkably like a little girl curtsying politely.

'Last night. What time did he get home?' asked Kelly.

'Oh, well after one o'clock.'

'You stayed up till then?'

'I usually read until well after midnight. I'd been in bed almost an hour before I heard him come in.'

'Drunk?'

'I suppose so.' She smiled. 'He didn't come in to see me.'

'I'll have words,' said Kelly. 'Mr Tallboy, Mr Kyle . . . they can stay here and listen?'

'Of course.' She turned to Tallboy and asked, 'Can I brew you a cup of tea?'

'That would be kind,' said Tallboy.

'Thanks,' said Kyle.

She waddled away towards the kitchen, leaving the three officers in a group in front of the fireplace.

Kelly said, 'Kidology?'

'You know him,' said Tallboy.

'I'll get it out of him,' promised Kelly. Then to Kyle, 'Have your notebook ready, son. Take it all down as you hear it.'

Kelly walked to a door leading from the living room, opened the door, walked into the bedroom, but left the door partly open in order that Tallboy and Kyle could hear the exchange.

The bed was a three-quarters metal, brass-knobbed affair. The bedclothes consisted of soiled sheets, an army blanket and an overcoat doing duty as an eiderdown. Cheap lino covered the floor. The furniture consisted of a cane-bottomed kitchen chair, a beer-crate covered by a flowered cloth 'remnant' and a fly-blown mirror hanging from a nail driven into one of the walls. These things – and the bed – the sleeping quarters of Ronald Peacock, self-employed 'general contractor'.

Kelly shook the man awake, then sat on the edge of the bed and waited until Peacock had hoisted himself into a sitting position and was reaching for an open packet of cigarettes and a box of matches from the beer-crate bedside table.

'Upper Neck, last night.' Kelly shook his head sadly. 'You acted stupidly . . . even for you. Were you drunk?'

Peacock chose a cigarette and struck a match.

'If some kid had picked up that torch,' said Kelly. 'Some kid. Picked it up. Switched it on. You'd have been in *real* trouble.'

Peacock inhaled his first lungful of cigarette smoke of the day. He doubled forward in a fit of coughing.

130

'Your dabs all over it,' continued Kelly sorrowfully. 'All over the battery. *And* your pick-up was seen in the village. I think you've gone doollally, Peacock. What the hell made you do it?'

'I'm not saying . . .' A second spasm of coughing denied the world of whatever it was Peacock wasn't going to say.

Kelly drawled, 'Constable Cooper . . . Christ, it could have *killed* him. Then what?'

'He deserves to be bloody killed,' croaked Peacock.

'If,' said Kelly slowly, 'Cooper — some kid — *anybody* — had picked up that doctored torch and switched it on. Bang! Wallop! I could be bouncing you down to the nick with a murder charge round your neck. Come *on*. Be thankful Peacock. Thank your lucky stars . . . that's what *you* should be doing.'

'Who says I was at Upper Neck?' asked Peacock shakily.

'Don't be bloody stupid. A village. *That* size. No boozer . . . nothing. A car stops, then starts up again. Use what little gumption God gave you. At that time of night. Every curtain had somebody behind it.'

Peacock remained silent. He drew on the cigarette.

'If that trick torch *had* worked . . .' said Kelly gently.

'It didn't, so it doesn't matter, does it?' Peacock's voice was ugly with bitterness. He continued, 'But it *should* have. Y'know what . . . I wish it *had*. I wish it had blown Cooper to hell.'

'Big talk,' mocked Kelly. 'You're safe. You can talk big.'

'No!' Peacock's mouth twisted. 'He put Tony away. It's what the bastard deserves.'

'Tony?' Kelly pretended ignorance.

'Tony Shanks. Molly's husband.'

'Molly . . . your daughter?'

'Cooper put him away. Left Molly with three kids to look after.'

'Rough,' agreed Kelly. 'You saying this son-in-law of yours was innocent?'

'What the hell's it matter? Innocent. Guilty. That's not important. Molly's left holding the mucky end of the stick. *That's* what I'm getting at.'

'So, you fixed the torch-bomb,' sighed Kelly heavily.

'He's bloody lucky. I'll get him next time. Next time I won't . . .'

'You got him this time,' said Tallboy coldly, as he walked into the bedroom. '*You* got *him* . . . *we've* got *you*.' Then, to Kelly, 'Thanks, sergeant. We'll take it from here.'

'Any time.' Kelly stood up from the bed, stared down at the

furious Peacock and said, 'Coppers, lad. Don't play explosive footsie with coppers. Your own kind? Who gives a damn? But not with coppers.'

Rowe. Poor old Rowe. Nobody wanted him, nobody needed him, nobody even remembered that he was still in the lounge of Bordfield General Infirmary.

William Henry Rowe; police inspector . . . and God in all His glory knew *how*! Not true, of course. There are various routes up the first rungs of the promotion ladder. You can graft; no guarantee, of course, but it *might* get you there. You can chase headlines; it won't make for popularity with your colleagues but, played cunningly, it'll make sure your name keeps cropping up. You can of course be the chief constable's son (or his son-in-law, or his nephew, or even his cousin three times removed) . . . that way you can't lose!

Or, as a last resort, there is always Rowe's way. Take no chances. Do as little as possible in order to make as few mistakes as possible. Smile and say 'Yes' to all the right people at all the right times. It'll get you chevrons, for sure. With luck, it'll get you a couple of stars on each shoulder (like Rowe) and with extreme luck — and assuming the powers-that-be of that particular time are *really* dumb — it could even make the stars three in number. But after that, forget it. If you make chief inspector on the strength of damn-all you're one of the lucky ones. Inspector, sure, Rowe had made inspector, and was living proof.

But, like his kind, he was never quite happy. Never *quite* happy. Come to that, never *quite* anything. Never *quite* respected; within weeks, the rawest recruit had developed the knack of by-passing Rowe's orders, in the happy knowledge that Rowe wouldn't *dare* sling a two-five-two in anybody's teeth, in case that Misconduct Form boomeranged. Never *quite* liked; never *dis*liked — to be disliked a man has to have some sort of personality — but never 'Bill' Rowe . . . always 'William'.

And Rowe knew he'd missed out somewhere. He'd forgotten something. No, not Blakey. He'd received Blakey's instructions second-hand, and this was something more direct. Something he'd . . .

Blayde!

If he was frightened of Blakey (which he was) Rowe was terrified of Blayde. Blayde, and the idea of crossing Blayde, gave poor old Rowe nightmares. Great God, Blayde wasn't above having a set-to with Harris. If the occasion demanded it, he'd eat Rowe as an *hors d'oeuvre*.

And Blayde had said, 'Send Burns back here.' That at some time before seven. And it was now past ten o'clock.

To the surprise of a handful of sad-faced occupants, Rowe stood up and scuttled from the lounge. Thereafter, his progress was a little like a scared rabbit in a strange warren. Up corridors, down slopes, round corners; opening doors, peering into wards and, eventually, having followed the signs, coming to a breathless halt at the cubby-hole of a brown-smocked ancient at one of the entrances.

'I'm — er — I'm looking for a police officer,' said Rowe.

'Oh, aye?' The brown-smocked ancient eyed Rowe from peaked cap to polished shoes. He observed, 'At a quick guess, I'd have thought *you* were one.'

'What? Oh, yes, of course. But I mean a constable. A Police Constable Burns.'

'A patient, is he?'

'No. Not a patient. He came here during the night — in the early hours — with a sergeant and a constable who'd been injured.'

'I see.' The brown-smocked ancient slowly released a Polo mint from its cylindrical packing and popped it into his mouth. He said, 'If he hasn't left, he'll be inside somewhere.'

'I realise that. But where?'

'Dunno.' The brown-smocked ancient explored the hole in the mint with the tip of his tongue. 'Might not have come in this way. Did he . . .d'you know?'

'I — I really don't know.'

'There y'are, y'see.' The mint played catch-me-if-you-can with the ancient's tongue. 'Three other entrances. Coulda come in — coulda left — at any of 'em. No way of checking.'

'For God's sake!' Rowe's temper did something unusual. It flew. 'You can't lose a damn *policeman.*'

'Mate,' said the ancient solemnly. 'In this place we can lose a bloody army. I've known men come in here to do a bit o' repair work. Weeks. Never see hide nor hair of 'em.'

'Of all the infernal . . .'

'Young man.' The ancient dropped his voice a semitone and glared. 'I don't run this hospital. I book 'em in and I book 'em out . . . *if* they use this entrance. What happens to 'em once they're past me is no concern o' mine.'

Rowe took a deep breath, turned and marched away from the entrance.

The ancient called, 'Who shall I book out?'

133

Rowe ignored the question. He had another problem to worry about. Where the hell had he parked his car?

It was the old quart-into-a-pint-pot caper and, around mid-morning, it happened every Friday. Every other day of the week, no problem. All the Market Square to park in. All the side streets. A socking great tarmac 'Official Car Park'. No sweat. Periodically — especially in the holiday season — odd moments of bumper-to-bumper work, but it sorted itself out. The trick was to nip round the nearest corner and let *them* sort themselves out; a copper waving his arms and jumping around like a demented jack-rabbit didn't help matters. They all knew where they were going (or if they didn't they *should*) and, given time, they'd get there.

But Friday — Market Day — oh boy, *Friday*!

The lunatic driving the Rover had tried a Stirling Moss cornering technique, the caravan being towed by the Rover had jack-knifed and, thereafter, following and approaching traffic had knitted itself into the tangle to end all tangles. Bread vans, a bowser, a beer delivery lorry, a Post Office van, a petrol tanker, local runabouts, cars of just about every make, size and model. For a hundred yards north and south of the Market Square nothing budged or was able to budge. Horns blared, people shouted, engines roared then quietened as accelerators were depressed, then released. And there, in the middle of the pandemonium, Sergeant Ramsden and a diminutive lady traffic warden rushed around attempting the impossible. They tried to disentangle the vehicular knot from its centre and, instead of helping, they made things worse.

From a table in a corner of The Market Cafe P.C. Witherham watched with open amusement. Witherham despised Ramsden. Come to that, Witherham despised most people. The human race (Witherham's considered opinion) was made up of two species; those who knew how to look after Number One, and mugs. Ramsden was one of the mugs. He, Witherham, was *not* one of the mugs.

He sipped tea, munched ham sandwiches and watched the street pantomime in comfort. His helmet was on the table in front of him, and alongside the helmet was a plate holding a cream bun and a bar of chocolate.

The cafe was only half full. Outside, and adding to the roar and yelling of hemmed-in motor cars and frustrated drivers, the market was reaching full pitch. It would stay at full pitch until late afternoon and the stallholders (knowing the pattern of their trade) had all returned to their businesses and would not trickle back into

134

The Market Cafe until the rush period was over.

A nearby customer glanced out of the window, and remarked, 'A bit of a mess, innit?'

'Aye.' Witherham chewed at his ham sandwich. With the air of an expert, he observed, 'They've no idea. No bloody idea at all.'

A tall, slim man entered the cafe, glanced around, then walked to the counter and purchased tea and buttered scones. He carried the beaker and plate towards Witherham, placed them on the table, and said, 'D'you mind?'

'Be my guest, mate,' murmured Witherham.

The stranger seated himself, tasted the tea, then said, 'They look as if they need a little help.'

'Them two?' Witherham moved his head to indicate the world beyond the cafe window. He said, 'They'll learn . . . the hard way.'

'Learn?' The stranger bit into a scone.

'Christ only knows how he made sergeant,' explained Witherham. 'He hasn't the gumption to leave 'em to it.'

The nearby customer added, 'They've no idea.'

'No?' The stranger raised a surprised eyebrow.

'That's what *he* said,' added the customer.

'And I'm right,' said Witherham.

'Is that a fact?' The stranger lowered his scone onto its plate. He took a notebook from an inside pocket, flipped the pages then slipped a ballpoint from the same pocket. He glanced at his wrist-watch and made an entry in the notebook. Then he tilted his head and read the numbers on Witherham's shoulder. He murmured, 'Fifteen-fifty-five. What name is it?'

'Eh?' Witherham stared.

'Your name, please,' said the stranger pleasantly.

'Witherham. But I don't see what the hell it has to do . . .'

'*That's* what it has to do with me.' The stranger wrote with his right hand and, with his left hand, felt in his jacket pocket and fished out a folded pastecard. Without looking up, he murmured, 'All questions answered?'

Witherham gaped at the pasteboard and muttered, 'I didn't know.'

'Obviously.'

'It's — it's my meal break,' blustered Witherham.

'I didn't hear that last word.'

'My meal break,' repeated Witherham.

'No, the word after "break".'

'I didn't . . .' Witherham closed his mouth, then said, 'Oh — er — *sir*.'

Blayde returned the warrant card to its pocket, looked up from his notebook, and said, 'You're on a fizzer, Witherham. Idling and Gossiping. Neglect of Duty.'

'It's my meal break, sir,' said Witherham weakly.

'I'll mention that to the chief constable,' said Blayde flatly. He held out a hand and snapped, 'Now, I'll have your book. Then you can get outside and show everybody how easy it is.'

In the Staff Lounge they seemed to have been there forever. Hilda Noble, Marian Cooper, Muriel Pearson and Tim Burns. That's who they were; not 'constable this', 'missus the other'.

10.30 a.m.   The outer skins — the unimportant externals — had been rubbed off, by waiting. Three women. One man. It had become as basic as that. All within a moderately narrow age group. For the rest of their lives, and however far they might be scattered, they would remember each other. The adhesive force of worry and waiting had bonded the four of them together forever.

Marian Cooper pulled her dressing-gown a little tighter around her waist and murmured, 'I'd like to . . .'

The other three looked at her and she, in turn, looked guilty.

'I . . . hadn't time to get dressed,' she muttered.

W.P.C. Pearson pushed herself upright from the armchair and said, 'I'll run you to Upper Neck and back. It won't take long.'

'They — they said within . . .'

'I'll wait for you.' Hilda Noble touched Marian Cooper's arm reassuringly. 'I'll wait. We'll go into them together.'

'I'd . . .' Tim Burn frowned. 'If it didn't mean leaving Mrs Noble here alone, I'd . . . '

'Go with them,' interrupted Hilda Noble. 'It's all right. You have a job to do.'

'If — if you don't mind. I mean . . .'

'I don't mind at all.' Hilda Noble smiled. 'I'll wait here. I'll be fine. The shock — that first shock . . . I'm fine now. I'll wait here until Mrs Cooper and Miss Pearson get back.'

Burns stood up, and stammered, 'I hope — y'know . . .'

'I know.'

W.P.C. Pearson said, 'Right. We'll get off. We'll be back in no time at all.'

'I'll be here. Waiting.'

Tallboy had telephoned the information from Lessford Regional Headquarters. Blayde had left for a quick snack only minutes before

136

Pollard had taken the call. Pollard had, therefore, passed the news onto Harris at Upper Neck Police Office, and Harris looked as if he'd won the football pool jackpot.

'That's it then, eh?' Harris beamed at the D.S. and the forensic liaison officer. 'Call off the house-to-house, sergeant.'

'Yes, sir.' The D.S. hurried from the office.

'And you.' Harris turned to the forensic liaison officer. 'All your crowd has to do is make it stick.'

'It's not quite as easy as that, sir,' said the liaison officer, airily.

'Isn't it, now?' Harris switched off the beam.

'We have to be strictly impartial. I'm sure you realise that.'

'I realise,' rumbled Harris, 'that you, and your test-tube babies, have to nail this Peacock character. He's coughed, right? That means he *did* it. That you *don't* have to prove. Just wrap him up in fancy jargon. That's all. He's been here. That van — pick-up thing — *that's* been here. Peacock drove it here, planted the torch contraption, then drove the bloody thing back to Lessford. You have what's left of the torch. You have the vehicle. You have Peacock. If necessary we can tear Peacock's home to pieces. What the hell more d'you want? A signed photograph?'

'We — er — we *should* be able to link them. Given . . .'

'You *will* be able to link them,' Harris's tone left no room for argument. 'Otherwise *you'll* be out of a very soft job, lad.'

'I'm sure, sir. I'm quite sure.'

A deflated forensic liaison officer left Upper Neck Police Office and, as he left, Rowe entered. For a moment — for perhaps the time it takes to blink an eye — Rowe seemed about to turn and run. He'd expected Tallboy. He'd accepted the frightening possibility of Blayde. But *Harris!*

'Well?' barked Harris, 'Where have *you* been hiding yourself?'

'The — er — um . . . the hospital. Bordfield General Infirmary.'

'And what news from Ghent?' asked Harris sarcastically.

'It's — er — well, nothing really *new.*'

'No?'

'Good news, sir,' stammered Rowe. 'Y'know — no news, good news.'

'A man gets blinded,' snarled Harris. 'Another man loses most of his arm. And that's "no news" — that's "*good* news" — and you have the blind bloody audacity to . . .'

'*All right!* All right!' Rowe raised his hands in despair, then flopped into one of the office chairs. The worm turned. The utterly unexpected happened. His voice was as squeaky as ever, the rage held a fair mix of hysteria, but the rage *was* there. The fury of a downtrodden man who's had enough; who no longer gives a damn. A trickle of spittle dribbled from one corner of his mouth as Rowe raged, 'From Blakey, from Blayde, from Mrs Cooper, from some old fool at the hospital entrance, and now from you. I've had enough. I've had *more* than enough. Since before five this morning. And nobody — *nobody* — tells me a thing.'

Rowe paused for breath and, in a strangely gentle voice, Harris said, 'Get it off your chest, son. It's better out than in.'

'A police inspector.' The rage was still there, but the hysteria had been replaced by disgust touched with self-pity. He rubbed the back of a hand across his mouth, and continued, 'It means nothing. Nothing! Sergeant Cockburn runs this section more than I do. Pollard commands more respect than I do. I try . . . God knows, I *try*. I try to be decent. I try not to be — y'know — an animal. And and for that I'm treated as a joke. Blakey . . . All right, he's my senior officer and I'm expected to obey his instructions. I'm not griping at that. But there's no pleasing him. Whatever I do, it's wrong. I'm there to take the blame. Like this morning. Dammit, there's nobody more upset about Noble and Cooper than I am. Nobody! But I'm a joke. Superfluous.' He waved a hand in defeat. 'So nobody *tells* me anything. So I'm . . .'

The voice trailed off. The movement of the shoulders said more than any words could say. The rage had spent itself and left Rowe looking sapped of all strength.

'Ballock 'em,' said Harris flatly. Like a father passing wisdom to a bemused son, Harris said, 'They're coppers. They're used to slinging their weight around. It's part of the job. You get that uniform on — pips on the shoulders — you're not one of the boys any more. What you call 'decency', forget it. I'm not saying be a bastard, but sling your rank around. It's what it's there for. You out-rank 'em, don't *ever* let 'em forget that. They'll respect you for it. That's what they expect. They don't want to love you, they want to *respect* you.' He paused, then said, 'Give it a month, eh? Bounce 'em around a little. Any back-chat, peg 'em. It's what they'd expect from Blayde. It's what they'd expect from *me*. Get 'em so they expect it from *you* . . . it's that easy, son.'

Rowe nodded, but looked undecided.

'For what it's worth.' Harris suddenly looked embarrassed. He continued, 'Tallboy's nailed some hooligan from Lessford. He's on his way back to Sopworth. I'm away to meet 'em. I'll leave you to clear things up here. Send the spare bods back to their sections. Then go for a meal.' Almost as an after-thought, he added, 'And forget Blakey. Blakey's burst his bloody balloon. Concentrate on Sopworth.'

Harris left and Rowe sat alone in Upper Neck Police Office. He sat, and thought, and felt sorry for himself. Because it wouldn't work. The advice — even if it had been good advice — wasn't advice he could take. Harris wouldn't understand — could *never* understand — because Harris used himself as a yardstick as far as mankind itself was concerned. Harris, Blayde, even Tallboy. They fitted into a matrix. The 'policeman' mould. The 'damn-your-eyes' templet. That was why they could work so well together; why they understood each other; why, with all its faults, they *enjoyed* police work.

But Rowe?

No way . . . not in a million years. He was Rowe, and he'd stay Rowe, to the end of his police career.

Back at Sopworth the traffic snarl-up was being gradually disentangled, with the assistance of Joseph William Witherham. In the Market Cafe Robert Blayde was enjoying an after-snack pipe, prior to resuming control of the Preston/Sutcliffe murder. William 'Taffy' Evans and Charles Wooley were hanging onto their stomachs as they arranged the headless victims on slabs at the public mortuary, to await post mortem examinations. In the Charge Office of the police station Edward Pollard was peeling the shell from a hard-boiled egg, prior to having his meal break. And at that moment Nellie Chambers was pressing the button at the public counter.

Nellie Chambers. As a child (possibly before she was even born) the pixies had touched her mind. Courtesy demands that she be described as 'late middle-aged' although, more than once, she'd suffered the description of 'that silly old hag'. It was a cruel description. She was quite harmless; something of a nuisance, perhaps, but really quite harmless. In her own private little world of fantasy she was a heroine. She smelled out spies. She recognised villains. She uncovered conspiracies. All this, umpteen times a week. Which meant that she regularly donned her ancient outdoor clothes, hurried down to Sopworth Police Station and there solemnly explained the imminent destruction of the world to the first policeman she could find.

Her favourite policeman — because he was always kind and ready to explain things — was Constable Pollard and, when he answered her ring, having laid aside the hard-boiled egg, she fairly beamed across the counter at him.

'Now then, Nellie,' he said. 'Are they still at it?'

'Oh, yes.' She nodded eagerly.

'Still signalling to each other with the clothes on the line on wash-ing day?'

'As busy as ever. But we've broken the code, haven't we?'

'We have, old darling,' agreed Pollard solemnly. 'So don't let on. Then when one of the squard cars pass the end of the street we can see what they're signalling and take appropriate action.'

'I'm glad.' She almost chuckled with delight. 'They won't get away with anything now . . . will they?'

'Never again.'

'Mind you.' She was suddenly very serious. 'They're trying to blind me these days.'

'Never!' Pollard looked obligingly shocked.

'Dust,' she said, *sotto voce*. 'They're sprinkling dust in my eyes. Even when I'm asleep. I think they've recognised who I am, y'know. That's why they're trying to blind me.'

'Dust?' mused Pollard.

'Even when I'm in bed,' she assured him.

'Mmmm.' Pollard rubbed his jaw, tilted his head to one side and said, 'Y'know, Nellie, I shouldn't be telling you this.'

'What? What?' She leaned over the counter, eager to hear the latest news from the undercover world of international shenanigans.

'It — er — it was last summer.' Pollard glanced first over his right shoulder, then over his left. Then he looked directly at Nellie's face and said, 'Y'know . . . I could get into real trouble.'

'Not a word,' she promised. 'I won't breathe a word to a soul.'

'In America,' he explained softly. 'That long drought they had last summer. Remember?'

She nodded.

'The harvest, y'see.' His tone was deadly serious. 'It affected the harvest.'

'Yes, it would.'

'And then the flour . . . and we get a lot of flour from America.'

'Yes, I know.'

'And now it's too late,' sighed Pollard. 'That flour — when it comes into contact with suet — it doesn't actually *explode*. It's not *that* dangerous. But — y'know — it sends off clouds of dust.'

'Ah!'

'And that's what it is, luv.'

'Oh!'

'Dumpling Dust. It's everywhere. It get into your eyes, into your clothes . . . *everywhere.*'

'Dumpling Dust?' She nodded her head slowly, sagely.

140

'You'd be surprised how many complaints we've had. But — y'know — we can't tell *everybody*.'

'No,' she agreed. 'That wouldn't be right. You never know who you're talking to.'

'That's it, then, Nellie.'

'I'm pleased.' The smile which lit up her face was one of pure innocence. 'I won't worry any more now.'

'There's a darling.' Pollard returned the smile.

'Dumpling Dust.' She shook her head in wonderment, turned and left the police station.

Pollard returned to his hard-boiled egg.

Pinter breaked the Minivan to a halt on the hard standing in front of his garage, then switched off the engine. He didn't 'book off duty'. He merely sat there, staring through the windscreen at the closed garage doors. He sat there for all of three minutes seeing nothing, hearing nothing, before he shuddered then slowly climbed from the van and walked into the house.

'Ma.'

He greeted his mother-in-law as he entered the kitchen.

She said, 'The doctor's been. About half an hour back.'

There was tea in the pot. He poured a beaker full, added sugar and milk, then joined her at the kitchen table. He opened a packet of cigarettes, she took one and he thumbed a lighter and held it to her cigarette, then lighted his own.

Tea and fags. . . and talk. Not too much talk. Mainly tea and fags. Because *she* was dying, the house itself was dying. Dying . . . it hadn't even life enough left to get untidy. Clean. Everything in its proper place. Nothing lost, nothing misplaced, nothing where it shouldn't be. *She* was dying, the house was dying, he was dying, ma was dying . . . the whole rotten world was dying.

'She's slipping away . . . peacefully,' the woman murmured. 'That's what the doctor said.' She paused, then added, 'He thought maybe the parson.'

'No parsons.' The words were low and harsh with heartbreak.

Very quietly, very gently, she said, 'She's Christian, Wilf. She was confirmed.'

He lowered his eyes and stared at the Formica surface of the table. Religion . . . at a time like this. Religion . . . with Hannah upstairs. Ma wouldn't understand. How *could* she understand? 'Gentle Jesus, meek and mild' . . . aye, but now read the Old Testament. About *God*. Assuming there *was* a God — that it wasn't all a con — that

141

Christ *was* the son of this God . . . hell, what a father! Those Old Testament prophets . . . if *they* were to be believed. Gorged on blood sacrifices. Page after page — chapter after chapter — of threats and terrifying punishments. The Old Testament, the New Testament — all part of the same book — all part of The Bible. The same religion. 'He shall break them with a rod of iron.' Who? Hannah? Dear, sweet Hannah? If religion meant *that*. If the blasted vicar represented *that*. It was — it was . . .

He drank deeply at the tepid tea then, without raising his eyes, muttered, 'If you think Hannah would want it.'

'The vicar?'

'I . . .' He moved one shoulder. 'Do what you think best, ma. What you think she might have wanted.'

'You're a good man, Wilf.' A hand reached across the table and squeezed his wrist. 'I'll — er — I'll ring him up.'

'If — y'know — if you think it's best.'

Blayde didn't like crowds. The late-morning heat, the jostle of the market crowds, the shouting, the noise of the traffic, the stink of petrol fumes, vegetables on the point of decay and the general smell of massed humanity. Christ, what a compound!

One day not too far in the future . . . He bent his head and shouldered a passage through the shoppers . . . Come retirement day, he'd put his feet up at the cottage . . . He zig-zagged a way through the now slowly-moving traffic . . . Read the books he'd always *meant* to read . . . He reached a pavement along which he could stride without having to force a way forward . . . Maybe buy himself a decent music centre and start a collection of tapes and records . . . He turned a corner, away from the Market Square, and seemed to be able to breathe again . . . Put all this filth and muck behind him . . .

He entered the police station and forgot the dreams.

In the Charge Office Pollard said, 'Good news, sir. Chief Inspector Tallboy and Constable Kyle. A tip-off. They've picked up a comedian from Lessford. They're on the way in now.'

'The Upper Neck job?'

'Seems so.' Pollard nodded. 'They sound pretty sure.'

'Back to here?'

'Aye.'

'How many cells? Three?'

'Three,' confirmed Pollard. 'Two occupied. Charlie Preston and a lunatic called Rayon . . . Barker nicked him last night for a smash-and-grab incident.'

'An Occasional Court tomorrow morning?'

'It's fixed, sir.'

'We could use it,' mused Blayde. 'If Tallboy's struck gold . . . we *could* use it.'

'Just the one cell, sir,' Pollard made his meaning clear by the tone of his voice. 'It's Friday night . . . we might need cell space.'

Harris bulled his way into the Charge Office. Following on Harris's heels were D.C. Evans and P.C. Wooley. Almost immediately Sergeant Cockburn, wearing a lightweight jacket over uniform shirt and trousers arrived. Suddenly the Charge Office seemed to be bulging with people.

'Have they arrived yet?' asked Harris.

'No.' Blayde answered the question. 'They're on their way.'

'I just heard,' said Cockburn. 'What's the latest?'

Pollard said, 'Noble's blind. Coop's lost a hand.'

'The bastards! Do we know who . . .'

'With luck, he's already in custody,' said Blayde, 'Detective Chief Inspector Tallboy and P.C. Kyle picked him up at Lessford.'

Harris said, 'They're bringing him here. They should be taking him to Beechwood Brook.'

'We'll have more cell room,' agreed Blayde.

Evans said, 'Sir, we've . . .'

'Where's Blakey?' asked Harris.

'Where's Rowe?' asked Blayde.

Harris said, 'I've left Rowe at Upper Neck, tidying things up.'

'Sir, we've . . .'

'But where the hell's Blakey?' demanded Harris.

'Sir, we've got the bodies ready.' Evans managed to make himself heard. 'Post mortem tomorrow morning.'

'Bodies?' Cockburn's eyes widened.

'A double murder.' Pollard spoke directly to Cockburn. 'Charlie Preston.'

'Dead?'

'No.' Blayde expanded upon Pollard's reply. 'He's the murderer. He shotgunned his wife and her fancy man.'

'Sutcliffe,' added Pollard.

'Bloody hell!'

'By the way,' said Harris, 'we don't object to bail. And I think Ranson may have advised him to make a statement.'

'He did, sir,' said Pollard. 'When he left — after I'd taken Preston back to the cell — he said Preston would be prepared to make a statement covering the basic facts.'

'So, we allow bail.' Harris frowned and added, 'Where the hell *is* Blakey?'

'Have you a minute?' Blayde moved his head.

Harris looked a question, then shrugged and followed Blayde out of the Charge Office and into Rowe's office.

Blayde closed the door. For a moment he hesitated then, without speaking, he took a sealed envelope from an inside *11 a.m.* pocket and handed it to Harris. Harris took the envelope, slit it open with a forefinger, took out the folded quarto sheet and read what was typed and signed without changing his expression. He refolded the quarto sheet and returned it to its envelope before he spoke.

He said, 'Do I have to tell you what it is?'

'No,' said Blayde shortly.

'Your idea?'

'Not altogether.'

'But . . . a nudge in the right direction?' Harris's lip curled.

'It's *his* resignation. It was *his* idea.'

'Coincidental . . . of course?'

'Even *you* can't ruin a man's life.' Blayde made the words hard and uncompromising.

'What bloody right have you to . . .'

'Hold it!' The tone silenced even Harris. Blayde said, 'Don't come the red-neck technique with me, Bob Harris. We tried our first helmets for size together, remember? A long time ago. I didn't jump when you yelled then. I don't jump when you yell *now*. Somebody has to slam your brakes on, periodically, otherwise you'd run riot. Let's say *I've* volunteered.'

'I could . . .'

'You couldn't do a damn thing. Beyond that door . . .' Blayde moved his head. 'My word carries as much weight as yours. That . . .' Again Blayde nodded. This time at the envelope which Harris was still holding. 'That's the easy way out. You get rid of Blakey . . . which is what *you* want. Blakey draws a chief superintendent's pension . . . which is what *he* wants. Your way merely draws blood.'

Harris took a deep breath, then growled, 'Nobody — *nobody* — in this whole bloody force would dare talk to me like that. Only you. And why the hell I . . .'

'Because you know I'm right.' Blayde's mouth curled into a sardonic grin. 'All you can see — *could* see — Blakey. But there's more than Blakey. He has a wife. Two daughters, neither of 'em yet married. Crucify Blakey and you crucify a whole family. I know you — I know you well — I don't think even you would want to do *that*.'

In the Charge Office Cockburn, Pollard, Evans and Wooley had been joined by a sweating Ramsden. The two sergeants were re-arranging their respective duties.

Cockburn said, 'You should be off at two. Anything fixed for this afternoon?'

'Nothing special.' Ramsden wiped his face with a large handkerchief.

'We'll need night cover,' said Cockburn. 'If we ask for a swinger that'll mean some poor devil being switched, without warning.'

'I suppose.' Ramsden mopped the back of his neck.

'Time you come on?' asked Cockburn.

'Five.'

'Okay. You hang on till five. I'll take over then and work a twelve-hour stint. Then if the swinger comes on at six, that'll only leave an hour uncovered and I'll drop back to nights tomorrow.'

'If Rowe doesn't . . .'

'I'll fix it with Rowe.'

'Fine. Fine.' Ramsden nodded. He blew out his cheeks and added, 'God . . . what a morning.'

Near the telephone/teleprinter ante-room, Pollard was listening to the troubles of D.C. Evans and P.C. Wooley.

Evans was saying, '. . . ever seen such a God-awful mess.'

'Pretty horrific,' agreed Wooley.

'You've fixed the P.M.?' checked Pollard.

'Tomorrow,' said Evans.

'And the inquest?'

'Monday. Opened and adjourned.'

'Identification of the bodies?'

'Oh, Christ!' breathed Wooley.

'They *can't*,' observed Evans. 'There's no — y'know — *faces*.'

'Something,' said Pollard heavily. 'Fingerprints. Rings. Operation scars. The coroner'll want 'em to *be* identified.'

Wooley moistened his lips and said, 'Sutcliffe's next-of-kin.'

'He has a mother,' said Pollard flatly. 'He also has a brother. I'd plump for the brother.'

'Today?' Evans sounded miserable.

'Before the pathologist gets cracking.'

'D'you — d'you know the address?'

'I'll find it,' promised Pollard. 'What about the woman?'

'There's — er — Charlie Preston.'

'Won't do.' Pollard shook his head. 'She has a sister — I think — I'll check with Charlie.'

Evans and Wooley frowned their wretchedness. Pollard was right — Pollard was *always* right — but that did little to comfort them as they visualised the thankless task of breaking the news and arranging for an official identification of the murdered couple.

Pollard said, 'Another thing. Charlie's going to get bail . . . tomorrow. Maybe he'll go to his sister's place. That's the best thing. But in case he wants to go back to his own home, somebody has to arrange for the mess to be cleaned up.'

Evans closed his eyes in despair.

'Maybe his sister,' suggested Wooley.

'If he wants it,' agreed Pollard. '*And* if she's willing. But it has to be done. We can't have him going back there with it just as he left it.' He paused, then added, 'Have a word with Ranson, his solicitor. He might know somebody.' He smiled, ruefully, and ended, 'They don't mention these things in textbooks, do they? That murder also means some mucky, bloody jobs.'

Rowe tapped on the door and W.P.C. Pearson answered the knock.

'Mrs — er — Cooper?' said Rowe awkwardly.

'She's getting dressed.' Pearson stared, flint-eyed at her inspector. 'Then I'm taking her back to Bordfield General.'

'I'd — er — like to see her.'

'Why?'

'We've . . .' Rowe moved his hands helplessly. 'That is to say, Chief Inspector Tallboy. He's arrested the man responsible.'

'You think that might interest her?'

'It might . . . give satisfaction.'

'Inspector Rowe.' Pearson's tone was uncompromising. 'You can order me. I'll obey that order. But . . .'

'No. I wouldn't dream of . . .'

'. . . you can't order *her*. She hates you — she hates the whole damn police force — and I can't blame her. Her man's lost a limb. As far as *she's* concerned the force is responsible. Indirectly. I don't think she cares who did it. I don't think that's important . . . to her. Just that it happened. That Coop was placed in a position where it *could* happen . . .'

'It could have happened anywhere,' said Rowe miserably.

'Yes, sir.' Pearson's tone softened slightly. '*I* know that. *You* know that. But it's something *she* won't yet accept.' She paused, then said, 'I'll ask you inside. I'll call her. If that's what you want. But it won't do any good. Only harm . . . for the moment at least.'

'All right, miss.' Rowe sighed heavily. 'I'll not — y'know . . . Just tell her. And stay with her. As long as you think it's necessary.'

'Yes, sir.' Pearson nodded, then closed the door.

Rowe turned slowly. For a moment he looked almost on the point of tears; the good man, misunderstood; the weak man, unable to handle contempt. With his head lowered he walked slowly to the gate.

At the gate the detective sergeant said, 'They're all dismissed, sir, all but one.'

'Eh?' Rowe jerked himself out of the sea of self-pity.

'You said round up the men. Send them back to their normal duties.'

'Oh — er — yes.'

'All except Constable Karn.'

'He's the Rimstone man.'

'Is he?' The detective sergeant's tone was grim. 'God help Rimstone.'

Rowe's mind was dragged from thoughts of Marian Cooper. He stared at the detective sergeant.

The D.S. said, 'If you'll follow me, sir.'

They walked perhaps two hundred yards. They stopped at a post-and-rail fence. They stared across a short stretch of meadow at a Dutch barn. Up there, atop of the hay, they saw a uniformed leg swinging gently alongside one of the bales.

'Karn,' said the D.S. flatly.

'Call him,' choked Rowe.

'KARN!'

Fury and disgust exploded in the single word. Chickens in a nearby farm yard fluttered and clucked as the unexpected noise hit them. A cluster of cows looked up from their grass-cropping. In the distance a dog started barking.

Karn sat bolt upright, gaped then scrambled down from his hiding place, allowing the fornicatory masterpiece to flap, unheeded, into the grass at the foot of the baled straw. He hurried across to Rowe and the D.S.

As he climbed the post-and-rail fence, he said, 'I was . . .'

'Shut up!' snarled Rowe and the voice, although still high-pitched, carried outrage Karn had never before witnessed in the inspector.

147

'You slimy bloody bastard,' breathed the D.S. 'Two of your mates. And this is how you . . .'

'Peg him,' snapped Rowe. 'Neglect of duty. And I want to see him in front of Chief Superintendent Blakey tomorrow morning.' Then, to Karn, 'You're finished, constable. If my word carries any weight at all . . . you're *finished*. Get home – get out of my sight – and start packing your furniture.'

'Living proof of E.S. bloody P.' growled Harris.

And, indeed, it seemed so. The Press and P.R. crowd at Head-quarters had done a lousy job. They'd trotted out the same tattered platitudes. 'An arrest is expected soon.' 'We're *11.30 a.m.* following a promising line of enquiry.' 'Obviously, we can't tell you all we know'. Harris wondered (and not for the first time) what the hell that bunch of useless long-stoppers were paid for. Certainly not to keep the news-gatherers at bay. They were all there, crowding the pavement outside Sopworth Police Station. Like vultures awaiting the last gasp of some mortally wounded morsel. The nationals, the provincials; reporters and photo-graphers. Two TV crews, BBC and ITN; two interviewers, two camera-men, two sound recordists.

'That one.' Harris squinted through the glass, above the frosted panes which made up the lower half of the window. He spoke softly and grimly to Blayde. 'The short-arse in the blue suit. Don't give him the time o' day. Twice, already, he's misquoted me and made me sound a right twat.'

Behind them in the Charge Office, Ramsden, Cockburn, Pollard, Evans and Wooley waited for the arrival of Tallboy and his prisoner.

'The old gag?' murmured Blayde.

'If he's any sense,' said Harris.

'Tallboy knows the tricks.'

Tallboy's car edged itself through the waiting newshounds and pulled to a halt at the police station door. Tallboy was driving. In the rear seat sat Kyle and a handcuffed figure with a cell blanket covering his head and shoulders.

Blayde turned and said, 'Sergeant, clear a way for 'em.'

Ramsden and Pollard left the Charge Office, pushed their way through the media people. Pollard opened the rear door of the car. Tallboy hurried around the front of the car then, with Pollard and Tallboy on one side of him and Ramsden and Kyle on the other side, the blanketed figure was rushed from car to police station, along the corridor and into the cell passage. Harris closed the door, firmly,

148

then walked with Blayde to the cell passage.

Sergeant Kelly stood there, grinning sheepishly and trying to straighten his hair with manacled hands.

'Good.' Harris nodded his satisfaction.

'Just in case some scoop-hungry type pulled the blanket clear,' said Tallboy. 'Peacock's tucked away at Beechwood Brook.'

'Nailed?' asked Blayde.

'I'd say.' Tallboy nodded. 'He's coughed . . . as near as dammit. Get the forensic round his ankles. He'll come.'

'If he did it, he'll sing,' promised Harris.

Kelly lowered his hands and said, 'He did it, sir. Nothing surer.'

Kyle unlocked the handcuffs and Kelly took out cigarettes and lit one up. Harris frowned his concentration, as he worked out possible permutations. He nodded, slowly, as he reached a decision.

He said, 'Right. You, lad, what's your name?'

'Kyle, sir.'

Tallboy chipped in, 'If it's cracked, Kyle cracked it.'

'Right, it's your case, Kyle.' Kyle coloured in slight embarrassment. Harris continued, 'Back to Beechwood Brook with Chief Inspector Tallboy. You, too, Kelly. I'll be along later. There's an Occasional Court fixed for here tomorrow morning. Get enough paperwork done to stand this Peacock character in the dock . . . and this time without bail.'

Kelly looked puzzled.

Blayde said, 'We've a double murder on our hands, as well as this lot.'

'Bloody hell!'

'We breed 'em . . . like rabbits.'

'That's yours, chief superintendent,' said Harris.

'Evans's,' corrected Blayde.

'With guidance and assistance from the expert.' Harris smiled. It was a very enigmatic smile.

'Evans.' Blayde's tone was equally non-communicative. 'Assisted by Constable Wooley. With the acknowledged expert keeping the trolley firmly on the rails.'

'As long as there's not a cock-up,' growled Harris.

'There won't be.'

For a moment, the two men locked eyes. This mock-antagonism had become part of their lives . . . if it *was* mock-antagonism. The unofficial 'Amos 'n Andy' act tended, at times, not to be funny. Not to be an act, in fact. Nobody knew for certain. Perhaps even Harris and Blayde weren't sure.

Harris said, 'Three cells here. Two of them are occupied. That doesn't leave much leeway. Preston — your man — we'll have *him* out at Beechwood Brook as soon as possible.'

'There's a statement to be taken,' said Blayde.

'That shouldn't take all day.'

'It *won't* take all day. We'll switch him to D.H.Q. as soon as possible.'

Tallboy said, 'Okay, we'll get back to Peacock. I'll take Sergeant Kelly. Will you bring Constable Kyle?'

'Half an hour,' said Harris. 'I'll shift those vultures at the door, then we'll be with you.'

Murder — in this case double murder — carries with it more than mere detection. Indeed, as far as Charlie Preston was

Noon

concerned, it carried *no* detection. But it carried all the other things. The tightening of the stomach muscles, because this was the 'big 'un'. The compassion for a good man who, for one moment in his otherwise blameless life, had lost control. The knowledge that this man (who has already been punished enough, by the fermentation within his own mind) will be subjected to judicial punishment, as a result of a ruthless machine called The Police Service. The sometimes forgotten realisation that the murdered *and* the murderer have kin to whom the crime will come as a monumental shock. And the boring, nit-picking, head-spinning paperwork; the 'How', the 'When', the 'Where', the 'Why' reduced into cold and impersonal 'statement language'; the Arrest Report, the Charge Report, the Summary of Evidence, enough to satisfy the Police Solicitor and the magistrate at an Occasional Court that the man in the dock had, indeed, slaughtered his wife and her lover. Not forgetting, of course, H.M. Coroner. Which meant Sudden Death Reports covering both victims. Forensic Science Reports. Post Mortem Reports. And that little lot only for starters.

Evans chain-lit a cigarette from the end of the one he'd just smoked, and said, 'Stone the bloody crows! We'll be up all night.'

'Relax, Taffy.' Wooley smiled. It was not a particularly happy smile. If anything it was a tired smile — hell he'd *been* up all night — but it was meant to counter the worried expression on the detective constable's face.

They were upstairs from the Charge Office. In a pokey room, little larger than one of the cells; a room which carried the euphemism of 'Canteen'. Canteen! A sink, a draining-board, a fold-away table, two kitchen chairs, an electric kettle and a wall cupboard in which the 'makings' were stored. Some bloody canteen. But for the moment they were clear of the huff and puff of the ground floor. Blayde and Harris were out of their whiskers. They sipped newly brewed tea from chipped beakers, and they talked.

'It's all wrong, y'know,' complained Evans. 'I mean . . . *murder*. What Charlie Preston's done isn't murder.'

'What else?' sighed Wooley..

'He's killed a rotten bitch who was two-timing him, that's all.'

'That's all?' Wooley raised an eyebrow. '*And* the bloke she was in bed with . . . *that's* all.'

'You think it should be classified as murder?'

'I think there are such things as Divorce Courts.'

'Charlie Preston wouldn't know how.'

'For Christ's sake, Taffy . . .'

'Look,' Evans held the cigarette between two fingers. He waved it around to give emphasis to his argument. 'Charlie's from, well, call it working class. His kind don't go in for divorce. They bugger off or they stick it out. They don't *divorce*.'

'Legal separation?' suggested Wooley.

'Maybe . . . if they're pushed.'

'But not murder. Murder isn't an alternative to divorce.'

'They don't go in for divorce,' insisted Evans.

'They go in for murder instead.'

'Look,' the cigarette waved frantically. 'Your father's a what . . .'

'A bank manager.'

'That's it, then.'

'I'm damned if I can see . . .'

'Middle class. They *believe* in divorce.'

'The hell they do. They believe in marriage.'

'Sure . . . if they're lucky. But if they're not. Divorce. It's the natural answer. My dad's a miner. Grafts his heart out at the coal face.'

'I can't see what the hell you're . . .'

'They *don't* divorce . . . see?'

'They murder instead?'

'Don't be daft, man.'

'It would seem,' mused Wooley, 'that those world-renowned valleys must hold more than their fair share of miserable bastards.'

Harris, too, was easing up on the speed a little. Temporarily. Not, be it understood, at The Market Cafe; assistant chief constables ignore such low class scoffing-spots. Nevertheless, and despite the price, the Ploughman's Lunch at The Sopworth Arms didn't have too much of an edge on The Market Cafe fare. The surroundings were posher; bags of glass, yards of chrome and, through the swing-doors, a snazzy ballroom, complete with tiny stage, an electric organ and a set of dust-sheet-covered drums. The brewery had spent a small fortune on The Sopworth Arms — on making it into a 'popular' night-spot-cum-road-house — but the beer wasn't the best in the world and, although the bread roll was locally baked and crusty, the apple was Golden Delicious, the butter was supermarket stuff done up fancy, the cheese was little more than 'mousetrap', the tomato was squelchy and the chutney came from a bloody great jar bought at sale price.

But so what? Harris was going to invoice a round three quid for 'lunch', so he should worry.

In the Charge Office Blayde and Pollard talked man-to-man.

'The statement from your pal,' said Blayde.

'Ranson gave the go ahead?' It was part-question, part-verification.

'Ranson gave the go ahead,' said Blayde.

'In that case . . .'

'I think you should take it.'

'Oh, no! I'm not . . .'

'Not officially.' Blayde waved the elderly constable silent. 'Just go into him. Get the details — whatever Ranson's advised him to say — come back in here and type it out.'

'That makes it . . .'

'That makes it nothing,' interrupted Blayde. 'You know each other. He trusts you. *You* won't work a flanker. Just get the details, type the statement, then give it to Evans. Evans'll take it back into the cell, read it over to Preston. *He'll* have taken it.'

Pollard looked suspicious.

'I'm trying to help him,' said Blayde heavily. 'Just because I hold this rank doesn't mean I haven't feelings. We do the job, but we can make things as easy for your pal as possible.'

Pollard sniffed.

'You don't believe me?' Blayde's mouth curled.

'I didn't say that, sir.'

'I'm not begging, Pollard. You won't find any dust on *my* knees.'

'No, sir.'

'So please your bloody self. He's your friend, not mine.'

'I'll type the statement,' sighed Pollard.

The fact is had Perkins, the cut flower man, not moved his stall — indeed had the traffic snarl-up been allowed to ram itself solid and stay there — a life might have been saved. But, come to that, had the Capri been driven by somebody else . . .

However . . .

The Capri rounded the corner which had caused Perkins such worry. Or, to be precise, it *half* rounded the corner, then opened up and aimed itself straight at the cut flowers stall. People shouted and jumped for safety. The obligatory screaming woman, who (as any copper will verify) is a vital ingredient at such a scene, let rip and the poor old guy hobbling around on two walking sticks knew he couldn't shift fast enough. His last living thought, before the nose of the Capri ploughed through the flowers and the struts of the stall, before it pinned him to the concrete lamp-standard and broke his neck, was that, indirectly, his slow-moving joints were going to be the death of him . . . and who was going to look after his cat? And all he'd wanted was to stand for a few moments alongside the flowers and catch a whiff of scent which reminded him of his youth; of the girl he'd married, and the country garden they'd tended before Old Man Time had torn them apart and forced him to live lonely and past comforting in one of a row of alms houses on the fringe of Sopworth. He tried to whisper her name with his dying breath . . . but couldn't make it.

Witherham heard the crash, heard the screaming woman and raced to the scene.

He didn't smell flowers. All *he* smelled was petrol fumes.

'Nobody strike a match!' he bawled, then tried to yank open the door by the driver's seat.

The occupant was middle-aged, unmarked and slumped forward as far as the seat-belt would allow. He was unconscious and his breathing sounded like a rip-saw hitting a rusty nail.

A heavily-built, well-dressed man pushed his way through the swelling crowd and, as he added his muscle power in an attempt to force open the door, he said, 'It's okay. I'm a doctor.'

'Ambulance,' gasped Witherham. He forced the door wide enough to get a firm grip then, as he braced his feet against the mudguard he turned his head towards the gapers and said, 'For God's sake! Don't just stand there . . . get an ambulance.'

The door was wrenched open and, as they leaned inside to unclip the seat-belt, the doctor said, 'The old fellow. I've checked. He's dead.'

'What I need,' gasped Witherham. Then to the crowd, 'For Christ's sake, nobody strike a match.'

As they lifted him from the car the driver stopped breathing.

The doctor shouldered the crowd back a few feet and they eased the driver onto the pavement. The doctor felt for the pulse at the neck, then bent down and listened to the chest.

Witherham unclipped his walkie-talkie, pressed the 'Send' button and said, 'Ted, I'm at the Market Square. I need some back-up'.

A metallic reproduction of Blayde's voice snapped, 'That's poor radio procedure, constable. I expect . . .'

'Sod what *you* expect.' Witherham threw politeness out of the window. 'I've a smashed car, two bodies and some injured pedestrians here, I need a hand. Fast.'

'Sit tight, son. They're on their way.' The tone altered, the words were a form of apology for jumping to wrong priorities.

The doctor turned his head, looked up and said, 'You're right, officer. This one's dead, too.'

'I can tell 'em,' grunted Witherham.

Perkins was nursing an injured wrist. A woman customer was dabbing a nasty gash in her calf with an already blood-soaked handkerchief. Other people were holding ribs, hips and hands; they'd jumped, but the passing Capri had caught them glancing blows before it had pinned the old man to the lamp standard. The crowd was building up; death and carnage being the finest magnet for gapers yet invented.

'Get back a bit,' bawled Witherham. 'Hell's bells! This isn't a peep-show.'

The doctor was feeling in the pockets of the driver's jacket. He held up a packet with the word 'Persatin' printed across its face.

He said, 'Heart failure. Angina, at a guess. This chap should never have been driving a car.'

'Tough guys,' said Witherham sardonically. 'They die . . . they take some other poor devil with 'em.'

Marian Cooper sat in the front passenger seat of the Volvo and stared, unseeing, at the road surface rushing towards the car's bonnet. Pearson drove the car fast and surely; she, too, watched the road ahead; she, too, was silent. Pearson wondered what was going on under the dome of Mrs Cooper's skull. She could make a crude guess, but she couldn't be sure. She was a woman . . . beyond that the differences between her and Marian Cooper were mountain high. Marian Cooper was an older woman and a married woman. But more than that – *much* more than that – she was Coop's wife.

A state of affairs of which Marian Cooper needed no reminder.

She was scared. That summed up the whole situation. She'd showered, she had chosen her clothes very carefully, she's used make-up and perfume sparingly; she knew that, for her age, she was an attractive woman – that men still turned their heads when she passed – but she was scared stupid. Coop was her man. Her only man. The only man she could ever contemplate as her husband. Okay – in a mild sort of way, he was her Svengali – but that didn't break any dishes. The rows – and there'd *been* rows, savage slanging-matches – they meant nothing. Rows were part of a marriage. Part of *their* marriage. Without rows – without an occasional exchange of near-spitting hatred – the bond would have been incomplete.

She knew Coop. Hellfire, did she know Coop! A hard man and, if the centre wasn't quite as hard as the exterior, it was still stringy and difficult to chew. Happiness? Odd, she couldn't remember one moment of their whole life together when Coop had given the appearance of 'happiness'. Not what the world understood by the word 'happiness'. Not the laughing, carefree picture of joy which went with that word. Satisfaction? Sure . . . she'd learned, over the years, how to satisfy him. The food he liked. The books he preferred. The silences he counted as more important than empty conversation. And – okay – even in bed she'd taught herself how to satisfy him. She'd once bought a manual. (For a split second she almost smiled.) Hell, if she'd tried half the things he'd have walked out on her.

That was Coop.

Straight up, straight down; two and two made four, and screw it around as much as you like, it didn't make three-and-a-half, and it didn't make four-and-a-half. It made *four*, period. The same with marriage – the same with every relationship – scales balanced, exactly, and if they didn't he wanted no part. He took nothing he couldn't pay for. He accepted nothing he couldn't return. He was the most bloody-minded, stiff-necked . . .

He was Coop.

And now he wasn't *quite* Coop. He was a hand and part of an arm short . . . and God only knew what that was going to mean.

It was one of those no-nonsense schools; red-bricked, steep-roofed and conveying the undoubted appearance of solemnity and determination; a place where generation after generation of pupils had been force-fed basic education. Nothing highfalutin' about this school. Within those walls you were *taught*. Facts were thrown at you, and you didn't argue or question those facts. 'George Washington borrowed his father's axe and chopped down an apple tree and, because of that, he became the first president of the United States of America . . . and stop fidgeting on the back row there'. That sort of school.

155

Daisy Wellington worked at this school. She worked in the kitchen. Sometimes she washed the cutlery and crockery, scrubbed out the pans and baking tins. At other times she stood behind the counter and plonked helpings of edible goo on to the plates of passing scholars. She didn't mind. It was a job. Anything and everything was a job, if it brought in a wage packet at the end of the week and, since the death of her husband, wage packets had been of supreme importance.

At the moment she was in the head's study, sitting uncomfortably on the edge of an ancient, horsehair armchair and waiting for these two young men to say what they had to say . . . to stop humming and hawing.

'It's — er — it's about Charlie, Mrs Wellington,' muttered Evans.

'*My* Charlie?'

'Your brother,' amplified Wooley. 'Charlie Preston.'

'Is he dead?' It was a simple question, simply asked.

'Good lord, no!'

'No, he's not dead,' added Wooley. 'It's just that . . .'

In the silence, Evans said, 'He's in police custody, ma'am.'

'He doesn't drink.' The light of battle glinted her eyes. 'Not to mean anything. Not to . . .'

'Not for being drunk,' interrupted Evans.

'For murder,' added Wooley.

'Double murder.' Evans dotted the last i, crossed the last t.

The light left her eyes. It was replaced by sadness and resignation.

'That madam he married,' she said sadly.

'And the bloke she was in bed with,' said Evans.

'I could see it coming.' Tears weren't far away. She felt in the pocket of her white smock, brought out a tiny handkerchief and blew her nose. In a steadier voice she asked, 'Where is he?'

'He's — er — he's either here at Sopworth. Or he's on his way to Beechwood Brook. He's up at court tomorrow morning.'

She nodded.

Wooley said, 'Is there anybody else we should notify?'

'No . . . just him and me.'

'He has a solicitor,' said Wooley. 'Ranson — Mr Ranson — he's a good solicitor.'

Evans said, 'Here. Sopworth Court . . . not Beechwood Brook.'

Evans and Wooley stood in silence for a few moments. Giving her time to accept the full realisation. She lowered her head, blew her nose again, then tucked the handkerchief back into its pocket and looked up at them.

'What can *I* do?' she asked.

'It's — er . . .' Evans floundered.

'The room,' said Wooley awkwardly. 'The bedroom . . .'

'The chances are he'll get bail tomorrow,' said Evans.

'And — and the bedroom. He shot them, you see.'

'With a twelve-bore. Both barrels.'

'While they were in bed.'

'It's — it's a terrible mess,' muttered Evans.

'He won't be going back there,' she said firmly. 'If he gets bail, he'll be coming home with me.'

'But — but the bedroom. It's . . .'

'I'll clean it up. Leave it to me.' Then in a grimmer voice, 'I'll even lay *her* out.'

'No!' Wooley took a deep breath. 'She's at the mortuary.'

'Where she should be,' said Daisy Wellington harshly. 'Where she should have been years ago.'

Meanwhile Witherham and Ramsden — who'd joined him at the scene of the fatal accident — were hitting snags with *their* cadavers. The ambulance men — specifically, the man who'd driven the ambulance to the scene and, obviously, the Number One of the two-man team — was being deliberately awkward. He didn't like coppers. Which, of course, didn't make him unique, but being what he was and where he was he could demonstrate his dislike via positive action. Or, more accurately, *non*-action.

'We're not a hearse,' he said dogmatically. 'The rules . . . we're not supposed to transport corpses.'

'We leave 'em here, that it?' snarled Witherham.

'That's your problem, mate.'

'Please!' Ramsden seemed to be on the point of tears. 'We have to get them moved. It's not as if . . .'

'Not in *my* ambulance you don't.'

'A bit of a Bolshevik bastard, eh?' said Witherham nastily.

'The book of rules . . .'

'Sod the book of rules.'

A squad car nosed its way through the crowd.

The ambulance man jerked his head and said, 'There's your transport.'

'For God's sake!' pleaded Ramsden.

They were grouped at the rear of the ambulance. The doors were wide open and they spoke in little more than whispers. The crowd

157

couldn't hear the exchange, but already outraged mutterings reached them from the onlookers.

Witherham hissed, 'You leave here without 'em, they'll lynch you.'

'They won't mate. I'm off.'

The ambulance man turned to return to his cab, then stopped as the doctor joined them and said, 'Trouble?'

Witherham said, 'This awkward sod won't move 'em.'

'Really?'

'They're dead,' said the ambulance man. 'We're not allowed . . .'

'Who says they're dead?' There was cold authority in the question. 'I'm a qualified medical practitioner *I* haven't pronounced life extinct.'

'You can *see*.' The ambulance man began to bluster. He'd lost his battle and he didn't like it. 'All you have to do is *look*.'

'I think they might still be alive,' said the doctor calmly. 'If you leave them here much longer they'll certainly be dead . . . but that's something *you'll* have to answer for.'

'All right,' choked the ambulance man. 'But if they *are* dead . . .'

The two ambulance men heaved the bodies onto stretchers, then lifted them onto the racks along one side of the ambulance. The 'walking wounded' clambered into the ambulance, and the doors were closed.

As the ambulance man climbed up into the cab, the doctor said, 'Beechwood Brook Cottage Hospital?'

'It's the nearest.'

'Good . . . they have a well-equipped mortuary.'

'I thought you said . . .'

'Indeed.' The doctor nodded. He looked up at the ambulance man's face, then said, 'The time you've taken, quoting from your rule book, the chances are they'll both be Dead On Arrival.'

Blakey suddenly realised how much he hated his wife; how much he hated her and how long he'd hated her. Her and her two damn daughters, each of whom were accurate reproductions of their ever-moaning mother. The realisation was sudden, but the hatred had been a slow-burning thing which had smouldered, unheeded and unrecognised, for years.

He prowled the lawn at the rear of their 'highly desirable' home on the outskirts of Beechwood Brook. And black thoughts and dark rememberings were his only companions. As for *her* . . . she was in the house, snivelling. That's how much use *she* was.

And okay — granted — he shouldn't have accepted the blasted

promotion. That in general. In particular, he shouldn't have accepted the promotion *and* Beechwood Brook Division. Beechwood Brook Division! Christ Almighty, it needed a giant to control it. It was too big by half. Ripley had controlled it, but in the end it had killed Ripley. Blayde had controlled it, but Blayde wasn't married and, anyway, he'd moved out of the Beechwood Brook D.H.Q. chair, and into C.I.D. before the damn division had had *time* to break him.

Whereas he, Blakey . . .

Stop kidding yourself, Blakey. Maybe you *could* have been another Ripley — another Blayde — but *she* put the kybosh on that particular dream. She didn't give a monkey's toss about you. Not *you*. Not Edmund Blakey. The only thing she was ever interested in was the rank. 'Chief Superintendent Blakey'. Big licks! That made her *Mrs* Chief Superintendent Blakey. Which sounded great at the W.I. meetings. Which went over great guns with the Townswomen's Guild. But you didn't matter. However many grey hairs it threaded through your thatch was of zero importance. Up you, Edmund, I'm an assistant chief constable's daughter.

Maybe that's why he'd married her. One of the reasons. Marry an assistant chief's daughter, then stand by for take-off. Some bloody assistant chief constable. Before amalgamation. Some piddling, fart-arsing force in the West Midlands. A nothing. Half a dozen fields and a farm-yard . . . not much more. But 'Daddy's the assistant chief constable'. 'Daddy does it this way'. 'Mummy does it that way'. He was pig-sick of 'Daddy' and 'Mummy'. He was equally pig-sick of their daughter . . . *and* their grand-daughters.

The truth was, he'd screwed up his life. Screwed it up solid. A
career flushed down the drain because he'd allowed

12.30 p.m.   himself to be brow-beaten by a stupid, toffee-
nosed bitch and (later) by her equally stupid, toffee-nosed daughters. How to fail. Chapter and verse. How to start big and fizzle out.

He stopped his pacing and stared at the bed of spindly-stemmed roses. His lip curled in self-contempt.

Sweet Jesus . . . he couldn't even grow roses!

Pinter grunted and opened his eyes. He hadn't meant to sleep. He'd flopped into an armchair, loosened the belt and buttons of his tunic, unfastened his shoe-laces, but he hadn't *meant* to sleep. Not with Hannah upstairs. It wasn't right. It wasn't . . .

'I'm sorry if I've disturbed you, Constable Pinter.'

Pinter blinked and hoisted himself into a more upright position.

159

The speaker was the local vicar. One of the 'modern' crowd. The dog-collar was there. So was the bib. But the light-blue safari jacket and the twill slacks and the Hush Puppies and the shoulder-length hair . . . they reminded Pinter of pop groups rather than pulpits.

The vicar smiled and said, 'I've just seen your sweet wife.'

'Has she seen you?'

The mother-in-law said, 'No, Wilf. She's . . . the same.'

'She's unconscious, I'm afraid.' The vicar still smiled. 'We knelt and offered up a prayer.'

'A prayer?' Pinter's tone was soft-spoken, but remorseless. The vicar stopped smiling. 'Any good?'

'I . . .' The vicar moistened his lips. 'We hope so.'

'D'you believe in it?'

'Prayer?'

'The lot. Prayer? The other place? What you're paid to preach?'

'Yes.' The vicar nodded.

The mother-in-law watched, silently. Sharing the hurt of her daughter's husband. Understanding, but unable to help.

'A loving God? An understanding God?' insisted Pinter.

'Yes.' Again the vicar nodded.

'Then why her?' Pinter glanced at the ceiling. 'She's never done — said — an evil thing in her life.'

'She's . . .' Again the vicar moistened his lips. 'She's going to a better place.'

'If you could ask her, she wouldn't want to.'

'Constable Pinter, I know how you feel. I know how . . .'

'The hell you do!'

'I assure you, I've . . .'

'Is *your* wife dying?'

'No, thank God.'

'When *that* happens.'

'I know.' The vicar's voice had dropped to a pleading whisper. 'But I try to understand . . . to truly understand.'

'Maybe.'

'And . . . comfort.'

'You can't comfort.' The argument was unyielding. 'You can't make her better, so you can't comfort.'

'Comfort you, then. Comfort those who suffer.'

'Vicar.' The words were as hard, as sharp, as flint chippings. 'I'd give what you call my soul to eternal damnation for one more day. One more hour. Make that deal, eh? That's the only comfort I want. The only comfort I'm interested in.'

160

The vicar closed, then opened, his eyes. He murmured, 'God bless you. Give you peace.'

He turned and left.

Pinter raised his hand to his face. He was surprised to feel the tears on his cheek. He hadn't known.

Dinner time (south of Potters Bar they called it lunch time, but up in Sopworth the meal was called dinner — a ham sandwich and a mug of tea but it was still *dinner* — therefore dinner time) and for an hour or so the market slowed down. Traders left their stalls in the keeping of neighbouring stall-holders. The Market Cafe was crowded. The pubs, too, had a sudden influx of Market Day customers.

In the main the talk was about the fatal accident. That and the same old topics of conversation . . .

'The price o' things, these days. Holy cow!'

'And it'll never be the same team again. I can remember when five Yorkshire players went to make up England. *And* against the Aussies . . .'

'Not that I've ever had it off wi' her, you understand. But from what I hear . . .'

'Bloody hell, this beer. Gnat's piss isn't in it. I'm gonna . . .'

'. . . the first pipe I ever had. A Dr Plumb's. Damn good pipes. Damn *expensive* pipes. An' it cost me half a dollar . . .'

'. . . Verity. Killed in Italy, during the war, so I'm told. They shoulda found the bugger who killed him, and strung him up by the balls . . .'

'. . . I mean — wi' a wife an' five kids — *I'm* not bloody interested. But that's what I hear . . .'

'. . . I mean, look at it. Just *look*. It hasn't a head on it worth calling a head. An' it tastes like washing-up water . . .'

The same old subjects. The same old topics. Permutated and cross-permutated. A rabble, a background noise, meaningless, fruitless and never-ending. In The Market Cafe and in the pubs. Dinner time on Market Day. Whirlpools of words spinning off from the wide flow of noise which filled the Market Square.

The side streets (the tributaries) were almost silent by comparison.

Witherham hurried along one of the side streets, taking a short cut to Sopworth Police Station. He kept his hands well clear of his clothes; the old man with the broken back had been reduced to pulp around his middle and Witherham's hands were caked in blood. Already the skirt of his tunic and his trousers were blood-spattered and would have to be sent to the dry cleaners. Something else the

161

barmpots who said it was 'a bobby's job' never mentioned.

As he reached the police station Harris's car, with a manacled Charlie Preston in the front passenger seat, pulled away from the entrance.

Witherham walked into the building, used his elbow to lift the flap of the public counter and to push open the Charge Office door.

Blayde nodded a greeting and said, 'All done and dusted?'

'Motor Patrol's taken over.'

'You *can* do it,' observed Blayde.

'Yes, sir.'

'Just — y'know — sometimes you don't *feel* like doing it?'

'I can do it, sir,' muttered Witherham belligerently.

'Nice to know, lad. Nice to know *somebody* can do it.'

They stood in the short corridor leading to Appleton Ward, four of them: four women; Bowtree, Pearson, Cooper and Noble; a nurse, a policewoman, a police constable's wife and a police sergeant's wife. Beyond them — through the glass-paned swing-doors — the beds of Appleton Ward were set alongside each wall; the high windows, the bedside lockers, the earphones and radio extensions above each bed. The men — in the main skinny, sexless creatures — slept or read or sat on the edge of beds and chatted to fellow patients. Even without being able to hear the conversation, and despite the hurrying nurses who flapped in and out of the ward via the swing-doors, there was that air of solemn desperation peculiar to a 'men's surgical'. In some strange way the patients had been mentally emasculated. They were no longer men; no longer bread-winners; no longer creatures of pride and authority. In their striped pyjamas and blanket dressing-gowns they suffered varying degrees of pain and apprehension. Pathetic creatures, eager to be fussed over and mothered.

The four women talked in lowered voices and, as they talked, two of them kept glancing through the glass into the main Appleton Ward.

Pearson said, 'Have they been told yet?'

'No.' This was Bowtree's world. She spoke with quiet certainty. 'The surgeon thinks it might be best coming from their wives.'

'Exactly what?' asked Marian Cooper.

'Your husband. He's had his hand and part of his forearm amputated. Sergeant Noble's blind.'

'Permanently?' asked Hilda Noble, and her voice was surprisingly steady.

"Fraid so,' Bowtree nodded. 'If you don't want to tell him — think you can't break the news . . .'

162

'I'll tell him.'

'It's not the end of the world,' said Bowtree. 'Be ready. At first, they'll think it is. Both of them. I'm sorry — but you want the truth — men are children. Much worse than women.'

'You mean they'll be shocked?' asked Marian Cooper.

'More than shocked. There'll be yards and yards of self-pity. There always is. It'll pass. Then bitterness . . . that's the thing to worry about. Bitterness. Get them over *that,* and you've won. They'll accept it. Sometimes — often — it makes them better people . . . once they're past the bitterness.' She paused, then added, 'Some don't pass the bitterness stage. Then you have trouble.'

The sister of May Preston was a different proposition to the sister of Charlie Preston. A very different proposition. Not to put too fine a point on it, she was a whore. This being the case, she could see no real fault in May Preston's having a bit of spare on the side. Sex being the name of *her* game, sex was the name of every other game.

Despite the time of day she was still wearing an ankle-length dressing-gown; a flashy imitation silk creation, with make-believe ostrich feathers at the neck; a garment as brash and vulgar as its wearer.

She strode around the living room of the self-contained flat — a gaudily furnished, remarkably untidy room — and smoked cigarettes in a fancy holder as she railed at Evans and Wooley.

'You'll put him away, I hope,' she stormed. 'You'll see he gets life.'

'He stands in the dock,' said Wooley bluntly. 'What happens after that doesn't concern us.'

'It had *better* concern you.'

'We don't sentence 'em.'

'Copper.' She stopped her pacing long enough to glare hatred at Wooley's face. 'I know people in this dump. Important people. He'd better get life. And I *mean* life. If he doesn't . . .'

She left the threat unfinished and resumed her pacing.

Evans said, 'We need you to identify the body.'

'You must be joking.'

'Somebody has to identify the body,' insisted Evans.

'Why?' Again, she stopped her pacing. This time she glared at Evans. 'Isn't the animal sure who he's killed?'

'He knows.'

'In that case, why the hell . . .'

'Cool it!' Wooley saw no reason to hang onto his temper. This bloody tart was too self-opinionated. Power without responsibility — that had been the claim made by harlots over the centuries — but not by this hick-town street-walker. Wooley barked, 'Cut out the act, lady. We don't give a damn who you've serviced, who you haven't serviced. All we want to know . . . can you identify your sister's body?'

'What do you think?'

'I don't know. I'm asking.'

'Sure I can identify her body.'

'Without a face? Without a head?'

That stopped her. Like hitting a brick wall, she stopped in mid-pace and almost buckled at the knees.

She croaked, 'Are you saying . . .'

'I'm *asking*,' snapped Wooley remorselessly. 'Without a head . . . can you *still* identify your sister?'

She nodded.

'How?'

'She has a birthmark. Just below the left armpit.'

'Anything else?'

'A bit of a scar — a moon-shaped scar — in the middle of her right palm.'

'Good.' Wooley nodded brief satisfaction. 'The public morgue. Eight o'clock tomorrow morning. Then you'll be needed at the inquest.'

Out in the street as they climbed into Evans's car, Evans said, 'Christ, you can be a hard man.'

'Why not?' The anger had simmered down to impatience. 'Her and her damn sister. People like that *create* murderers.'

They knew. Noble and Cooper. They'd been told; stammered words; half-finished sentences; trembling voices. They both understood. The after-effects of their operations still clouded their minds, but the information had penetrated the mist and they both knew.

1 p.m.

It was a tiny, two-bed ward. A room off the short corridor which led to Appleton Ward proper. Small enough for intimacy, but large enough to allow the three women (Muriel Pearson, Hilda Noble and Marian Cooper) room for easy movement between the two beds.

Both men were on saline drips; plastic tubes led from their bandaged upper arms to plastic containers hanging from chrome stands alongside each bed. Each had been stitched and patched, where flying fragments of metal had slashed face and chest. Noble wore a skull-

164

cap of bandaging which extended to the tip of his nose; where his eyes were – where his eyes had been – the packing was thick enough to cause the bandage to build itself up into a tiny, elongated mound. Cooper's right arm was bandaged to well above the elbow; the stump had been padded and protected until the arm-length seemed to reach as far as the wrist of his left hand.

And now they both knew the worst. Knew . . . but didn't yet appreciate.

Noble croaked, 'God, I could do with a drink of water.'

He ran a dry tongue across parched lips and turned his head a little, to where he thought his wife was sitting alongside his bed.

'Not yet, pet.'

Hilda Noble reached out, took his hand and squeezed it.

She said, 'Later. The surgeon should be coming in later. I'll ask. But they said nothing – nothing at all – until this evening.'

Slowly, he raised his hand. She guided it to her face and the tips of the fingers explored the face; gently; as if *she* was the one who'd been injured. She guided the hand to her mouth and touched the palm with her lips.

'I wish,' said Higginbottom, 'that doctors would speak the same language *we* speak.'

'And can't you remember?' Mabel, his wife, sounded very cross.

'Libby-something,' grunted Higginbottom. He bent to massage his aching ankle. 'Nothing serious . . . not from the way he said it. Summat to do with her age. That's the impression *I* got.'

'You're a fool,' grumbled his wife.

Higginbottom didn't argue.

As was his habit when he was on 'nights', Mabel had given him a shake in order that he might come downstairs and listen to the News Headlines, prior to the one o'clock magazine programme on radio. He still wore his pyjamas under the Marks and Sparks dressing-gown. His cheeks, chin and neck showed grey stubble. His hair was stuck out in every direction. Maybe he'd go back to bed, after hearing what lunacies the world leaders had concocted throughout the last twenty-four hours. Maybe he wouldn't. Maybe he'd have a spell at the allotment . . . get out of everybody's way for a couple of hours.

'You should have asked,' insisted his wife.

'I *did* ask,' he lied. 'He said every girl her age caught it.'

'It's catching, then?'

'Seems so.'

'*I* didn't catch it when I was her age.'

'Happen you were lucky.'

'Aye . . . an' happen *we'll* catch it, if we don't take precautions.'

'Gargle wi' salt and water,' he suggested.

He straightened, curled his hand around the pint pot of scalding tea, and swallowed half the contents in one gulp.

As always — as with ninety per-cent of ordinary English couples — John Henry and Mabel Higginbottom were blissfully unaware that their normal, every-day life could, with little exaggeration, form the base line for a TV situation comedy. How they lived, how they acted, how they talked . . . to an outsider it would have been side-splitting. To them, it was slightly dreary if not downright boring.

'Can't see how those pills can help,' she mused.

'They have side-effects.' He bent and began to massage his ankle again.

'Not good side-effects. Not from what I hear.'

'We dunno. *He's* the doctor.'

'D'you think he's a good doctor?' she asked anxiously.

'Not much cop. He can't even get my bloody ankle better.'

'Coop.'

Marian Cooper willed her husband to turn his face towards her; to stop staring up at the ceiling of the tiny ward. To *respond*. That's all . . . to respond! His eyes were out of focus. Dull, yet with a sheen which reflected a terrifying fury which blazed somewhere deep inside. A self-destructive emotion. Something she'd witnessed when she'd been a nurse. Not often, but just occasionally. The look of a man — never a woman — who *wanted* to die. Who'd finished with a life he'd never treasured, and wished to throw it aside, like a worn and filthy shirt.

'Coop,' she repeated softly.

But if he heard her he didn't heed. He stared at the ceiling and (she knew) yearned for death.

Rowe arrived back at Sopworth Police Station and, without calling in at the Charge Office, went straight to his office.

Blayde heard his arrival and said, 'If I'm wanted, I'm in with Inspector Rowe.'

As Blayde opened the office door Rowe was reaching for the desk telephone. He withdrew his hand, gave a half-smile and waved to an empty chair.

As Blayde sat down, Rowe said, 'All the men from Upper Neck have been sent back to normal duty.'

'Good.' Blayde brought pipe, tobacco and matches from his pocket and began the rigmarole of cleaning, filling and lighting his pipe.

'I was about to telephone Chief Superintendent Blakey,' said Rowe.

'Uhuh?'

'We — er — that is the detective sergeant and myself . . . we found one of the officers skiving. Hiding away on top of some hay when he should have been on enquiries.'

Blayde blew down the step of his pipe.

'I — er — I told the sergeant to put him on a Misconduct Report.'

'What else?' Blayde knocked the loose dottle from his pipe and into the palm of his left hand.

'I've never done it before,' said Rowe slowly.

Blayde leaned forward and dusted the dottle from his palm, into a heavy glass ashtray on Rowe's desk.

'It — it wasn't easy.'

'Not the first time.' Blayde began to finger shredded tobacco from pouch to pipe. 'In time, it gets *too* easy.'

'I — I wouldn't know.'

'Had a break yet?' The finger continued to curl the shreds into the bowl. 'You've been on since . . .what time?'

'About half past four.'

'Without a break?'

'I had coffee at the hospital. I'll slip out for a . . .'

'Your wife's a teacher, isn't she?'

'Yes.' Rowe nodded.

'You'll be eating alone?'

'I always do.' Rowe looked puzzled. 'I don't count my midday meal as being important. I usually . . .'

'Home-cured ham and fresh farm eggs,' said Blayde as he placed the stem of his pipe between his teeth.

'I'm sorry, sir. I don't . . .'

'That's what *I'm* going to have. Care to join me?'

'That's — that's very nice of you, but . . .'

'Forget Blakey, for the moment.' Blayde stood up, returned the pouch to its pocket, then struck a match. 'There's an ancient constabulary monument out there in the Charge Office.'

'Constable Pollard.'

'Let him know where you are — at my place — he'll be glad to get us from under his feet.'

A strange expression flickered across Rowe's face. Part joy, part shock, part relief. He blinked. Just for a moment — just for a split second — he seemed to be on the verge of tears.

'Take it or leave it.' Blayde stroked the flame of the match along the surface of the tobacco.

'I'll take it.' A smile — a genuine, honest-to-God smile, and the first he'd enjoyed for as long as he could remember — illuminated Rowe's face. 'I'll take it . . . gladly.'

Tallboy was already seated at a table eating his midday meal. He'd left Kelly and Kyle at Beechwood Brook D.H.Q. Peacock was tucked away in a police cell. At a guess (and if they'd any sense) Kelly and Kyle would have found some decent cafe. The case was as good as cracked — certainly there was already enough to slap Peacock in front of tomorrow's Occasional Court and enough to oppose any suggestion of bail — from here on it was simply heads down and keep grinding. Brother Peacock would, eventually, end up where the pigeons couldn't mess on him for a long, long time.

Meanwhile . . .

As she fed more freshly fried chips alongside the egg and sausages, Susan Tallboy said what a few thousand police wives had said a few thousand times before.

'You have to eat.'

'I'm eating.' And, to prove the point, Tallboy spoke through a mouthful of food.

'I mean really eat.'

'This.' Tallboy moved his knife and fork, like twin magic wands, over the plate. 'Egg, sausage and chips. Couldn't be better.'

'Not everything from a frying pan,' insisted Susan.

And, having delivered the remark, she joined her husband at the table and began eating . . . egg, sausage and chips.

She said, 'You'll end up with ulcers.'

'A bad tempered old devil.'

'You can be that, already.'

'Maybe I already *have* ulcers.' He grinned at her.

'I've known you . . . ' She waved her fork at him accusingly. 'I've known you to go three days — three days — without *anything*. No sleep. No proper meal. No rest. Nothing!'

'Fags and tea, sweetheart.' His smile was a tease. 'I reckon a copper — any copper worth his salt — could circumnavigate the world on fags and tea.'

'Don't you try it, that's all.'

They were quite a pair. Quite a combination. In their middle years, with a marriage old enough to have begun to go stale on many people, they were (in effect) still on their honeymoon. It didn't often happen, but it had happened with *them*. Susan Tallboy was getting just a little wide around the waist, her brassiere size was two up on the size she'd worn on the day of their wedding but, to Tallboy, she remained female perfection personified. Chris Tallboy, too; with the greying hair had come those facial creases which men earn as the years pass; he was still fit, but not as fit as he'd once been; he tried to be adaptable, but only partly succeeded, which meant he was more set in his ways (therefore more prone to impatience than he'd once been) and tended to suffer fools less gladly than had once been the case. And yet each could see no fault in the other. A little thing called 'love'. They had it in abundance. Nor were they ashamed of it,

1.30 p.m.   nor saw any reason to be ashamed of it. It was what made them tick. It was the bedrock of their life. Other men were policemen first, husbands second. Chris Tallboy was Susan Tallboy's husband, and that before *everything*. And she — because she was the daughter of a policeman who had once almost allowed the job to ruin a similar marriage — knew the value of this, and gave as much as she received. They were husband and wife, lover and mistress and — which was also of vital importance — pals. No secrets. No 'nights out with the boys'. No 'evenings with the other ladies of the district'. Complete in themselves.

She said, 'You think this Peacock man did it?'

'Nothing surer.'

'What sort of man is he?'

'A slob.'

'Chris, that's no answer.' She was serious. Worried. 'A man who wants to kill a policeman because . . .'

'There's your answer.' Tallboy forked food into his mouth. 'He wants to kill a copper, because that copper did his job.'

'That's no reason.'

'It's *his* reason.'

'And you *understand* it?' She looked amazed.

'No, my pet.' His seriousness matched hers. 'I don't understand it. I'm not paid to understand it.' He paused, then said, 'The old days are past, sweetheart. The days your father knew. The days *I* knew, when I first joined. The scum are still scum, but they're being written about by learned people. Our attitude . . . they're scum, because they do these things. It's been reversed. They do this sort of thing *because* they're scum, and we — the police — have *made* them scum.

That's the modern theory. It's crazy. It's like saying a soldier — a P.B.I. — is responsible for a war. We don't prevent trouble. We *make* trouble. The great 'low profile' tactic. Have the coppers there, but don't let anybody *see* 'em. It's pure bullshit. Let 'em see the coppers. Hundreds of 'em. Thousands, if necessary. Let 'em know what's going to happen if they step out of line. Then they *won't* step out of line. As it is . . .' He sighed. 'We're being dictated to by high-minded amateurs. And what's happened to Noble and Cooper is a spin-off.'

The last call — the last 'notification' — was at Jack Sutcliffe's farm, and Evans and Wooley had already agreed that a meal-break would be very nice up on The Tops. A decent, country cafe, with home-made grub. Good scoff at reasonable prices. After what *they'd* done, they deserved it.

Meanwhile Mr Jack Sutcliffe . . .

Jack Sutcliffe had been up since before six; up and about; working and shooting. His 'place' (as he called it) was Spa Top Farm; originally a holding of eighty-seven acres which, over the years and by dint of careful purchase, he'd extended to almost two-hundred acres. And he was still open for expansion . . . if the price was right.

The marvel was that he worked it alone. He asked no help from his wife; a wife's place was in the home and, as far as Jack Sutcliffe was concerned, that's where she stayed. His two sons? Such men drive their children (sons or daughters) out of their lives without consciously wishing to do so. They refuse to bend and nothing can break them. He *had* two sons. Where they were, what they were doing . . . he didn't know and he didn't care.

Question him as to what sort of farmer he was and he'd say, 'A bit of owt . . . as long as it pays,' and he'd be telling no less than the truth. A few pigs, a few score head of cattle, sheep, poultry, a dozen or so goats. He worked livestock. He bought 'em young, fattened them on the tough grass of his fields, then sold them for a profit. And everything — *everything* — that walked, ran or flew over his land was his.

And that included his wife and family . . . as long as they slept under his roof.

A truly strange man. Thick-limbed and bull-necked, he removed the stained cap which sat squarely upon his close-cropped head only when he undressed for bed. It was a gesture. 'I doff my cap to no man.' That was his creed, and he lived it every minute of his waking life. His pride was a terrible thing. It kept him apart, and aloof, from his fellow men, and that was how he wished it. He was a deeply religious man, but no church- or chapel-goer. Once (years ago) he'd tried The Plymouth Brethren for size, but had found even that organisation far too wishy-washy for *his* taste. His creed was pure Old Testament stuff; man in the image of God and only fractionally less all-powerful than God; a hellfire-and-damnation belief, based upon fear, necessary cruelty and absolute domination. A strange and terrible man.

He'd stumped into the stone-floored kitchen of his farmhouse, dropped two brace of pigeons on the large, plain-topped, deal table, then placed the single-shot .22 on its rack on the wall beneath the companion twelve-bore.

He'd growled, 'I'll have my meal now, woman,' then sat at the table, away from the blood-marked pigeons, pulled a huge, black-backed Bible nearer and, opening it at a marked page, had begun reading. As he read his lips had silently mouthed the words and a thick index finger had followed the text.

His wife, Martha, had brushed a wisp of iron-grey hair from the front of her face, then scurried between the massive, old-fashioned 'Yorkist' range and the table, setting out a meal large enough to have satisfied three normal men.

And now he'd finished eating. He still fingered and read the Bible, while his wife collected the plates and cutlery and carried them to the huge stone sink.

They heard the car brake to a halt, heard the engine stop, heard the car doors open and close, then heard the knock on the kitchen door.

Martha Sutcliffe glanced at her husband for instructions.

'Answer it,' he grunted and continued reading.

Evans and Wooley entered the kitchen and Evans said, 'Mr Sutcliffe?'

'Who wants to know?' Sutcliffe continued reading and mouthing the words.

'Police.'

'Oh, aye?' Still Sutcliffe didn't look up.

'It's about your brother.'

'Oh, aye?'

'He's dead.'

Sutcliffe growled, 'Oh, aye?' a third time, then slowly — very reluctantly — raised his head. His finger pinned the point at which he'd stopped reading.

'He's dead,' repeated Evans.

'I 'eard you.'

171

'A violent death,' amplified Wooley awkwardly.

'Nobody'll miss him,' rumbled Sutcliffe.

'He was . . . murdered,' gulped Evans.

'Oh, aye?'

'He was with a woman — another man's wife — and the man came home unexpectedly and — and . . . shot them both. Both of 'em.'

'Fornicators.' Sutcliffe's lips curled.

'Well — er . . . yes. That's — that's what they were,' stammered Evans. 'That's what they were — y'know — *doing*.'

'Cursed are the fornicators,' growled Sutcliffe.

'Eh?'

'Their souls shall be devoured by everlasting fire.'

'Oh!'

'We — er — we need you to identify the body,' said Evans, getting down to business.

'His body?'

'Yes. But — y'see — there isn't a head. There isn't a face.'

'He was a weak man,' rumbled Sutcliffe.

'Yes, but, y'see, without a face . . .'

'Are you being deliberately offensive?'

'Eh?' Evans gaped.

'Are you suggesting I can't recognise my own blood?'

'Well — er — no . . . not exactly. But . . .'

'When?' growled Sutcliffe.

'Tomorrow. Tomorrow morning.'

'Where?'

'Sopworth. Sopworth Public mortuary.'

'I'll be there at half past five.'

Evans made as if to say something, but Wooley said, 'I'll be there, Mr Sutcliffe.'

Sutcliffe nodded his head once, rumbled, 'Good day young men,' then returned to his reading of the Bible.

Mrs Sutcliffe shooed them from the kitchen and, as they climbed back into the car, Wooley said, 'A bit of a one-off job.'

'A bloody good job they don't give one of *him* with every packet of jelly babies.'

Thereafter food; food and, with some officers of Sopworth Section, a shift change. It varied. Each day was different. Some days those last thirty minutes of an eight-hour spell dragged; each minute seemed like an hour and that last half-hour seemed longer than the previous seven-and-a-half. On other days, one o'clock became two o'clock with the speed of light. But sometimes — and at each shift change the men going off duty dreaded the possibility — with ten, sometimes even five, minutes to go something happened. A suicide. A motor car pile-up. A wounding. Anything. It could happen within minutes of knocking-off time . . . and it couldn't be left for the next shift to deal with. Then there was frustration, ill temper and overtime.

But not on this day.

On this day Pollard and Witherham packed away their bits and pieces and made ready to hand the section over to *2 p.m.* Bob Sowe and Fred Hinton. Sergeant Ramsden slipped home for a quick snack; he and Cockburn had arranged for a change over at five. Pinter was still doing a 'twenty-four-hour-cover' of Upper Neck and Rimstone Beats; Cooper was in hospital, Kyle was at Beechwood Brook and Karn was at home, feeling sorry for himself and wondering whether his future career in the Police Service could now be counted in days. As for W.P.C. Pearson, she was doing a 'vamp-till-ready' stint at Bordfield General Infirmary; in effect, she had two badly injured police officers and their distressed wives under her wing, and *she* was off duty only when she was satisfied that some sort of equilibrium had been reached.

Harris was in his office at Bordfield Regional Headquarters, catching up on the paperwork. Scrawling his name on forms and documents . . . and hoping to hell the day had seen its full quota of general cock-ups.

At his cottage Blayde was a changed man. Or so it seemed to Inspector William Henry Rowe. A small thing, but who would ever have equated Blayde with real culinary skill? Okay, he lived alone, therefore he looked after himself, but the man could *cook*. Equally ham and eggs — who *can't* fry ham and eggs? — but few men, few women, can fry them to perfection. Two eggs each; free range, fresh and done not a second too little or a second too long. A slice of ham each; quarter-of-an-inch thick, newly sliced, covering more than half the dinner plate and fried in its own juice until it almost melted in the mouth. Freshly baked bread rolls. Farm butter. And real coffee — ground, then percolated, then served — not in thimble-sized cups but in half-pint beakers.

Rowe dabbed his mouth with a napkin and said, 'Delicious.'

'I live well,' chuckled Blayde. 'The perks of bachelorhood. It has its advantages.' Then, almost as a throw-away remark, 'What makes you so scared of Harris? Of Blakey, come to that?'

'I'm — I'm not *frightened* of them.' Rowe coloured.

173

'You are,' contradicted Blayde, 'and it interests me.'

'They're my superior officers. Like you are.'

'No.' Blayde shook his head. '*Senior.* There's a world of difference. Senior, not superior.'

'Very well . . . senior officers.'

'Tell me to mind my own business.' Blayde topped Rowe's beaker with more coffee, then topped his own. 'We'll change the subject, if that's what you want.'

Rowe spooned brown sugar into the coffee, seemed to give thought to the proposition then, in a quiet tone, said, 'No. I'm open to advice.'

'Blakey.' Blayde reached across for the sugar bowl.

'He's my chief superintendent.'

'You let him walk all over you.'

'I tend to take the easy way out . . . that's what my wife tells me.'

'It's not. Not in the long run.'

'She tells me that, too.'

'A sensible woman. You should listen to her.' Blayde stirred his coffee slowly. He continued as if voicing a creed, as if Rowe wasn't there. 'Above a certain rank. Superintendent and above. Especially uniformed officers. Divisional officers . . . like Blakey. They can make their mark one of two ways: they can choose their underlings with care, that's the easy way. Gather a team — a *good* team — inspectors, sergeants, constables. Weed the no-goods out. Then sit back and let 'em get on with it. Don't interfere. Don't meddle. Keep in the background and collect the kudos. I've known a lot of men end up with reputations they didn't deserve by working things *that* way.

'The other way. Let's call it "Ripley's Way". I followed Charlie Ripley, as chief super of this division. Nobody has to tell me what sort of man *he* was. Those men *earn* a reputation, personally. They can take anything — anybody — the good, the bad, the indifferent — and *make* them into a team. Some of it's by setting an example, but it's more than that. Charisma, that's part of it, a special personality. Ripley had it by the ton. And another one. Collins.' Blayde glanced up. 'Heard of Collins?'

'He was in the old Lessford City Force?'

'That's him.' Blayde nodded. 'Chief Superintendent. Hallsworth Hill Division. A little bit like you.'

'That I very much doubt,' smiled Rowe.

'Uhuh.' Blayde nodded slowly. 'Quiet. Never swore. Rarely raised his voice. Very gentlemanly. Blue chip, though, scared of damn-all.'

'Therefore, *not* like me.'

'You,' said Blayde solemnly, 'have let Blakey squeeze all the vinegar out of you. That's all. You pegged a man today.'

'Karn. My first.'

'So did I,' said Blayde. 'Witherham, and I didn't enjoy doing it any more than you did.'

'I don't see . . .'

'That's what made Collins great. And Ripley. To my certain knowledge neither of 'em needed a Misconduct Form . . . ever. They led from the front. They didn't wield a big stick and drive from behind.'

'It's the best way,' sighed Rowe.

'The hard way.'

Rowe looked puzzled, and said, 'I still don't see what . . .'

'Let's talk about Blakey.' Blayde sipped his coffee. 'How many years?'

'Since he became my superior — er — *senior* officer?'

Blayde nodded.

'Four. Closing five.'

'He's ridden you,' said Blayde flatly.

'Sometimes,' admitted Rowe.

'*Always*. I know the type. Everybody plays long-stop to his kind. You've picked red-hot goolies up for him for four years.'

Rowe shrugged.

'And never passed them down the line.'

'I accept the responsibility of the rank, that's all.'

'Your responsibility . . . plus Blakey's.'

'I — er — I don't like talking about my chief superintendent behind his back. I appreciate . . .'

'Don't be loyal to a man who no longer exists,' said Blaye, gruffly.

'What?' Rowe's eyes widened.

'Edmund Blakey.' Blayde sipped at his coffee. 'But no longer Chief Superintendent Edmund Blakey.'

'Oh!' Rowe frowned, then said, 'Harris dropped a hint. Earlier today. But I didn't know . . .'

'Blakey didn't know.' Again Blayde sipped from his beaker. 'Harris was all set for sacking him. Blakey beat him to the punch . . . resigned.'

'Blakey did?' Rowe looked amazed.

'So, forget Blakey.' Blayde smiled. 'Start a new page. Start a whole new book.'

Rowe took a deep breath and let it out slowly.

'Tallboy?' suggested Blayde gently.

'What about Tallboy?'

'Harris has him lined up. For Blakey's chair. He might be able to do it, too. He's *sure* he can.'

'That would be nice.' The pleasure wasn't feigned. It lit up Rowe's face. 'That would be *very* nice. I like Chris very much indeed.'

'Who knows?' murmured Blayde. 'Maybe even a new library.'

Fred Hinton took over from Pollard at the mighty Wurlitzer . . . this being Hinton's pet name for the switchboard-plus-teleprinter-plus-microphone. Hinton had a very personal — very private — sense of the ridiculous. It did much to keep him sane. With a Mongoloid child and a forever-griping father-in-law who lived with them, Fred Hinton *needed* something to keep him sane. 'It could be worse,' he'd say with a grin. 'I could have a Mongoloid father-in-law and a bitching bugger for a kid.' He was known to have a weakness for the old tonsil varnish, but who the hell could blame him? That, too, helped to keep him on an even keel.

He glanced at the entries in the Telephone and Teleprinter Message Book, scrawled his signature along with the time and date in the margin alongside the last entry, then answered the buzz of the bell-push at the public counter. And, as soon as he saw the visitor, Hinton knew.

Captain Cecil Harvey was what the Victorians might have called a 'card'. What many of the less polite coppers of Sopworth called 'a bloody nuisance'. At a guess, Harvey spent sleepless nights figuring out ways in which the minor laws of the land might be by-passed; how he, one of the lesser lords of creation, might not be inconvenienced by the operation of such laws. The seat of his pants was nearer to the ground than most men's, and God only knew what he'd ever been 'captain' of, but his ego was such that he refused to acknowledge any remark which didn't include the full style and title. He was an active member of, and an acute embarrassment to, the local Freemason Lodge; he claimed to be a good friend of the chief constable (which was false) and a form of blood-brother to Chief Superintendent Blakey . . . which was true. He demanded preferential treatment (which he sometimes got) and treated every police officer as a personal lackey . . . which, had he had the gumption to realise such things, made life just that mite more harrowing for him.

Hinton saw him, smiled broadly, then said, 'Ah, Captain Cecil Harvey. About your car, I presume?'

'What?' Harvey glared.

'It's been stolen,' said Hinton happily.

'How the devil did *you* know?'

'It always is,' explained Hinton. 'This is the fourth time in as many weeks. It's getting to be an addiction . . . don't you think?'

'What?' Harvey had been caught one-footed. He expected – indeed he *demanded* – that mere police constables fawn in his presence. And this one wasn't fawning. This one was grinning like a loon, and quietly removing all the oil from Harvey's lamp . . . and it was something Harvey wasn't used to.

'You parked it – don't tell me . . .' Hinton eyed the ceiling for inspiration. 'You parked it very carefully, somewhere where parking is allowed. When we find it, it'll be somewhere where parking *isn't* allowed . . . and there'll be a traffic warden's ticket under one of the wipers.'

'Are you being impertinent?' barked Harvey.

Hinton's smile broadened, as he said, 'I'm the seventh son of a seventh son, didn't you know?'

'I'm here to report the theft of my motor car. And I'm damned if . . .'

'And we'll find it for you. Never fear – we'll find it for you – if we have to use hazel twigs.' Hinton flipped a mock-salute at the red-faced Harvey, then disappeared into the Charge Office.

He picked up the microphone and said, 'Bob. Are you with me, yet?'

From the loudspeaker Sowe's voice said, 'Just about.'

'Captain Cecil Harvey.' Hinton spaced each word very deliberately. 'Guess what?'

'He's had his Merc pinched.'

'Such a careless man. No wonder it took us five years to win the bloody war.'

'As we arranged?' Sowe's voice sounded solemn and mysterious.

'I think so.' Then, Hinton added, 'He has a very juicy smell about his breath. Try the area around The Constitutional Club.'

'I'll be back,' promised Sowe.

Hinton returned to the public counter and beamed bonhomie at the irate Harvey.

'It's happening,' he promised.

'I don't know what the devil you . . .'

'We have,' said Hinton cheerfully, 'perfected a system. For finding motor cars . . . specifically *your* motor car. I doubt if you'll have need to report it stolen again. This system. It's foolproof.' He opened a drawer on the official side of the counter, took out a sheet of foolscap, slipped a ballpoint from his tunic pocket, then said, 'Now, the details.'

'You already know the blasted . . .'

'Captain Harvey.' Hinton looked as if he might wag a reproving finger. 'A man who holds Her Majesty's commission. You should *know*. Forms. Duplicate, triplicate. We start from square one every time. Now, your name and address, please. And please spell each name and word very carefully. You never know. We don't want any mistakes, do we?'

In the corridor outside Appleton Ward, Marian Cooper broke all the rules by smoking a cigarette. The 'No Smoking' notice was ignored. Nurse Bowtree and the white-coated medic made no comment — raised no objections — it was a situation in which the smoking of a cigarette was of no importance whatever.

'I'm a qualified nurse,' said Marian Cooper in a low voice. 'I'm not some hysterical wife, here to be calmed down and fobbed off with the usual he'll-be-better-after-a-good-night's-sleep garbage. He can hear me. He can understand me. But he just doesn't want to *know*.'

The medic glanced questioningly at Bowtree.

Bowtree said, 'He's — er —awkward, doctor. He won't even answer questions.'

'Why d'you think that is?' The medic looked at Marian Cooper.

'He's . . .' She sought around for words. 'He's a proud man. A sensitive man.'

'Self-pity, perhaps?' The medic raised questioning eyebrows.

'Self-disgust,' said Marian Cooper.

'I'm sorry.' The medic smiled. 'I don't follow.'

'It's . . . hard to explain.'

Hard to explain? *Impossible* to explain. These people — these doctors and nurses — they were babes in arms when it came to the more subtle forms of suffering. She knew; she knew this as one of the great weaknesses of a well-functioning hospital. Open it up, take it off, stitch it together again. The answer to all things. Run a few tests, find the seat of the pain, diagnose the symptoms, dope it down or whip it out . . . next patient, please.

The medic murmured, 'I'd better have a word with him.'

But you fool — you poor, benighted, text-book-blinded fool — you *can't* 'have a word with him'. That old bedside manner won't work unless there's somebody in the bed. A dummy. A zombie. A *nothing*! You can talk till your teeth rot, but he won't answer. He won't

178

react. He won't smile back at you and obediently say, 'Yes, doctor,' or 'No, doctor' . . . or *anything*. You don't exist. As far as he's concerned *you* don't exist, because he doesn't *want* to exist. To acknowledge you would be tantamount to acknowledging himself.

God in all his glory! Don't they even teach *basic* psychology these days?

The three of them single-filed into the room. Pearson and Hilda Noble looked up.

Noble muttered, 'What is it? What's . . .'

'It's all right, pet.' Hilda Noble squeezed her husband's hand.

The medic unhooked the clipboard from the foot of Cooper's bed. He made great play at reading the dots and graphs. He took a step towards Cooper, lifted Cooper's uninjured hand and held the wrist while he stared solemnly at his own wrist-watch. Cooper offered no resistance. Didn't turn his head. Continued to stare up at the ceiling.

The medic lowered the hand back onto the bed, cleared his throat, smiled, then spoke.

'Now, old man, feeling a little under the weather, are we?'

Marian Cooper almost screamed. It was so infernally senseless. So monumentally stupid. He wasn't talking to a child. Come to that, he wasn't talking to a man who'd just come from the operating theatre . . . not *just* a man who'd come from the operating theatre.

'Mustn't feel *too* sorry for ourselves, y'know,' waffled the medic. 'Everything's going on fine.'

No, damn you . . . everything is *not* 'going on fine'. Everything has been screwed up to hell and beyond. That human being you're talking to is my husband. *Was* my husband. I'm the one he trusts. Nobody else, and certainly not a bumbling idiot like you.

'Everything's going on fine, y'know,' repeated the medic. This time in a more authoritarian tone. 'We need your help, of course. Can't do much without the help of the patient.'

Cooper stared at the ceiling. Not so much as blinking. Not listening, not hearing, not responding.

In a much sterner tone the medic began, 'Cooper, I'm not . . .'

'That's enough!' choked Marian Cooper.

'Mrs Cooper, I assure you . . .'

'Enough!' The tone allowed no room for argument.

Hilda Noble touched Marian Cooper's hand. Pearson watched, silent and helpless. Bowtree sighed and shook her head. The medic tightened his lips, replaced the clipboard and led Bowtree and Marian Cooper out of the side-ward and back into the corridor.

179

As Bowtree closed the door, the medic said, 'Mrs Cooper, that was a . . .'

'You're a fool,' flashed Marian Cooper. The medic took it like a slap across the face but, before he could reply, she continued, 'You think you can *bully* him into responding? You think he's some sort of child? That he's *afraid* of you . . . or ten more like you?'

'He's obviously afraid of something,' said the medic tightly. 'Of life, perhaps. Of life with only one hand. If that's the case, the sooner . . .'

'He's afraid of nothing.' Marian Cooper's tone was cooler. Cooler, but as determined as ever. 'That's my man, in there, doctor. I know him better than you know him. Better than you'll ever know him. And neither you nor I can frighten him into altering a decision he's already made.'

'I can see no signs of a decision. All I can see . . .'

'All you can see is a man without a hand. All *he* can see is a future he wants no part of. The future of an incomplete man . . . and he won't accept it.'

'He hasn't much option, has he?' said the medic nastily.

'*He* has.'

'I really can't see the sense in . . .'

'With a man like you, there'd be no option. And — all right — that's what you're taught. That's what you've learned. But to him . . .' She allowed herself the luxury of a twisted smile. A quick smile of triumph; as if she knew something the medic would never know. 'With him there's an option. Death. He's willing himself to die.'

Police Constable Robert Sowe, 2564, found the Merc where his buddy had suggested it might be. Within two streets of The Constitution Club. And, moreover, standing almost alongside a socking great notice which read 'No Parking'. The cellophane envelope tucked behind one of the windscreen wipers told its own tale; some traffic warden had strolled that way.

So, of course, had Captain Cecil Harvey who, having spotted the cellophane envelope, had continued on his way to the police station, there to report the 'theft' of his car, and thus provide himself with a water-tight answer to the unlawful parking charge and, at the same time, saddle hard-working coppers with a bundle of useless bumpf. The smart-Alicks of the motoring fraternity knew the gag off by heart. Harvey pulled it with a regularity which bordered upon the monotonous.

Sowe strolled up to the Merc. He slipped a box of matches from his pocket. Near the front nearside wheel he bent to check his shoe-laces, and at the same time he unscrewed the dust-cap from the tyre-valve and jammed a match against the tiny spindle of the valve. He checked his shoe-laces four times; front nearside, rear nearside, rear offside and front offside. Then he walked casually to the nearest corner and waited until all four tyres were flattened.

He continued his patrol and, as he neared the market, he raised his walkie-talkie to his mouth and spoke to Hinton.

Detective Constable Evans was not amused. The realisation that, without Wooley, he'd be steering a one-man course *2.30 p.m.* across an uncharted ocean filled him with trepidation. Without Wooley he would be lonely and alone. There'd be no back-up. Only Blayde . . . and the greater the distance between himself and Blayde the happier Evans would be.

'Look, Taffy,' said Wooley, in a reasonable voice, 'we've done all the dirty work.'

'Easy,' grumbled Evans. 'It's the paperwork that takes up the time.'

'It's *your* case.'

'How the hell can it be *my* case? A double murder. How the hell can one man handle a double murder enquiry?'

'I was on patrol duty all last night,' said Wooley patiently. 'I was lumbered — all right I volunteered — to give you a hand, because I called in at the nick to see how Coop and Noble were going on. I'm on patrol duty again tonight. I need sleep, Taffy. And it *is* your case.'

'You can fix things with Cockburn.'

'I don't want to fix things with Cockburn. I don't want some other poor sod to do my night shift.'

'It was okay when it was easy, eh? You didn't mind . . .'

'Easy?' Wooley's voice tightened. 'Y'mean when you were puking your heart out? When you didn't even want to *look*?'

Evans stared ahead through the windscreen. His mouth took on a petulant curve. Okay, so he hadn't the stomach of this Wooley bastard. Blood upset him. He didn't like handling corpses. But that was no reason. He, Evans, was the jack. Wooley was a bloody door-knob-turner. A uniformed jerk. And now Wooley was being stroppy. Moving out when he'd had enough.

In a more friendly tone, Wooley said, 'I'll meet Sutcliffe's brother. Get that particular identification sewn up.'

'Don't bother,' snapped Evans.

'What the hell!' Wooley stared.

'I'll drop you at your lodgings.'

'Okay.' Wooley shrugged. 'I *won't* meet Sutcliffe's brother.'

'Don't do another damn thing,' said Evans angrily.

And (although, in time, neither of them remembered) that was how it began. Such a tiny, unimportant thing. And yet, years later — when Evans had made Detective Sergeant and Wooley had made Uniformed Inspector — the needle was as sharp as ever. Dislike had bloomed into outright hatred. And that silly exchange (although neither realised it) was the tiny seed from which the hatred grew.

Police Constable 1956 Hinton returned to the public counter from the Charge Office. He smiled at the fuming Harvey and said, 'That's service for you, sir. We've found your car.'

'Really?'

'Felix Lane. Know where Felix Lane is, sir?'

'Of course I know where . . .'

'Not too far from The Constitutional Club.'

'I *know* that.'

'You might have parked it there yourself,' mused Hinton in a friendly tone.

'What? Are you . . .'

'I'm not suggesting you *did*,' interrupted Hinton. 'I mean, *you* wouldn't break the parking laws . . . would you? And, if you did, you wouldn't leave your car with four flat tyres.'

'I wouldn't . . .' Harvey's jaw dropped.

'"Fraid so.' Hinton smiled a sympathetic smile. 'Somebody in this town doesn't like you, *Captain* Harvey. They're forever pinching your car. And now they've started letting the air out of your tyres.'

'You — you mean to tell me . . .'

'All four.' Hinton nodded.

'They were perfectly all right when I left the car.'

'Of course.' Hinton stared, mockingly, into Harvey's eyes. 'But *you* didn't leave it in Felix Lane . . . did you?'

'Dammit . . . of course I didn't.'

'Of *course* you didn't,' agreed Hinton.

'What the — what the devil are you going to do about it, then?'

'Do about what, sir?'

'My blasted car?'

'It's in Felix Lane, sir. Waiting for you to collect it.'

'But the damn tyres. You say they're . . .'

'Ah, now that doesn't come within our province, sir.'

'What?'

182

'You need a garage, sir. Not a police station.'

Harvey would have liked to stay and argue. Indeed, he would have liked to reduce Sopworth Police Station, and its full complement of police officers, to a heap of demoralised rubble. But the imp of mockery which danced at the back of Hinton's eyes dared him to even try. Instead, he stormed his way back to the street.

He passed the returning Sergeant Ramsden and, after glancing at the retreating Harvey's back, Ramsden said, 'What did *he* want?'

'Directions.' A po-faced Hinton ripped the time-wasting documents he'd completed, then dropped them into the wastepaper bin.

'Directions?'

'Street directions. The way to Felix Lane.'

'But . . .' Ramsden turned to stare at the door. 'That was Harvey. He must *know* where Felix Lane is.'

'He's getting old, sarge. Doting a bit. He couldn't remember where he'd parked his car.'

And in Bradford at street corners, in sleazy cafes and on patches of waste ground one would-be punkie sought assistance from his kind in the regaining of his ruptured pride.

Woman Police Constable 1324 Pearson was feeling the pace. She'd been up since just after five; wet-nursing two police wives and, at the same time, worrying herself stupid about two injured colleagues. Never had eight hours − little more than eight hours − seemed so long. The bone weariness produced a vague, indefinable ache which seemed to permeate her whole body. It hunched her shoulders. It brought a mild, but irritating pain in the small of her back. It seemed to have wrapped her brain in thick layers of cotton wool.

'God, you look *awful.*'

Tony, her boy-friend, was on duty and they'd almost collided with each other before she'd recognised him.

'I *feel* awful,' sighed Pearson. 'And God only knows how long I'll have to stay here.'

'Your two wounded warriors?' grinned Tony.

'It isn't funny.' She ran fingers through her dishevelled hair. 'It's not a bit funny. Coop's behaving like a spoiled brat, and it's driving his wife up the wall.'

'Coop? Oh, y'mean Cooper? The one who's lost his sight?'

'No, that's Noble. He's fine. He's that sort of bloke. Coop's lost a hand.'

'It's not the end of the . . .'

'For Christ's sake!' It was a whispered scream. 'Don't say "It's not the end of the world" . . . *please*. That bloody phrase. Everybody's used it. For Coop it *is* the end of the world. His world.'

'You sound . . .' He stopped, and a watered-down version of the grin took over.

'What?'

'As if — y'know — you fancy him.'

'Oh, my God!'

'That's what it sounds like.'

'Tony,' she pleaded in a tired voice, 'at this moment I don't fancy anybody. Not even you. Coop? Okay, he'd make a smashing brother. An elder brother. Somebody I could *really* bawl out when he behaves like he is doing now.'

'Bawl him out,' suggested Tony bluntly.

'With his wife there? With Noble — blind— listening in the next bed?'

'Tell his wife. Tell *her* to bawl him out.'

'I'm tired,' said Pearson heavily. 'I'm tired and I'm hungry. I can't think straight. I need a breather.'

'Eat,' said Tony simply. 'There's a canteen — a very good canteen — you've used it before.'

'Uhuh.' Pearson nodded. Then she said, 'I'll collect the two wives. They have to eat, too.'

'You,' said Tony, 'are a glutton for punishment.'

'Could be.'

'Good luck, my love.' He glanced around, then stooped and kissed her quickly on the mouth. As he turned to go about his duties, he added, 'My place, tonight. It'll save you a long drive.'

'I'll be there,' she promised.

Ramsden took the call from Leeds City. He flexed his shoulders in an attempt to ease the tiredness. Having identified himself to the Leeds City switchboard operator, he waited for the clicks and buzzes to cease.

A man's voice said, 'C.I.D. Office, here. We have a guest you might want to talk to.'

'Who's that?' Ramsden frowned. He didn't like this off-handed manner of the big city boys.

'A character called Alfie Bingham. Know him?'

'No.'

'Motor Patrol picked him up last night. Nicking timber.'

'Timber?'

'From a wood-yard. A length of wood. Just after midnight.'

'I don't see what . . .'

'No Fixed Abode. Living rough. He's been through your area.'

'You think he might have committed crime over here?'

'*Think?*' There was a quick chuckle. 'He's coughed a murder . . . that's all.'

'Whaaa . . .'

'Last year. A teenage girl.'

'But that's impossible. We haven't any record of . . .'

'He'll tell you. We'll hoick him across. It should make your crime stats look much healthier.'

'I tell you. We haven't any . . .'

Ramsden stared at the dead receiver and wondered just what the hell next. Just what the hell *next*? A double murder. A double wounding. And now this!

He returned the receiver to its rest, then lowered himself onto the chair which stood within the alcove-cum-ante-room.

It just wasn't on. Damn and blast it . . . it just wasn't *on*. This section — Sopworth Section — seven working coppers, a detective constable, a police woman, three sergeants, plus four outside-beat men and a useless bugger for an inspector. That when they were at full strength. That when they were firing on all cylinders. They could cope. Given any ordinary, run-of-the-mill day they could cope. Things were stretched a little on market day, the bloody traffic was a weekly headache, but they could cope. Get some homicidal lunatic leaving exploding torches around for unwary coppers to pick up, but they could still cope . . . it meant switching the shifts around a little, but they could still cope. Get some bloke like Charlie Preston going berserk and blowing his wife and her fancy man to kingdom come, they could *still* cope . . . more shift changes, a bit thin on the ground, but they could still cope.

But this!

Always in bloody threes. For no reason — but there had to *be* a reason —everything in threes. Something magical about that number. Get a suicide . . . stand by for the other two to come up. Get a house-breaking . . . two more on the way. A sexual assault . . . stand by the switchboard for the next brace. As if the fairy stories and the nursery rhymes held some hidden secret. The three bears; three blind mice; three little kittens; every princess had three suitors; every lamp, every ring had three wishes. Three of everything.

And now this little lot. Three on top of three. Three dead 'uns. Three major incidents.

There was no way. No blasted *way*. Sopworth Section was going to be sunk without trace.

Meanwhile, Sowe had found the tinkers.

Sowe didn't like tinkers. Once upon a time he'd worked a rural beat; open countryside, fields, hedgerows, the lot. That was before he'd been switched to Sopworth. Some of the happiest years of his service had been spent pushing a pedal cycle along the country lanes. Sowe, therefore, knew all about gypsies. The Romany – the genuine article – was a rare breed; they no longer called themselves 'gypsies'; they were too proud to share that name with what the country folk called 'didekei'. You got Romanys parked on a verge and, when they left, that verge was as clean – sometimes cleaner – than when they'd arrived. They didn't leave a trail of muck and damage in their wake. They loved nature far too much to crap in its face. But the others – the 'didekeis' – the tinkers . . . Jesus wept! Some of 'em were horse-traders, some of 'em were scrap-dealers, *all* of 'em were petty thieves and trouble-makers. They'd steal anything, dammit, they'd even stolen the name 'gypsy'.

And here they were on the spare ground at the rear of the disused railway station, with garbage scattered in all directions. And more kids and dogs than the parson preached about. Two vans; one of them had shafts, the other was a trailer attached to a lorry. A fire was smouldering about a yard from the shafted van. Water-cans and cooking pots were lying where they'd been dumped. About fifty yards away two horses were tethered and seeking grass from the cracked and rubble-strewn tarmac. Other than the swarm of kids, five adults – two men – three women – made up the human complement.

Sowe stopped and waited.

The elder of the two men pushed himself upright from a three-legged milking-stool on which he was squatting and wandered over.

He gave a tentative leer, then said, 'Good day, sir. A fine day, sir.'

'Till I clapped eyes on this lot,' agreed Sowe coldly.

'We'll be moving, sir. We'll be moving very shortly.'

'When?'

'Oh, a coupla days, sir. No more.'

'A bloody sight less,' growled Sowe.

'This morning, sir. We only arrived this morning.'

'And it's already a shithouse.'

'You'll not . . .'

'Lee or Smith?' cut in Sowe.

'Sir?'

'The name. It's always one or the other. Lee or Smith?'

'Oh! Er – Smith, sir. That's my name. William Smith.'

'Right "William Smith".' Sowe stared aggressively into the dark eyes. 'I'll be around this way again this evening. Make sure you've vanished.'

'Sir, you wouldn't . . .'

'Like a dose of salts,' promised Sowe.

'We aren't doing harm, sir. We . . .'

'Fine. Don't do harm somewhere else. As far away as possible.'

'Tomorrow morning, sir?' suggested the tinker tentatively.

'Tomorrow morning,' promised Sowe grimly, 'you'll be in a police cell, if you're still here this evening.'

'And what would the charge be, sir?' The tinker tried a little naughtiness for size.

'There's a book,' said Sowe solemnly. *'Stone's Justices' Manual,* about four inches thick. Full of charges. There'll be summat in there, lad.' He swept his eyes over the general tinker's filth. 'Don't worry about that problem . . . there'll be summat in there.'

'You wanna leave us alone, copper. You wanna find summat better to do.'

They'd been joined by the younger man, and the younger man was of a very belligerent nature.

'Yours?' Sowe asked the question of the older man, and jerked his head.

'Sir?'

'The lunatic with the mouth?'

'My brother, sir.'

'Oh, aye?'

'He's – er – he's a bit hot-headed, sir. He doesn't mean . . .'

'Any more lip,' growled Sowe, 'and I'll cool him down. He'll need *thawing* out.'

'I'll – I'll watch him, sir.' The elder man raised a hand in a token touching of the forelock. He stammered, 'And – er – we'll be away, sir. Leave it to me. We'll be away.'

'Do that. Now . . . and as far as possible.'

The exchange with the tinker typified Sowe's technique. No bluster. A straight, up-and-down 'Do it, or else'. Sowe asked no favours and gave none. The job wasn't a popularity parade, but that was okay. Sowe didn't expect to be loved. At times bobbying called for going in, bull-headed – accepting a certain degree of danger sometimes – but that too was okay. You said 'Please', if 'Please' was called for. But if 'Please' was likely to earn you a raspberry — even a delayed raspberry when you were out of earshot — you didn't say 'Please'. You didn't fanny around. You were boss . . . because you'd *better* be boss.

Ramsden told his tale of woe. Blayde listened.

Ramsden ended, 'They're out of their minds, sir. I've checked for the last year just in case. Nothing!'

Ramsden had collared Blayde the moment he and Rowe had entered the police station after their meal. The look of panic-stricken urgency of Ramsden's face had made Blayde allow himself to be bustled into the Interview Room.

And now the Big Decision was awaited. The reason for Blayde's rank. The reason for his salary. Lowly sergeants *3 p.m.* didn't cop onto things of this nature; they slung 'em a few more rungs up the ladder. As quickly as possible they let the Brains Department in on the secret, then settled down to keep the Section Diary up to date.

Christ! If only it *was* as easy as that.

'Missings from Home?' said Blayde.

'Nothing. Nothing even *likely* to fit the bill.'

'Sudden Deaths?'

'I've checked. Nothing.'

'Right.' Blayde pinched his nose in thought. 'Widen the scope. Don't tell 'em why, just ask for a check on records. The whole police area. County, Lessford, Bordfield. Anything even remotely possible.'

'Yes, sir.'

'When . . . what's his name, again?'

'Bingham, sir. Alfred Bingham.'

'When he arrives, bung him in a cell. No questions. Nothing. Get Hinton out on the street . . . out of the way. Chief Inspector Tallboy? Does he know about this, yet?'

'No, sir. You're the first . . .'

'Get Mister Tallboy across here. Kelly and Kyle should be able to handle the other thing, for the time being. Tell the chief inspector — from me — nothing till we've had a chance to weigh things up.'

'Yes, sir.'

'And — er — sergeant.'

'Sir?'

'I take it you've told nobody else about this yet?'

'No, sir. You're the first . . .'

'Keep it that way. When Bingham arrives, straight into the nearest cell . . . and chase whoever's with him back to Leeds as soon as possible.'

Ramsden hesitated, then said, 'It's — er — it's in the log, sir.'

'The log?'

'The Telephone and Teleprinter Message Book. It seemed important. A message like that . . . so I logged it.'

'Lose it,' said Blayde bluntly.

'Sir?'

'Lose the bloody thing. Temporarily. Sit on it. Lock it away in a drawer somewhere. Just lose that book for the time being. This thing stays tight, till I give the word.'

'But sir . . .'

'Look — sergeant — some twit's coughed a murder to a Leeds jack, right?'

Ramsden nodded.

'A murder he says he committed a year ago?'

'Yes, sir.'

'But we don't *have* an undetected murder on the books.'

'That's what I told . . .'

'Don't the . . . Blayde blew out his cheeks. 'Don't those idiots at Leeds know *anything*? Haven't they heard of headline-chasers?'

'He seemed sure, sir.'

'How the hell can he be sure? How the hell can anybody be sure . . . yet?'

'Sir, I'm . . .'

'We have a murder enquiry, maybe. What we *don't* have is a murder. We don't even have a corpse. About the only thing we *do* have is some putty-brained, snotty-nosed little tealeaf who tells an equally putty-minded idiot, from the Leeds mob, that he killed somebody here, in Sopworth, last year. And from *that* we have a murder enquiry? The hell we have a murder enquiry.'

The food was tasteless. The mashed potato was lumpy, the boiled cabbage sloppy and over-done, the beef tough and stringy. As a meal it was a wasted effort. Hospital food. Something with which to fill an empty stomach . . . nothing more than that.

W.P.C. Pearson passed her cigarettes round and, for a few minutes, the three women smoked in silence. Everything had been said . . . or so it seemed. All emotion had been squeezed from the two wives and, if the truth be told, Pearson herself had been unable to steel herself into an attitude of non-involvement. Cooper and Noble were her friends. Her colleagues. Carnality had no place in her feelings for them, nevertheless she 'loved' them. As brothers, perhaps, but no . . . as something *more* than brothers.

One day the various police authorities would realise something very fundamental. That, by their very nature, women cannot *not* become involved. Put them in uniform, train them, give them absolute equality, but women can never be like men. When they see hurt, they themselves hurt. They suffer with the suffering. They weep with the mourners. They have feelings, and a depth of feeling rarely found in men . . . *very* rarely found in policemen. Send a police-woman to a Sudden Death, to a fatal accident, to some act of barbarity and, although she may hold herself in check whilever duty demands that she remain objective, she will weep before she sleeps that night. Sex equality can only ever be skin-deep. The inner emotions are well beyond mere legislation.

Burns had left the hospital hours before . . . and this not because he didn't care. He cared. But he was a man. W.P.C. Pearson *couldn't* leave . . . because she was a woman.

As she smoked, Pearson became aware of her vulnerability. Of the basic vulnerability of every complete woman in a world where violence, or the threat of violence, is part of her working life.

She muttered, 'He has to be made to talk,' and the words almost choked her.

Marian Cooper screwed up her eyes against the smoke, then said, 'I've known him a long time. I've never known anybody make him do something he didn't want to do.'

'But he's . . .'

'I know.' The gentleness of the interruption contained tiny barbs of frustration. 'We *all* know.'

'Let's . . .' Hilda Noble squashed what was left of her cigarette into the ashtray. She opened her handbag, then said, 'Let's all have another cigarette . . . then we'll get back to them.'

'Snap out of it, Coop.'

Noble, too, 'knew'. He'd been able to sense it. There, in the tiny side-ward, he'd felt the growing atmosphere. He couldn't see. He'd never be able to see again — and that was something *he'd* have to come to terms with eventually — but for the moment the rock-hard determination of his colleague not to . . .

Not to what?

'You're breaking your wife's heart, Coop.' It hurt him a little to talk; the movement of his face muscles pulled at the stitches which held the lips of facial wounds together. But small pain was unimportant to the killing, mental pain of his friend. He said, 'You've lost a hand. That's all . . . as far as I can make out. I'm sorry you've lost a hand. But it could have been a thousand times worse.'

There was silence. Noble couldn't even hear the sound of Cooper's breathing.

'You've still one hand, Coop.' Noble fought hard to give the performance of his life; to get through to this buddy of his who refused to be comforted. 'One hand, Coop.' He chuckled and the stitches pulled like hell. 'You can still wipe your own bum . . . and that's something.'

Silence. Not even the sound of slight movement from the other bed.

'Nelson,' continued Noble. 'Remember? One eye, one arm, one arsehole . . . and *he* didn't do too bad. Give it a try Coop, old son. Don't let the bastard who did it crow.'

Silence. No breathing. No sound of bed-movement. Nothing!

'Maybe I'm talking to myself.' Noble's voice hardened a little. 'I wouldn't know. Maybe they've shifted you. Maybe you're standing there, grinning at me. *Are* you there, Coop?'

The silence remained unbroken.

'No, you're not there, Coop.' The voice dropped to little more than a murmur. Sad. Resigned. 'You'd talk, if you were there. You're not *that* gutless.'

Matilda Blakey, red-nosed and red-eyed from crying, said, 'We'll have to move to another town . . . you realise that?'

'Why?'

Blakey was beyond caring; this morning he'd been the Big White Chief and now he was nothing. He was Edmund Blakey . . . and *Mister* Edmund Blakey, if somebody was being particularly polite. That from a chief superintendentship was rather like stepping down an unseen well and ending up to the neck in ice-cold water. It was an experience. A very sobering experience.

'This town.' Matilda Blakey sniffed. 'This whole division . . .'

'It was never mine.' Blakey sat in the window-seat, staring out at the straggle of the garden. His voice was low-pitched, and he didn't turn his head as he spoke. 'This division was never mine. Never would be. Never could be. It belongs to a dead man.'

'Ripley?' From her the word sounded like a profanity.

'Ripley,' he agreed, but the way he spoke the name was totally different.

Strange how disaster — humiliation — become some men. How it can give weak men strength; fools wisdom; arrogant men humility . . . *real* humility. Even his wife noticed it. For the first time in their married life he was the man she wanted him to be. Had *once* wanted him to be. But now? Now she was frightened. The bombast had gone. The bawling and shouting she'd been able to control wasn't there any more. He was the man she'd once *thought* he was, but that was long ago and she wondered. She wondered whether the man she'd once thought he was would have married *her* in the first place. That was the question . . . and the possible answer terrified her.

Still gazing out at the garden — still in a low, controlled voice — he said, 'You've been a poor wife. A useless wife. You've always wanted me as a peg upon which to hang your silly pomposity. That's *all* you've wanted me for.' He paused, sighed, then continued, 'I'm not blaming you . . . not wholly. I've allowed it to happen. You. My two daughters. Not *my* wife. Not *my* daughters. The wife and daughters of "Chief Superintendent Blakey". And now, when you're not that, you want to run. Okay . . .' He nodded, still without taking his gaze from the garden. 'You have my permission. You have my blessing. Run, all three of you. I'll accept my responsibilities. As a husband. As a father. Run. But I'm not running with you.'

He stood up and, hunch-shouldered, made for the door.

'Where . . .' began his wife.

'Out.' For the first time he looked at her. 'I'll be back. I've already said . . . I'm not running away.'

Markets vary. Each has it own pattern; its own life; its own characteristics. Leeds Market is a sprawling giant; Tuesdays and Saturdays it stretches its massive limbs and overflows into all the side-streets at its rear; it gobbles up the shoppers by the thousand, then spews them out, bag-laden and leg-weary, with empty pockets and aching arms. Knaresborough on a Wednesday is ridiculously busy for its size; the open-air stalls huddle within the limits imposed by the square and, because it sells cheaply, because Wednesday is early-closing day in many neighbouring towns, the shoppers surge in, bargain-hunting, and seem to swirl and tumble around the stalls like a river hitting rapids. Ripon on a Thursday has a schizoprenic quality; despite the busy market it tries to maintain its 'genteel holiday' image; the rows of stalls are surrounded by a steady flow of touring cars and gaudily-dressed families breaking their journey en route for the dales or the east coast.

With Sopworth there was no messing about. The market was the market, period. Few strangers had reason to visit Sopworth on market day other than for the market. Therefore, from the start, it rolled its sleeves up, spat on its hands and got down to it. The stall-holders shouted themselves hoarse. By mid-morning the tarmac of the square was littered with packing paper, cabbage leaves and the general garbage which is a concomitant to all open-air markets. By mid-afternoon the bulk of what was going to be sold had *been* sold, throats were strained and a gradual packing away of non-perishable goods was in progress.

The tall, skinny guy in charge of the second hand book stall was humping an occasional carton of grubby paperbacks into the rear of his van.

'Good day?' asked Hinton casually.

'Fair,' admitted the skinny guy. As a qualification he added, 'They don't read much these days.'

'Television,' observed Sowe solemnly.

Hinton and Sowe (as was their periodic practice) had linked up and were working 'double'; strolling lazily around the stalls, keeping their eyes skinned for petty 'lifters' and, now and again, pausing to exchange small talk with stall-holders.

Sowe thumbed his way through the 'Crime and Detection' section. His expression reflected his mild disgust.

'A right load of crap,' he murmured critically.

'Depends,' defended the skinny guy. 'Some good, some bad.'

'It's all been told,' proclaimed Hinton with an air of some authority. 'Some of the bloody turds get their *ideas* from these things.'

'Authentic?' suggested the skinny guy.

'Not *much* like the real thing,' scoffed Hinton. 'But,' he added, 'on the other hand . . . tell the real thing, people wouldn't believe.'

'Been on many murder enquiries?' asked the skinny guy.

Sowe said, 'Don't make me laugh. Anything under a detective inspector . . . he brews the tea and fetches the fags.'

A certain detective constable might have argued the point with some vehemence. Evans had the distinct impression that he was being suffocated with paper. It wasn't that he didn't know the 'How'. Or even that he didn't know the 'What'. Looked at *3.30 p.m.* from one angle the file was as easy — as uncomplicated — as one for nicking a bike. But the bloody *size!* A copy for the D.P.P. A copy for the Police Solicitor. A copy for Bordfield Area Headquarters. A copy for Beechwood Brook D.H.Q. A so-called 'working copy' (presumably to take the teacup rings). Then one for his knob. Every statement, every report, every everything. Six of 'em . . . and on a typewriter weak from rough usage. A man could go cross-eyed in next to no time. They'd given him the Lumber Room — the gash room which did duty as Lost Property Cupboard, Broom Cupboard and General Junk Shop — and the bloody place was like a pig-pen *and* the window wouldn't budge. He'd removed his coat and rolled up his sleeves, but the sweat dripped from his chin and his nose end and, if he wasn't careful, stained whatever it was he was wrestling with at the time.

The door opened, Blayde poked his head around the jamb, and said, 'Coping, son?'

'Er . . .'

'Straightforward. Nothing to it. If you hit any snags, give me a yell.'

'Yes, sir,' croaked Evans.

'Good lad.'

Blayde closed the door and left Evans to his misery.

'You've shifted,' growled Ramsden.

'Orders.' The Leeds City motor patrol man unlocked the handcuffs which linked him to Alfred Bingham. 'You need him in a hurry.'

'Your blokes seem to want to *part* with him in a hurry.'

The motor patrol man shrugged.

'Alfred Bingham?' Ramsden asked the question of the prisoner.

'Yes, sir,' said Bingham meekly.

The motor patrol man said, 'Body receipt. Property receipt. Statement and previous cons.' He dumped a large envelope and two receipt books on the Charge Office desk.

'Everything in there?' Again Ramsden asked the question of Bingham and, at the same time, nodded at the envelope.

Bingham said, 'Yes, sir.'

Ramsden scrawled his signature in the two recepit books and the motor patrol man left.

'C'mon, lad.' Ramsden picked up a large key, attached by means of frayed string to a wooden label, then guided Bingham from the Charge Office. He said, 'Just sit in a cell till somebody comes to talk to you.'

'I committed murder, sir,' said Bingham in a toneless voice.

'So you say.'

'It's true, sir. I'm not what you think I am.'

'What's that?' asked Ramsden gruffly.

'Sir?'

'What we *think* you are?'

194

'Soft in the head,' said Bingham solemnly.

'Nobody's said that, lad.'

'That's what you think.'

'Is it?'

Bingham smiled sadly. As if at a private, not-very-funny joke.

Ramsden unlocked the cell door, then stood aside to allow Bingham to enter.

Ramsden said, 'Shoes, braces, belt. You don't have a tie?'

'No, sir. Nor braces.'

'Okay, shoes and belt.'

Bingham removed his shoes, then slipped his belt from the loops around the top of his denims. He rolled the belt around his hand, then held it and the shoes out to Ramsden. Ramsden took them and placed them neatly alongside the cell door in the corridor.

As he straightened, he said, 'Anything else? Something to read?'

'No, sir.' Bingham hesitated, then added, 'I'd — er — I'd like something to eat, sir. If it's not too much trouble.'

'I'll fix it. Tea? Corned beef sandwiches? That okay?'

'Thank you, sir.'

'I'll fix it,' repeated Ramsden.

'Sir.' Bingham looked into Ramsden's face. 'I *did* kill her. I'm not — y'know — just *saying* it.'

'Save it for now, lad. Just sit down. I'll fix you some grub.'

Ramsden closed and locked the cell door. He walked from the cell passage, tapped on the door of Rowe's office, then opened it and said, 'Bingham's tucked away in a cell, sir.'

'Good.' Blayde nodded his satisfaction.

Rowe made as if to rise from the desk chair and said, 'In that case, we'll . . .'

'Let me know when Chief Inspector Tallboy arrives,' said Blayde.

'Yes, sir.'

Rowe relaxed on to the seat of his chair once more. Ramsden closed the door of the office and returned to the Charge Office.

Tallboy drove with the window down. He drove with his elbow resting on the sill of the window, and with the tips of his fingers caressing the rim of the steering wheel. He drove at a very moderate speed; taking his time and enjoying a June afternoon, the like of which he had not known since the previous year. As he drove he sang softly to himself. Softly and unmelodiously; a deliberate take-off of the Nat King Cole classic, *That Old Black Magic*.

Tallboy was happy. Peacock had already coughed his heart out;

thanks to Kyle's local knowledge and the cunning of Detective
Sergeant Kelly, Peacock hadn't had much of a choice. Meanwhile,
Tallboy was nobody's pet lapdog. He took his own good time. He
didn't come running just because some whoopee Leeds City jack
hit panic stations; just because some grass-green collar-feeler heaved
a dead duck over the boundary.

Murder? In a pig's ear, murder!

'Please, Mr Detective, sir, I'm a murderer.'

'Please, Mr Detective, sir, not today, not yesterday, but last year.'

'Please, Mr Detective, sir, it wasn't *here*. It was way and gone to
hell Sopworth way.'

Holy cow! And some dim bulb had sucked it.

He – Detective Chief Inspector Tallboy – would give the snivelling
little nothing murder. *He'd* give him murder. The little yuck would
wish he *had* committed murder. He'd think murder was about to *be*
committed . . . on him!

Other than such thoughts – which in their own back-to-front way
were not unpleasant thoughts – Tallboy was happy. It was a glorious
afternoon. The car was running as sweet as a nut. Peacock was trussed
up, stuffed and ready for the oven. The world wasn't a bad place,
after all.

The three women wandered back towards Appleton Ward. Slowly.
Almost reluctantly. Their burden was one of utter helplessness, and
it weighed them down and bowed their shoulders. Things had gone
well beyond the stage of mutual sympathy. They each *knew* – they
each *felt* – and there wasn't a damn thing they could do, other than
wait and hope.

Sowe and Hinton strolled, side by side, into and away from the
Market Square. Their present problem was one of boredom. A thing
– one of the many things – never mentioned by the Join-The-Police-
Service ads. Bashing the pavements. Walking a pattern along the
same limited number of streets.

'I wonder how Coop's going on,' said Sowe but without real
interest.

'Cool, clean hospital sheets.' Hinton sounded almost envious.

'A bugger about Noble, though.'

'He'll catch a nice pension.'

'Blind, though.'

'Aye . . . a pity,' agreed Hinton.

At Sopworth Police Station Blayde and Rowe waited in Rowe's
office. Blayde smoked a pipe. Rowe smoked cigarettes.

Rowe said, 'Mind if I sit in?'

'Eh?' Blayde dragged his mind from its meanderings.

'When you interview what's-his-name?'

'Bingham?'

'D'you mind if I sit in?'

'Why not?' Blayde moved one shoulder. 'Chances are it's all a load o' crap.'

Rowe looked vaguely disappointed.

In one of the cells Albert Rayon sprawled on the cell bed and cat-napped. It was a game, see? Like cards. Like snooker. Certain rules, certain regulations. Sometimes you could play a fast 'un . . . some-times. But not often. Still, never mind, eh? A few months inside. Meet up with some of your pals. There was always *somebody* you knew. Keep your nose clean. Serve it day at a time. It passed. Nothing lasted forever.

In another cell, Alfred Bingham worried.

He sat on the edge of the cell bed, linked his fingers between his thighs and stared at the tiled wall.

Supposing . . .

Supposing they didn't believe him. Supposing that blurted remark to the Leeds jack was pushed aside; dismissed as one more potty attempt to attain petty notoriety. A nothing little lifter out for front page space. Or — worse still — an all-out barmpot with a bee in his bonnet.

He'd met 'em. A few years on the road, living rough, and you met 'em. My God, yes! You met 'em, you felt sorry for 'em and you hoped to Christ *you* wouldn't end up like that.

They believed what they claimed to be. It wasn't a joke. They were serious. Wrong-side-of-the-blanket offsprings of royalty. Some of 'em even believed *that*. Millionaires fiddled out of their wealth. Duke this, Count that, Lord the other. They truly *believed.*

Follow a railway line. Find a station, go to the darkened carriages parked in some bay for the night, try the compartments till you found one unlocked. There was an even chance you'd find one of 'em settled in. Or in barns, tucked away among the bales. Bus shelters, maybe. Waiting rooms. Any of the hundred places where man (and sometimes woman) curled up to keep dry; waiting for a dawn and what heat the sun could offer.

They'd be there. Wanting to talk. Wanting to tell you . . . to tell *themselves.* People with nothing — less than nothing — eager to explain all the reasons.

The coppers knew 'em. The coppers had heard all the hard-luck stories a thousand times. So many times, they didn't even listen.

And supposing . . .

Odd . . .

Blakey relaxed and allowed the Rover to be carried forward in the stream of mid-afternoon traffic. And he *could* relax. That was the oddity. Having accepted the inevitable, having delivered the ultimatum, the farther he travelled from the orbit of his wife's control the easier it was to relax.

It wasn't that he wanted another woman . . . or, come to that, had *ever* wanted another woman – it was just that . . .

God, she'd been like a ton weight across his shoulders. Her and her infernal daughters. Not *his* daughters. Sure, he'd fathered them – they were from his loins – but from the start Matilda had grabbed and held tight. According to every book on the subject a daughter has that extra affection for her father . . . like a son has that extra affection for his mother. Parlour psychology. But that was the only brand of psychology he knew anything about. And, within the Blakey family, it was all balls.

And now it didn't matter. Come to that (and with hindsight) it hadn't mattered for years, but he'd been too dumb to realise.

There was a freedom. A *feeling* of freedom. No pressure from the top office, no pressure from home. Like a schoolboy on the first day of a school holiday.

Blayde? Blayde had done him a favour. One hell of a favour. Harris had been after his blood. God, if Harris had had his way. But thanks to Blayde he'd been able to beat Harris to the punch. A neatly typed resignation . . . 'for personal reasons'. A chief super's pension. A nice house. And *freedom*. Something he didn't deserve. Oh, sure (again with hindsight) he hadn't deserved this let-out. Matilda had made damn sure of that. What he *had* deserved was the boot and, without Blayde, that's what he'd have *got*.

His thoughts reinforced – ratified – the realisation that he truly hated his wife. Nor was it that hatred which is within wafer-thin distance of love; that sudden upsurge of rage when a goddess behaves like a goddess should *not* behave; when a man worships a woman and, for a moment, that woman forgets and heels that worship into the muck. No . . . this was *real* hatred. A cold, calculated detestation which had flowered unseen, unfelt, *unknown* for years. It was far too big, too deeply rooted ever to admit of forgiveness. The 'fresh start' thing needed some peg upon which to hang the clean slate. The peg wasn't there. Over the years of their marriage his wife had nagged and complained, whimpered and bullied and had, in effect, sandblasted the wall flat and clean. No peg. Nothing! A blank wall of loathing, uncoloured by even a speck of understanding. No peg. No place for a peg. Ergo, no forgiveness.

And yet that realisation, too, seemed to add to his sense of freedom.

Tallboy replaced the receiver onto its prongs. Blayde and Rowe waited. Blayde tapped the photostat of Bingham's previous convictions.

'Know thine enemy'. Blayde was a great believer in 'knowing' as much as possible. That was one reason why he'd pulled Tallboy back to Sopworth from Beechwood Brook. Tallboy knew one of the Leeds City inspectors; had been asked to contact that inspector and ask questions. Questions about Bingham. Questions about the Leeds detective who had questioned Bingham when the great heart-opening had taken place.

'Well?' asked Blayde.

'Possible,' said Tallboy carefully.

'A little off-key.' Blayde touched the photostat. 'A lot. A list to be proud of. But *not* the list of a potential murderer.'

'Murder's a one-off job,' observed Tallboy.

'Quite. Very often no list at all. But when there *are* previous convictions, they tend to be for violence.'

'G.B.H. About a year ago. That's about the time he says he committed the murder.'

Blayde glanced at the previous convictions, then said, 'Suspended sentence at a magistrate's court. He'd already done two short stretches. That means a very *technical* G.B.H. or mitigating circumstances.'

'Still, a rare old list.'

'Prior to the G.B.H.' Blayde consulted the photostat. 'A three-month stretch for petty theft. Before that a three-month for drunk in charge.'

'He — er — he had a motor car?' queried Rowe timidly.

'In those days he had a motor car,' agreed Blayde. 'He even *lived* somewhere.'

'Otley,' contributed Tallboy.

'Otley,' Blayde murmured in agreement. 'But even in those days, petty pilfering. And since . . . *more* petty pilfering. Nothing of any weight.'

199

'He's been living rough.' Tallboy grinned. 'You don't plan a second Great Train Robbery in a hedge bottom.'

Rowe contributed, 'No convictions for sexual deviation?'

'No.'

'Assuming,' said Blayde slowly. 'Assuming for the sake of argument that he's telling the truth. What motive for murdering a teenage girl?'

'Sex,' said Tallboy bluntly.

'Right.' Blayde leaned back in his chair. 'Your friend, the Leeds City inspector?'

'Well now . . .' Tallboy chose his words. 'Like the rest of us, he's not too keen on knocking one of his own blokes.'

'But?'

'A fair-to-middling copper. Run of the mill.'

'It doesn't tell us much.'

'No Joe Mounsey . . . that was *his* expression.'

Blayde murmured, 'No Charles Ripley,' and it was almost like an echo. And, having said it, Blayde wondered why the hell he *had* said it, and wished to hell he *hadn't*. It was one of those unintentional Freudian bricks dropped by even the most careful of men. He looked directly at Tallboy and said, 'Your father-in-law.'

4 p.m.

'Yes, sir.' The use of the word 'sir' went with Tallboy's tone and expression.

Rowe murmured, 'Quite a man, so I've heard.'

'A good copper,' growled Tallboy.

Blayde said, 'Which means . . . *everything.*'

'No, sir.' Tallboy's jaw muscles hardened.

'No?' Blayde sounded genuinely surprised.

'Sir.' Tallboy hesitated, then said, 'You're asking me about Ripley? My father-in-law? Is that it?'

Blayde nodded.

'He had flair,' said Tallboy slowly. 'He also had luck. More than his fair share. But — y'know — no real copper shits rose petals. Ripley wasn't the exception. If he was alive — if you asked him — he'd admit that. His marriage blew up in his face. At a guess — I've never probed too deeply — but at a guess his wife couldn't take what the force had made him. He changed his ways. Not a lot, but enough to mend his marriage. After that, he wasn't the old Ripley. By that time he'd made his name, so it wasn't too important. But *we* knew. *We* could see it. Those of us who'd been with him when he was a real bastard. When he really *didn't* give a damn.' Tallboy paused, then continued,

'He's left a name. A reputation. Deserved, I reckon. But — if that's what you're asking — it can be equalled. Bettered. Not by Blakey, but by the right man.'

Rowe's packet of cigarettes was open on the desk. Blayde leaned forward, helped himself to a cigarette and lighted it. He took his time; made each separate action a deliberate movement. He waved out the match, dropped it into an ash-tray and inhaled cigarette smoke before he spoke.

Then he said, 'A thing worth remembering.'

'What?'

'That little speech you've just made.' Then, before Tallboy could press the point, he continued, 'Bingham's in the cell. You bat first. Inspector Rowe and I will wait here . . . with eager anticipation.'

At Bradford a detective sergeant sipped foul tea, forced himself not to pull a face, and said, 'You're sure of that?'

'In the front. I 'eard 'em. They're cooking up a right bloody pantomime.'

'Sopworth?' The D.S. moistened his lips from the contents of the chipped cup.

'That's wot *I* 'eard.'

The D.S. believed the man. The man was a snout, he ran just about the most sleazy cafe in the city, he consorted with whores, pimps, hoodlums — you name it they were his 'friends' — but his quiet tip-offs in the squalid kitchen of his establishment could be believed. One day somebody would cotton on and, when that day dawned and if the person cottoning on was of a certain type, a rather nasty mess would be found in some dark alley.

The D.S. wondered why, in hell's name, any man chose to run with the hare and hunt with the hounds in this way. Why he deliberately courted danger. The thrill? In order to give the outward appearance of being a respectable citizen? As a form of sucking up to the police? Maybe all those reasons. Maybe for some other reason well beyond the comprehension of a mere detective sergeant.

He pushed the puzzle from his mind and forced himself to suffer another taste of the foul tea.

He said, 'Thanks. I'll pass the word.'

Bingham swallowed the last of the corned beef sandwiches, then gulped hot, sweet tea from an enamelled mug.

Maybe . . .

Oh, Christ, what was the point? Who'd understand? Who *could* understand? A man – *any* man – no, the hell with it, a *weak* man, that's what he was, a *weak* man. All right, any weak man might have done the same. Might have. Maybe . . . There was no excuse – he wasn't making excuses – but a *weak* man . . .

One thing after another. Y'know . . . a log-jam. No way out. No way of changing things. Just . . .

His nose felt as if it was about to drip. He ran the back of his hand across his nostrils, then stood up from the cell bed and, still holding the enamelled mug, stepped to the window of the cell. He stared through the tiny panes of inch-thick glass. He stared up at the sky.

The sky. He loved the sky. The colour . . . its present colour. Crackpot novelists used expressions like 'duck-egg blue'. Knackers! Duck eggs *weren't* blue. Not *that* shade of blue. Duck eggs had a greenish tinge. He should know. He'd pinched enough of 'em. No hen eggs to nick, so duck eggs. Raw duck eggs. Break the shell. Gulp the lot. Don't think about it. The sort of taste you hadn't to think about. Not exactly sour. More 'strong' . . . sort of 'earthy'. But the shells were never blue. Never the same blue as the sky.

Duck eggs. He'd once had a go at a goose egg. Jesus! He'd almost choked. Too much of it. A whole mouthful of slime, and too much to swallow. Jesus!

Bumming. 'Knights of the Road'. Don't let 'em kid you, mister. Tramping around, not knowing where your next meal's coming from, not knowing where the hell you're going to sleep come night. A very over-rated pastime, mister, a *very* over-rated pastime.

Except for the sky.

It made you appreciate the sky . . .

Pinter radioed off-duty, locked the doors of the Minivan, climbed the fence and walked slowly towards the cool shelter of the trees. He swayed slightly, as if he was a little tipsy. He wasn't aware of the fact. Only two things filled his mind. Hannah was dying and he was tired enough to wish *he* was dying, too.

Somewhere inside his aching skull a babble of voices refused to be quietened. Like a crowd heard from a distance. Words couldn't be made out . . . just the rise and fall of crowd noise. In the van it had mingled with the sound of the engine; he'd thought it *was* the engine; that a combination of weariness and the hum of the engine had been playing audible tricks on him. But, even without the engine, the distant crowd noise persisted.

It stayed with him as he entered the shade of the conifers. The ground was springy underfoot and the scent of pine was on all sides. It was one of those tiny Forestry Commission pockets of cool silence. The occasional rustle in the undergrowth spoke of timid life. The birdsong seemed to echo around the trees, as if it was not a wood but a cathedral. The insects danced and buzzed in the shafts of sunlight which pierced the overhead curtain of branches.

But it was cool . . . a little like taking a cold shower to clear the head.

He found the log – the log he knew was there, the log the foresters used when they broke for a meal – and he lowered himself into a sitting position. There was peace. Cool, soft solitude . . . but still the hum of a phantom crowd deep inside his brain. And the steady ache behind his eyes. And the sorrow and hopelessness which wrapped him like a second skin.

'God, let her live.'

A voice detached itself from the crowd. A whispered voice. A voice hoarse with heartbreak. It came as a shock when he realised it was his own voice.

'God, let her live. Not Hannah. Don't take Hannah. Please! As she is . . . I don't mind. Better that than nothing. As she is . . . but don't take her. Take me. Anything. *Let her live.*'

The word 'runt' described Alfred Bingham to perfection. Small, scared and (very obviously) unloved. The Leeds Bridewell boys had not yet allowed him the use of a razor, and the stubble of an overnight beard added nothing to his sex appeal. He wore torn denims and an unwashed, open-necked shirt. He sat awkwardly on the cell bed and watched Tallboy muse his way through a three page list of previous convictions.

'Quite a busy little lifter,' observed Tallboy flatly.

Bingham blinked, but said nothing. He was well used to these cheerful little sessions with members of various police forces. He was content to sit there, not answer back and, wherever possible, give full co-operation. It was the easier way . . . you kept your teeth!

'Alfie Bingham,' droned Tallboy.

'Yes, sir.'

'A lovely string of previous.'

Bingham nodded.

'The Leeds lads picked you up last night. Nicking timber.'

'Yes, sir.'

'Born Harrogate?' Tallboy raised his eyebrows.

'Yes, sir.'

'Where all the millionaires come from?'

Bingham remained silent.

'Married?'

'Yes, sir.'

'Where's your wife?'

'I left her, sir.'

Again, Tallboy raised his eyebrows in mock amazement.

He murmured, 'Last known address, Otley?'

'Yes, sir.'

'Quite a come-down from Harrogate?'

Bingham didn't answer.

'Let's see, now . . .' Tallboy ran his finger down the entries.
'Doncaster. Wetherby. York. Darlington. You lifted a pig in Darlington . . . how the hell do you nick a *pig*?'

'Strictly speaking, I didn't steal it, sir.'

'It just followed you?'

'No, sir. I found it.'

'I know. You can't move for 'em.'

'Sir?'

'Pigs . . . especially in Darlington.'

'Sir, it was lost.'

'And you tried to sell 'em *that*?'

'Sir?'

'That a stray pig was hoofing around Darlington and you "found"
it.'

'Sir, that's the . . .'

'No wonder you earned three months.'

'Yes, sir,' sighed Bingham.

Tallboy studied the list again, then murmured, 'Local boy makes
good . . . or should it be bad?'

'Sir?'

'Nothing south of Doncaster. Nothing north of Darlington.
Nothing west of the Pennines.'

'I — I like these parts,' muttered Bingham.

'Obviously. If it isn't welded to a six-storey office-block, it's
yours.'

Bingham moved his lips. It might have been a smile, it might *not*
have been a smile. Bingham was out to please; if Tallboy was being
jokey, it was a smile; if Tallboy was making a serious observation . . .
okay he'd never yet lifted a six-storey office-block.

Tallboy tossed the list of previous convictions onto the cell bed.

'Okay, Alfie, you were picked up last night.'

'Yes, sir.'

'What was it? Seven foot of six-by-two from a woodyard?'

'Yes, sir.'

'For kindling wood?'

'No, sir. A chap I met said he'd like . . .'

'In the Leeds area?'

'Yes, sir.'

'You were interviewed?'

'Yes, sir.'

'And you coughed a murder? Just like that?'

'Yes, sir.'

'Just like that?' repeated Tallboy.

'Yes, sir.' Then, in a whispered groan, Bingham added, 'It's true, sir. I don't wanna live with it any longer.'

'And if I say it's all balls?'

'You'd be wrong, sir. You'd be terribly wrong . . .'

Sowe and Hinton stopped a fight. It wasn't much of a fight; it came to an abrupt end before it could develop into a genuine set-to. The two men were neighbours — more or less — if you can call a five-mile stretch of desolate hill-farming country a 'dividing line' between one broken-down farmhouse and another broken-down farmhouse. The hill farms had, for years, bred men of quick temper and suspicious mind; sheep farming on The Tops was no 'Garden of England' cake-walk; you fought the bloody elements and, if you didn't fight hard, the elements won; you trusted nobody, you took lip from no man and, if you were lucky, you survived . . . just!

That then . . . and the booze.

Having been told, Sowe and Hinton strolled into the yard at the rear of the pub. Sowe had already slipped his truncheon from its pocket and hidden it up the right sleeve of his tunic. They were old hands. A team. Neither had to be told what to do.

One man's mouth was bleeding and he had his head down ready to rush, bull-headed, at his opponent. As he started the rush Hinton stepped behind him gave him a gentle ankle-tap and the man tripped over his own feet and sprawled. Sowe moved forward, confronted the second man and murmured, 'That's enough.'

'That bleeding' . . .'

Sowe tapped the man gently on the cheek — at least it *looked* like a gentle tap — in fact the truncheon had been allowed to slip down until it was hidden by the palm and the 'tap' was travelling somewhat. In effect the man received a hefty clout across the ear with a piece of turned hickory. He staggered sideways and clapped a hand to his injured ear.

'That's enough,' smiled Sowe, flipped the truncheon back into its hiding place and spread empty palms in a gesture of reasonableness.

Hinton stared down at the fallen warrior, then said, 'You're both pissed.'

'The hell they're . . .'

'And *you* . . .' Sowe eyed the outraged spectator coldly. 'You are going to incite a breach of the peace . . . if you aren't *very* careful.'

'Drunk and dizzy,' contributed Hinton laconically.

'Both of 'em,' agreed Sowe.

The small crowd thinned out as its members wandered away from the scene. The two would-be-fighters glared at each other.

'The choice,' said Hinton. 'Inside or home.'

'We don't give a damn,' added Sowe.

The man with the aching ear growled, 'Wot the 'ell did you 'it me with?'

Sowe spread his empty palms and smiled.

'*If* you've homes to go to,' said Hinton pointedly.

The two men collected their coats and, still scowling, left the pub yard.

Sowe slipped his truncheon back into its pocket then he and Hinton continued their 'double-harness' patrol.

The psychiatrist said, 'There's nothing really wrong with him, madam. Nothing really *wrong.*'

Marian Cooper merely sighed.

Hilda Noble snapped, 'He won't talk. *Something's* wrong with him.'

'I assure you, madam . . .'

'Don't be such a damned fool!'

Marian Cooper's lips bent into a slow, sad smile.

Such a lot, since the early hours. Since she'd been at the centre of the pain and panic resultant upon the explosion. Then she'd been the strong one; the person capable of handling things; the one to whom all the others had turned for guidance. But now. From some hidden reserve Hilda Noble had found strength which she (Marian Cooper) had lost. Hilda Noble was standing up to the psychiatrist. Standing up to him, and blasting off as the man's smooth manner made things worse than they were.

The psychiatrist . . .

God, they all oozed that same supercilious charm. Big, small, fat,

206

thin . . . they all had that smooth insolence. This one, tie askew, hair stuck out in rat's tails, front of his white coat stained where he'd dribbled drink or food, a comic-opera 'professor' . . . and yet that same scornful air. As if the mysteries of the mind were, to him, little more than a primer in simple English.

In the main, con men. Not deliberately so, but afraid to admit ignorance. The one branch of medicine that was still not far removed from witch-doctoring.

'A shock,' he smiled. 'A sudden shock might . . .'

'He's *had* a shock.' Marian Cooper spoke, before Hilda Noble could jump in with another explosive remark. 'He's lost his hand. That's a shock, doctor.'

'What do you suggest?' spat Hilda Noble. 'That we should chop the other hand off?'

And now one man believed.

Tallboy walked slowly from the cells, back to Rowe's office, and scowled unreasonable annoyance at himself. It was all cobblers, of course, but it wasn't! Nutters — kinky buggers — they were *always* claiming this, admitting the other. They were a damn nuisance. Not quite daft enough to be put away, but daft enough to create more unnecessary work than *that*, but not this one.

Tallboy was a very solid man. Solid in build, and solid in his mental outlook. 'Uncouth', that's what his wife called him sometimes. Okay, 'uncouth'. It was part of the job.

4.30 p.m.   Years of sorting out yobs, of bouncing scum off the street, of squashing smart-arsed bastards who thought they were well above the law. It left jagged edges. It played merry hell with a man's patience. Maybe it even tended to sour him a little.

But you knew all the gags. You'd heard all the funnies. You knew every trick in the book . . . plus a few dozen they daren't print. By that time — after working C.I.D. for *that* many years — you took nothing at face value. Your eyes, your ears and your nose. If *they* told you certain things, well, maybe.

On the other hand . . .

For Christ's sake don't make sense of bobbying. Don't try to break it down into its component parts and see what makes it tick. It can't be done. Monty Python himself couldn't do it.

Get the years under your belt and you believed nothing. On the other hand, get those same years under your belt and you'd believe *anything.* Reasons? Who needed reasons? For theft, for rape, for murder . . . who needed *reasons*?

For kicks. That was reason enough . . . reason enough even for murder.

And the end-product of this immaculate contradiction was a man like Tallboy. For want of a more accurate description, he called it 'gut policing'. Part experience, part having been sold a dummy too many times in the past, part something neither he nor anybody else could ever explain. 'Gut policing'. It *never* let you down.

And for these obscure, ethereal reasons, Tallboy believed Bingham. Believed that Bingham *had* committed murder. And the belief worried Tallboy because unless somebody else (that 'somebody' being Blayde) *also* believed Bingham . . .

Tallboy muttered, 'Sod it. Why should *I* worry?'

But, nevertheless, he did worry . . .

The stall-holders were packing away. Slowly. Piece at a time. The market shoppers were still around; the wiseacres who deliberately arrived late, in the hope of picking up something cheap on the vegetable stalls. Or on any other stall, come to that. Bargain hunters. Men and women who gauged the temper of the weary stall-holders. Something that wouldn't keep. Something they'd had for weeks and couldn't shift. Something they were tired of lifting in and out of the van. Just before the final hauling down of the tarpaulin covers there'd be a sudden flurry of buying and selling. It always happened. The old hands at the open-market caper waited for it and had the junk ready; something partly hidden throughout the day then, as the close of the market began, exposed and treated as if it was rare and unique. Crap . . . waiting to be foisted off on the bargain hunters.

Sowe and Hinton strolled to the spare ground behind the disused railway station. Smith, the tinker, was hitching one of the horses between the shafts of a van. His brother sat behind the wheel of the lorry, scowling at the two approaching coppers.

'We're on our way, sir.' Smith tightened a harness buckle and leered at the two officers.

'Good lad,' said Sowe flatly.

Hinton peeled off to the right, took out his notebook and jotted down the registered number of the lorry.

'Wot's 'e doin'?' demanded Smith's brother.

Sowe said, 'We might want to see you again.'

'You might have lifted the town hall,' amplified Hinton as he closed his notebook.

'Wot the bleedin' 'ell . . . '

'We're on our way, sir,' interrupted the elder Smith hurriedly.

He led the horse forward and the van rumbled in its wake. The younger Smith spat from the open window of the cab, started the engine of the lorry and, with much crashing of gears, moved the lorry forward after the horse-drawn van.

Sowe said, 'Have a safe journey . . . and a long one.'

The two constables continued their patrol and, the call of nature being what it is, a few minutes later they descended the steps of a public toilet. They were alone — or thought they were — when they heard boyish voices coming from behind one of the closed lavatory doors.

'Betcha daren't do it on the floor.'

'Betcha I dare.'

'Go on then, I'll *dare* you.'

Having emptied their bladders, Sowe and Hinton zipped up, sighed and waited. From behind the closed door came the sound of movement. The breaking of boyish wind. The suppressed giggles of youngsters misbehaving themselves.

'By gum, that's a real pile.'

'I told you I dare, didn't I?'

The door opened and the two schoolboys stopped as if they'd hit a brick wall; two stern-faced policemen blocked their way and eyed the 'real pile' with open disapproval.

'Not nice,' observed Sowe.

'*Very* nasty,' agreed Hinton.

'Clean it up, lads,' ordered Sowe.

'And *not* with toilet paper,' amplified Hinton.

'I'm — I'm sorry, sir.' One of the youngsters seemed about to break into tears.

'Wot wi'?' The other youngster glanced at the offending 'pile'.

'That.' Sowe nodded at the folded comic which protruded from the pocket of the second youngster's jacket.

'I haven't read it yet,' protested the second youngster.

'Dear me,' sympathised Hinton.

The first youngster moaned, 'C'mon, let's clean it up.'

He pulled a soiled handkerchief from his pocket.

'Where did you get the handkerchief?' asked Sowe.

'It's — it's *mine.*'

Hinton said, 'Nobody says it isn't. Who bought you it?'

'Me mam.'

'Not to do *that* with.'

'Use the comic,' said Sowe.

The first youngster returned the handkerchief to its pocket.

Five minutes later two very subdued youngsters climbed the steps into the street. The lavatory floor was cleaner than it had been for weeks. Sowe and Hinton gave them a few moments to get clear, then they followed them up the steps.

'Child psychology,' observed Hinton. 'It's as easy as falling off a log.'

'Because he says so?' Blayde did little to hide his disgust.

'Because he says so,' agreed Tallboy. 'And because I believe him.'

'I thought you were a copper. A detective chief inspector.'

'That's what it says on my record.'

'And you let a little yuck like that . . .'

'You sent me in there to find out,' Tallboy reminded him.

'I expected something positive.'

'You've *got* something positive. I believe him.'

'Right, who the hell has he murdered?' Blayde glared.

'He doesn't know.'

'It's — er — possible,' murmured Rowe timidly.

'The hell it's possible!'

'Some young slag on the road?' suggested Tallboy.

'Did *he* say that?'

'He doesn't know. *He* was on the road, how in hell's name can *he* tell us what *she* was?'

'Just that he strangled her?'

'It makes her dead,' said Tallboy flatly.

'Y'know what I think?' said Blayde.

'I can guess.'

'I think you bought a painted sparrow, and you still think it's a canary.'

'Okay, *you* listen to him sing.'

'And don't think I won't.'

Muriel Pearson and Tony Armstrong knew the cubby holes in Bordfield General Infirmary; knew where they could snatch a few minutes of precious privacy in the heart of this massive complex of wards, corridors, offices, departments, waiting rooms, theatres and God only knew what else. The storerooms, for example. In particular one storeroom; a place in which new broom-heads, giant tins of wax polish, bundles of yellow dusters and the like were kept. It was cool, it was clean and it was rarely visited.

Nor, at that moment, were they policewoman and male nurse. They were two people, young and very much in love.

Pearson looked bone-weary and infinitely sad. Armstrong looked worried and unusually protective. He'd guided Pearson gently, but firmly, into the storeroom, closed the door, turned the key then touched her lips in a token kiss. Nothing passionate — in her present mood it was no time for passion — but as a gentle reminder that he was *there* . . . and that he understood. Then she'd held him close, he'd folded his arms around her and she buried her face into his shoulder and wept a little.

'Cooper?' he asked softly.

'And Mrs Cooper.' She'd sniffed; annoyed with herself at her own weakness. 'It's breaking her up, Tony. She's a fine woman, but he's pushing her through hell.'

Armstrong sighed and tightened his arms.

What *did* a man do in these circumstances? The man's place. His place in life. To protect and comfort his woman. But *how*? Tony Armstrong suddenly realised a great truth. That when the chips are down, and despite all the studying, all the textbooks, all the urge to become a truly fine nurse, certain situations are well beyond the scope of a mere man's ability to *do* anything.

He muttered, 'You're too involved.'

She nodded, and he felt the movement of her head against his shoulder.

'You're a lousy policewoman,' he whispered.

Again she nodded and the tears still crept from her eyes.

After a few moments of silence he breathed, 'Marry me.'

She seemed to stiffen.

He waited, then murmured, 'I — er — I made a suggestion.'

Again he felt the single nod of her head.

'A *good* suggestion?' he asked timidly.

'A *wonderful* suggestion.'

Then the tears flowed more freely, but they weren't quite the *same* tears.

The trouble with Harris . . .

Quite simply, the trouble with Harris was that he counted himself larger, higher and more important than he actually *was*. A natural mistake. 'Assistant Chief Constable (Crime) — Bordfield Region'. It was there on the door of his office, picked out in letters of gold. Which meant he was a bit of a whoopee wallah as far as rank was concerned and in effect, if not in fact, the 'chief constable' of Bordfield Region and the socking great area that region covered. Nor would that, of necessity, have been a bad thing . . . had he *been* chief constable. He had the required built-in bounce; the growling hauteur; the glaring grandiosity. Robert Harris was a lad-and-a-half . . . especially in the considered opinion of Robert Harris.

But he had a boss.

Bordfield Region (sprawling as it was) was but one of two such regions which went to make up Lessford Metropolitan Police Area, and that police area *had* a chief constable.

Gilliant by name and not (like some so-called chief constables) a mere figurehead. When the occasion demanded it, Gilliant could chew skyscrapers and spit rubble. He knew every underling paid to obey his orders, down to, and including, chief inspectors. He knew them by name and by reputation; he knew their names, their strengths, their weaknesses, their foibles . . . at a guess, the colour of their eyes and their choice of after-shave lotion.

He knew Harris.

'Before you go off duty, Bob,' he said. And even over the telephone wire the tone had a 'you *will*' quality, as opposed to a 'will you?' quality.

'Seems pointless.' Harris put up token resistance. 'The man responsible's already in custody.'

'Nevertheless . . . before you go off duty.'

And, having delivered an undoubted order, Gilliant rang off.

Harris frowned at the dead receiver. He slowly replaced it on its prongs. Telephones, teleprinters, radio transmitters and receivers. He hated 'em all. Their occasional usefulness was more than offset by the fact that they were too handy. A bloody sight too handy. A man had things organised – rolling nicely – then some clown, merely by reason of electronic jiggery-pokery, screwed everything to hell and beyond . . . *and* from a distance.

Noble? Agreed, Noble had had a rough passage. Take away a man's eyes and he was knackered. That was rough. White sticks, guide dogs, Braille. A man could go potty faced with that sort of situation. But what was a hand? One bloody paw. It wasn't as if they were still in the 'hook' era. Artificial hands were damn near as good as the real thing these days. And anyway . . .

Cooper had been a stupid sod. A one-man crusading outfit. Of course Shanks had been guilty, no argument. But that wasn't the point. Without actually *manufacturing* evidence Cooper had slapped it on with a trowel. Given the force a bad name. Handed the civil libertarian lunatics one more stick to wave. Jesus Christ! Hadn't

212

they enough trouble with the fairy-minded twats without helping 'em?

Shanks. A ball-brained little lifter who was going to spend the rest of his natural life in and out of nick. In and out, like a fiddler's elbow. As sure as God made green apples. And, already, he'd been mentioned on the goggle-box. Already he was something of a hero. Something of a martyr.

And all because Cooper couldn't bide his time.

Cooper! Detectives! These days they gave 'em away with corn-flakes.

'This girl you — er — murdered,' said Blayde. 'Tell us about her.'

They were in Rowe's office. The set-up was classic inquisitorial Blayde sat in the desk chair, on his right sat Tallboy, on his left sat Rowe. In front of the desk, in a particularly uncomfortable chair brought in from the Charge Office, sat Bingham; shoeless and with his hands clasped tightly between his gripping thighs. He looked remarkably like an unhappy schoolboy with a bladder on the point of bursting. He looked terrified.

'Tell us about her.' repeated Blayde.

'Sh-she was a girl,' muttered Bingham.

'How old?'

'Oh — er — in her teens, I think.'

'Thirteen? Fifteen? Eighteen?'

'Eighteen . . . I think. I dunno. About eighteen, I'd say.'

'And you — as they say — "had your way with her"?'

'Sh-she offered, sir. It wasn't *that*.'

'What?'

'Y'know . . .' Bingham swallowed. 'Rape.'

'Oh, it *wasn't* rape?' Blayde put surprise in his voice.

'No, sir.'

'Just . . . murder?'

'She — she offered, sir.'

'How?'

'She — she just said — y'know . . . did I want to.'

'And of course . . . you *did*?'

'Sir?'

'*Want* to?'

'Oh! Er — yes, sir. It seemed . . .' He ran out of words.

'A good idea?' suggested Blayde.

'Yes, sir.' Bingham nodded, miserably.

'What was she wearing?'

Bingham turned almost eagerly towards Tallboy as he asked the

213

question. He seemed to sense that here was a man prepared to give some degree of credence to his words.

He said, 'Trousers . . . jeans. A shirt. A sorta belted mac, plastic, I think. It mighta been leather. And sandals.'

'That all?'

'And — y'know — underclothes. Not many, though.'

'A belted, leather mac in June?' Blayde took up the questioning again.

'It — it mighta been June. Maybe before, maybe after. About a year ago. I dunno exactly.'

'But summer?'

Bingham nodded.

'A belted leather mac in summer?' said Blayde mockingly.

'She was on the road, sir. It can get chilly of a night.'

'Did she have a name?' asked Blayde.

'Maggie . . . I think. Or Madge. I can't remember.'

'Just that you killed her?'

'Yes, sir.' It was softly spoken, but without hesitation.

'Strangled her?'

'Yes, sir.'

'Having screwed her?' said Blayde bluntly.

'Yes, sir,' breathed Bingham.

'Why?' Rowe asked his first question.

'Sir?'

'Why did you kill her?'

'She — she was diseased, sir.'

'Oh!'

'Pox? Or clap?' Blayde was as blunt, as harsh as ever.

'I — I dunno, sir. Just . . . that she was diseased.'

'You catch anything?'

'No, sir.'

'Then how the hell d'you know?'

'She — she told me, sir.'

'Before? Or after?' Tallboy took up the questioning.

'Oh, after, sir. If I'd known *before* . . .' Bingham looked sad and didn't end the sentence.

'After?' murmured Tallboy.

'She laughed at me,' mumbled Bingham. 'She thought she'd given me summat . . . and she laughed at me.'

'You're a lying hound,' said Blayde flatly.

Karn was not merely a bad copper, he was a bad human being. There are such men; parasites of the human race; organisms who derive substance without rendering service. They give nothing, but expect everything. They are the whores of the Police Service — male and female — and they wield whatever power they possess, but refuse any responsibility.

When a man or woman applies to join a police force certain enquiries are made. Obvious enquiries. That (for example) he or she is not up to the neck in unpaid debts. That, within their immediate community, they carry a certain degree of respect. That they are not related to, or friends of, known criminals.

5 p.m.

But the net is wide-meshed and sometimes men like Karn are 'passed' as fit and proper police officers when, in fact, they are not even fit and proper human beings.

Karn stood in the front garden of his police-provided house and, with his hands deep in the pockets of his trousers, scowled across the lane at the blossoming cow parsley on the opposite verge. He'd lost his job. Not much doubt of that. That flaming detective sergeant and that nancy-boy Rowe had ganged up on him beautifully. That two-five-two Misconduct Form was going to be a dinger. *They'd* see to that! The way of the world, mate. Sods like that climbing to the top of the heap by stamping on the necks of poor buggers who only want to live and let live.

Karn truly believed his own argument. He truly believed that, in hiding himself on top of hay and reading cheap pornographic literature when he should have been asking questions concerning the maiming of two of his colleagues, he hadn't done anything wrong. Jesus Christ, it was his Weekly Rest Day. He shouldn't have been on duty in the first place. All this house-to-house crap . . . a waste of time and everybody knew it. And because he hadn't gone along and played silly-buggers with the rest of 'em . . .

But what to tell Elsie?

Elsie had a good job. Good shorthand typists weren't — y'know — weren't thick on the ground. They brought home good pay. And she was happy in that office where she worked.

So . . .

She'd go on, and on, and on. She'd give him hell. Chances were she'd make out it was his own fault. She'd blame *him*. She wouldn't see *his* side of things. In the past . . . nag, nag, nag. She didn't understand. She never *had* understood.

From behind his back he heard the telephone bell ring inside the house. So, let it ring. It was *still* his Weekly Rest Day. He couldn't be farther in it than he was. So let the bloody thing ring its stupid bell off . . .

'Where was she from?' asked Blayde.

'I tell you . . . she was on the road.'

'Living rough?'

'Yes, sir. Like me.'

'Where did you pick her up?'

'I — I didn't.'

'Come on, Bingham. If you're telling the truth . . .'

'It's the truth, sir.'

'. . . you must have picked her up from somewhere.'

'She — she came into this barn, sir.'

'Barn?'

'Up there. A few miles from here. I'd found this barn. More of an outbuilding, really.'

'You found this barn.' Tallboy took over the interrogation. 'This outbuilding.'

'Yes, sir.'

'The evening, was it?'

'Yes, sir. I was settling in for the night.'

'And she — this Maggie, this Madge — came along?'

'Yes, sir.'

'Used it before?' asked Blayde.

'Sir?'

'This outhouse? This barn?'

'Oh — er — yes, sir. A few times.'

'You'll know where it is, then.'

'Well . . .' Bingham hesitated.

'If you've used it before, you'll know where it is,' pressed Blayde.

'It's — y'know — in a corner of a field, sir.'

'Which field?'

Before Bingham could answer, Rowe said, 'A barn — an outhouse — it should be attached to a farm. *Near* a farm. Do you mean a plough-shed?'

'I — er — yes, sir. It's not near a farm. It's well away from anywhere . . . in a corner of a field.'

'It doesn't bloody-well exist,' growled Blayde in disgust.

And now she felt guilty. Such a mix. Such a compound. Joy, excitement, sorrow, trepidation, a touch of fear for the future and a certain sour taste of guilt.

For the second time that day the three of them shared a table in the hospital canteen. Muriel Pearson, Marian Cooper and Hilda Noble. It seemed right that they should remain together until all three could smile and know the worst was over. More than once Marian Cooper had been on the point of suggesting that, if they wished, the other two might leave. Already Noble had come to accept the fact of his blindness; the full realisation hadn't yet hit him — that would come when he left his bed and *then* the shock might drive him to a despair he hadn't yet touched — but for the moment, and even if some of it was play-acting, he was on an even enough keel to be left until tomorrow. As for W.P.C. Pearson . . . already she deserved a medal for what she'd done. But to even suggest that the trio should yet become less than a trio seemed (to Marian Cooper) a minor profanity.

And yet Muriel Pearson . . . The pastiche of her feelings was reflected in her changing expression.

'What is it?' Marian Cooper asked the question in a quiet, gentle tone.

'It's nothing. It's . . .' Then it burst with the suddenness of a high-speed blow-out. 'I'm going to be married. He's — he's . . . This afternoon. He proposed and I accepted.'

And — women being women and because they're women, romantic creatures whatever the circumstances — there was much excitement, and kissing, and hand squeezing, and a touch of tears. For the moment Noble and Cooper were thrust to the back of the mind. This — that Hilda Noble and Marian Cooper were at Bordfield General Infirmary because marriage also carries the certainty of heartbreak — was forgotten. At that moment there was a band of love which held the three women close; a band unknown to mere men . . . a band which would never be completely loosened.

'I've tried to get hold of Karn.' Ramsden seemed to be on the point of wringing his hands. It had been *some* day . . . and now this. There was near-wildness in his eyes and he continued, 'Pinter. He's been on since early morning. And there's his wife. We can't . . . And Coop's in hospital, and Kyle's across at . . .'

'Easy, Bob.' Sergeant Cockburn removed his helmet and placed it and the lunch-box on top of the green, steel filing cabinet. 'I'll take it. Where's the log?'

'And that's another thing,' wailed Ramsden. 'Blayde — he's in Rowe's office with Tallboy — they're questioning a roadster Leeds picked up last night. He says he killed a lass here — at Sopworth — sometime last year.'

217

'Big licks.' Cockburn showed no sign of surprise. No sign of panic. 'The log. I'd better . . .'

'It's locked away. Blayde's instructions. I logged the message from Leeds and . . .'

'Away home, Bob. Get your feet up. The old story . . . log on spare bits of paper, till they've checked the murder cough.'

'I don't like it,' moaned Ramsden. Then he took a deep breath and said, 'It's locked away in the safe. The messages . . . you'll find 'em scribbled on flimsies by the switchboard. And this domestic thing up at Rimstone. Karn mustn't be at home. He should have . . .'

'We'll fix it.' Cockburn grinned. 'I'll take Sowe. Who knows? It might be *another* murder.'

'So?' There was a distant snarl in Blayde's tone. 'You know where it is? You *don't* know where it is? In short it's all bloody moonshine.'

'No, sir. That's . . .'

'If you've used the barn before?'

'I have. Once or twice.'

'Once? Twice?'

'A — a few times.'

'A regular dossing spot, is it?'

'When — when I'm round this way.'

'How often's that?'

'Sir?'

'When you're round this way . . . how often *are* you round this way?'

'About once a year, sir. It — it varies.'

Rowe asked, 'Why did you leave home, Bingham?'

'Sir?' There was almost eagerness in the way Bingham turned to answer this less belligerent officer.

'What sent you on the road?' Rowe re-phrased the question.

'I — er — my wife left me, sir. I — I couldn't handle things.'

'*She* left *you*? Not the other way round?'

'She — she left me, sir.' Then, as a hurried addendum. 'I'm not blaming her, sir.'

'Why?'

'I'm no good to her, sir. I'm — I'm not much good to anybody.'

'You can say *that* again,' growled Blayde.

'This barn,' said Tallboy. 'This plough-shed. You must have some idea.'

'It's — it's going up to the moors, sir.'

'From here?'

'Going to where?'

Bingham snapped his attention back to Blayde, as Blayde barked the follow-up question.

'Going to where?' repeated Blayde.

'It's . . .' Bingham shook his head. 'I dunno, sir. I don't look at signposts. I'm — I'm never making for anywhere in particular.'

'So, it could have been *anywhere*?'

'Sir?'

'Half your life you don't know where the hell you are. Assuming — for the sake of argument — you *did* murder somebody . . .'

'Yes, sir. I did.'

'. . . it could have been *anywhere*?'

'No, sir.' Bingham's voice was low, but certain.

'From what you've just said . . .'

'I — I came down, here. To this police station. I was — I was gonna give myself up, see?'

'And?'

'I — I daren't.'

Evans flexed his fingers, blew out his cheeks, then muttered, 'To hell with it. If that won't do . . . to *hell* with it.'

He leaned back in the chair, lighted a cigarette and surveyed the six identical stapled thicknesses of quarto and foolscap. One complete crime file . . . plus five copies. More than that, even. One complete *murder* file . . . plus five copies. And in a single day. It was something to write home about. Something for which to stick out his chest. And (discounting Wooley, of course) all his own work.

Pollard had been right in his voiced assessment to Blayde. That file, headed 'Regina *v.* Preston' was the making of Detective Constable William 'Taffy' Evans. It was what he'd needed. The deep end; the sink-or-swim treatment.

There are such days in the lives of men. Particularly in the lives of coppers. Something happens, the Big Hurdle looms ahead and you either dodge round it or try for a leap. If you dodge round it, you're finished and you know it. From then on you're a frightened man; you know you can be licked; you know that, given certain circumstances, you'll turn and run. As a copper, you'll never be completely trustworthy and that, although you keep it a secret throughout your whole service, it is a bitter truth you must live with. Take the Big Hurdle and fall? At least you've tried and that, of itself, eases the shame, because next time you might not fall. But clear the hurdle? There is a new sparkle in the eye, a new spring in the step, a new self-assurance in the manner in which you do your job. You're a *copper*! Complete, rounded and three-dimensional. Nothing will ever again frighten you. Nothing will intimidate you. Nobody will out-face you.

Evans inhaled cigarette smoke and looked, with pride, at the six thicknesses of official documents.

He felt good . . . but didn't quite know why.

'Hold the fort, Fred.' Cockburn reached for his helmet and, from long practice, placed it at its normal, slightly rakish angle on his head. He fastened the button on one of the breast pockets of his tunic, then added, 'Right, Bobby Sowe, one domestic disturbance coming up.' Then, as he and Sowe were leaving the Charge Office, 'Fred — the Telephone and Teleprinter Message Book — it's locked away. Orders from on high. Use buckshee flimsies for any messages. We'll log 'em in later.'

'Will do.'

Cockburn and Sowe left. Hinton moved purposelessly around the Charge Office and (as always when he was alone) thought about Rob.

Mongolism. One of those ailments — like cancer, like leprosy — the name itself frightened people. Maybe they should wear a placard around their necks with the word 'Unclean' printed on it. Maybe they should carry a bell and ring it to warn of their approach.

Instead they were treated like loonies. Cut the mealy-mouthed crap, Hinton. Loonies! That's what the world *5.30 p.m.* thought they were. And the world was wrong. Rob was living proof that the world was wrong. Rob had more love — more honest-to-God, no-strings-attached love — in his little finger than . . .

Like a child. A very honest, unsophisticated child. Okay, he'd *always* be like a child. A child, hampered by a teenager's body. In time, a child hampered by an adult's body. But as long as you remembered that however big he was — however old he was — he was still this child . . .

Like a child, he knelt by his bed and said his prayers every night. Like a child, he *believed*. A very uncomplicated belief. 'Our Father' *was* in heaven and no questions asked. That was the choking beauty of it all; he never went to church because to take him to church would mean putting him up on view and people who only professed their belief would stare and frighten him. But unlike those people, Rob believed. The Bible — The Prayer Book — he couldn't read them, couldn't understand them, couldn't . . .

And yet *nobody* was more certain than Rob . . .

Thus Police Constable 1956 Frederick Hinton. Externally a man dedicated to his profession. On the face of it a man who enjoyed being a police officer . . . as, indeed, he did. A man who, when he was off duty, occasionally drank a little too much. A steady, reliable copper. No tearer-up-of-trees, no headline cracker. He'd soldier on, do his service, complain a little, laugh a little and end with the rank he'd been given on the day he'd taken the Police Oath.

Yet secretly and for the rest of his life . . .

Blayde said, 'You claim you strangled her?'

'Yes, sir. When she told me . . .'

'What happened to the body?'

'I . . . buried it, sir.'

'Where?'

'Not far away. About a hundred yards from the barn. In a – in a field.'

'You buried it?'

'Yes, sir.'

'How?'

'Sir?'

'With your hands? How did you dig the hole?'

'With the spade.'

'The *spade*?' Blayde raised a sardonic eyebrow. 'Something you carry around in your pocket, is it?'

'Sir?'

'This spade you've suddenly produced?'

'It – it was there, sir. In the barn.'

Tallboy said, 'You buried the body?'

'Yes, sir.'

'Where?'

'About a hundred yards from . . .'

'No, I mean *where*? In a hedge-bottom? Where?'

'Oh – er – in a field, sir. There's this field.'

'Near the barn?'

'Yes, sir. Not far from the barn.'

'And the spade was in the barn?'

'Yes, sir.'

'A new spade?'

'No, sir.'

'An old spade?'

221

'I – I dunno about that, sir. It was – y'know – well used. Sharp. It wasn't hard to dig the hole.'

The way he said it. That last sentence. The solemn, quiet way in which he mouthed the words. 'It wasn't hard to dig the hole.' For the first time Blayde accepted the possibility. Even the *probability*. His nape hairs tingled. Cold-footed spiders seemed to scurry along his spine.

In a changed voice, he said, 'Tell us about the barn, Bingham. The spade. What else was there in the barn?'

'A bath, sir. An old bath. I think – y'know – I think it must have been used as a cattle trough. Sometime. I've seen 'em. Old baths used as cattle troughs. I think that's what the bath must have been used for, then – y'know – dumped in the barn.'

'The girl?' Rowe took up the questioning. 'Was she from round here?'

'She was on the road, sir.'

'No, I mean her accent. Her dialect. The way she talked. Could you . . .'

'Oh, she wasn't from round here, sir.'

'Where from?'

'Liverpool, I think. Maybe Birmingham.' Bingham hesitated, then added, 'Maybe Welsh . . . I dunno much about these things.'

Blayde breathed. 'Hell!'

'Sir?'

Blayde sighed, 'You've widened the scope, lad. You've *really* widened the scope.'

'Railway Cottages, obviously near the station.'

Cockburn allowed the Ford Capri to ease along at a steady forty. It was a new car, the engine parts hadn't yet worked themselves into their smooth-running best. Anyway, there was no hurry. That official expression 'Domestic Disturbance' covered just about everything. An irate wife locking her drunken husband out of his own home; a teenager at the receiving end of a long-overdue thrashing from his father; a straight up-and-down, man-and-wife row . . . they were all 'Domestic Disturbances'. So, you took your time. What the hell happened – however tactful you tried to be – *you* were going to end up as villain of the piece. Common gumption. A domestic barney . . . who the hell wanted some hairy-arsed copper in on the act? Best thing to do . . . arrive late, add a few tut-tuts to the kiss-and-make-up scene. That way they didn't think too badly about things.

Because they were on their way to Rimstone Beat – because that fact jogged his memory — Constable Sowe said, 'Pity about Pinter's missus.'

Cockburn grunted.

'Not much hope, I reckon.'

'I think Wilf's a mug,' growled Cockburn, in a low voice shot with a little disgust. 'I can see his argument, but he's wrong.'

'Keeps his mind off things.'

'Seen him lately?'

'Not within the last week.'

'If he keeps this up, she'll see *him* out.'

They rode in silence for a while, then Sowe said, 'Nick doesn't help a lot.'

'Karn.' Cockburn seemed to spit the word. 'Why the hell do men like him join the force?'

'A soft touch?' suggested Sowe.

Again Cockburn grunted. This time the disgust was far more obvious.

They found Railway Cottages, they found the house and they talked with Lizzie and William Ackroyd, and, while not wholly believing, there was a quality about the telling which denied complete *dis*belief.

It was, you see, Friday and Friday was 'fish' day. And William Ackroyd liked his bit o' fish on a Friday; in particular he liked his kippers when he arrived home from work. He'd *always* had kippers when he arrived home from work on a Friday. Always! Ever since they were married and that was going back a bit. Two nice, fat, juicy kippers. Summat to look forward to. Summat he *always* came home to on a Friday evening.

And the kippers had been bought for him. No question about that. His Lizzie was a good lass. She knew her place. She knew what pleased her husband. And, indeed, she'd actually been frying the kippers when Ma Sutcliffe had called.

Old Ma Sutcliffe. A funny woman. Y'know . . . laying bodies out, sometimes helping the midwife at births. Sometimes without even the midwife. Not many of her kind left. Unmarried. Who'd ever marry a crone like that? Who'd marry her kind, whatever their age? Not a woman to cross. She could do things. Strange things. Frightening things.

Anyway, Ma Sutcliffe had called and seen Lizzie Ackroyd frying the two kippers. She'd just started frying 'em. Just put 'em into the pan, see? And Ma Sutcliffe had seen 'em, then *asked* for 'em. Just like that. 'I like kippers, Lizzie. Bring 'em across to my place when tha's fried 'em.' As brazen as *that*. Not even a 'will you?'. Not even a 'please'. Just − y'know − 'bring 'em'.

And Lizzie had done it.

When the kippers were done to a turn, she'd opened the door and, frying pan in hand, had hurried across the street to Ma Sutcliffe's home. And, moreover, Ma Sutcliffe had been waiting. Plate ready on the table. Knife and fork in hand.

'I knew tha'd come, Lizzie. Tha'd no option.'

As for William Ackroyd . . .

To be faced with jam and bread when his belly was eager for kippers. That was more than flesh and blood could stand. He'd gone mildly berserk. He'd roared his fury and, in order to underline his disappointment, had fisted his wife in the eye . . . and *meant* it.

The shouting and screaming had upset the nextdoor neighbour and a nine-nine-nine call had been made to the police.

That (minus all the bad language in the telling thereof) was the story listened to by Sergeant Cockburn and Constable Sowe.

'Just like that?' murmured Cockburn.

'As God's my judge,' sobbed Lizzie. 'There . . .' She pointed. 'There's t' frying pan. I dunno why. They were Bill's kippers. I dunno *why* I took 'em across.'

Life had dealt Lizzie Ackroyd a bad hand, and whatever tricks she might have called had been blocked by her marriage to William. She was skinny and hunch-shouldered, as if half a century of too much sorrow and too many tears had squeezed all the fight and much of the liquid content from her body. She could be dominated. That much was very obvious.

And yet . . .

Cockburn and Sowe. They didn't believe in ghosts, hobgoblins − all that crap − their size tens were firmly placed on Mother Earth. And yet, *she* believed. Not a shadow of doubt. This frail, broken woman with the swelling and discoloured eye would never willingly have taken those bloody kippers to the Sutcliffe crone. She'd have *known*; known what the consequences would be; known she'd be bounced off the nearest wall by this animal she had as a husband. But, knowing all this, she'd taken the kippers.

Therefore . . . *something*.

'I think,' said Cockburn slowly, 'we'll have a short statement. Bare details, plus the fact your husband poked you in the eye.' He paused, then added, 'Maybe a photograph. That might help.'

'Eh?' William Ackroyd looked puzzled.

'Of the eye,' explained Cockburn solemnly. 'If we pick the court date — pick the right bench — you should get a month, at least a month.'

'*Me*?' William Ackroyd looked flabbergasted.

'Assault,' said Cockburn coldly. 'Give the boat a bit of a push, maybe even G.B.H.'

'Look, wot the 'ell . . .'

'Wife-bashing isn't yet recognised as a field event, mate.'

'I – I . . .'

'Kippers or no kippers.'

'No, sir, please!' Lizzie looked as if she might drop to her knees in beseechment.

'It's up to you, madam,' said Cockburn in a gentle tone.

'Please, sir, I don't want anything else to . . .'

'You're the boss, madam.' Then to Sowe, 'A short report in your pocketbook, constable. The complaint and what we've found.'

'Sarge.' Sowe flipped the pages of his notebook open.

'And *you*.' Cockburn faced Ackroyd. 'We record this visit . . . understand? If we have to come here a second time for the same reason, you'll get a real draught up your kilt . . . am I reaching you?'

'If – if she . . .'

'*She* won't have a say in the matter next time, mate. All your wife'll see is a following cloud of dust.'

Blayde, Tallboy and Rowe walked into the Charge Office. Blayde tossed the cell key onto the nearest desk.

He said, 'Teenage girl . . . make it between fifteen and twenty. Thereabouts. Liverpool and Birmingham. Madge or Maggie, that's all we know. Ask 'em to check their Missings From Home for the last couple of years. Suspected murder. It's *that* urgent.'

'Yes, sir.' Hinton frowned, then added, 'A tip-off from Bradford, sir. We're in for some sort of raid.'

'A what?'

'Some of the Bradford wide-boys. Tearaways. They're planning a visit to Sopworth this evening. Looking for trouble.'

'Is that a fact?' Blayde sniffed. 'Sergeant Cockburn know?'

'Not yet, sir. He's out at . . .'

'Tell him. We'll be ready . . . just in case.'

'Yes, sir.'

'I'll be back. And . . .' Blayde glanced at Rowe. 'The inspector.'

'I'll be back,' echoed Rowe.

'And me,' added Tallboy.

'Why not?' For a moment Blayde's grin made him look ridiculously boyish. 'Ask the Bradford people to keep us posted. Bingham's back in his cell, see he gets fed and watered. Oh, and – er – bring the log book up to date.'

'Yes, sir.'

Out in the street, Rowe said, 'I owe you a meal, sir.'

'What?' Blayde didn't understand for a moment. 'Oh, that's . . .'

'My wife's a good cook, sir. There'll be plenty.'

'There's no need to . . .'

'Please.'

The word was more than a politeness. It was an implied request to be 'accepted'; in effect, an assurance that things were now different.

'Thanks.' Blayde nodded. 'If you're sure it won't inconvenience Mrs Rowe, I'd be delighted.'

Ma Sutcliffe's place stank to high heaven of cats. It was a beautiful June day, but in some inexplicable way dark and murky inside her cottage. Think of the witch in *Snow White* – Disney's cartoon wasn't too much of a caricature of Ma Sutcliffe. Even the wheezy cackle when she laughed conjured up images of cauldrons boiling with some filthy brew. The plate, holding what was left of the two kippers, was still on the table.

There was little said, but what *was* said carried a world of meaning. The woman had long ago convinced even herself that she possessed some secret well of power; that she could 'will' people to do things if she so desired; that witches – albeit without flying broomsticks or 'familiars' – walked the earth and that she was one of them. Cockburn and Sowe, on the other hand, were coppers. Sane and paid to retain their sanity. Paid to take a situation – any situation – and reduce it to a two-plus-two-equals-four simplicity. Hocus-pocus was definitely out, as far as their thinking was concerned. Ma Sutcliffe was merely an evil old bitch who battened on to what few dark superstitions still lurked in the backwaters of rural communities.

'It could be described as theft.' Cockburn eyed the plate coldly. 'You conned her into it.'

'She *brought* them.' Sutcliffe grinned, and the grin was a leer. 'I didn't even *ask*.'

Sowe said, 'You're an evil old cow.'

'Careful.'

'Of what? Will you turn me into a toad?'

'*You* be careful, old woman.' Cockburn's tone carried an open threat. 'There's an answer to everything . . . even you.'

'Sergeant, you mustn't . . .'

'Don't tell *me* what to do. What not to do,' snapped Cockburn. 'Next time, I'll have a doctor with me. I'll make damn sure you're certified.'

'You can't . . .'

'Try me,' snarled Cockburn.

'Or try *me*,' added Sowe.

'The last time.' Cockburn nodded at the plate holding the remains of the kippers. 'The next time I'll put salt on your tail, old woman, won't I just!'

They drove much of the way back to Sopworth in silence. These days the cult religions sprouted and grew like fungi in the worm-wooded structure of a civilisation gone rotten with hate and greed. Witchcraft? It was practised. It was believed in. Much of it for kicks, as a relief from boredom. But in the Dark Ages . . .

'All balls, of course,' murmured Sowe as they moved into the outskirts of Sopworth.

'Make out your report.' Cockburn stared straight ahead at the road as it sped towards them. 'I'll add a few comments.'

The bustle of Bordfield General Infirmary was easing. Gradually. Almost imperceptibly. It would never be completely silent; even in the small hours there'd be the squeak of rubber soles on polished floors, the sound of an ambulance drawing to a halt, then being driven away, the murmur of voices and the soft rumble of a stretcher-trolley being rushed along corridors. Nevertheless, many of the ancillary workers had left, the meals had been served, the operating theatres were standing empty, awaiting whatever emergency might arise before morning. Therefore, the bustle was easing.

6.30 p.m.

Harris walked slowly and without seeking directions. He followed the signs leading to the wards. Then the sign which read 'Appleton Ward', and only then did he enquire from a nurse the whereabouts of Sergeant Noble and Police Constable Cooper.

He knocked and opened the door of the side-ward in a single movement.

Pearson stood up from a chair.

'Sit down.' Harris waved a hand, then moved to the side of Noble's bed. In a gruff, awkward tone he said, 'How's he going?'

'He's blind,' said Hilda Noble simply.

'I'd heard. That's bad.'

'Who is it?' Noble turned his head.

'Harris,' said Harris. 'The chief asked me to call in.'

'Nothing spontaneous, of course.'

The observation came from Marian Cooper. It held contempt and loathing in equal measure.

'I've been kept informed.' Harris moved across to Cooper's bed and, in a voice which almost matched that of the woman, said 'How's *he*?'

'You've been kept informed,' she reminded him.

'The thing was meant for him,' said Harris flatly. 'A good man has lost his sight. *His* — your husband's — fault. Should I feel sorry for him?'

'Could you?' She joined battle with this huge, thick-limbed assistant chief constable. It was something to do. Something *positive*. She accepted the challenge with something not too far removed from joy. Her eyes blazed and she snapped, 'Could you feel sorry for *anybody*?'

'It's been known,' he taunted.

'Yourself, perhaps?'

'Often.'

'But very few other people . . . right?'

'Not for coppers who aren't fit to be coppers.'

'You make me sick. Sick to the stomach.'

'And people like him?' He glanced at the bed. 'What do *they* make you? Gutless fools who think themselves a law above the law. Who ask for trouble and, when they get it, sulk like spoiled brats. They *don't* make you sick?' His lips twisted. 'And the women they choose. As gutless as themselves. As brainless, as self-centred, as . . .'

'Shut up you fat bastard!'

Cooper shouted the words in a hoarse, heart-broken voice. Despite the saline drip, he struggled to free himself from the bedclothes. His expression was kill-crazy and, as he fought to free himself, he mouthed his hatred of Harris.

'You talk to my wife like that, I'll break your stupid neck. What the hell do *you* know about . . .'

'Coop!'

Marian Cooper threw herself across the body of her struggling husband. Muriel Pearson joined her and, despite the threshing, they held him down. Harris watched and, gradually, the smile became one of triumph.

It took the two women a full three minutes to quieten the struggling, cursing Cooper, then the two men stared at each other. One with loathing. The other with victory.

'I've been kept informed,' growled Harris. 'They said you wouldn't talk. They were wrong. They didn't know how to *make* you talk.'

He favoured Marian Cooper with a frosty smile, turned and walked from the tiny ward.

Muriel Pearson stared at the closed door for a moment, then breathed, 'Y'know what? *That's* why he's an assistant chief constable.'

Elsie Karn felt like only a woman can feel. Her feet ached; every month at this time, her damn feet seemed to swell and shoes which, for the rest of the month fitted comfortably, nipped and rubbed and gave her minor hell. Her back ached; the loonies who designed typist's chairs should be made to use them for hours on end and while bent forward deciphering hurriedly scrawled shorthand. Her head ached; a subtle ache which wasn't *quite* an ache, but which happened at this time and went on, and on, and on.

And now this.

For God's sake, why couldn't Nick understand? The world didn't owe him a living. Nobody owed him a living, and sure as hell *she* didn't! She owed him nothing. She'd given him everything. Even before they were married, she'd ended up paying every piper who happened to have played Nick's tune. And, by God, she was tired of it all. She was tired of being substitute-mother to him; tired of making all the decisions; tired of working her guts out while at the same time being forced to listen to his everlasting griping about a job which, if he'd only do the damn job properly, would be a good job.

She pushed herself out of the armchair and said, 'I'm going to bed.'

'Eh?' Karn gaped. 'I've just told you. Rowe's likely to get me booted out. That means . . .'

'That means,' she interrupted wearily, 'you'll be out of work. It means you'll get another job. But you won't like *that* job, so you'll be out of work again. You're a pain, Nick. Did I ever tell you? *You're* a pain and *I'm* tired, so I'm going to bed.'

Sandwiches. Said to have been invented by the fourth Earl of Sandwich in the 18th century, as a means of playing cards and eating at the same time. A neat trick; something not too far short of the invention of the wheel. Without sandwiches what would men banged up in a police cell eat? This time it was cheese sandwiches, washed down with the obligatory mug of hot, sweet tea.

Bingham chewed and drank, and began to wish he'd kept his mouth shut. Well, no, not altogether. A man walks around with murder on his conscience. It grows. It becomes a weight too heavy to carry any farther. No dreams, you understand. No nightmares. Maybe if he'd known her; thought something about her; liked her . . . even a little bit. But as it was . . . he'd just *murdered* her.

Like killing a rabbit. Like wringing the neck of a stolen chicken.

But she hadn't been a rabbit, and she hadn't been a chicken, therefore, although no bad dreams, the conscience thing had bothered him. And when the Leeds jack had pushed him, he'd coughed. Out, almost before he knew he'd said it.

And now . . .

All the details. When? How? Where? Why? Unimportant things. Questions he couldn't answer. Christ, he'd trudged *miles* since then. Hedgerows, haystacks, cowsheds, half-built houses. Last winter he'd found the door of a school boiler-house unlocked . . . he'd slept *there*. Prison was like Butlins. It really *was* like a holiday camp. A few years — ten years, even twenty years — no hardship. Christ, *not* being in prison was the hardship.

And this dead little cow was the key, but they wouldn't let him use the key.

Sod 'em.

He'd kill some other miserable bugger towards the end of the coming summer, and he'd leave the corpse up top. They'd believe him *then*.

Meanwhile, Hinton was snatching a meal at home before relieving Sowe. Hinton went home for his meals; a small concession because of Rob; he usually worked with Cockburn and Sowe and they didn't mind. He lived less than a quarter of a mile from the nick and he was on the telephone; he could be up and on duty in the time it took somebody to dial his number.

Rob was eating with him. Just the two of them. They had their meal in the kitchen — this time it was sardines on toast — while Con and her father sat in the front room, gazing at the box. That's the way they usually worked things. Today was no different.

Hinton put out a hand and touched his son's arm.

'Easy, Rob. Don't push too much into your mouth at once.'

Rob said he enjoyed sardines on toast. To a stranger the mouthed words would have been unintelligible, but Hinton heard and understood.

'Me, too, old son. But they're all yours. Eat slowly. Take your time. Enjoy the taste.'

Rob nodded his head eagerly. Anxious to please this man who

was his daddy. Nevertheless, he continued to push food into his mouth at the same rate.

Hinton sighed.

He couldn't blame Con. Jesus — Connie Bradshaw, the girl all the young blades of the village had had their sights on, and she'd married him, Fred Hinton — and Rob, here, had been the result. No, he couldn't blame Con. No more kids — *definitely* — and he couldn't blame her for that, either. Come to that, he couldn't really blame her for — y'know — that faint flicker of distaste which touched her expression sometimes whenever she had to handle her son. It wasn't *her* fault. She couldn't see beyond the exterior — couldn't see all that simple happiness, that limitless love locked up inside and fighting to get out — all she could see was what she *could* see.

'Fred, we should arrange for him to live somewhere.'

'Y'mean locked up?'

'No — not actually locked up. But there are places.'

'No.'

'Nursing homes. Nice places where he'd be happy, where they'd . . .'

'No way!'

And the argument to which there was no real answer.

'Fred, what happens when we die? We won't live forever.'

'We're not old. We've a long way to go, yet.'

'We'll die. The chances are we'll die before him.'

'Don't call him "him". He has a name. Use it.'

'All right . . . Rob. He'll outlive us. He'll . . .'

'Forget it, Con. I don't want to talk about it.'

'Because you know it's true. Because . . .'

'Forget it!'

Always the same argument; the same, unresolved argument. Because to look beyond tomorrow — beyond next week at the most — holy Christ, what *would* happen?

Their marriage was crumbling. Sure it was. Like rotten plaster falling away from a sodden wall. That's how it was crumbling. And it hurt. It hurt like hell . . . it hurt like hell to know he didn't love her as much as he had once upon a time. That each day saw a little less love; a little more plaster falling away.

For no reason. For no *real* reason. For no . . .

Almost automatically, he said, 'Rob, old son. Not too much of a mouthful, eh? Easy does it. It tastes better.'

Tallboy spread a thickness of paté onto his toast, bit into it and, with his mouth full, said, 'Kyle.'

'If,' complained Susan Tallboy, 'you'd let me have *some* idea. However vague . . .'

'Kyle might be able to tell us.'

'. . . Just some *idea* . . .'

'He knows that area. His own beat and Rimstone Beat.'

'. . . I might be able to feed you properly . . .'

'It's at least evens it happened on Upper Neck or Rimstone.'

'. . . I might not have to sit here and watch you starve yourself to death. Or eat the wrong sort of food. Or . . .'

'Were you saying something, sweetheart?' smiled Tallboy.

'Oh, my God!' Susan Tallboy blew out her cheeks in exaggerated desperation.

'I'm listening,' Tallboy assured her sweetly.

'You've finished with this mysterious Kyle?' she enquired.

'What? Oh – er – yes. What is it you want to say?'

'About meals.' Her voice was deliberately controlled.

'Yes?'

'Even *you* have to eat.'

'I'm eating.' He waved the toast.

'Great heavens! I mean a *real* meal.'

'I had . . .'

'*Not* from a frying pan.'

'Okay.' Tallboy sighed. 'List my faults, then tell me how lucky you are to be my wife.'

She tried and he listened. But (as always) it was hopeless. This man of hers was almost unique, and part of the quality which made him unique was the fact that he counted himself a very *ordinary* guy. Her wifely annoyance dissolved when faced by his smiling calm. Maybe she *could* twist him round her little finger, but because of what he was, she didn't *want* to.

One day (she told herself) he'd get her *so* mad . . .

But this wasn't the day.

Hannah Pinter died.

No fuss, no bedside drama, no famous last words. She just ceased to be alive . . . as simple as that. She was alone at the time; her mother was in the kitchen preparing a makeshift meal. Pinter was out on patrol in the Minivan; 'out on patrol' meaning he was alone – deliberately alone – seeking what solace he could away from the immediate heartbreak of his home, and dredging up memories with which to torture himself.

Her mother didn't find her until after eight. Having eaten the meal, she washed the dishes, wandered around the kitchen and the living room, then flopped into an armchair and she, too, dragged memories from the past; memories which made her weep a little. At eight o'clock she climbed the stairs, splashed cold water onto her face then, having dried herself, she walked softly into the bedroom.

But Hannah Pinter had died.

Cycles. Wheels within wheels within wheels. The pattern of policing. There are certain periods of inactivity; the sweep hand of time hits a certain point and, as if to order, the world seems to pause in its spin. The nine-to-fivers have gone home; the office blocks, the banks, most of the shops all stand empty. The public houses, the bingo halls, the cafes and restaurants have not yet moved into top gear. Even the streets seem strangely deserted.

Thus in the small hours — between midnight and dawn — this comparatively 'dead' period is when coppers relax a little, and bring the paperwork up to date. Similarly between five o'clock and seven o'clock, there is a second slowing down of the day; a breathing space; a time for taking things easy, a time for 'making up' notebooks, a time for stretching the limbs in preparation for the evening's activity.

At Sopworth the market stalls had all been dismantled. The various struts and boards had been stacked neatly *7 p.m.* away in the yard behind the Council Offices. Two council employees swept and tidied the square; clearing the leaves, the squashed fruit, the general garbage into piles, then shovelling the piles into a lidded, box-like container on wheels to be trundled away and left for the refuse-collectors to dispose of next morning. By seven o'clock the square had reverted back to its normal function of Official Car Park.

'Go home.' Cooper's voice was mild and resigned. 'You've had a hell of a day, all three of you.' He paused, then added, 'I haven't helped.'

'If you'd sooner we stayed . . . ' began Marian Cooper.

'He's right.' Noble interrupted from the other bed. 'Go home. Get some sleep. We'll be okay.'

Hilda Noble said, 'If you're sure.'

'I'm sure.'

Cooper added, 'We're both sure. And . . . thanks.'

The three women stood up. They were tired; drained of both energy and emotion. Without saying much else, each of them kissed both men on the cheek, then trooped out of the tiny ward.

There was a few moments of silence, then Cooper said, 'I'm sorry, sarge.'

'What the hell for?'

'That thing. Harris was right . . . it was meant for me.'

'Harris.' Noble chuckled. 'He's a wily old sod. All that bullshit, pretending to be . . .'

'It wasn't *all* pretence.'

'Hey, Coop.' Anxiety touched Noble's tone. 'Don't hoist that railway sleeper onto your shoulder again.'

'It *was* meant for me,' insisted Cooper.

'It was meant for the first person picking it up.'

'Me.'

'Or it could have been me. Some kid. Anybody.'

'At that time of night? You know damn well it . . .'

'Your wife. *She* might have picked it up. A nice night. A quiet stroll to the gate. Anybody.'

'She rarely stays up for me.'

'Who knows that? Who knows *who* might have picked it up. Don't make things harder on yourself than they are.'

'I'd like the bastard,' said Cooper grimly. 'Just with one hand. For five minutes. I'd *love* the bastard.'

There was some silence. Friendly silence. Masculine silence . . . assuming silence is capable of taking upon itself a gender. But the previous bitterness wasn't there. A little sadness, perhaps. Certainly companionship which included mutual respect.

Then, in a slightly dreamy voice, Noble said, 'Y'know, Coop . . . I'll need a partner.'

'Eh?'

'Not being able to see. At least, not yet. Not properly.'

'I'm sorry, I'm not with . . .'

'Something I had worked out. For when I retired. Hilda and I . . . we agreed it was a good idea.'

'Sarge, I'm not . . .'

'The name's Harry.'

'Okay – Harry – I'm not . . .'

'Nothing big.' Noble's voice retained its hint of dreaminess. 'Small. Y'know . . . small, but *very* reliable. Local. Staffed by ex-coppers. Hand-picked.'

'Harry, I've lost you. I've never been with you.'

'A security firm, Coop.' The dreaminess was replaced by the enthusiasm of a project long talked about. 'There's a tunnel – a railway tunnel – the tracks are up, the line's no longer in use. I can lease it. I know, I've made tentative enquiries. Imagine, Coop. A railway tunnel, sealed off – *really* sealed off – reinforced concrete, the lot. That as a base. In effect an underground strongroom. A couple of purpose-built trucks. And men we can trust. Just to move cash and valuables from place to place. Maybe store them for a while. One hundred per-cent reliable. We know all the tricks, we know all the gags, we can . . .'

'We?' Cooper interrupted Noble's flow of dreams.

'I'd need a partner, Coop,' said Noble softly. 'I have a nest-egg. Maybe not enough, but I can get the rest. But I need a partner.'

There was silence from Cooper's bed.

'Somebody I've known,' urged Noble gently. 'Somebody I've *seen*. Can trust . . . absolutely. A partner, but a damn sight more than just a partner.'

'Give me time,' breathed Cooper.

'We've time.' Noble smiled to himself. 'We aren't going anywhere . . . not for a few weeks.'

Meanwhile, Albert Rayon was feeling very hard done by. Here he was in a police cell. Been there hours, he had. Eff-all to read, eff-all to do. Every few hours they opened the door and threw some grub at you. Other than that . . . nothing.

His missus – some bloody missus – she hadn't been near. A lot *she* cared. Out in the boozer tonight. Nothing surer. Getting nice and cut on the strength of her old man having been nicked. Always some berk ready to stoke 'em up when their husbands were inside. And you didn't need three bloody guesses why.

It was right, y'know, what the barmy civil liberty nuts said. They treated you like dog dirt once they'd got their claws on you. Sling you in a cell . . . forget you. Nothing to do. Nobody to talk to. Nothing to read.

Bloody dog dirt!

He eyed the inset bell-push, alongside the cell door. *For Emergency Use Only*. That's what it said on the notice. Well, so what, he was bloody lonely. As far as *he* was concerned, that was an 'emergency'.

Hinton answered the ring. Hinton was back at the nick, spelling Sowe. Sergeant Cockburn was in the Charge Office, catching up on the official bumph.

Hinton stood at the open door of the cell, and said, 'Well?'

'I – er . . .'

'What's the "emergency"?' demanded Hinton.

'Er – nobody's been to see me,' grumbled Rayon.

'*I'm* here,' said Hinton in a reasonable enough tone.

'No — I mean — whether I'm still here. Still alive.'

'You under the impression you're dead or summat?'

'I don't like this,' said Rayon.

'You shouldn't go round lifting things.'

'I — er . . .' Rayon had a sudden inspiration. 'I want some exercise.'

'Oh, aye?'

'I'm entitled to exercise,' insisted Rayon.

'And where does it say *that*?' asked Hinton with interest.

'It's — it's an understood thing.'

'You want summat to read?'

'Exercise. That's what I . . .'

'Exercise your eyeballs,' said Hinton laconically.

'I've a right to . . .'

'Your rights,' said Hinton solemnly, 'boil down to this. You can stretch out on that bed and count the bricks. Half a brick counts as one. Do that three times, Rayon. You'll end up with three different totals. That . . . or something to read.'

'I don't want owt to read,' grumbled Rayon. 'And I *still* think . . .'

'Suit yourself . . . start counting.'

Hinton slammed and locked the cell door.

When you think about it . . .

Get the guy (or the girl) with that little extra oomph; with that gramme more conscience; with the hair's breadth addition of care. That's all it needs. Sometimes his compatriots taste sour grapes and call it luck. The hell it's luck! It's pride; it's the refusal to accept anything less than as near perfect as he can reach; it's doing the thing as it *should* be done, but as it's very rarely done.

With a copper, it means knowing things. Not just guessing, not just thinking, not just taking a chance. *Knowing*. The difference between 'Yes' or 'No' or 'Maybe'. Eventually it gets that copper noticed, and by people who matter.

As with Police Constable 2121 Angus Kyle.

Without hesitation, he said, 'Yes, sir. If it's the one I think you mean, it's on Tippet's land. At the corner of one of his fields.'

'Rimstone?' asked Tallboy.

'Well,' Kyle smiled. 'Tippet's land crosses the boundary. Most of it's in Upper Neck, but that particular field's in Rimstone.'

Tallboy nodded his satisfaction. He'd called in at Beechwood Brook D.H.Q., climbed the stairs to the C.I.D. Office and there had interrupted Detective Sergeant Kelly and P.C. Kyle as they were putting the finishing touches to the file against Peacock.

'How's it going?' he'd asked.

'Laced up tight.' Kelly had waved a hand at the neatly stapled documents. 'Even a statement from his wife . . . in case he tries a blinder and calls her as an alibi.'

'Fine.' Then Tallboy had turned to Kyle and said, 'A puzzler. A shed — y'know — an outhouse thing. Part of a farm, but not near the farm. Broken down. Maybe an old plough-shed. Up on your patch somewhere, we *think*. Roadsters use it sometimes. A kipping spot.'

And Kyle hadn't hesitated.

Tallboy mentally crossed his fingers and said, 'This place. What's it like inside?'

'Filthy. God only know how they sleep in all that muck.'

'Anything else?'

'It's broken down.' Kyle frowned. 'Rubble. Old slates from the roof. Weeds. Nettles galore. There's an old bath, half filled with broken bricks. It's the usual thing. Bird droppings all over the place. Swallows nest there every year. I don't know what Tippet uses it for these days, but . . .'

'Can you manage without Kyle?' Tallboy broke in and asked the question of Kelly.

'Sure. We've just about finished, anyway.'

'Fine.' Then to Kyle, 'Feel like detecting another crime for us, constable?'

'Aye.' Kyle looked puzzled, but nodded. 'I'll — er — I'll give home a ring first, if you don't mind.'

'Do that,' said Tallboy. 'I'll see you in my car outside.'

Nor was Hannah Pinter the only person to die that day.

Hinton took the call from Doctor Wilkinson — the same medic who that morning had baffled Higginbottom while discussing Betty Higginbottom's contraceptive pills — and the gist of the message was that one of his patients had died that afternoon. Not much doubt about the cause of death. Ex-miners die daily from pneumoconiosis, and William Wath was an ex-miner. Wilkinson, therefore, had no reason to doubt that Wath's death was due to 'the dust'. But, unfortunately, Wath had all his life been a stubborn old cuss, and at the end had refused medical aid. Ergo, because he hadn't seen a medic for at least six months the death was 'reportable', which meant a post mortem followed by an inquest . . . and, as far as the police were concerned, that amounted to a Sudden Death.

Wilkinson ended his telephone call with, 'The old girl thought he was asleep. She tumbled when he started going cold. I'd get there as soon as possible . . . he's starting to stiffen.'

Hinton logged the message, then telephoned the Sopworth undertaker who assisted at such times. Less than fifteen minutes later, Hinton and the undertaker were in the hearse on their way to Curzon Street, with the 'shell' bumping gently in the back of the vehicle.

Hinton had a body, but no crime. Blayde, on the other hand, had a murder (at the very least a *confessed* murder) but no body.

'There was no corpse in the Camm case,' murmured Rowe. 'He pushed her through the porthole.'

'Bags of circumstantial evidence,' grunted Blayde.

'Still . . .'

'We haven't a damn thing, other than a roadster who's probably lying.'

'You don't believe him?'

'It's called "an open mind",' sighed Blayde.

The two men walked slowly from Rowe's parked car towards Sopworth Police Station. In a few hours each had found a colleague. Perhaps even a friend. Certain it was that Rowe no longer feared Blayde. Nor did Blayde despise Rowe as he had done twenty-four hours previously. Two meals and a great deal of talk had worked wonders.

Had anybody lashed Blayde to a psychiatrist's couch, he would have described himself as a 'loner'. 'A lone wolf'. 'He travels fastest who travels alone' . . . all that sort of stuff. And, indeed, he *was* a 'loner' insofar as he was a lonely man. He made friends slowly. Carefully. Almost suspiciously. Self-educated, he was actuely aware of the great gaps in his knowledge of all things other than Police Law. Beyond the area of his own experience he trod cautiously; ever ready for the trap which might illuminate his lack of knowledge.

Not quite a pathetic creature – not quite as bad as that – but a man deserving sympathy. A proud and lonely man, unaware of his own loneliness. Too proud to admit that loneliness.

Had anybody lashed Blayde to a psychiatrist's couch . . .

Sowe was in the Charge Office and, as Blayde and Rowe looked in, he said, 'Message from D.H.Q., sir. Chief Inspector Tallboy. He thinks he's found the plough-shed . . . said you'd understand what he meant. He's on his way over now.'

Hannah would die. The hum of the engine, the 'crowd noise' effect, the pump of the blood into his tired brain repeated the three words over and over again. Hannah would *die*.

Like the incessant clack-clack of an unseen harvesting machine. Like the regular thump of a trip-hammer. Like the monotonous thud of a pile-driver forcing a timber of truth through the tenacious goo of his mind. Hannah *would* die.

To see needed deliberate concentration. Merely to *see*; to force the lids of his eyes to remain open. Not for himself, but for the sake of other road users, he deliberately kept the Minivan in third — never moving beyond the twenty mark — and braked, in order to inhale gulps of fresh air, at every lay-by. What he was doing was madness, but necessary. To sleep would be to admit defeat. To go home would mean sitting in an armchair and to sit in an armchair would mean sleep. Instant and overpowering sleep.

Awake he could fight . . .

What could he fight? Great God, what *could* he fight? No matter. Whatever it was, however powerful it was, however awful, however overwhelming . . . awake he could fight it.

But if he slept . . .

Hannah would die!

Poor, despairing Pinter. He didn't yet know. Nobody knew. Hannah was already dead.

Number 43 Curzon Street. It was a terrace house; a back-to-back, two-up-two-down. A number of years ago the whole street — the whole area — had been condemned but, thanks to the activity of those who lived there, thanks to their pride and their personal refusal to allow the area to descend into what is usually meant by the word 'slum', the condemnation had become merely an excuse to be used by the local authority in order to evade responsibilities of upkeep. Not that the inhabitants of Curzon Street minded over much. They were a community. To outsiders they were 'The Curzon Street Lot', but what matter? They were like one huge family . . . and that was *all* that mattered.

The undertaker's name was Longman. Short, stocky and obviously a very strong man, he wore the near-obligatory grey-striped trousers, black coat, black shoes, black tie and white shirt. His upper-arm muscles made the arms of the coat stretch a little and his jaw moved rhythmically as he chewed gum. If, to the poet, a rose was a rose was a rose, to Longman a corpse was a corpse was a corpse. His trade demanded that he be able to put on a long face, when the occasion

7.30 p.m.

239

called for a long face, but his natural disposition was that of a phleg-matic, rather droll individual.

As he braked the hearse to a halt outside 43 Curzon Street, he said, 'Wath?'

'William Wath,' verified Hinton. 'His wife's name is Mary.'

Before opening the door of the cab, Longman eyed the house frontage and said, 'I know these places. If he's upstairs, we have problems.'

'Take it as it comes,' said Hinton.

They climbed from the cab and, after a perfunctory knock, Hinton opened the door and stepped directly into the living room of the house. Three women were huddled together. One was weeping, quietly.

'Mrs Wath?'

The weeping woman blew her nose, straightened her shoulders, then said, 'That's me, constable.'

'Your — er — husband?'

'He's upstairs in bed.'

Hinton heard Longman's heavy sigh from behind his right shoulder.

'We — er — we have to take him away, Mrs Wath,' said Hinton, gently.

'I know. The doctor said so.'

'He'll be treated with respect,' promised Hinton.

Mary Wath nodded miserably.

Before Hinton could make the suggestion one of the women said, 'I live next door. I'll take Mary into our house . . . until you've gone.'

Hinton smiled his gratitude, then he and Longman stood aside and allowed the three women to walk slowly out into the street.

Longman closed the door to the street, walked across the room, opened a door, and said, 'We'll never get the shell up those stairs.'

'Let's see the body first.'

They climbed the stairs; ten directly from the room, then a pokey landing with a grandmother clock ticking away time relentlessly, then the stairs climbed back upon themselves for an additional eight steps. The front bedroom — the *only* bedroom, discounting what was little more than a store-cupboard, but which some enterprising architect had once described as a 'little bedroom' — smelled of death. That sweet, nauseous smell which, while not strong, is invariably *there*. The body had the parchment pallor, the pinched nostrils and sunken eyes of a man who had lived within easy reach of death for many years. He wore a fresh linen shirt, with a napkin carefully folded, positioned under the chin and tied on top of the sparse but combed hair. A stubble of white showed at the hollow cheeks and Hinton found himself wondering . . . *was* it all moonshine, this old wife's tale about the hair, the beard and the nails continuing to grow for days, some said weeks, after death?

Longman chewed his gum, like a cow chewing grass, gazed at the body with professional interest, then observed, 'That one wasn't too unhappy about leaving.' He folded back the bedclothes, felt at one of the skinny arms and added, 'Good job they laid him out. He's like a board.'

Hinton cleared his throat and said, 'The shell?'

'Leave it downstairs. I'll carry him down in my arms.'

Hinton nodded and they returned to the downstairs room, out into the street and manhandled the shell into the house.

They called it the 'shell'. Coppers, Longman, everybody . . . the 'shell'. It was a coffin; a strongly made, very large coffin. Large and strongly made, because it was used as a means of carrying every size and shape of corpse possible to the public mortuary. Nothing fancy. It was painted black. Inside it had been coated with black bitumen paint; thicknesses of the stuff, in order to make it completely watertight. The lid was held in place by six large wing-nuts, and hefty rope handles, at the foot and at the head, were the means of lifting and carrying. A monstrous, macabre thing, they man handled it from the hearse and into the house. Hinton closed the door to the street, while Longman unscrewed the wing-nuts. They lifted the lid and (as always) the stench of death wafted up from the shell; scores of deaths, even hundreds; death brought about by every ailment and every accident under the sun. And, although the shell was hosed out each time after use, the smell of putrefaction remained.

Longman leaned the lid against a wall and said, 'Stay here. I'll fetch him.'

Wath was no weight at all to a man as strong as Longman. He folded the body in his arms and, like a child, carried him from the bedroom. Because of the rigor mortis Longman found it easier to turn and back down the narrow, awkward stairs. The top eight steps presented no problem, and he backed around the tiny landing, twisting his head to see where the first of the final ten steps began. The stiffened corpse was, for a moment, more awkward to manoeuvre and (unknown to Longman) one of the feet wedged itself behind the grandmother clock. Longman gave an impatient tug, lost his balance and corpse, clock and Longman rolled and clattered down into the living room.

It was a very rowdy descent and, almost before they arrived at the foot of the stairs, Hinton had dived for the street door and turned the key.

It was the perfect sandwich; Longman, with the corpse on top of him and, on top of the corpse, the clock.

Hinton breathed, 'Holy cow!' and lifted the clock clear.

Longman hauled himself upright, then dumped the body of Wath into the shell. For a moment the grandmother clock took precedence over everything. It was unmarked; even the glass of the face wasn't cracked. They carried it carefully back up the stairs and positioned it, with great exactitude, in its place on the landing. It had stopped, of course, and the pendulum hung stationary, but neither Hinton nor Longman were prepared to open the front in an attempt to start the thing going again.

Longman dusted himself down, they lidded the shell, then carried the shell outside and into the hearse.

Hinton tapped on the door of the neighbour's house, entered, then said, 'That's it, Mrs Wath. I'll be along tomorrow morning for a short statement.'

'Thank you, constable. Thank you very much indeed.'

And, thereafter, Hinton and Longman delivered the body of William Wath to the public mortuary without further mishap.

And yet . . .

To her dying day Mary Wath insisted that there were 'things' beyond human explanation; for example Bill's favourite clock – a most reliable grandmother clock – had, and for no reason, stopped at the very moment they carried Bill's body from the house.

'It sounds like it,' agreed Blayde reluctantly. Then, to Kyle, 'If it is . . . your case?'

'That's up to you, sir.'

'You've had a long day, old son.'

Rowe said, 'I'll give you a hand, constable. Plain clothes till further notice.'

'Then,' said Blayde, '*Detective* Constable Kyle.'

'I wouldn't want that, sir,' said Kyle gently.

'C.I.D.?' Blayde looked surprised.

'Being the Upper Neck copper. That suits me fine, sir.'

'You've an aptitude.' Blayde sounded a little annoyed.

'If you don't mind, sir.' Kyle was adamant.

Tallboy stepped in and said, '*If* it's the right place.'

'There's only one way to find out.' Blayde stood up. 'Let's have Bingham out of his cell. Two cars, right? Inspector Tallboy's with

Kyle. Mine with Inspector Rowe and Bingham. Not a word to Bingham. We'll just follow the other car, watch his reaction when we get to the place.'

Police Sergeant 1871 William Henry Cockburn slipped the completed Overtime Cards into their manilla folder, then placed the folder in its allotted position in the stationery cupboard. He returned to his desk in the Charge Office, took a cigarette from an opened packet on the desk top, lighted the cigarette, then leaned back in his chair and silently contemplated the state of the Police Service in general and, in particular, his place in that service.

A way of earning a living. These days a *good* living. But, there again, *these* days . . .

Time was — just after Hitler's war — there was fun in bobbying. That was the only word for it . . . fun. The characters. The *real* characters. These days? All the pith had been squeezed out of the job. By comparison it was a dried-up occupation. There had to be a reason. Maybe the candy-floss-minded do-gooders; it *could* be them; they cared sod-all about the victim, they were too busy feeling sorry for the bastard who'd been caught. That was wrong. Hell's bells, that was *all* wrong. And they couldn't see any farther than their stupid noses; they couldn't see — maybe *wouldn't* see — that the lout they were wasting their sympathy on was conning them out of their cotton-picking minds. Sure, he was sorry — sorry he'd been caught — *that's* what he was sorry about. Maybe the proliferation of the do-gooders had taken the juice out of bobbying.

On the other hand . . .

Corruption had to have something to do with it. The Met mainly. London had more than its fair share of bent coppers. Maybe because the temptation in the Big City was greater than anywhere else. But — hell! — a bent copper. And not just the lower ranks. Men on the take, all the way up the ladder. And where the Met led, the rest followed. If a bloke working the West End could take back-handers, why the hell couldn't everybody? That *had* to have something to do with it.

And moonlighting . . .

Oh, sure. The moonlighting. Before the big money arrived men had stripped off their uniform and worked a second job . . . strictly for cash, of course. They'd become used to it. So they still did it. Some, not all. Some, too many. A man learned a trade, then joined the force. Maybe painting and decorating. Maybe some branch of the building trade. Maybe . . . whatever. Come the end of his shift, who could *really* blame him for using that skill to under-cut and make a little pin money? Who could blame him? *He* (Cockburn) could blame him. Bobbying was a full-time job. Time was it had *been* a full-time job. The good times. The happier times. Maybe that was *why* they'd been happier times.

On the other hand . . .

The telephone bell cut across his musings. Sowe stepped into the switchboard alcove, lifted the receiver from its hook and grunted a few words in answer to whatever was being said over the wire. He replaced the receiver, and stepped back into the Charge Office.

He said, 'Attempted suicide.'

'Where?'

'Tong Road. I'll call.' Sowe clipped his walkie-talkie to the lapel of his tunic, and donned his helmet. 'If I need transport, I'll give a yell.'

They rode in Blayde's car. Blayde drove. In the rear seat Rowe sat alongside Bingham. They followed Tallboy's car. It wasn't bumper-to-bumper work; that would have been too obvious. But while allowing the occasional car or van to overtake and slip between the two vehicles, Blayde never lost sight of Tallboy's car.

It was a mite spooky. Other than Blayde's, 'Get your shoes and belt on', when he'd opened the cell door, nobody had spoken to Bingham. Nobody had spoken to *anybody*. Bingham had tried a few tentative questions, but nobody had answered.

Tallboy and Kyle had left the police station first, then a few moments later Rowe and Blayde had led Bingham out to Blayde's car, and they'd set off.

Spooky. Bingham wondered why. He was of an intelligence capable of believing anything. Anything! For a kick-off, who the hell knew he (Bingham) was here? In this car? Being driven to Christ knows where. Off the face of the earth for all anybody cared. For all anybody knew. I mean — y'know — *coppers*. Anything!

He moistened his lips, then muttered, 'We're — er — going somewhere, are we?'

Rowe looked straight ahead. Blayde concentrated upon his driving.

'Are we — are we *going* somewhere?'

Without turning his head Blayde spoke.

'Shut up and sit down.'

And that was it. What else? Bingham shut up and sat down.

To appreciate the absurdity of the situation it is necessary to mention that Tong Road was no back-alley. Tong Road left the market square

— the very heart of Sopworth — and arrowed its way towards Bord-field; without being a dual carriageway, it was certainly a wide and well-used thoroughfare; one of the two main roads into and out of Sopworth.

And Tong Road was the site of the 'attempted suicide'. Not inside some house or office along the side of Tong Road. Tong Road itself.

Sowe pushed his way through the usual crowd of rubber-necks, stared, then breathed, 'Bloody hell! What next?'

The single-decker bus — destination board reading 'Sopworth' — was pulled into the kerb, the driver was out of his cab and, all in all, the schemozzle might have earned top billing at Blackpool Tower Circus. The little fat guy — a nutter if ever there was one — was stretched out on the road surface, little more than a yard in front of the wheels of the bus. He was hammering the tarmac with clenched fists and sobbing with frustration.

'I wanna die! I wanna die! Get back in the bus and run over me. I wanna die!'

'He wants to die,' observed the driver drily.

Sowe grunted, 'Aye . . . what colour d'you think he'd prefer?'

'He's buggering up my schedule.'

'Get back in the cab. I'll shift him.'

The driver turned and walked back to his cab. Sowe squatted on his heels alongside the nutter.

'On your feet, idiot,' said Sowe *sotto voce*.

'I wanna die,' sobbed the nutter. Tears ran down his pudgy cheeks and he repeated, 'I wanna die.'

'Not here. It's too messy.'

'I wanna . . .'

'I know. But find a quiet corner somewhere. Don't make a pro-duction number out of it.'

'Please. I wan . . .'

That's as far as he got. Sowe leaned forward, shoved the first and second finger down the back of the nutter's collar and twisted. The words and the air were both suddenly cut off. Still gripping the twisted collar Sowe straightened himself. The nutter came up with him. Strangulation was, obviously, *not* the nutter's first choice of means to his own end. He struggled for breath, but he struggled in vain until Sowe waved a hand and the bus moved forward and on its way. Then, before releasing his grip, Sowe marched the nutter onto the pavement.

'What's your name, barmpot?' asked Sowe without sympathy.

'You shoulda . . .'

'What's your name?'

'Samuel.'

'Samuel what?'

'No. Samuel . . . Richard Samuel.'

'Right, Richard Samuel.' Sowe frowned paternal disapproval. 'What's the big idea?'

'I wanna . . .'

'You lot.' Sowe turned to what remained of the crowd. 'Move along. You're obstructing the pavement.' Then, as the gawpers thinned out and went on their way, to Samuel, 'Behaving like a prize pillock. What's the big idea?'

'My — my wife's left me.' Samuel looked as if he might break down and cry again. In order to emphasise the point, he repeated, 'She's *left* me.'

'Is that all?'

'You don't understand. We've been married for . . .'

'Find a restaurant,' advised Sowe bluntly. 'Find a restaurant. Scoff a good meal. Then go get yourself plastered, and spend the night with some whore. Tomorrow morning you'll be glad your wife's left you . . . you won't have any explaining to do.'

It was the place. As Blayde watched Bingham climb from the rear of the car; as he watched the slight tremble of the legs, the wild look in the eyes, the near-stumble as Bingham walked slowly towards the derelict plough-shed, he knew. Rowe and Tallboy also knew. Kyle knew . . . even though he didn't know all the details. This man — this Bingham — was staggering through a personal nightmare. They watched as he dragged his feet through the grass, through the gap in the hedge and to the open frontage of the wrecked and rotting building. They allowed him to stare at the muck and filth which made up the floor and, when he turned, they saw the glisten of tears in his eyes.

8 p.m.

'The place?' asked Blayde gently.

Bingham nodded.

'And the burial place?'

Bingham raised his head, looked slightly to his left, then muttered, 'Over there, sir. A hundred — maybe two hundred — yards, that's where, sir.'

Tallboy breathed, 'Oh, my God!'

The heavy, linked-wire fence stood eight-foot high less than twenty yards from the broken-down plough-shed. Beyond the fence, like

246

some geometrically perfect concentration camp, stood the long rows of huts in which the battery-fed hens were housed. The whole concern stood on a 'raft' of reinforced concrete.

'Last year?' said Blayde.

'Y-yes, sir.'

'You buried her in there somewhere . . .' Blayde nodded at the battery hen sheds. 'Last year about this time?'

'Yes, sir.'

'Not last year,' said Kyle. 'That thing was up last year.'

'Sir, it wasn't. It *wasn't*.' Terror flickered in the eyes of the man who sought to clear his conscience. 'It wasn't like . . .'

'It wasn't up the year before,' interrupted Kyle. 'Two years ago, they were still at the planning permission stage.'

'*Two* years ago?' suggested Blayde.

'No, sir. I . . .' Bingham shook his head in utter incomprehension. 'Last year. I'm sure it was . . .'

'What's *this* year?' asked Rowe.

Bingham answered without hesitation. He was a year out. Somewhere inside his tormented mind a pawl had slipped; a whole year of his life had gone by unnoticed. Nobody had any doubt; the brand of truth being handled by Bingham left no room for doubt.

Blayde sighed, then said, 'Let's get one thing clear. *This* is the place? This shed?'

'Oh, yes. Yes, sir. This is where I . . .' The voice trailed off into silent misery.

'Let's get back to Sopworth,' said Blayde wearily.

Blakey ended up at Sopworth. There was no real reason; no reason other than some crackpot reason which might have been culled from Blakey's subconscious by a psychiatrist. Maybe because Sopworth represented Blakey's 'Waterloo'; because Sopworth, and what had happened at Sopworth and its consequences, had led to this newly-found freedom.

Or, on the other hand, maybe because Blakey's car needed petrol and, having driven nowhere in particular, he'd spotted a garage which sold his favourite brand on the outskirts of Sopworth and, having filled the tank, he'd realised that he, himself, was in need of a 'top up', and the nearest place in which he might buy a decent meal was The Sopworth Arms.

At Upper Neck two women (Marian Cooper and Hilda Noble) relaxed in armchairs, sipped tea and munched their way through a plateful of buttered scones . . . and, very gradually, allowed the tension to flow from their minds and bodies. The emotional beating they'd taken throughout that day had left its mark in dark-rimmed eyes and a complexion akin to the colour of ancient candle-wax.

And yet they'd won. And when Marian Cooper had suggested the stop-over for a quiet snack, before Hilda Noble continued on her way to her home, Hilda Noble hadn't hesitated.

They spoke little. They were each content to allow their tired limbs the opportunity to ease away the aches; to allow their weary minds to gradually acknowledge the glorious realisation that the bad part was finished with.

Later they smoked cigarettes. Then, as dusk thickened into true night, Marian Cooper drove Hilda Noble to her home and, as they parted, the kiss was far more than a token gesture.

And a mother found her daughter had died alone.

That she had died alone upset her far more than the death itself. The death was a release; a freedom from the drug-clogged mind. But alone! Supposing, as death had folded her into its arms, she had opened her eyes? Not in fear. Not in pain. In (say) blessed thankfulness. Supposing that . . . and nobody there. Her last living thought a misunderstanding?

Dear God, not that. Let her have understood. Let her have *known*. That her husband, Wilf . . . That her mother . . .

She stared down at the face she'd loved and known for so long. Since birth; since it had been placed in her arms, and the tiny mouth had reached towards a nipple. Since . . .

People talked foolishness about death. People talked foolishness. That it could be beautiful. That death could look like a deep sleep. That it brought with it a serenity; a *look* of serenity. Foolishness. Death was death. It was ugly; a vacuum where there should have been life; a nothingness where there should have been joy and anticipation. No more present — no more future — only a past which in time would fade.

Poor Wilf. Poor, poor Wilf. He'd have to be told and yet . . . No! To be told over a loudspeaker would be wrong. A heresy. At its lowest level, it would be a cruelty. An unnecessary cruelty. His pride . . . That he'd refused to apply for compassionate leave . . . That he'd refused the rest of the world — even his colleagues — access to his grief . . . The telling had to be a personal thing. Between the two of them. The way Hannah would have wanted it. The way Wilf would want it.

Cockburn was following a hunch. Perhaps a little more than a hunch. He'd heard rumours. Hints. Nothing specific — mainly because nobody really knew how it was *done* — but enough to make him suspicious, and a quiet talk to a friend, who *knew* a friend, who *knew* a friend. The way good bobbies work.

With Hinton strolling alongside him, Cockburn entered the portals of The Golden Nugget Bingo Hall. Very plush. Very 'with it'. All mod cons, including the cylindrical gadget inside which all the numbered ping-pong balls bounced around on a jet of air, until one of them was caught in the chute which delivered it into the caller's hand.

The proprietor, complete with frilly shirt, bow tie, slicked hair and fixed smile, greeted the two officers.

'A flutter, gentlemen?'

'Just a look round,' murmured Cockburn.

'See how the other half lives,' added Hinton.

'Make free. Make free.' The proprietor waved a magnanimous arm.

'These 'em?' Cockburn picked a 'book' of bingo cards from their housing alongside the entrance. 'These what they buy?'

'Ten pence a card,' said the proprietor. 'Fifty pence a book . . . six cards in each book. One on the house, as it were.'

'As it were,' echoed Cockburn. He flipped the cards, reached out for a second book, then flipped through *those* cards. He asked, 'Who prints 'em?'

'We buy them wholesale.'

'The hell you do,' said Cockburn pleasantly.

'I assure you, gentlemen . . .'

'Any decent printer would have his name on the things.'

'And', added Hinton cheerfully, 'you need your eyes testing. We're not "gentlemen". We're coppers.'

'That doesn't mean . . .'

'Nit-picking,' admitted Cockburn. 'But that's what the law demands. The name and address of the printing firm. It's missing.'

'I'll — I'll see to it.' The smile became a little more fixed. 'I — er — I didn't know.'

'You *should* know,' observed Hinton. 'All this flash — all this expense — that's how people get in the family way.'

'What?'

'Not knowing what they *should* know.'

'I've been collecting 'em,' Cockburn led the way down the carpeted aisle between the rows of tables and chairs. He strolled towards the stage and, as he talked, he felt in his hip pocket and pulled out a wad of used bingo cards. Various colours. All similar to the ones he'd returned to their housing. He thumbed through them as he continued, 'All from here. Over a period. A fairly long period. No printer's name. Nothing.'

'Sergeant, you have my solemn assurance . . .'

'I'll bet I have. These cards, though. What is it . . . twenty-two?'

'Two little ducks,' contributed Hinton.'

'Two little ducks. Every card . . . two little ducks. And sixteen . . .'

'Never been kissed,' murmured Hinton.

'Only one of 'em *doesn't* have number sixteen.'

'It's — it's the luck of the draw, sergeant. I've — y'know — no means of knowing . . .'

'Balls.'

'What?'

'These balls.' Cockburn smiled. 'Table-tennis balls?'

'Yes.' The proprietor followed Cockburn onto the stage. 'That's all they are. Table-tennis balls. Numbered.'

'Neat.' Cockburn picked one of the balls from its rack and tossed it to Hinton. 'Neat?' he asked.

'Works of art.' Hinton stepped onto the stage. As he handed the table-tennis ball back to Cockburn he said, 'Must be worth a fortune.'

'Oh, they are. They are,' agreed Cockburn. He touched the equipment, as if explaining its function and working to some ignoramus. 'Very fancy. Very clever.' Then to the slightly perspiring proprietor, 'Switch it on, son.'

'There's — there's no balls in the . . .'

'*I'll* provide the balls,' promised Cockburn.

The proprietor leaned forward and flicked a switch and an unseen electric motor began to hum.

'A sort of inverted Hoover, see?' explained Cockburn.

'Clever.' Hinton entered into the straight-faced act with enthusiasm.

'Shove the balls in — if you'll pardon the expression — and off you go.'

'Easy when you know how.'

'Pass me a couple of balls, constable. Not twenty-two. Not sixteen.'

Hinton obediently lifted two of the balls from the frame and Cockburn fed them into the machine.

'See 'em,' he said triumphantly. 'Bobbing about there. Having the time of their lives.'

'Enjoying themselves,' agreed Hinton.

'But,' said Cockburn, 'just pass me number twenty-two, and you have a decko at number sixteen.'

Hinton chose the two balls and handed one to Cockburn.

250

'Now.' Cockburn turned the ping-pong ball in his fingers. 'If you look carefully – *very* carefully – you'll see where the hole is. Where the needle and that little drop of wax went in. If you hold it up to the light you'll see it a lot easier.'

'I see it, sergeant.'

Then, to the worried proprietor, 'Put 'em both in, lad. With the other two. Let's see what happens.'

'Look, I don't know what . . .'

'Put them in!'

The proprietor reluctantly fed numbers twenty-two and sixteen into the blast of air. They rose . . . but not as high as the other two balls.

'So, y'see,' explained Cockburn. 'That's how the fiddle's worked. They rarely go high enough to reach the chute, and all the suckers are there with twenty-two, or sixteen, on their cards waiting for the prize they are *not* going to win.'

'I call that cheating,' said Hinton solemnly.

'Aye.' Cockburn nodded. 'And if you make sure your pals have the cards *without* twenty-two or sixteen.' Then to the proprietor 'Stop the machine, son.'

The proprietor switched off the electric motor.

Cockburn shoved his hand into the plastic cylinder and removed the two doctored balls.

He said, 'Souvenirs, constable.'

'Ta.' Hinton caught the ball tossed to him.

'You – you can't . . .' protested the proprietor.

'I *can*,' Cockburn assured him. 'Just watch. *And* the cards. New cards . . . complete with printer's name and address. New balls . . . *not* doctored. Then you're in business again.'

'I – I open at nine. The players . . .'

'They won't be playing tonight, son. Not, of course, unless you want to explain the twist to a bench of magistrates.' The white-faced proprietor almost trembled with rage. Cockburn murmured, 'Send the staff home. Then lock the doors after we've gone.'

The shadows were lengthening. Much of the heat of the day had been dissipated by a breeze which had sprung up from the north-west. The pubs and clubs were winding themselves up for the busiest period of the day. The disco joints had already turned up the volume and started the lights flashing. The eating-places were almost full. Sopworth – small

8.30 p.m.

251

town that it was — was putting on its nightly make-believe mask. The hick-town metropolis.

In a thousand homes the staid folk were settling in for an evening's T.V. viewing. A Bible Class was getting under way at one of the vicarages. At a meeting of Sopworth Literary Society a tiny audience was settling down to a lantern-slide lecture on 'Tropical Birds and their Habitat'. The Gilbert and Sullivan Society were crashing their way (not too musically) through the choruses of *Pinafore*.

At Sopworth Police Station, Bingham had been returned to his cell and Blayde, Tallboy, Rowe and Kyle were gathered in Rowe's office.

'He's telling the truth,' said Tallboy.

'Maybe.' Blayde wouldn't yet openly commit himself.

'I'm inclined to agree with Chris,' said Rowe.

'And you?' Blayde asked the question of Kyle.

'Unless he's an awful good actor, sir.'

'He has the timing wrong,' insisted Blayde irritably.

'He doesn't possess a watch,' argued Tallboy. 'He certainly doesn't possess a diary. It's a warm day, that's all he knows. All he cares. I doubt if he knows what day of the week it is. I doubt if he knows what month it is.'

'But a year out,' growled Blayde. 'Always assuming he *did* kill her. That she even exists. That she ever existed.'

Rowe murmured, 'We can't leave it open-ended.'

'Hell, we can tear that battery-hen place down,' agreed Blayde. 'But we need authorisation, and we won't get authorisation without some sort of proof. And,' he added, as Tallboy was about to speak, 'when I say "proof" I mean a damn sight more than the say-so of some half-wit who doesn't even know what year it is.'

'A holding charge,' murmured Rowe.

'The wood he nicked at Leeds,' said Blayde heavily. 'What else? We tell the bench it's a holding charge . . . then start asking around. Express Message to all districts. Missings from Home within the last two years. Emphasis upon tarts who spoke with Brum or Scouse accents. Bloody hell!' He blew out his cheeks in disgust. 'Talk about needle-hunting in haystacks.'

'Two years,' sighed Tallboy.

'Unless,' said Blayde nastily, 'he's *two* years out.'

'Give him a cigarette,' said Cooper.

'I'm pushed for time,' said Armstrong crossly. 'I just looked in because Muriel's been so . . .'

'So, *you're* the lucky man?' Noble asked the question.

252

'Yeah.' Armstrong's face coloured.

'So, give him a cigarette,' teased Cooper.

'A celebration,' said Noble.

'It's — it's not allowed. Not after . . .'

'You notice anybody come into this room?' asked Noble.

'Not a soul,' said Cooper. 'Just you and me.'

'And *I* can't see a thing.'

'Look,' pleaded Armstrong. 'If I'm caught . . .'

'I'll tell her,' threatened Cooper. 'So help me, next time I see her I'll tell her.'

'What?'

'That because of you,' said Cooper, 'I was forced to pull this stupid drip thing from my arm and give my sergeant a cigarette.'

'I *ordered* him,' grinned Noble.

'Strewth,' breathed Armstrong. 'You two . . .'

'You'll find 'em in my bedside locker,' said Cooper.

'Okay.' Armstrong nodded, then solemnly added, 'But — y'know — Sergeant Noble can't see. If he sets the bed alight.'

'I'll fix it.' Cooper met solemnity with solemnity. 'Just put the ash-try where I can see it. I'll do a left-left-steady routine till he hits the right spot.'

As he handed them cigarettes and lighted them — as he carefully positioned the ash-trays — Armstrong said, 'Real dead-heads, you two. My guess is you'll be up and about in no time. Between you you'll be running the place within a month.'

'We won't *be* here that long,' promised Cooper.

In Bradford the punkie who'd tangled with Police Constable Witherham was feeling pleased with himself. And why not? Five of his pals. Four more geezers on their hot-rod motor bikes. A nicked van. Ten of 'em. They'd show the Sopworth animals a thing or three. *They'd* give the bleeders summat to think about. They wouldn't be so ready to sling boots and clothes over walls next time. My Christ not!

'Like a dose o' bleedin' salts,' grinned the punkie.

'Just do 'em . . . then out,' agreed a youth with a shaven head.

One of the motor cyclists revved his machine until the roar of its engine seemed to fill the narrow back street in which they'd assembled; the noise seemed to physically rattle the decaying bricks and stones. He eased the throttle and gradually the engine died to a perfectly tuned purr. He was in his early twenties; tanned and well-built. He wore no crash helmet and his long, blonde hair was slicked back from his forehead. He'd taken over from the punkie: like a lion

253

in the prime of its manhood, he was born to lead. He wore black 'leathers', complete with gloves, and the wind-cheater was zipped open to reveal his chest. Around his neck he wore a thin gold chain, and from the chain hung a single tear-drop-shaped paste ruby. Everybody called him 'Gaffer'. That was the only name he ever answered to . . . 'Gaffer'.

The punkie was behind the wheel of the stolen van. He leaned from the cab and said, 'You'll be following us, Gaffer?'

'*You* do the following.'

'Look, I organised this bleedin' . . .'

'You couldn't organise your prick through the zip of your trousers.' The Gaffer didn't raise his voice. Indeed he didn't even look at the punkie as he spoke. He leaned forward a little on the saddle of his machine and brushed a speck of non-existent dust from the chrome of the petrol tank. 'Just keep behind us. And keep your cake-slit buttoned.'

Just for a moment, the punkie looked as if he might argue. He had his own 'respect' to think about. All day *he'd* run around gathering a makeshift gang of hooligans with which to descend upon this Sopworth dump. It was *his* rumble. And now this . . .

After some brief hesitation, and in a mock-friendly tone, he said, 'Okay, Gaffer. You be the shock troops, eh?'

Gaffer ignored the remark. He was far more concerned about the gleam of his machine's petrol tank.

Blakey, having enjoyed as nice a meal as he'd eaten for months, strolled from the dining room and into the main room of The Sopworth Arms. A nice pub. Something of a road-house, really. The room was big enough to allow for a moderate dancing space, with tables and chairs around. On the tiny stage a trio — electric organ, drums and bass — made foxtrot and quickstep tempo, as a pleasant change from the ear-splitting cacophony which a younger generation had been conned into believing was 'music'. Beyond this main room was the bar of The Sopworth Arms, and waiters carried trays of drinks to the tables around the dance floor.

Blakey lowered himself into a chair at one of the tables and, when he'd caught the eye of a passing waiter, ordered a fifty-fifty whisky and water.

It was a nice place. The hum of conversation was sufficient to provide warmth and companionship, and not raucous and nerve-grating. There was an air of efficiency and orderliness about the place; no fumbling with change, no drips from the base of the glass as the waiter lifted it from the tray. Via some magic of furnishing and decor the place looked at once modern and old-fashioned; as if somebody very knowledgeable had taken the best of all ages and combined them without clashing.

Blakey sipped his drink and relaxed. If his mind wandered towards his wife and family — towards the chief superintendentship he'd relinquished that day — he dismissed such thoughts with a mental flick of the finger, sat back and enjoyed himself. Relaxing. Listening to the trio. Watching the handful of dancing couples. *Enjoying* himself.

Sowe and Hinton were out on the street, Cockburn was bringing the Sopworth Sectional Diary up to date, when Daisy Wellington pressed the bell-push at the public counter. Cockburn sighed and walked from the Charge Office.

'Is — er — is Constable Pollard . . .'

'He's off duty, ma'am. Went off at two. He'll be on again at six tomorrow morning.'

'It's just that . . .' She hesitated, then said, 'I've just left my brother.'

'Your brother?'

'Charlie. Charlie Preston.'

'Oh!' Cockburn smiled. What little officiousness there had been vanished. 'You Charlie's sister?'

She nodded and said, 'I've just left him. It's about his house. I've — er — I've cleaned it all up. It's taken most of the day, but — y'know — all the mess has gone. Not that he's going back there. He's coming to my place. But it's empty. Charlie's place, I mean. And I dunno when . . .'

'We'll keep an eye on it for you, luv.'

'That's — that's what I called about. That's all. Only Charlie's a bit worried about . . .'

'You say you've just seen him?'

She nodded.

'How is he?' asked Cockburn.

'He's . . .' She sought for the right word, then settled for, 'worried.'

The truth was, she didn't know. How *was* he? How *could* a man be who'd just murdered his missus and her fancy man? And doing it . . . Making such a *mess*!

God, it had turned her stomach. What it must have been like with the *bodies* there. And that was what Charlie — her Charlie— had done. Such a nice lad. When he was younger. When they were both at school. He wouldn't lie . . . he *couldn't* lie. Some men — y'know — deep inside, from the moment they're born, there isn't any wrong. More than that, even. They can't see wrong in others. They're surprised — shocked — when they find the world isn't the straight-up-and-down place they think it is. Like Charlie. Like Charlie *was*.

But now . . .

Killing people — killing people like that — committing murder — whatever those people have done . . . it *had* to have an effect. Her Charlie. He *had* to be different.

'Will he go to prison?' The words were a whispered plea for some explanation she could understand.

'I'd be a liar if I said "No",' said Cockburn gently. 'But not for long. Not long at all.'

'He'll go mad.' There was a faraway look in her eyes, a faraway tone to the words. 'I've just come from Beechwood Brook. He'll go mad in that cell if he's there much longer. He'll go mad if they send him to prison.'

'Look, missus . . . what's your name?'

'Daisy. Daisy Wellington.'

'Daisy, he's worried. That's all. *Worried*. You've said so yourself. Who wouldn't be?'

'He's remembering.' She tried so hard to explain. To find the words. To use a limited vocabulary as a vehicle for subtleties beyond its range. Elusive, delicate nuances she felt but couldn't describe. 'He's — he's alone you see. By himself in that cell. In prison. And all he can do is *remember*. That's all he'll be *able* to do. Remember and blame himself. Because that'll be why he's there. He won't be *allowed* to forget.'

'He killed two people,' Cockburn remined her softly.

'D'you think *he* doesn't know that?'

'Of course he knows. But . . .'

'That's why he'll go mad,' she said flatly.

The motor cyclists rode, two abreast, in front of the van. They left Bradford and kept in perfect formation. There was a menacing precision in the manner in which they handled *9 p.m.* their machines; the precision of a beautifully balanced, high-powered rifle. Deadly, but superb. Gaffer set the pace, not too fast but not slow, never deviating from his chosen path, leaning into corners with immaculate balance, swinging out to overtake vehicles, but not allowing an inch when other vehicles overtook the tiny cavalcade.

256

In the following van, the punkie and his hooligan companions shouted and cat-called. They banged the sides of the van and screamed obscenities at every other user of the road they passed. They had one hell of a time and, in doing so, reduced the main weapon in their armoury, the element of surprise.

The driver of an overtaking Jaguar and his wife were subjected to their moronic insults and, less than ten minutes later when he arrived home, that gentleman dialled nine-nine-nine and made a formal complaint.

Thus the Sopworth police, while not ready and waiting were, nevertheless, not caught one-footed.

There is a point of mental and physical exhaustion which, of itself, defeats sleep. Equally there is a point, not far from a state of complete collapse, where sleep — even death — is a thing to be prayed for.

Woman Police Constable Pearson had reached that former point. Tony's flat was a delightful place. It had an intriguing air of masculinity. The choice of autumn tints in curtains, carpets and furniture gave subtle hints of protection; the twin bullfighting posters — framed and carefully positioned — were a man's choice. Even the ash-trays; polished steel, with tiny replicas of vintage motor cars on each rim. A man's flat. Tony's flat.

Having showered, she'd climbed into the three-quarter-sized bed and waited for sleep which had refused to come. She'd left the bed, walked barefooted into the main room and now sprawled in one of the deep armchairs, tired but unable to assuage her tiredness. She had one of Tony's artificial silk 'shortie' dressing-gowns wrapped around her otherwise naked body. And she chain-smoked and explored the possible future.

To be 'Mrs Armstrong'. The thought intrigued her. Not a flat, but a house. If possible a house in the country; not deep in the country, but within easy walking distance of fields and woods. Not on some red-brick estate. Definitely not *that*! She wanted no neighbours a mere fence-width away; no conforming privet hedge, no identical front lawn, no equally identical vegetable patch at the rear of the house. 'Mr and Mrs Armstrong'. They had to be 'different'. Not eccentrics, but at least themselves.

To remain a policewoman? No, that was out. As they were at the moment, it was okay. But as man and wife — as *real* man and wife — no way. The force shattered marriages. It shattered marriages when the man was in the force. When the wife was in the force no marriage

257

was safe. Policing made for tenseness, for irritability, for strain and, the hell with women's lib arguments, that was no basis upon which a wife might subscribe to a successful marriage. Some other less demanding job, perhaps? Well, perhaps.

And kids. And kids meant . . . motherhood? Fatherhood? Christ, could she *be* a mother? Not physically. Emotionally. Mentally. Could she cope? The dirty nappies, the runny noses, sure, that part was easy. Messy, but easy. But the other part. The bit about bringing 'em up right. The important bit.

And Tony? Would he . . .

Sure he would. He was a dead ringer as a father. Made for the job. Easy going, without being soft. Soft, without being mushy. Mushy, without being . . . Jesus, he'd spoil the little brats to hell! He'd be a lousy father. The hell he would. He'd be a great father. A pip of a husband. He'd be . . .

At which point the tightened spring of the day's activities began to unwind a little. A few tears crept from her eyes. She smoked one last cigarette, then blew her nose, went back to bed and, within minutes, was fast asleep.

With Pinter it was the other way. He would have given ten years of his life to be allowed to sleep. To allow *himself* to sleep. To climb into a bed — or even lean forward over the Minivan's steering wheel — close his eyes and know that, when he opened them Hannah would still be with him. But to sleep without that knowledge . . .

He was parked on a lay-by. Both windows of the van were wide open. The cool dusk breeze helped him a little, the fact that he no longer needed to concentrate upon driving helped him a little, and the family in the Cortina which shared the lay-by helped him a little. It was something to watch; something with which to keep his aching eyes occupied. The man, obviously weary but happy; at a guess on his way to or from holiday if the cases on the roof rack were anything to go by. The woman (the man's wife) measuring out hot liquid from a Thermos jug; one for her husband, one for each of the two kids and what was left for her. A nice lady. A nice guy. Two nice kids. Funny how you *knew* these things. That they were nice, that they were happy, that there was love in the family. Funny . . . how you knew. Okay, the kids were well-behaved, but laughing. Giggling a little. Nice kids were usually born gigglers. Openly. Not behind the hand. As if laughter was never far from the surface and, now and again, some of it leaked out. And the guy . . . the way he nodded and spoke a word Pinter couldn't hear. 'Thanks' . . . that was the word. A tiny politeness. He didn't take the woman for granted. When she handed him the beaker he still had manners enough to thank her. Nice guys did that. Louts merely held out their hand, took things . . . sometimes without even *looking* at the giver. The world was populated with too many louts. Too few nice guys.

Maybe that's why you knew. The louts were the norm, therefore the nice guys could be identified without too much . . .

Pinter heard them, before he saw them. In the distance and coming nearer. The roar of the machines then, as they closed, the yelling and shouting. As they passed, he'd already turned the ignition key and, for the moment, his tiredness left him as he pulled into the road and gave chase.

At sixty he was gradually overtaking them. He knew the roads; knew the straight stretch ahead. He pressed the pedal down a little and, as they hit the straight stretch he was poised for overtaking, if the road was clear of oncoming traffic.

The road was clear. He overtook the van and from the open windows heard the catcalls. Okay, let 'em yell. Let 'em use their mouths. A few minutes from now and he'd use *his* mouth. He kept the speed and overtook the two pairs of motor cyclists. Saw them clearly in his rear-view mirror. He leaned forward slightly and flicked the switch which illuminated the *'Police Stop'* sign at the rear of the Minivan. He eased up on the pedal and the images in the rear-view mirror grew larger. They continued to grow larger, and his dulled senses took a little longer than usual to realise that neither the motor cyclists nor the van were going to stop. They weren't even going to slow down.

Pinter held the speed of the Minivan steady. The following vehicle began to fill the rear-view mirror. On his right, Gaffer gradually drew abreast. On his left the second lead motor cyclist kept pace with Gaffer. As the two machines levelled with the cab of the Minivan they pulled in closer, as if threatening to deny Pinter road space. Gaffer grinned contemptuous triumph. His colleague on the nearside of the Minivan turned his head and deliberately spat at the nearside cab window.

And these scum — these animals — were to be allowed to live. The world would be a better, cleaner place without them, but they were to be allowed to live. It was so monstrously unjust. So foul. So iniquitous.

The two lead motor cyclists pulled ahead, then closed immediately ahead of the Minivan. The second pair moved up to cab-level and in the mirror Pinter could see the van almost nudging the rear bumper of the Minivan.

Subjectivity aside, it was magnificent machine-control on the part of the motor cyclists. At any gymkhana it would have earned deserved applause. But this wasn't a gymkhana. This was the Queen's Highway. And Pinter was a police officer and Pinter's wife was dying — in fact, already dead — and the injustice . . . And the tiredness . . . And the great surge of uncontrollable fury . . .

It was not an accident in the true sense of that word. It was a deliberate action by a man whose brain was incapable of coherent thought, whose body was weary to the point of utter exhaustion, whose emotions were shredded far beyond control. He turned the steering wheel of the Minivan and, at the same time, increased the speed slightly. He jockeyed the nearside motor cyclist nearer and nearer to the grass verge then, when there was no more road space left, he yanked the wheel and slammed the gate.

The Minivan tore across the verge, taking the motor cycle and its rider with it. Across the grass, nose-diving into the ditch, then smashing itself, and the motor cycle, into the hawthorn hedge.

Somewhere in the distance — a thousand miles away — Pinter heard the scream of tyres as the following van swung out to avoid being part of the pile-up. For perhaps five seconds Pinter marvelled that he was still alive. Even unhurt, other than a foot which was trapped firmly in the pedals. The windscreen was smashed, the bonnet of the Minivan was twisted and tilted upwards, and the safety harness had held. He'd slipped forward in his seat, and he rested his head against the back of the driving seat . . . then he sighed, closed his eyes and slept.

Wooley looked in at the police station to enquire about Noble and Cooper. He laughed genuine delight when he heard (to use Cockburn's expression) that they were 'sitting up and taking nourishment'.

'Where's Taffy?' he asked tentatively.

'Away home. He's finished the Preston file.'

'Oh!'

His smile went and was replaced by a frown of vague disappointment. It was a pity; had Evans still been on duty he'd have made the first move to patch up their quarrel. And (again) there might not have been that running sore between them for the rest of their service. Fate. Kismet. Not being at the right place at the right time. Not, perhaps, the course of history, but certainly the lives of two men might have been altered.

The bell at the switchboard rang and Cockburn answered the call.

As he replaced the receiver his face was dark with combined anger and worry.

'Something?' asked Wooley.

'Bloody hooligans from Bradford,' growled Cockburn. 'We've had the word . . . they're heading for Sopworth. Trouble.'

'I'd better stay,' suggested Wooley.

'There's been a shunt-up.' Cockburn shook his head in disgust. 'Some ton-up lunatic and Pinter. A passing motorist dialled Beech-wood Brook.'

'Ambulance . . .'

'It's on its way. And a squad car.' Cockburn headed for the door of the Charge Office. 'I'd better notify the boss.'

When he heard the news Blayde said, 'Right. We'll organise a reception committee.'

Rowe said, 'How's Pinter?'

'In one piece,' said Cockburn. 'Little more than cuts and bruises from what I can gather.'

'And the motor cyclist?' asked Tallboy.

'Broken arm, I think. Shaken up, obviously. The ambulance is on its way.'

'How many of 'em?' asked Blayde.

'Hard to say, sir. Two — maybe three — Hell's Angel types and a van load of tearaways. Enough,' he added grimly.

'Where are they heading?'

'Sopworth.'

'Specifically?'

Cockburn moved his shoulders.

Kyle said, 'I'll stay, if I may, sir.'

'You *may*.' said Blayde. Then, to Cockburn, 'Who's on the street?'

'Sowe and Hinton.'

'Get 'em in here. We don't want to be picked off one at a time.'

'And Wooley,' added Cockburn. 'He's in the front office. Ready to give a hand, but he's not in uniform.'

'We'll use him. Then get onto D.H.Q. Have a couple of motor patrol units head in this direction. Ready to back-up, if necessary.'

'Right.'

Cockburn left Rowe's office.

They had a pride. One must presume that within their own worlds every creature on earth has something which might be called 'pride';

261

that even the common flea, the everyday house fly, has a degree of 'pride'.

The punkie had righted the stolen van. Gaffer had moved slightly ahead of his two companions and now led an arrow-head formation of motor cycles immediately in front of the stolen van.

They'd seen the accident; the Minivan and one of their fellows smash into the ditch and the hedge. They hadn't even slowed their pace. That, too, was part of their pride; that injury, or even death, left them unmoved.

To understand them?

If they have a cause, it is the cause of anti-everything; anti-life itself. They are more than mere non-conformists. They are more than mere rebels. Their arrogance is such that they truly believe that they are above the law, above common decency, above every restraint which might deviate them from their chosen life style. They vandalise, they maim, they even kill . . . *because*.

Because, at that moment, they feel like it. Because not to do so would be a form of self-restraint, and they will not be restrained. Their courage is that they defy the world. They refuse to acknowledge convention in any form. They cannot 'win' . . . ever. And they know this, too. But the knowledge does not deter them. If anything it goads them onto even greater outrages. They have been called savages, and the term fits them perfectly. But, to give the devil what little due he deserves, they are noble savages. That it is a twisted, perverted nobility is the choice *they* make.

9.30 p.m.

Thus the pride with which Gaffer headed the 'raiding party'. What had happened earlier in the day concerned him not at all; the punkie's treatment at the hands of Police Constable Witherham was merely a looked-for means to an end. He needed no real excuse. That possible carnage was his to commit was excuse enough.

And at Sopworth Police Station they waited. Eight of them — Blayde, Tallboy, Rowe, Cockburn, Kyle, Sowe, Hinton and Wooley — and to some of them it was a re-run of riots and near-riots they'd been part of in the past. To others it was a new experience.

'Where d'you think?' asked Wooley tentatively.

'Boozer. Disco.' Cockburn smoked a cigarette. Perhaps he wasn't as cool as he looked, but years ago he'd mixed it with the race-course gangs and, although organised baton charges weren't the 'in' thing these days, the set-up differed only slightly. He said, 'A lot of it's noise. Wherever they hit, they'll break.'

Sowe added, 'They *have* to break. Queensberry Rules don't apply. It's not who's the best. *We're* the best . . . we'd *better* be.'

Hinton was worrying a little. About Rob. About what might happen to Rob if anything happened in the coming punch-up. If anything happened to *him*. It had happened once before; a street fight and he and two colleagues had had to go in, bull-headed. A fractured skull and a few weeks on his back in a hospital bed. But when he'd arrived home . . . Hell's teeth! The bloody idiot of a father-in-law of his had talked Con into 'making tentative enquiries'. Rob had *almost* ended up in some institution. Rob. Poor old Rob . . . wouldn't hurt a fly, wondering where his daddy was, only wanting love and a little understanding. And they'd seriously considered the ins and outs of putting him away. Of burying him. Of . . .

Hinton worried a little.

Blayde, Tallboy, Rowe and Kyle entered the Charge Office.

Blayde said, 'The golden rule. Wherever possible back-to-back. That way they can only come at you from one direction.'

Rowe moistened his lips.

He, too, was worried. A man can only change so much within the course of one day, and Rowe *had* changed. But enough? Or, come to that, did he desire to change so drastically? It was one thing to admire a man like Blayde, but it was another thing to approximate him. Anne, his wife, had married William Henry Rowe. She had *not* married Robert Blayde, nor anyone *like* Robert Blayde. Moreover, at that meal. She'd been intimidated by Blayde. She was not the sort of woman to be the mate of a man like Blayde.

On the other hand . . .

Policing had taken upon itself a new dimension within the last few hours. A dimension whose culmination was to be a fight — a very physical conflict — between law-enforcement and lawlessness. What policing was all about, surely? The reason for the uniform, the reason for the legal authority, the final, pristine reason for the force itself.

Rowe was one of the men who worried.

Blayde said to Wooley, 'You here, at the station, son.'

'Sir, I volunteered to . . .

'I know.' Blayde smiled understandingly. 'You're anxious to air your muscles. But two things. I don't want Sergeant Cockburn, or Hinton, or Rowe to be talking to thin air when they use their walkie-talkie sets. And you're on nights, right?'

'Yes, sir. But . . .'

'End of argument, son. I want a full night shift. That's important, too.'

Wooley nodded, but looked disappointed.

They hit the outskirts of Sopworth and every yard of the way advertised their arrival. Gaffer claimed the crown of the road. The two out-riding motor cyclists zig-zagged between vehicles coming from or going to Sopworth; when necessary they mounted the pavements or roared over the frontages of filling stations. The van rocked as the punkie spun the wheel in an attempt to equal the dare-devilry of the motor cyclists.

Nine of them and this was what they lived for. To terrify. To vandalise. To destroy.

Disciplined, and within the context of war, they might all have been heroes. That small thing to their credit. Indeed, it *was* war; a form of war. Themselves against Sopworth . . . against the rest of the world, if necessary.

Ordinary people were scandalised. Ordinary motorists braked to a halt and hurled curses after the disappearing raiding party. But (sometimes) ordinary people and ordinary motorists felt an illogical, primaeval envy.

To be so free. To be so untamed . . .

Tallboy knew it was wrong. To feel this way. To have the old adrenalin pumping away inside him. To know that if there *wasn't* a confrontation he'd be a disappointed man.

It was wrong, because it was the negation of everything deserving the description 'civilised'. Force against force, terror against terror . . . and no holds barred. His memory looked behind him, and he recollected the other times. Not a lot, but not a few. When his dead father-in-law, Charles Ripley — Chief Superintendent Ripley — had roared into battle with jutting chin, blazing eyes and clenched fists. Great days, but long-past days. When he (Tallboy) had gloried in a gloves-off scrap with hooligans and tearaways. Golden days, but long-past days.

Today — what the hell happened — they were on a losing wicket. Let the law-breakers win, and the police would be criticised to the high heavens for allowing 'rioting in the street'. Let the police win and, equally, the police would be just as sternly criticised for using 'strong arm methods'. The bloody public couldn't make up its silly mind. It demanded protection, but refused its protectors the freedom to protect. The outcome of the threatened shindig was going to be trouble — headline harassment — questions asked in Parliament — stick from every direction on the compass . . . whoever came off best. So, what the hell? Go in there swinging. Hope to Christ the odds aren't stacked *too* much in the other guy's favour. Keep a one-track mind. Bugger the so-called 'consequences' until every last animal was on his back and pleading for mercy.

Bobbying!

At once the best and worst job on God's earth. But he wouldn't change it . . . not for all the oil in the lamps of China.

And yet a pea-sized feeling of embarrassment made for discomfort. Stick or bust, he was going to enjoy himself, and good men — 'decent' men — shouldn't enjoy the prospect of a coming battle.

'Staffs?' Blayde broke in on Tallboy's thoughts.

Sowe said, 'Ready for use, sir.'

Hinton nodded and pulled his truncheon part-way out of its pocket, then let it fall back.

'Aye.' Then Cockburn added, 'What about you, sir? And Mr Tallboy? And Inspector Rowe?'

'If necessary, we'll find something,' said Blayde flatly.

Kyle remained silent.

The truth was, Kyle never carried his staff, nor his handcuffs, other than on the few occasions when he knew he'd be required to 'produce' these articles of equipment; on parades, on race-course details, on strike or demonstration duties. In the first place they were clumsy; to sit in a cramped Minivan (which was his normal mode of transport) with a truncheon down the right leg of his trousers and a pair of handcuffs in his hip pocket merely made discomfort even more uncomfortable. And in the second place, Police Constable 2121 Angus Kyle held the firm belief that, without mechanical aid of any description, he was quite capable of knocking any Sassenach from the face of this planet . . . should the occasion demand it.

Not, mark you, that Kyle was an aggressive person. He could control his temper better than most men, and had as much patience as any man, but dirks and broadswords had had their place in his ancestry, and the glens and lochs, the Highlands and Islands breeding the men they bred, Kyle hadn't it in him to back down to any man.

'Cars?' said Blayde. 'Seven of us. Mine and who else's?'

Cockburn kept his mouth shut. The last thing he wanted was his new Capri scratched and buckled.

'Mine,' said Tallboy.

265

'Fine.' Blayde nodded. 'You take Inspector Rowe and Constable Kyle. I'll take the others.'

In The Sopworth Arms they heard it coming before it arrived. The customers at the bar glanced at each other as the roar of the motor cycles moved closer from the distance.

The landlord frowned his worry. Motor cyclists — *any* motor cyclist — tended to equate with trouble. At the very least some would-be-drinker who clumped through the place dressed up like a spaceman . . . and who tended to lower the tone of the pub. And — obviously — there was more than one. The landlord frowned and absent-mindedly polished a glass which didn't need polishing.

He relaxed a little as the roar of the engines retained their decibel-level. They obviously weren't stopping. They weren't slowing down. They were *not* visiting The Sopworth Arms.

When Gaffer rode his machine up the shallow steps, through the swing-doors and into the bar itself, the landlord realised just how wrong a man can be.

The three machines — Gaffer leading — snarled and skidded the length of the bar. Tables went flying, customers jumped from the path of the motor cyclists, women screamed, the roar of the machines filled the room and the air was heavy with the smell of exhaust fumes.

The landlord dived for the behind-the-bar telephone and fumbled his fingers through a nine-nine-nine call.

Gaffer reached the far end of the bar first. He brought his machine into a controlled ninety-degree skid, then rode back down the front of the bar. His left arm was outstretched and, as he passed, he swept every glass, every ash-try, syphon, bottle and even beer-mat from the surface of the bar counter. His two companions caught the mood. They, too, turned and weaved their way between tables and chairs, smashing and vandalising as they performed a mad obstacle race along the length of the room.

Then the swing-doors were flung open and the punkie and his five fellow-hooligans raced into the premises to add their own yells and obscenities to the reprisal raid.

Wooley had the receiver off its hook before the strident tone of the 'emergency call' bell could reach its second ring. The others watched, like sprinters at starting-blocks.

'The Sopworth Arms,' said Wooley. 'They're tearing the place apart.'

266

Even before he'd finished speaking they were on their way from the Charge Office, out to the cars.

On the tiny stage the trio had stopped playing. The few couples dancing stood, turned their heads and wondered what the hell was happening in the bar. Customers were on their feet, some moving tentatively towards the emergency exit. Blakey stood up from his table and frowned at the archway leading from the main room.

Then Gaffer led his motor cyclists into the main room, and the hooligans surged after him hellbent on destruction.

One man (a would-be hero or a born fool) stepped directly into the path of the punkie and his mob. He swung an ineffectual fist and, for his pains, became the first serious casualty. The punkie had come armed with a home-made flail — a hammer-shaft to which was fixed a length of bicycle chain, with the links honed to razor sharpness — and a back-handed swipe opened the man's face bone deep. The blood gushed out and the sight of the injury sent women, and some of the men, up onto the padded benches which lined the walls of the room.

Blakey breathed, 'You bastard,' and moved into action.

He used a chair, much as a big-cat trainer uses a chair against a threatening charge, and rushed towards the punkie. Again the punkie swung his flail and this time it caught on a cross-bar on the underside of the chair, but not before it had sliced the back of one of Blakey's fingers. The punkie couldn't jerk the flail loose and for a moment Blakey had the advantage, but because he was ignorant of the technique of rough-house fighting, he did the wrong thing. He should have either thrown the chair at the punkie's head, or dropped the chair and waded in with his fists. Instead, he tugged at the chair in a futile attempt to make the punkie loose his grip on the flail. It wasted precious seconds. It gave a football-shirted hooligan time to rush in, wield a pick handle and knock Blakey cold.

Meanwhile, Gaffer had dismounted from his machine for a moment. He jumped onto the stage, and when the musicians raced from their exposed position, Gaffer took the cymbals from their stands and skimmed them across the room at the tinted mirrors which decorated the walls. He ended this escapade by taking first the snare drum, then the two tom-toms and, finally, the bass drum and hurling them into what was developing into a mass of screaming, fighting raiders, public house employees and customers.

Blayde's car screeched to a halt at the main entrance. Tallboy literally

267

threw his car into the car park and, with equal style, burned rubber from the tyres as he stopped at the rear, emergency exit.

They knew before they entered that this was no normal pub brawl. One of the windows had gone and the noise from inside told its own tale.

Sowe muttered, 'Christ!' and had his truncheon in one hand and his handcuffs snapped and ready for use as a makeshift knuckle-duster in the other.

Blayde led the charge from the main entrance. Kyle was at his heels. Kyle dodged and twisted his way the length of the main room — ignoring for the moment the thrashing ear-splitting din of men gone fighting-mad and women on the point of hysteria — he reached the emergency exit, threw himself at the crash-bars and opened the way for Tallboy and his men.

Kyle turned in time to see a shaven-headed tearaway wearing a tartan shirt and skin-tight jeans coming at him with an open cut-throat razor. It was the tartan shirt that did it; that a mad loonie like this should have the impudence to wear *anything* with a tartan weave.

'Ye wee bugger,' he snorted, fended off the cut-throat, then smashed a fist into the curled-back lips.

As the tearaway staggered, Kyle moved in. He damn near broke the wrist of the hand holding the razor, and the weapon fell to the floor. Then he twisted, grabbed a handful of the shirt at the neck, gripped the jeans at the crotch and, as the tearaway howled, Kyle yanked him off his feet and his testicles took the strain. Kyle kept the momentum going, straightened his arms above his head, then grunted as he literally threw the tearaway onto the stage at the feet of Gaffer.

Sowe and Hinton hadn't needed telling. They fought back-to-back and refused to be drawn forward. It was no picnic; truncheons and fists — even fists with handcuffs wrapped around them — make their mark, but the chairs swung by the opposition did equal, if not more, damage. Nevertheless, around Sowe and Hinton grew a limited area of pure carnage, until one of the motor cyclists roared his machine straight at Hinton, broadsided at the last second and sent Hinton flying with the rear wheel.

Police Constable Higginbottom limped into the Charge Office, saw Wooley not yet in uniform, and said, 'What's up?'

'The Sopworth Arms. There's hell on.'

'A bit of a punch-up?' Higginbottom wasn't really interested.

'*Hell* on,' emphasised Wooley.

Higginbottom sniffed. Trust Sowe and Hinton to find trouble. They looked for it. They sought it, hunted it out, went out of their way to find it. So . . . sucks to 'em. Whatever it *10 p.m.* was they'd brought it on themselves. Bound to have done. Ergo, they could bloody-well sort it out. He, John Henry Higginbottom, had his own worries. An ankle that was giving him merry gyp, and a pea-brained daughter who was apparently on the game. He'd looked the damn word up in the family dictionary. 'Libido'. Hellfire and damnation! 'Vital sexual urge'. Wait while he saw Doctor bloody Wilkinson next time. A fine thing, eh? A daughter – little more than a kid – with a 'vital sexual urge'. Tomming it all over town, you could bet. All the young Turks sniffing round. And if Betty, his wife, ever got to know. He'd hidden the damn dictionary. And that hadn't been too much of a brainwave either. Because Betty usually spent the last hour or so before bed fannying around with some crossword puzzle. And when the dictionary wasn't in its proper place, she'd wonder. And if – supposing – she found it . . .

Hell, if *she* looked up 'Libido', she'd have a fit!

Wooley said, 'If you're Night Office Reserve . . .'

'I wouldn't be here, else.'

'I'll – er – I'll nip on . . . see if they need a hand.'

'Where?'

'The Sopworth Arms. They might . . .'

'You're on night shift, lad. You should be in uniform.'

'I'll be back.'

As he reached the Charge Office door Wooley bumped into P.C. Barker.

'Where the hell . . .' began Barker.

'Sopworth Arms,' gasped Wooley.

Barker saw the look on Wooley's face, dropped the tiny case containing his meal and said, 'I'm with you, mate.'

Together they raced through the streets.

A man in his early twenties – slim, elegant, wearing a lightweight suit, complete with flared trousers – was taking on the punkie whose injured pride had started it all. He wasn't doing too bad, either.

He'd come to The Sopworth Arms for a quiet drink with the lady in his life and suddenly, out of nowhere and for no reason at all, a bunch of louts had ruined a nice evening. The young man's name was Percy, and had any doubts been attached to that fact it would soon have been dispelled by the screams of his girlfriend.

'Percy! Percy! Let's get out of here, Percy. Don't. Don't! Percy, let's get out of here.'

But Percy's dander was well and truly up. Thanks to the loose booze which was flying in all directions as bottles and glasses went, his nice new suit was ruined and somebody was going to pay for it, if not in cash, in kind.

Man for man, the punkie might have been the master; he knew enough tricks in the art of dirty fighting to make him boss-cat. But equally Percy was a fit man and in a roped ring would have made circles around the punkie. But the punkie still had his bicycle-chain flail and when that landed it drew blood. Sometimes it bit bone-deep.

Nevertheless, the punkie's face was showing signs of wear and tear; the chair wielded by Blakey had left its mark and more than one other person had had a passing swipe.

Percy dodged a swing from the bicycle chain, nipped in and planted a beaut full on the punkie's nose. Which, whether intended or not, was a wise thing to do. The nose gushed blood, but what was more important the punkie's eyes almost squirted water, and for a vital moment the punkie couldn't see.

At which point the girlfriend did a particularly stupid thing.

As Percy stepped in to really hammer some sense into this hooligan, she grabbed his arm and held on. The punch he was throwing pulled her off balance and for a moment she was between Percy and the punkie.

Percy yelled, 'Leggo, you silly bitch!' but it was too late.

The flail swung wildly and the sharpened links cut through the dress material and bit deep into the shoulder. The girlfriend shrieked and backed into a corner.

'Right . . . that *does* it.'

Percy reverted to pure brute. At that moment a dozen 'punkies' would have been squashed like so many flies. He ducked a second swing from the flail, grabbed an already broken chair and, with left and right swings smashed the punkie backwards the breadth of the room. The punkie tried – oh, how he tried – to raise the arm holding the flail and 'do' this ponced-up berk who was knocking ten shades of shit out of his hide, but no way. He didn't know it, but the collar bone had gone. He couldn't feel the pain; nobody can in such circumstances. He was still trying to raise the flail when his back touched the wall, and then it was 'Goodnight Nurse' and Percy was *still* belting away with a chair which was almost kindling wood.

Percy glared at the unconscious punkie, turned and, still using what was left of the chair, fought his way back to his girlfriend.

'You – you called me a *bitch*,' she complained tearfully.

'Did I?' Percy flung the remains of the chair into the thresh of arms and legs which covered the dance floor. He took his girlfriend by the uninjured arm and said, 'We'd better get out of here before I call you something worse.'

Meanwhile Kyle had fought and pushed his way to where Sowe straddled the fallen Hinton. Sowe gave a quick grunt of approval and, back-to-back, they defended their fellow copper.

There was an air of cold indestructibility in the way Sowe fought. There was neither retreat nor advancement. Already he had taken a beating lesser men might have gone down under; forehead, cheek and mouth were opened up and his face streamed blood. He had a savage pain in his side; he didn't yet know it but one of his ribs had been broken. But no matter. The pain was of secondary importance; a scrap – especially a scrap of this magnitude – equated with pain and the pain could be considered *after* the scrap. Like a scythe in the hands of a craftsman, his truncheon swung steadily but never stopped, and around him there was a tiny island of devastation.

Tony Armstrong called in to see Noble and Cooper before he went off duty. The tiny 'night light' bulb gave the two-bed ward a look of warm comfortableness. A peace in which bodies and minds could do much to mend themselves.

In a low voice he said, 'See you tomorrow, chaps.'

'Eh?' Noble turned his head on the pillow and faced the direction of the voice.

Cooper grunted, 'No sleep for the wicked.'

'Sorry.' Tony Armstrong smiled. 'Just to say "Goodnight" . . . that's all.'

'Goodnight.'

'Goodnight.'

'And no smoking till there's some light.'

'Good*night*.'

Noble said, 'Goodnight, mate, and thanks.'

Tony Armstrong closed the door on two men on the very rim of sleep.

Splintered glass crunched under the shuffling feet. Smashed tables and chairs tangled with legs. The snarl of motor-cycle engines filled the room with sound, and the stench of exhaust fumes mingled with that indescribable scent of men locked in battle. And it *was* a battle. It was almost a bloody war!

271

Thanks to a Bradford informer, thanks to the inter-force liaison which had prompted a Bradford police officer to pass the word, the raiding gang had met unexpected resistance. *Real* resistance. Not the in-out-and-away foray they'd planned, but instead a prolonged bash-up in which quarter was neither asked for nor given; in which men, outraged by the mad vandalism of gangs of rampaging youths, were determined to teach at least one such group a lesson.

The landlord and the male members of the staff had hauled tables and chairs into a barricade at the opening from the bar and the main room. They'd isolated the rumpus; whatever else, nobody was going to tear around the pub committing mayhem *everywhere*. Most of the women had been hustled from the premises. Most of the more timid men had already left. Only the scrappers remained, and the more hefty members of the pub staff climbed the barricade and joined in the blood-letting.

The football-jerseyed hooligan was down and out and, as he advanced with some timidity the landlord stooped and picked up the pick handle.

Then within seconds he was alongside Rowe, forcing two of the punkie's pals into a corner from which there was no retreat.

Rowe? It must be admitted that Rowe fought like a woman . . . but with the proviso that some women can fight. Nevertheless (and in golfing terms) he didn't 'follow through'; he pulled his punches far too often; where he could have drawn blood he merely caused his opponent to blink. But what he lacked in quality he tried to make up in quantity. His fists and arms were never still and that almost fifty per-cent of his blows missed their mark nevertheless caused the two hooligans to dodge and, in their dodging, miss with their own roundhouse wallops.

Not that they missed every time. Rowe's face was already shiny and swollen but, as yet, not bloody. And the odd thing (to him) was that although he knew he'd collected no small amount of punishment, he felt no *pain*. One of his eyes was closing, fast, but he felt no pain! It was an unexpected bonus. He was breathing heavily, and he had the distinct impression that he was wading through treacle, but he kept flinging his fists in the general direction happy in the realisation that he must be unique . . . a man mixing it in a mêlée of titanic proportions, and yet impervious to pain.

The landlord (plus pick handle) joined him and suddenly there was only one hooligan to deal with. A sideways swing with the pick handle landed on one of the hooligan's neck. Had it been an axe it would, without doubt, have decapitated him. As it was, it knocked him a full two yards and draped him, unconscious, over one of the broken tables.

The second hooligan backed into the corner, crossed his arms over his head, cowered and gasped, 'Enough! Enough!'

'Not by a mile,' snarled the landlord.

The first downward chop with the pick handle broke one of the hooligan's forearms. The second, on the now exposed head, put him in hospital for the next four weeks.

'Enough . . . *please,*' gasped Rowe. 'Any more and you'll murder him.'

Wooley and Barker arrived at The Sopworth Arms breathless, and not quite ready for the crowd which had gathered outside that building. Here and there men, and some women, carried marks from the merry hell going on inside.

'Ambulance?' snapped Wooley to one of the onlookers.

'I dunno. I haven't . . .'

'Get one.' Wooley jerked his head in the direction of a nearby telephone kiosk.

'Look, I dunno who the hell you are, but . . .'

'He's one of us.' Barker's uniform answered the unasked question. 'Don't arse around. Get an ambulance, otherwise we might need a hearse.'

Then Wooley and Barker raced through the front entrance, to add weight to what was happening inside.

Both Tallboy and Blayde were a little past it. Ten, fifteen years ago they'd have been having the time of their lives; they were the type who *join* the Police Service for battles royal with the ungodly, and between them they'd broken a few bones. But years of snatched meals and loss of sleep had taken their toll, and both men, while fighting, were also fighting for breath. They fought together; sometimes back-to-back, sometimes side-by-side. Experience told them that the hooligans were beginning to buckle. The question was . . . who'd buckle first?

'The motor cyclists,' gasped Tallboy.

Blayde saved breath by merely nodding.

There are degrees even among scum and, of the raiding party, the motor cyclists were the elite. Squash them and the others would fold without too much trouble. The problem was . . . how to squash 'em? Gaffer was still on the stage; a very personal, very bloody vendetta had developed between Gaffer and Cockburn; theirs was a fight apart and separated from the general skirmish of the main room.

But the other two motor cyclists were, literally, using their machines as weapons. Plunging them at any man who wasn't one of their own kind and, if skidding a split-second before the actual collision, giving one more hooligan the opportunity to get in one more punishing blow.

'One each,' panted Tallboy.

'Pick one,' gasped Blayde.

Tallboy 'picked one'. There was a moment's respite between himself and a heftily built, but rather stout, hooligan and at that moment one of the riders slewed his machine into a broadside less than two yards from Tallboy.

Tallboy forced himself to think — to time things properly — and, as the machine was at an angle, prior to being *10.30 p.m.* hauled upright, Tallboy hurled himself at the neck and shoulders of the rider. The momentum carried both Tallboy and the rider clear of the machine. They rolled and fought among shattered glass and broken furniture. The rider ended on top and fastened his hands around Tallboy's throat — which with anybody having mere basic knowledge of self-defence is a silly thing to do — and Tallboy grasped the little finger of each of the rider's hands, bent those fingers back and, quite deliberately broke them at the lowest knuckle. The high scream of pain rose above the general din, and Tallboy rolled over until he was on top of the motor cyclist with his knees pinning the rider's arms to the floor, above the elbow. Then Tallboy started swinging punches. Lefts and rights, lefts and rights, at a head which couldn't be protected and which gradually rolled without life as the accumulation of blows hammered consciousness from its owner.

Tallboy sucked in breath and began to haul himself upright when a boot lashed out, landed full on the side of his face and knocked him cold alongside the motor cyclist he'd just tamed.

Blayde did things the hard way. The terrible way. He dispatched his immediate opponent by linking both hands into a double-fist and, using just about every muscle in his body, smashing that double-fist in a side-swipe at the hate-filled face. And one more hooligan went and stayed down.

Then Blayde took a deep breath and looked for the second motor cyclist.

Tony Armstrong unlocked the door, then walked into his flat. It was a ground-floor flat, therefore he had no stairs to climb. In rubber-soled shoes he entered the bedroom without a sound. His girl — the girl he'd asked to marry — was curled up in the bed, fast asleep.

Muriel — Woman Police Constable 1324 Muriel Pearson — and there were things about her he'd never know. A depth he'd never be able to plumb. Today had proved it. Today he'd glimpsed part of the monumental compassion of which she was capable. It had to do with the uniform she wore, but that was only part of it. That was only one of the *reasons* for it.

At present — whilever she was in the force — she was a woman in a man's world. Equal, yet *not* equal. Those men she worked with. Her colleagues. They weren't supermen. Some (he knew) were scoundrels; little better than the people they were paid to police. But the others . . . The majority . . . Like Noble and Cooper. They treated her as an equal, but at the same time they protected her. She treated *them* as an equal, but when they were hurt she suffered. God, how she suffered! Equality, with a plus and minus sign attached. A strange — almost mystic — balance.

Love, without even a hint of carnality. Brotherly love. Sisterly love. All that, and more. He, Anthony Armstrong, handled filth and pain; it was part of his job; it was what he'd been trained for. But she handled a different brand of filth and pain. Something deeper — much deeper — than burst ulcers, the end-product of a road accident, those sort of things. Torn personalities. Shattered emotions. The hell which crouched deep inside some people's minds. She handled it — and had handled it for years — and was able to handle it, because of the men she worked with.

And those men . . .

As a husband, he'd have to measure up to those men. Not deliberately, not even consciously, she'd measure him up against those men for the rest of her life. And when she left the force (and she *would* leave the force) memory would take over, and she'd forget what weaknesses they'd had. Her faulty recollection would make them little short of gods. The way the mind worked. Every mind. *Her* mind.

He'd *better* be good!

He smiled down at her sleeping figure. So comfortable. So relaxed after a murderous day. It would be a small blasphemy to disturb her.

He stripped, showered, towelled himself, then hauled a sleeping-bag from a wall cupboard. He rolled the sleeping-bag out alongside the bed, wriggled into it, then blew her a kiss before settling down to sleep.

* * *

Blakey regained consciousness, wondered where the hell he was, what the hell had happened and what the hell all the noise was about. He half-remembered, rolled onto his front and began to push himself upright. Somebody stumbled backwards against his rising figure, planted a shoe on the nape of his neck and ground his face into a carpet confettied with broken glass. For a moment he wondered what Matilda would say . . . then remembered Matilda didn't matter a damn any more.

Nevertheless, he was no hero. Nor (theoretically speaking) was he still a police officer. His ticket had gone in; technically he was on Resignation Leave. He rolled onto his side, tucked his knees into his stomach, covered his face and head with his arms and hoped to God not too many people would kick or tread on him.

Blayde, on the other hand, was moving into action.

The truth was Blayde, too, had forgotten he was a police officer. Discipline be damned! This thing had grown too big — had gone on too long — to be tooling around playing at 'disciplined bodies of men'. The bastards had to be tamed and, if to tame them it was necessary to carry a corpse or two from the pub . . . who the hell started it, in the first place!

The second motor cyclist roared towards him. Biayde held his ground. The rider braked and broadsided and Blayde grabbed and swung himself across the pillion seat. They went down with the machine, and the engine roared and the rear wheel continued to spin.

The rider was on all fours, with Blayde astride his back. Blayde grabbed a fistful of black, curly hair with his right hand and, with his left, pulled the rider's left arm up and hard behind his back.

'Tough guy,' rasped Blayde. 'Just *how* bloody tough?'

Blayde jerked the arm until it was almost out of its socket, then he shifted his position until his right knee was throwing all his weight onto the nape of the rider's neck. The rider's face was only inches above the spinning spokes of the machine's rear wheel. His right arm was bent at the elbow, and he hadn't the strength to straighten it and lock it stiff against Blayde's weight.

'Tough baby,' panted Blayde. 'Against old women and kids a real tough baby. Just *how* tough?'

The rider heaved upwards, but Blayde threw more pressure on the neck and the fingers in the rider's hair pushed his face fractionally nearer to the spokes. Both men were panting. For the moment they represented the two extremes of a spectrum; lawlessness and law-enforcing; terror and counter-terror. And yet the spectrum was more than a mere arc. It was a continuation of that arc, until it formed a perfect circle. 'It takes a bastard to tame a bastard'. They were the final proof of that remark. Such was the rage of Blayde that he trully *wanted* to ram the driver's sweat-soaked face into the murderous spokes of the spinning rear wheel of the machine. The hell with courts, the hell with juries, the hell with prison sentences. This animal — this motor-cycle tearaway with the twisted mentality — this rebel whose only cause was the infliction of pain and the terror-isation of decent people . . . what the devil else did he deserve?

The rider gathered his strength, gave a final heave, Blayde pushed harder, the rider knew he couldn't make it and snatched his right hand from the carpet and flung it as a guard between the wheel and his face. The spokes caught the fingers, broke bones, whipped the hand until it jammed between the wheel-brace and the spokes, tore flesh and sinew from the hand, then the bones of the wrist became an effective wedge between the spokes and the wheel-brace . . . the wheel stopped turning and the engine died.

The rider dropped his face onto the stilled spokes and wept with pain. His shattered hand was as locked as in any mantrap. Blayde pushed himself upright and, for a moment, felt a strange shame.

Pinter nodded and sighed. The mother-in-law searched his face for signs of a breakdown, but all she saw was tiredness.

He'd refused to stay in hospital. He'd allowed them to strap up his injured foot — he'd refused them time to X-ray it to check whether bones were broken or not — a couple of stitches in his calf, some balm for an assortment of very minor cuts and bruises . . . then the motor patrol vehicle had taken him home.

'There was no pain. She didn't regain consciousness.'

The mother-in-law didn't know. She *knew* she didn't know, but she silently prayed that she was telling the truth.

'I was with her, holding her hand,' she lied.

It was a good lie; a lie for which she could be readily forgiven. She *would* have been there, had she known. She *would* have held her daughter's hand. To be told that his wife had died alone — perhaps (God forbid!) *knowing* she was alone — wouldn't help this good man who'd already suffered enough. Let the dead rest. Concentrate on the living; give the bereaved what little comfort was possible.

'Do you . . .' She continued to watch his face. 'Do you want to go up and see her?'

'No.' There was no hesitation. He shook his head slowly.

'I — I think you should. I think . . .'

'Ma.' Pinter pinched his nose to counter the utter weariness. 'She was a fine wife. None better. I tried to keep pace.'

'Wilf, you've been a good husband. You deserve . . .'

'I don't want to see her dead.' The interruption was almost savage. 'You want the truth? I'll not see her dead. Not even in her coffin. The good times. The happy times. *That's* what I want to remember. I don't want them blotted out — spoiled — I'll not *have* them spoiled.'

She nodded understandingly. She said, 'I'll make some tea.'

'Please.'

As she left for the kitchen, he fumbled in his pockets, found a crumpled packet of cigarettes, then lighted one.

When she returned, carrying a tray, she placed it on a side table, went across and removed the smoking cigarette from his fingers. He was fast asleep.

Nick Karn — Police Constable 1235 Nicholas Karn, a law enforcement officer responsible for Rimstone Beat — staggered home as drunk as a fiddler's bitch. He'd been 'supping it' at the local boozer as fast as he could pour it down his silly throat. The lads of the village had had a night to remember pouring it down his gullet by the yard. And cheap at the price. Here was one bobby who could be made to look an idiot. Who *behaved* — who *talked* — like an idiot once his skin was full.

No more would he be a menace . . . if he ever *had* been a menace. No more would he command even token respect. Karn? That ale-pot? The village drunk in uniform . . . that's what Karn was and ever would be.

He staggered and almost sprawled as he entered the hall.

He pulled himself upright, felt his way to the foot of the stairs, and bawled, 'Elsie! Elsie! It's only me. I'm home.'

There was sound of movement from the main bedroom.

Karn yelled, ''S all right, luv. It's only me.'

Elsie Karn stood at the top of the stairs and stared down at her drunken husband. In heaven's name, what had she ever seen in this drunken, no-good slop of a husband? What had she ever *seen* in him?

He held onto the rail and gingerly placed one foot on the bottom stair.

'Don't,' she snapped.

'Eh?' He gazed up at her, slack-mouthed and puzzled.

'Don't come any nearer,' she warned coldly.

'Look, luv, I commin' t'bed. I wanna . . .'

'I'll kill you,' she said solemnly. 'I'm going back to bed. I'm going to close and lock the bedroom door. If you come up these stairs – if you so much as *touch* that door – somehow, I'll kill you.'

Karn gawped up the stairs as his wife disappeared. He heard the bedroom door close. He heard the click as she turned the key in the lock. He remained gazing up at the landing for some few moments. Unable to get his brain to focus upon what he'd done wrong. Why this stupid wife of his was behaving in this ridiculous way.

He muttered, 'Bloody women,' then groped his way into the sitting room, flopped out on the sofa and snored his way to dawn.

Three years later – a wiser, sorrier man – the divorce was made absolute and, looking back, he figured that the rot set in (*really* set in) the day Rowe and that bloody detective sergeant had found him reading a paperback on top of the hay, when he should have been tramping around asking silly questions on his Weekly Rest Day. To the end of his life he swore that being a bobby had screwed up his marriage. Just that . . . nothing to do with him as a man.

And, suddenly, it stopped. The fighting, the screaming, the sound of breaking furniture and shattering glass. Like the closing of a door.

11 p.m.   Like the flicking of a switch. Like a blazing match dropped into a bucket of water. Comparative silence. A few groans. The gentle sound of panting breath. The soft crunch as men trod splintered glass into the carpet. But other than that . . . nothing.

Barker and Wooley swore that their arrival had convinced the hooligans that the game was up. That *they* were the reason for the sudden peace. Well, maybe. On the other hand . . .

Up on the tiny platform Cockburn and Gaffer ignored the end of the scrap. To them it was a very personal thing. That the rest of the world turned sane and took up rose-growing . . . so what? Two men still lived who hated each other's guts. Each wanted to kill the other.

Gaffer had a switch-knife; a blade all of six-inches long, double-edged and razor-sharp. He knew how to use it, too; thumb along the flat of the blade, weaving the steel in tiny patterns, then stabbing or slashing whenever Cockburn came within range. Cockburn had armed himself with the snare-drum stand; chromed steel, longer than the knife and with the arms which held the drum broken off and the feet folded back to the shaft; a make-do-and-mend sword with which to open up flesh or pierce an eyeball.

Both men wore marks of their conflict. Gaffer's forehead was opened to the bone where Cockburn's weapon had slashed at the face and landed too high; the still-flowing blood tended to blind him

279

a little, and it had matted the blond hair which had fallen forward during the fight. Nor was Cockburn unmarked. He'd used his left arm to ward off knife slashes, and the sleeve of his tunic was ripped and blood-soaked. Each had a neat collection of other cuts and bruises. The floor of the stage was streaked with blood; it was splashed on the electric organ and on the drapes and, despite the quiet of the rest of the room, these two men continued to circle each other, each intent upon seeing the liquid life of the other spill onto the floor of the stage.

Blayde walked to the stage and said, 'It's over.'

Neither Gaffer nor Cockburn heeded . . . assuming they even heard.

'It's finished.' Blayde raised his voice.

It made no difference. Gaffer sprang forward, arm outstretched and blade sweeping for Cockburn's stomach. Cockburn stepped back and the drum-stand hissed as it cleaved the air above Gaffer's ducking head.

'Damn it!' Blayde glanced around for a weapon.

Miraculously — almost, it seemed, as a jest of fate — there was an open, but unbroken wine bottle on the apron of the tiny stage. Blayde grasped it by the neck. The wine spilled unheeded and soaked his sleeve. With what energy he had left, he hoisted himself onto the stage.

He said, '*Stop* it!' and smashed the bottle across the back of Gaffer's head.

Gaffer went down and, still holding the wine bottle by its neck, he advanced towards Cockburn and snarled, 'I gave an order, sergeant.' The shards of the broken bottle were threatening. Nobody in the room even *thought* Blayde was bluffing. 'Drop that thing, sergeant. Drop it . . . or you'll carry scars to the grave.'

Cockburn froze. Gradually, the brute savagery left his expression and his eyes moved into focus. He lowered his arm and, as if locked and requiring great physical effort, his fingers straightened and the drum-stand clattered to the floor.

He whispered, 'Yes, sir,' and the words barely reached Blayde.

Blayde dropped the broken bottle, stepped forward and helped Cockburn from the stage.

Two newly-arrived motor patrol officers were helping the landlord and the staff to dismantle the table-and-chair barricade. One of them knew Tallboy. He walked across and saluted.

'Anything we can do, sir?'

'Ambulances?' Tallboy still had difficulty in controlling his breathing.

'There's two outside.'

'The badly injured. Not the walking-wounded. Then we need a police van to take the others to the station.'

'I'll fix things, sir.'

'Somebody stay with 'em. When they've been patched up, I want them back at Sopworth.'

'Yes, sir.'

The patrol man left to arrange things. Barker arrived alongside Tallboy and asked for instructions.

'The . . . animals.' Tallboy shook his head, as if to clear his brain. 'Those not needing immediate treatment. Cuff 'em together. Right wrist to right wrist. Then . . .' Tallboy managed a tired and twisted grin. 'If they run, even *we* can catch 'em.'

Barker returned the grin.

'Those bloody motor cycles. Impound 'em for evidence.' He paused, then added, 'They might be — y'know — smashed up a bit. Accidentally. Made unrideable for the time being.'

'I'm very accident-prone, sir,' said Barker solemnly.

Within the minor chaos of clearing up and sorting out the hooligans from the staff and customers, Blakey edged his way from the main room, across the bar and out into the car park. He climbed into his Rover and, for a few minutes, sat quietly rubbing his still aching head.

The name of the game was self-preservation. As far as he was concerned, it always had been. It always would be. For a moment in The Sopworth Arms he'd thought he'd re-discovered his lost manhood. Just for a moment. When he'd faced the hooligan with the bicycle-chain flail. The memory made him lower his head; look almost sadly at the dried blood on the sliced finger. Then he raised his hand again and massaged the bump where the pick handle had landed.

It couldn't be, of course. All this 'freedom' was a complete de-lusion. A mirage. A few hours of delightful self-kidology. What he was he *was*, period. He was the final product of Matilda and his two daughters. He'd go back. He'd take their complaints and their silly yardsticks of what was 'nice' and what wasn't 'nice', and he wouldn't complain.

Men — other men — left their wives and walked out. How? How did they do it? Were they weak or were they strong? To take what he'd taken, year after year — what he'd continue to take for the rest of his life — that was a form of strength, surely? Accepting it. Absorbing it. Not running away from it. In God's name, that was being strong, wasn't it? The other thing was being weak.

Funny, though, for those few hours. It *had* been different. Like — y'know — when some bird of prey escaped from a zoo . . . a very heady but very temporary freedom. But in its way once the novelty had worn off, strangely frightening.

He sighed, turned the ignition key and headed the Rover back towards Beechwood Brook.

And in a cell at Sopworth Police Station Alfred Bingham stared into the darkness and he, too, wondered.

Dammit it *was* the place. That building — plough-shed what the hell they called it — it *was* the place. Last year, too. *Last* year. That place — that hen place hadn't been there. Not *last* year.

She'd deserved it. The diseased little bitch. She'd deserved it . . . last year. A man shouldn't have to . . .

On the other hand, a man shouldn't kill. Shouldn't strangle, then bury. That wasn't decent. It wasn't nice. Nice people didn't go around strangling teenage kids. Whoever they were. Whatever they were. Not if they wanted to . . .

That was why, he supposed. Guilty conscience. That and a bloody police station. Asking questions, making a man feel lower than *that*, pushing and leaning . . . all for the sake of a length of timber. The usual bullshit; 'Come on, get it all off your chest', or 'Let's have everything, then when you come out, you'll know we won't be waiting for you'. The number of times. And each time you swear you won't do it again. Never again. But you always do. You always 'cough'. Everything.

And this time. My God *this* time!

He didn't know it — how could he possibly know it? — but Alfred Bingham was going to get away with murder. All the circulations. All the delving through Missings From Home. They never traced her. They never heard a hint of her . . . and she was buried with a battery-hen complex as a headstone.

Police vehicles and ambulances gradually carted the injured off to Beechwood Brook Cottage Hospital. Coppers took names and addresses of witnesses, and arranged for a mass statement-taking within the coming weekend. The 'walking wounded' ended up at Sopworth Police station, along with Blayde, Rowe, Tallboy, Sowe, Hinton, Wooley and Barker. Cockburn too, despite the savage knife-wounds, insisted upon going back to the nick. The police surgeon was

282

called, and he examined everybody, including the hooligans before they were bundled into the cells.

Higginbottom watched the performance with a set face, but with mildly contemptuous eyes.

'Quite a barney?' he observed drily.

Sowe grinned and said, 'The right side won. That's the main thing.'

'Aye . . . I reckon.'

'Affray?' Tallboy asked the question of Blayde.

'All of 'em,' agreed Blayde. 'Affray as a basic charge. Then do 'em all for conspiracy. G.B.H., conduct likely to cause a breach of the peace, wilful damage . . . every blasted combination you can come up with Chris. Throw the book. I want 'em tamed . . . legally as well as physically.'

'Sowe and Hinton?'

'The lot of us.' Blayde's eyes held the sheen of near-fanaticism. 'I don't have to tell you. When the candy-floss merchants get hold of this they'll have a flag day.' He sneered, 'Poor, underprivileged little boys having hell smacked out of 'em by wicked coppers. That's the line they'll take. *And* they'll be backed to the hilt by vote-catching loonies in Parliament.' His voice dropped to a growl as he continued, 'You, me, Rowe. Cockburn, Sowe, Hinton, Kyle. I want every damn copper who even *saw* anything up there in the box. I want photographs of that room showing the damage. I want every witness you can get your hand on ready and willing to tell what *really* happened. And the bikes — have *them* in court — they're not cheap and that'll scotch the 'poverty' plea. *And* the weapons.' He sighed, then ended, 'Sopworth is going to have a name, Chris. It's going to hit every head-line in the country. And what happens to those bastards is going to scare the living crap out of every one of their kind capable of reading. That's how it's going to be played . . . and at a Crown Court with a jury listening to every word.'

'Ten stitches. At least ten stitches,' said the police surgeon, impatiently. He eyed Cockburn's opened-up arm and shook his head in disgust. 'And it has to be rested. Damnation, man, you could lose the arm. Get infection in there and . . .'

'Start stitching,' said Cockburn flatly.

'And if it goes wrong?'

'I'm on duty till five.'

'Sergeant, you're not . . .'

'Hospital.' Tallboy joined the medic and the sergeant. 'Hospital, then a fortnight's sick leave. A month, if necessary.'

'Sir, I'm . . .'

'Not for your benefit.' Some of Blayde's savagery mixed with his own ill-temper had made Tallboy's voice ugly. 'I don't give a damn if your arm falls off. But I want you to be able to get up in court and say you were incapacitated . . . for as long as possible.'

Cockburn compressed his lips.

'I'm not arguing, Cockburn. I'm not *asking*. It's known as tactics. Agreed tactics . . . between Chief Superintendent Blayde and myself.'

Cockburn nodded. He couldn't trust himself to speak, and he could recognise red warning lights when he saw them.

Wooley had nipped home to put on his uniform, Barker was out on the streets, giving token coverage to a town already either in bed or going to bed. Higginbottom fannied around between the Charge Office and the teleprinter/telephone alcove. Inspectors and above were not his chosen playmates, and the place was crawling with 'em.

'There's a van reported stolen at Bradford.'

He spoke to nobody in particular, therefore nobody took any notice.

Blayde examined Rowe's face with open interest.

'You've a real shiner coming up there,' he remarked.

'The first.' Rowe tried to smile, but other facial bruising made the effort too painful. 'I've never had a black eye in my life before. Heaven only knows what my wife will say.'

'She'll be proud of you,' promised Blayde.

The police surgeon stepped over, fingered Rowe's eye and the swellings at his jaw and cheekbones.

'I'm all right,' murmured Rowe.

'Another hero,' grunted the police surgeon.

'Really,' Rowe assured him. 'It's painful, but not serious.'

'That's a contradiction in terms.'

Blayde smiled at the surgeon and said, 'By morning, it'll be all the colours of the rainbow.'

'I'm not interested in the artistic effect. I'm thinking of possible concussion.'

'As bad as that?' The smile was replaced by a frown.

'Rest,' pronounced the surgeon. 'At the very least, rest.'

'Look, I can't . . .'

'You can, inspector,' interrupted Blayde. 'See how you feel on Monday.'

'A van stolen at Bradford,' said Higginbottom in a lost voice.

'What number?' Rowe pushed the surgeon's hand aside.

284

Higginbottom gave the registered number and the make of the stolen van.

Rowe said, 'That's it. That's the one they came in.'

'Is it, by God?' Blayde's eyes shone at the news.

'I noticed it. Noticed the number, when we arrived.'

'Chris.' Tallboy came across at Blayde's summons. 'Get that van. Fingerprinted . . . the lot. Find who was driving it. Check the driving licence and the insurance. Conspiracy to steal. Joint theft. Joint *everything*. Aiding and abetting. The whole bloody book — page at a time — spitting in the street if somebody saw 'em do it.'

'That's — er — that's vicious,' said Tallboy tentatively.

'And they *weren't* vicious?' Blayde took a deep breath, then in a calmer tone said, 'That's what they're going to say, Chris. However we play it . . . we're "vicious". Let's enjoy ourselves for a change. Let's *be* vicious.'

Wooley was back in uniform. He'd linked up with Barker and they strolled the streets side-by-side. They talked of the rumpus at The Sopworth Arms. In a roundabout way, what they'd *11.30 p.m.* seen made them envious; they'd both liked to have been 'in there' with their mates. This despite the possibility of being seriously injured. It was what they were paid for. Why they wore the uniform. Why they'd joined.

As they passed shops they tried handles, shone torch beams up at first and second floor windows. They eyed and remembered the few pedestrians they passed. They noted the passing cars; a rough description; the direction; when possible the number of occupants; they ignored the registration numbers, because it would have been impossible to carry them all in their heads.

Bobbying . . . doing what you can do, but knowing what you can't.

Wooley stifled a yawn and said, 'Quiet night.'

'Like last night.'

'Eh?'

'At this time . . . quiet.'

Wooley chuckled and said, 'I've had quite a day.'

'Keep your fingers crossed.'

But had he been pressed, Barker would have retracted that remark.

Men — men like Barker, men like Wooley — don't join the Police Service because they enjoy boredom. They *accept* the boredom. The hours of boredom is payment (usually in advance) for moments of high excitement and wild activity.

Their turn would come . . .

The motor patrol car dropped Kyle at his home on Upper Neck beat after delivering Cockburn to Beechwood Brook Cottage Hospital for running repairs. He waved 'Goodnight', walked up the path to the house and suddenly realised how dog tired he was.

Quite a day. An uncommonly long day. As far as he was concerned, it could have been a day of change; one of the milestones of his career, possibly of his life. The rank of detective constable had been his for the taking and he'd refused . . . and the force being what it was, he wouldn't be readily offered that rank a second time.

As he peeled off his tunic and hung it with his peaked cap on the pegs of the hallstand, he experienced a slight twinge of regret. And yet . . .

He was a detective — *the* detective — as far as Upper Neck was concerned. And to a lesser degree as far as Rimstone was concerned. Head of *their* C.I.D. *Their* chief constable. (He strolled into the kitchen where he knew the Thermos of warm cocoa and the cheese and biscuits would have been left by his wife before she'd followed the kids to bed.) Something the Big Daddies never quite grasped. That within a limited area a man could know just about everything. But expand that area, and the more you expanded it the less a man could know. (He chewed biscuits, bit into the cheese and sipped cocoa.) This, as far as he was concerned, was the ultimate. The only truly successful way to police.

Meanwhile . . .

In plain clothes tomorrow. A lot of loose ends to sort out. A heap of paperwork to get through. But with Tallboy, and Tallboy was a bonny man to work with. No panic. A steady jog-trot through the various stages; the umpteen charges; the nine pieces of trash who'd had big ideas about 'taming' Sopworth. And a rare fighter — for his age — when the aggro started.

Police Constable Kyle munched cheese, popped the last piece of biscuit into his mouth then took a final drink of cocoa.

It had been a busy day . . . and tomorrow was yet to come.

William Henry Rowe was rather enjoying himself. Never before had his wife fussed and fretted about him so much. Never before had she been so obviously worried. It made a very pleasant change.

Very gently she stroked liniment onto his bruised face; the cool fingers and the oily balm had a distinctly erotic effect . . . and that, too, was nice.

'You might have been killed,' she murmured.

'It was unlikely.'

'But you might. It *has* happened. Then what about me?'

'We couldn't let them run riot, darling.'

'I know. But . . .'

'Could we . . .' Rowe hesitated, then took the plunge. 'Blayde told me not to report for duty until Monday . . .'

'I should think not.'

'. . . so why not take the car, find a quiet hotel somewhere. The Lake District, perhaps. Have a weekend together.'

The way he pronounced the word 'weekend'. His own insolence almost frightened him. Twenty-four hours previously he wouldn't have *dared*.

'Your face . . .' It was a half-hearted protest.

'We needn't . . .' He swallowed, then said, 'Apart from meals, we needn't leave our room. Just — y'know — the rest.'

'The "rest"?' She smiled and (good Lord!) her smile held a coquettish quality.

'I love you,' he whispered and the words came out without conscious effort. Without conscious thought.

'That's nice to know.' She kissed him gently, full on the lips. 'It's nice to be told. This — er — weekend, tell me lots of times.'

The truth was, Cockburn felt his age. The red-necked cop image was a little hard to keep up after a certain point. Sure, he'd have stayed on duty until five o'clock. Sure, he'd have taken the slashed arm in his stride. A matter of pride. A matter of self-esteem. A matter of — all right — a matter of blind, bloody-minded stupidity.

Once upon a time . . .

Ah, once upon a time he'd have taken that switch-knife and rammed it down Gaffer's throat, hilt first. No trouble. No sweat. But at *his* age? Blayde had stepped in, and thank God for that. Because Gaffer had been on top. Man-to-man Gaffer was cock o' the walk, switch-knife or no switch-knife.

But, y'see, a copper couldn't allow a tearaway like Gaffer *be* cock o' the walk. It wasn't allowed. Coppers couldn't retreat from people like Gaffer. They had to stand their ground. Take what the hell was coming. Yes, die if necessary, but *never* retreat.

Funny, though. Odd. On the point of collapse he really *hadn't* heard Blayde's voice. Hadn't even recognised Blayde. The whole world and everybody in it . . . all his enemies. That was the truth. His precious manhood – his precious pride – Christ, for a moment he'd almost gone at Blayde himself! To prove something.

To prove damn-all, if the truth be told.

The nurse patted the bandage where she'd just fastened it, and said, 'That's it, sergeant. A good long sleep . . . you'll feel a new man.'

Cockburn grunted.

'We've contacted your wife. She'll be here with your pyjamas very soon.'

'Look, I don't need . . .'

'This is a respectable hospital, sergeant.'

'I don't need to *stay* here.'

'This way.' The nurse spoke as if to a naughty, but well-loved, child. 'I'll show you your bed. Then when your wife's been, I'll come and see you're comfortable.'

Cockburn sighed and followed the nurse. And why not? The hell with being tough. The hell with being a brass-faced bastard. The hell with everything . . . for the time being.

Tallboy drove home, with all windows down. He needed the air. He needed as much freedom as he could claim. Noble, Cooper, Preston, Bingham and the punch-up at The Sopworth Arms. Hell's teeth! The feeling was one of being hemmed in on all sides by mad buggers. The sheer weight of evil . . . like being imprisoned in one of those Iron Maidens of the old-fashioned torture chambers.

Not what you might call a 'usual' day, of course. But not a particularly *un*usual day. Busy. At times verging on the disorganised. But never *quite* beyond control.

Thank God for people like Blayde. Even for people like Harris. Nor had Rowe come out of it too badly. A good section. A good divsion. A good team.

Mind you . . .

One more – two more – at the boozer and the wrong side might have won. This wasn't the Met. Hand-picked men trained specifically for riot situations weren't part of the provincial set-up. And the communication had been ropey. Very ropey. The sporting one-to-one situation was *not* the way to police. Swamp 'em, jump on 'em, then sit on 'em. That was the way. The sensible way. Fewer people got hurt. Like blanketing a fire with foam, eliminating it before it could spread and cause real damage. Assuming (for the sake of argument) fifty uniformed coppers had marched into The Sopworth Arms. Just marched in . . . that's all. That's all it would have *taken.*

There'd have been an immediate unconditional surrender and no heads broken. And it could have been done; with good communication, with a scheme already worked out . . . fifty coppers from various parts of Beechwood Brook Division could have arrived.

Something to think about. Something to put forward at the next Senior Officers' Conference. Modify the Train Disaster Scheme a little. Same set-up. Same lines of communication. Nothing difficult . . . just that it hadn't entered anybody's mind.

Bobbying . . . Christ it was getting more like a never-ending war every day. Too much energy flying around. Too much wrongly-directed energy.

Meanwhile — he grinned at the thought — Susan would be waiting up with her own brand of energy bottled up and ready. The usual routine. Too many hours, not enough to eat, too many cigarettes, not enough relaxation. She was scared . . . that was it. She'd seen the job drive a wedge between her parents, therefore she was scared. Silly lass. Her mother had been a copper's wife, but she hadn't also been a copper's *daughter*. Ripley's daughter. It made a difference. All the difference in the world.

Nevertheless . . .

They'd have a holiday before the summer was out. A real holiday. Away from it all. Somewhere — y'know — where he could wear snazzy shirts, and Susan could bring the wolf-whistles in a bikini. Somewhere where . . .

Oh, the hell with it. He'd let her decide where. Tomorrow the whole thing had to be reduced to cold official language. But after that . . .

Blayde garaged his car and walked slowly to the kitchen door of his cottage. As he opened the door he felt something rub against his left leg. He looked down and saw the moggy which had adopted him.

'You're out late, cat.' He opened the door, switched on the strip-lighting and was surprised to see that the cat had followed him indoors. He said, 'You don't live here, mate.'

The cat purred, as if in contradiction.

Blayde poured the cat a saucer of milk, then plugged in the electric kettle for his own last drink of the day. He loosened his collar and kicked off his shoes and padded around doing the odd jobs necessary to his bachelor existence.

He, too, mulled over the events of the day.

Everything done well, everything done properly. Except . . .

Would he *really* have driven the rider's face into the spinning spokes? Would he *really* have opened Cockburn's face with the broken bottle? Had this lousy job *really* turned him into that sort of a man? Fire with fire, okay, but you don't fight a TocH candle with a flame-thrower. That was the difference.

'If . . .' He spoke to the cat. 'If you're taking up with me, cat. Certain rules. Okay? I'm not a very nice man to know. Ask around. Just realise that before you move in.'

The teleprinter began to chatter and Higginbottom walked into the alcove. He read the message as it came through. One more stolen vehicle . . . The sweep hand of the Charge Office *Midnight* wall-clock moved past the vertical, and it was the start of a new day.

SATURDAY, JUNE THE TWENTY-SEVENTH

So easy. So little pother. Time, like the geometrician's dot, didn't exist other than in the imagination; 'now' became 'then' merely by reason of noting it . . .